The DECENT PROPOSAL

A Novel

The DECENT PROPOSAL

A Novel

KEMPER DONOVAN

HARPER

An Imprint of HarperCollinsPublishers

This book is a work of fiction. The characters, incidents, and dialogue are drawn from the author's imagination and are not to be construed as real. Any resemblance to actual events or persons, living or dead, is entirely coincidental.

FIRST EDITION

Designed by William Ruoto
Palm tree illustration by Dana Rose Mendelson

Donovan, Kemper.
  The decent proposal : a novel / Kemper Donovan.—First edition.
    pages   cm
  ISBN 978-0-06-239162-9 (Hardcover)
  ISBN 978-0-06-249842-7 (International Edition)
1. Motion picture producers and directors—Fiction. 2. Women lawyers—Fiction. 3. Los Angeles (Calif.)—Fiction. 4. Love stories.
  PS3604.O56685 D43   2016
  813'.6—dc23   2015045248

16 17 18 19 20   OV/RRD   10 9 8 7 6 5 4 3 2 1

For Adam

Only connect!

—E. M. FORSTER, *HOWARDS END*

The DECENT PROPOSAL

A Novel

THE MEETING

BEFORE GRAY HAIR, or crow's-feet, or achy backs and fickle knees, there is one sign of aging that makes its appearance early enough to bewilder its young(ish) victims instead of alarming them, as it should. And so one morning a few weeks after his twenty-ninth birthday, Richard Baumbach awoke in a state of bewilderment:

Since when had the hangovers gotten *this* bad?

Lifting a twisted rope of bedsheet from his naked chest, Richard placed it beside him with a tenderness usually reserved for more sentient occupants of his bed, and braced himself for vertical alignment. *Here goes,* he thought. *You can do this. Come on. One, two, three . . . go!*

Nothing moved other than his brain, which beat steadily against his skull.

He tried picturing the bright green Brita pitcher inside his refrigerator door: the cool, refreshing water it contained. But the mere thought of brightness made his eyeballs retreat painfully in their sockets like hermit crabs darting inside their shells, and his stomach lurched at the suggestion of anything green. He switched to the aspirin waiting for him in his medicine cabinet: chalky-white, inoffensive, holding out the promise of an end to his misery. Two tablets was the recommended dose, but for this *Hindenburg* of a headache he would allow himself four . . . if he ever managed to get up.

Nothing to it, he pretended. *Piece of cake, easy as pie.*

Ugh, dessert-based idioms were not the way to go.

Get. Up. Now!

For one glorious moment the throbbing sensation disappeared inside the *whoosh* of upward momentum and he became a believer in miracles. His headache was gone; he was cured! Then his feet hit the floor and his head came to a stop, igniting in a series of fiery explosions that—even in the midst of his pain—he likened to the climactic sequence of one of those nineties action movies viewed routinely on his DVR. Thinking about his DVR only added to his pain, however, his wince deepening from minor toothache to full-blown lemonface as he shuffled to the bathroom. Just yesterday the cable guy had come at his request to take away everything, including his beloved DVR. He had no Wi-Fi now, and in a fit of martyrdom he'd even canceled his Netflix streaming account, which he supposed he could have used on his laptop in coffee shops. But he had decided the eight bucks a month was eight bucks he could no longer afford in the face of a credit card bill that had begun not so much accumulating as metastasizing from one month to the next.

Richard dumped six aspirin into his shaky palm and lapped up a mouthful of water directly from the tap. (Screw the Brita.) For one who supposedly worked in film and television, it was more than a little mortifying to lose the ability to watch films and television inside his home. But this was what his life had become.

He collapsed onto his couch, facedown, like a corpse. It was thoughts like these that had led to several rounds of homemade cocktails the night before with his "business" partner, Keith. They'd only recently begun adding the quotation marks, and when Keith had pointed out halfway through the evening that they were having a *literal* pity party for themselves, Richard had pretended to be amused. He turned his head aside now and eyed the Bombay Sapphire still sitting, uncapped, on his coffee table. *Et tu, Bombay?* he asked it silently, unable, even in his dejection, to overcome his weakness for terrible puns, which was nearly as acute as his weakness for gin-and-tonics, and for madcap plans like starting his own production company with nothing to recommend him other than his (alleged) wits and youthful audacity. Three years ago, he and Keith had quit their jobs as glorified assistants for an established film producer to strike out on their own, and Richard feared that "striking out" was precisely what they'd done. Nowadays they worked out of each other's apartments with extended stints at a Coffee Bean in the Valley alongside all the other unemployed writers, actors, and producers whose irregular schedules ensured L.A.'s world-famous traffic would never be confined to a few simple "rush" hours in the day. True, they'd made some progress: Two Guys One Corp had sold a few feature screenplays, a pilot script or two. But despite considerable hustling and bustling, the much-sought-after green light to production remained elusive, a distant mirage always *just* out of reach. And until they reached it, there would be no money coming in.

Keith's parents had been supporting him for a while now, but Richard couldn't ask his parents for money they didn't have, mainly for fear they'd try to give it to him anyway. He'd finally exhausted the last of his savings from his previous job; he'd even depleted his pathetic little IRA. The time had come to be a cog in someone else's wheel again, but the Great Recession had affected Hollywood as much as any other industry, and he wasn't even sure he could land a job as solid as the one he'd left three years ago. Was he going to have to *work* at the Coffee Bean in the Valley? Maybe move there too, abandon the fashionable Silver Lake neighborhood he loved so much? *First-world problems*, he reminded himself. And yet they were real problems; they were his problems, because he wasn't ready to give up on the dream he'd dreamt beneath his *Star Wars* sheets twenty years ago in the suburbs of Boston.

Richard sat up, buoyed somewhat by the aspirin beginning to work its way through his system, but also by the blessings of a native sanguinity. So what if he had to work a soul-sucking job for a while? He'd do what needed to be done; he'd get back on his feet. Every time he contemplated his ongoing struggle to become a successful Hollywood producer, it wasn't long before that struggle began resembling the training montage from *Rocky* (any of them, though if pushed, he preferred the one from *Rocky IV*). Now he imagined himself toiling away at some sort of backbreaking manual labor involving lumber, or slabs of concrete, and copious smudges of grease across his face. He pictured himself waking up before dawn (it didn't matter that this had never happened in his life, not even once), putting in a hard day's work and then conferring with his faithful business partner late into the night, too virtuous and exhausted to spend the money that accumulated—slowly, but surely—in his ravaged bank account. Each week he'd check his balance online—no, forget that, he'd be paid in cash—and every Friday he'd watch the dollar bills rise, the pile growing steadily as the weeks went by, slowly at first, then faster, until the pile became a *tower*, so tall that down it came, bills swirling in a seamless smashcut to the confetti at the premiere party for his and Keith's first movie, to which he would invite all his brothers in arms from the . . . lumberyard/drilling place. And as he entered the banquet hall they'd cheer, clapping their red and calloused hands, and there might even be a few man-tears as they hoisted him on their shoulders and he looked down upon the astonished world, and beamed.

If, just then, a supernatural creature with powers of teleportation and prophecy had wiggled into view and announced that by the end of the week Richard's money woes would be over, first, he would have put on some pants, because at the moment he was wearing only boxers and they were by no means fit for company. Second, he would have feigned disbelief, but only, third, while secretly believing that *of course* it was true, it *had* to be true. Because he was still innocent enough to believe only good things would come his way, in a life that had every appearance of stretching endlessly before him.

Richard jumped up from the couch and this time the miracle stuck: headache gone, stomach settled. He retrieved his phone from underneath a pile of yesterday's clothes, yelping when he saw the time. 12:45, *yikes*. He had a meeting in less than two hours. Time to start his day.

"LA MÁQUINA!"

Elizabeth Santiago looked up from her desk, suppressing with great difficulty an intense urge to roll her eyes. From the hallway outside, a muscular man in suspenders was pointing at her. She stared at his perfectly manicured fingernail.

"Time to get yo lunch on!"

Oh, hell no. She tilted her head in the direction of a thermal lunch bag sitting on one of the chairs opposite her desk.

"La Máquina strikes again!" the man bellowed, shaking his head and grinning. Elizabeth grinned back, trying not to focus on the gelled rhino-horn of hair glistening atop his head. He was a fourth-year, wasn't he? What was his name? Jake? Jack? Jock? Why was she so terrible with names?

But it didn't matter, because he was already on the move again:

"La Máquina, La Máquina, La Máquina!"

He sounded like Speedy Gonzalez shouting *arriba arriba, ándale ándale!* As his voice faded down the hallway, Elizabeth unleashed the eye-roll she'd been suppressing. She glanced at the bottom of her screen: 2 hours, 26 minutes, and 41 seconds had elapsed since she'd begun reviewing the inch-thick document lying in pieces on her desk, and she hadn't looked up once. It was no mystery why everyone called her La Máquina (Spanish for "the Machine"). At first it was a nickname her colleagues used behind her back when she billed the most hours of any first-year associate at the firm, worldwide. (For the record: 3,352. Which was insane. And unsustainable.) At some point in her second year an accidental cc had clued her in, and it had required only a few seconds of calculation to craft a good-natured reply and sign it, "La Máquina." No harm done. But from there, the moniker had exploded till every lawyer in every department, and even a few of her clients, were using it.

She clicked off the timer at the bottom of the screen. There were those who suspected her of inflating her numbers, so she was especially vigilant about her timekeeping. For every two hours billed, a standard corporate lawyer spent approximately three hours in the office. This ratio accounted for regular human activities such as chatting with coworkers, surfing the Internet, eating lunch, and going to the bathroom. But in a ten- to twelve-hour workday, Elizabeth billed a staggering nine to ten hours regularly. She was always polite but never friendly; most days she brought her lunch instead of eating in the Lawyers' Dining Room with everyone else; she even made a habit of not drinking too many fluids throughout the day, thereby limiting her bathroom breaks to two: one midmorning, one midafternoon. She never went above 3,000 hours after that first year, but she routinely hit the high 2,000s.

Elizabeth knew she ran the risk of creating enemies by committing the double sin of shunning her coworkers *and* outpacing them, which was why she endured her nickname. It helped neutralize her otherness, which didn't come so much from her Mexican descent as from her steely reserve, her robotic ability to block out the noise others found so enticing. She was simply "La Máquina," the weird Latina who kept to herself and whose social life was a mystery, but who *more* than pulled her weight in the Mergers & Acquisitions Department of Slate Drubble & Greer, despite outweighing every female colleague in the office (stick-thin white girls, for the most part). She had become one of the family, even if she was the eccentric spinster aunt who kept to herself, an "odd duck," as the original Drubble's great-grandson had put it to her drunkenly one holiday party while invading her personal space. And as an eighth-year associate, she was practically guaranteed at a mere thirty-three years old to become a partner sometime in the coming year. All she had to do was keep on grinning, or nodding, or pointing whenever one of her colleagues accosted her with those two magic words she could just as easily have complained about to HR. Good ol' La Máquina.

Elizabeth closed her door, grabbing her lunch on the way back to her desk. She was expected to keep her door open unless she had a meeting, but she reasoned that lunch was a sort of meeting—*food, meet mouth*—and closed it for the five minutes spent inhaling whatever it was she brought from home. Today, however, she lingered over her PB&J, staring at the hideous painting behind her desk, a cartoonishly simplistic portrait of a scowling, peach-colored career woman in an eighties-era power suit, a sleeve of which had been pulled up to flex an absurdly oversized bicep. "We Can Do It!" the woman bellowed by means of a neon-yellow dialogue bubble above her head. It was a play on the famous World War II image often incorrectly identified as Rosie the Riveter, which was how Amber Hudson had referred to it while bestowing it on Elizabeth with great fanfare. Amber was Elizabeth's unofficial partner mentor, a woman who used phrases such as "having it all" and "you go, girl!" without a scintilla of irony, and while Elizabeth never would have chosen this ugly, distracting piece for herself (it looked like the work of an eighth grader), it had been impossible to decline. Once she made partner, her office would be hers alone to decorate. She turned away from the painting, glancing automatically at the time on her computer screen. At two thirty that afternoon she had a meeting with another lawyer, which was unremarkable except that she didn't know the lawyer, or his firm, and had been instructed the meeting was of a "personal nature." When she had asked for more information, she'd been told that all would be revealed in the meeting. Elizabeth did not like surprises, and had taken it upon herself to discover what little she could ahead of time.

She knew that Jonathan Hertzfeld was a partner at a boutique law firm in Century City specializing in estates planning—wills and trusts and other instruments meant to stave off or at least temper the vagaries of passing through this uncertain world. The most likely scenario was that someone had died and left her property, except that she didn't know anyone who had died, or who was rich enough to leave her anything in the first place. Elizabeth had grown up less than twenty miles from her office in Beverly Hills, but it was a neighborhood she was willing to bet Jonathan Hertzfeld had never visited, or even passed through in his car. And there was no one from her adult life she could imagine wanting to make her a gift significant enough to require a lawyer. For at least the tenth time since setting the meeting yesterday, she wondered what it could possibly be about. A shiver might even have run up her spine in this moment if it hadn't been thwarted by the mundane business of crunching into an apple, upon which she focused for the next minute and a half.

If that same supernatural creature from Richard Baumbach's apartment had shimmered into view right now and told Elizabeth she would bill exactly zero hours after her meeting today and no more than eight hours total for the rest of the week, she would first have insisted on knowing through what sleight of hand the shimmering effect had been achieved and, second, she would have ushered the poor deluded creature out of her office while placing a discreet call to security. But third, she would have cursed her weakness for secretly believing the creature had spoken the truth, because its prediction would have confirmed what she had suspected since yesterday: that some form of calamity awaited her at this meeting of a "personal nature," something to derail the quiet, orderly life she'd worked so hard to build for herself.

Lunchtime was over. Elizabeth opened her door. She restarted the timer on her screen and immersed herself once more in the work at hand.

RICHARD SQUINTED THROUGH the windshield of his used Toyota Corolla, notorious among his crew for being the only car they knew that still had manual locks and roll-up windows. His best friend Mike said it was like entering a time capsule whose contents no one wanted to remember. It was a little past 2 p.m., and still overcast: typical for an afternoon in L.A. in the beginning of June. Most other times of the year, the "marine layer" of clouds that blew in overnight from the coast would have burned off by now, if it existed at all, but anywhere from May to July, when the rest of the Northern Hemisphere was bursting into the full bloom of summer, L.A. was often shrouded in "June gloom" until the late afternoon. Like many transplants, Richard still obsessed over the weather, disappointed every time it failed to match the stereotypical perfection of sunny warmth and azure heavens. If they were headed toward a post-apocalyptic, *Mad Max*–ian hellscape in a few years anyway (sporadic El Niño effect notwithstanding), it could at least be sunny all the time.

Turning onto Santa Monica Boulevard, he became mired suddenly in lunchtime traffic: a single false step sinking him helplessly, like quicksand. Rather than railing uselessly against the traffic, Richard forced himself to focus on his upcoming appointment, even though it was just a general, with a lawyer he couldn't even remember meeting. The guy had called him yesterday and asked for a face-to-face, something of a "personal nature," which meant he had a nephew, or a neighbor, or a nephew's neighbor, or a neighbor's nephew who'd written a script. If he were busier, Richard would have insisted the lawyer spell it out over the phone and simply e-mail him whatever it was he wanted him to read. But what else did he have to do? Besides, you never knew where the next great script might come from. Heartened by this thought, he snagged a CD from among the debris on his passenger floor and slid it in the player (he had a tape deck too, not that he had any cassettes). It was a homemade mix and he skipped ahead to the eighth track, "Eye of the Tiger," the vestiges of his *Rocky* montage still lingering inside his head, a happy dream half-remembered. He began shouting along:

"Rising up! Back on the street . . ."

The light ahead of him turned green and he lurched forward with the rest of the traffic, bleating the whole time. The light was faster than expected, however, and turned yellow while there was still one car ahead of him. Richard glanced at the intersection; it was clear, and he allowed his car to drift, head nodding along to the beat, assuming they would both keep moving forward:

"And he's watching us all with the eeeeeeeeeeeeye—"

The car ahead of him stopped suddenly. Richard had to jam on his brakes, causing the CD to skip and leaving him to shout on his own:

"OF THE TIGER!"

He shook off this humiliation by honking a rebuke to the slowpoke in front of him, whose shiny bumper he'd missed by an inch, maybe two. Richard eyed the car; it was immaculate, probably brand-new. That was all he needed—to shell out an ungodly sum for some minuscule dent or scratch, or, worse, risk jacking up his insurance.

ELIZABETH SHRUGGED AT the filthy car behind her. It was true; she could've made the light. But the rule was to slow down at a yellow light, not speed up, and the fact that no one else seemed to remember this made her all the more eager to remember it herself.

A dreadlocked man who had been standing at the side of the road began shambling drunkenly between lanes, begging for change. When she lowered her window, his head swerved toward her, and he stopped so abruptly the top half of his body had to compensate in a liquid bend from the waist that reminded her of those Gumby-ish air funnels that twist and dip from the roofs of used car dealerships and secondhand furniture stores. He hurried toward her.

"Mocha chip or yogurt honey peanut? Or both?" she asked him brightly, holding out two Balance Bars retrieved from her glove compartment.

He blinked. "Both, I guess."

"Here you go!" She handed them over. The window rose between them; he had to yank his hand back to avoid being nipped. As he stumbled toward the sidewalk, Elizabeth watched his lips working furiously in what was probably a torrent of abuse leveled at her (surely he would have preferred money), but barely a minute later, he'd ripped open one of the bars and begun devouring it.

The light was still red. Elizabeth used the extra downtime to close her eyes for five seconds, counting on her left hand with "Mississippis" in between, her way of ensuring she took enough time to acknowledge something good in her life, no matter how small. In fact, the smaller the better, and especially when it was a blessing in an otherwise unfortunate situation. A new friend of hers (*yes*, she thought, with the tiniest thrill of pride, *La Máquina can make new friends*) had inspired her recently not to ignore these destitute men and women she saw from time to time on the road, as long as she didn't compromise her safety. For almost six months now, she'd kept her glove compartment stocked with Balance Bars for this exact purpose, and this was only the second time she'd been able to use them.

The light turned green.

RICHARD FOLLOWED THE car ahead of him through the intersection and then left onto Avenue of the Stars. But instead of proceeding to the address he'd been given, he turned off at the Century City Mall, where parking was only a dollar an hour for up to three hours. (He'd forgotten to ask if parking at the lawyer's building would be validated, and he couldn't afford to leave it to chance.) By the time he extricated himself from the mall's labyrinth of a garage, jaywalked across the street, snagged an elevator, tracked down the correct suite, and supplied his name to the modelesque receptionist at the front desk, it was 2:38. He was ushered immediately into a conference room where a man and woman sat waiting in silence.

WHEN ELIZABETH HAD been shown into the room exactly eight minutes earlier, the old man she assumed was Jonathan Hertzfeld had told her they were waiting for one more, and he hadn't said another word. He was wearing suspenders, and she couldn't help thinking of him as an age-progressed version of Jake/Jack/Jock. When the second guest arrived, Elizabeth felt a jolt of something akin to surprise. She hardly knew what she was expecting, but it wasn't this: a boyish-looking man sweating visibly through his T-shirt, a sizable rip in one knee of his undeniably grimy jeans. What was he, twelve? Who wore jeans to a meeting anyway? He was attractive, admittedly, but this was nothing special. So were a lot of people in L.A.

RICHARD TOOK A chair opposite the woman, who looked straight out of *Working Girl* with her high heels and tailored business suit. Obviously she was another lawyer. Maybe she was the one who'd written the script? On the side? *Doubtful.*

But she did have the best breasts he'd seen in a while.

"I'M SURE YOU'RE both wondering why you're here."

Richard Baumbach and Elizabeth Santiago eyed each other across the Formica vista of the conference room table.

"At this point you're probably aware I'm an estates attorney."

Huh? thought Richard, while the woman nodded owlishly. *Like wills and stuff?* His heart began to race. Someone had died and was leaving him a boatload of cash. He *knew* it! He was saved!

"No one has died," said the lawyer. "I represent my clients when they die, but I represent them while they're living, too—in particular, when they wish to dispose of property. And one of my clients is offering you five hundred thousand dollars each, *if* you'll agree to spend some time together. At

least once a week for two continuous hours, for one full calendar year."

Richard's eyebrows tilted downward in an exaggerated V
that looked almost comical, like a vaudeville pantomime, but
Elizabeth's face didn't move at all. It was her frozen mask—
suggestive of horror—that made the lawyer pause, and inside
this pause his brisk manner fell away. He took refuge in his
notes, slipping on a rimless pair of reading glasses with a flus-
tered, fumbling air. Though he wasn't quite sixty-five, in this
moment he looked older, almost feeble, while struggling to find
his place.

"Please understand that my client wishes to remain anonymous. I can tell you nothing about this individual."

His eyes flicked upward in apology. He forced them down
again.

"Let's see . . . a few points: There cannot be any third parties
present except for incidental reasons—waiters at restaurants and ·
so forth—and you must conduct yourselves in a substantially
conversational manner. That is to say, it is not enough to merely
remain in each other's presence for the two hours. You must *talk*
during them. But please note that conversation is the only re-
quirement, and the subject of this conversation is immaterial."

He removed his glasses and began polishing them on his
silken tie with an air of relief.

Richard was the first to speak. He laughed: a single, disbe-
lieving bark of a laugh.

"Half a *million* dollars? *Each?*"

The lawyer nodded.

"You're kidding, right?" Richard made a show of whipping
his head around the room, as if he were looking for a hidden
camera, but even now, seconds after hearing the proposal, a part
of him was wondering if he could ask for an advance.

The lawyer put down his glasses and shook his head, *no.*

"But . . . why?" Richard asked. "I mean, we've never met before—"

He swung his head in the woman's direction.

"—right?"

She nodded, which was the first time she'd moved since the lawyer had spoken.

"So why us? What's the point?"

The lawyer spread out his hands. "I'm afraid I can't give you any reasons, just the proposal itself. These were my client's express instructions."

Elizabeth felt as though she were watching them from inside a glass bottle, or some sort of aquarium or other transparent tank. It was hard to follow what they were saying, but she could see them perfectly, and she tracked every hand gesture and head movement now as if her life depended on it. The lawyer's proposal was a trap, obviously, or a joke, or something equally cruel. She wanted nothing to do with it. If there was one thing she knew, it was that nothing came for free.

"I've made two copies of the formal agreement, which lays out in more detail what I've already told you, along with standard and customary supplementation: representations and warranties, a no-publicity clause, the pro rata payment schedule, and so forth."

With a jerk of his hands, he pushed two stapled documents in opposite directions over the glossy tabletop, as if they were air hockey pucks. Richard caught his copy and turned over the pages without reading them. No matter what ended up happening, he couldn't wait to tell Mike, who was going to *Freak. The Hell. Out.*

Elizabeth let her copy slide off the table and fall to the ground. She stared at it, and then at the lawyer, as if to say: *that's what I think of your proposal.*

"How were we selected for this?" she asked finally, her dark eyes boring into him.

Richard looked up: *yeah, how?*

"I'm afraid I can't tell you that either," the lawyer said. "But no one has violated your privacy. And I give you my word no one ever will."

"But we don't know you," said Elizabeth, her exasperation lending her voice a degree of animation it didn't usually have. "And we don't know who's making the offer. You can't seriously expect us to go along with this? Without more information?"

The lawyer stared at her.

"Would *you* accept this proposal?" she demanded.

"I know this is a very, ahem, *unusual* disclosure to receive, and in so sudden a manner," he said. "But I thought this was the best way."

There was a long pause, during which Elizabeth conveyed with perfect eloquence the unspoken notion that sometimes, the best wasn't good enough. She stood up. "I have to get back to work," she said. "It was nice meeting you both."

The flatness of her tone couldn't have articulated the opposite meaning more clearly than if she'd spat on them.

"You have until the end of the week to think it over," the lawyer called out a little desperately, and Elizabeth gave him the courtesy of stopping while he continued. "I suggest you exchange contact information and talk it over in a day or two. Maybe over coffee? And of course you know how to reach me."

Richard sprang up. He couldn't let her go without having some way of contacting her. He pulled out a business card from his wallet and shoved it in her direction.

"Here, just in case. It's got my cell and e-mail."

"I don't have any cards on me," she said, accepting his reluctantly.

"That's okay, what's your e-mail?" His fingertips hovered over his phone.

She rattled off a Gmail address he hoped she wasn't making up on the spot. And then, after an awkward pause, she swooped down to retrieve her copy of the contract, and for a moment he caught a bird's-eye view of those spectacular breasts. The next moment she was gone. Richard rolled his contract into a cylinder, batting it against his leg while saluting the lawyer ironically. By the time he reached the elevators, she was nowhere to be seen. He opted for the stairs so as to call Mike immediately.

THE TASK WAS done, but Jonathan Hertzfeld felt no sense of accomplishment for having completed it. He walked to the window of the conference room and looked down. The Century City Mall spread out below him, the crown jewel of the neighborhood, a giant outdoor maze lined with high-end shops like Armani, Coach, and Louis Vuitton. The mall's food court was as elaborate as a food court could possibly be without becoming something better, but it always struck him as the block of cheese reserved at the center for the lucky rats that managed to find it. Usually he pitied the hordes that scurried below him. He had no taste for shopping, and was the rare attorney who enjoyed his job. He took old-fashioned pride in spending long hours inside his air-conditioned box on high, and had been doing so for forty years. But today he envied the vermin their simple pleasures. He rubbed his tie pin between his right thumb and middle finger, a fidgety habit from prep school days. Today, he would rather be anywhere but here.

The worst of it was that he was almost as clueless as the two young people who had just left him. He had no idea *why* his client had insisted on making this proposal. He had no idea *how* two perfect strangers had been selected, neither of whom was a family relation. He had simply been given two names and an assurance that there *was* a connection, along with a set of instructions. And he had done his duty to the letter, as always.

Elizabeth Santiago, at least, had been a pleasant surprise. Jonathan had liked her reserved manner and businesslike attire. He had been able to admire her dark, watchful eyes and pleasing figure without feeling unwholesome, the way he did when noticing more . . . obvious women. (One of the many pitfalls of aging was how easily he could be made to feel like a dirty old man.) He guessed that her quiet brand of comeliness went largely unobserved, and forty years ago this would have been enough for him to single her out from inside a crowd, to do whatever he could to make those serious features relax into a smile. (It *had* been enough, though the woman, of course, had been another.)

Richard Baumbach had left a less favorable impression. Jonathan knew it was an old-fashioned term, but despite Mr. Baumbach's careless way of dressing, he had struck Jonathan as a "playboy," one who would have been more in his element at a nocturnal social gathering surrounded by an adoring, mainly female crowd. Such men were no more likely to be good or bad men than others, but they didn't interest him much, and he wondered if Miss Santiago felt the same way.

But what he *really* wondered was what his wife would have to say about it all. Jonathan didn't usually take Rivka into his confidence on professional matters—she had more interesting things to think about, she liked to say—but every now and then he breached confidentiality when he felt it was necessary to his peace of mind. That evening, he told her everything while they were washing up the dishes. (They owned a state-of-the-art dishwasher, but preferred, much to their grown children's amused disbelief, to wash up together by hand—a tradition dating back to the first years of their marriage.) Rivka cackled over the folly of the proposal and predicted with sadistic glee that it would do more to harm than help the supposed beneficiaries, should they be so idiotic as to accept it. Jonathan secretly agreed, but true to his profession he played devil's advocate now for the sake of teasing out the argument:

"I'm sure it's perfectly innocent. I can't see what harm will come to them."

Rivka shook her head impatiently, setting free a cluster of soap bubbles. "With that much money? Nothing's innocent. You be careful, Jonathan."

She pointed a knobby finger his way, and he grabbed hold of it, kissing its shiny tip.

"Little cynic," he murmured, causing her to blush like a teenage girl, though she too was nearly sixty-five years old. Over time this phrase had become something of an endearment. "Nothing bad will happen, except more headaches for *me*."

"The way they work you," she grumbled.

Jonathan had given up reminding her he was no longer a bright-eyed young associate but his own boss now, with the luxury of choosing how hard he worked on any task. Rivka's scrubbing turned vicious, and he paused in his drying to admire her as she continued:

"It's too much! But you listen to me. Those two'd better forget it if they know what's good for them. Whatever it is connects that boy and girl, it's got to be some *trick* or else they'd know it from the start. It's meddling, and no good ever comes from *that*, let me tell you."

It was, Jonathan reflected, one of the tragedies of his life that he could never prove his wife wrong. So rather than pursue a hopeless argument, he opted to pop a tiny bubble that had landed on her wrinkled cheek, and kiss the soapy remains.

"Get back to work!" she scolded him.

"I thought you said I work too hard?"

"I take it back!"

For him, this was victory enough.

THE COFFEE

ELIZABETH SAW HIM before he saw her. She lingered at the condiments station, clearing away the milk stains and sugar granules left by previous customers to observe him a little longer. Okay, fine: he was unusually good-looking, even by L.A. standards. *You could practically cut yourself on that jawline*, she thought. *Cheekbones too*. His face may as well have been carved from marble, his nose was so straight, his forehead so perfectly smooth. True, his mouth ruined the illusion partially by curling a little at the edges—even while at rest—and he had sweeping, crescent lashes no man had any business having, but why hide it? He was striking. Or as striking as someone wearing the same ripped and dirty jeans from four days earlier could be. *Hello, old friends*. At least he'd changed his shirt. This one was a little thinner, a little tighter, showing off a lean, lightly muscled build that either came naturally or had been acquired with great discipline, and she was willing to bet he rarely saw the inside of a gym. There was an aura of effortless, even *careless* health about him—the way he kept thumping his leg against the floor, for instance—the by-product of a hyperactivity she remembered now from their meeting, a cheerful energy, more brisk than manic, the boyish vigor of playground antics and long afternoons in the sun.

There was no use denying it. If this were a party, or—God forbid—some sort of singles mixer, he was hands down the unlikeliest person for her to approach on this sun-drenched, jam-packed terrace in the middle of the day. But this is precisely what she did now, drawing in her breath and striding forward like an actress who'd been waiting in the wings and was finally making her grand entrance center stage.

The sun blinded her—a spotlight gone awry—and she paused, unsure of her mark, flailing already for her opening line. *What the hell am I doing here?* she asked herself.

WHEN RICHARD CAUGHT sight of her, she was blinking into the sun, a ceramic cup the size of a cereal bowl hoisted in front of her like a shield. His right leg thumped a little harder, a little higher. It was he who had e-mailed, and insisted they at least meet to talk things over. Urth Caffe had been his idea, a busy spot below Wilshire in Beverly Hills, one of his favorite neighborhoods, so different from its popular depiction in movies like *Pretty Woman* (Julia Roberts sashaying down Rodeo Drive, oversize shopping bags dripping off her arms). The real thing was cozier, more like a village center back east: a walkable grid of streets whose buildings were crammed together so tightly, it wouldn't have surprised him if one of them buckled one day like an overcrowded tooth shifting sideways. Tiny cafés and restaurants spilled, European-style, onto sidewalks crammed with pedestrians (a rarity in L.A.), and yet there was none of the darkness or dirt that stuck to other city blocks. The sun shined more brightly here thanks to the white façades of high-end jewelry and clothing boutiques. This was where the fussy geriatric crowd came for old-school breakfasts at Nate 'n Al and ornate lunches at La Scala. In the afternoon, packs of Persian-American preteens released from school prowled the streets trailing tailwinds of designer scent, while overworked talent agents from the surrounding office buildings zoomed past them in fancy suits. Even now, on a Saturday, Richard saw a few of these industry types dotting the terrace, clad in workout gear and toiling away at "weekend reads" on their iPads and Kindles. *I should be reading too,* he thought, lifting his hand to wave at her, but he hadn't read a thing since the meeting at the lawyer's office. He *had* gotten past his initial shock, though. Before returning to his car in the mall parking lot, he and Mike had already concocted a nickname for the whole ridiculous situation: "The Decent Proposal," which was a twist on *Indecent Proposal,* of course, which they'd hate-watched recently on DVD (he owned a copy, though he had no idea why). The next day, a Wednesday, he called his mom in a rare violation of their Sunday routine, which usually consisted of a brief summary of his week (briefer than ever, recently), followed by a maternal roundup of hometown gossip and political outrage punctuated at some point by an obligatory three-minute interlude from his father checking in on his health, his finances, and his car, always in that order. (All three were invariably "fine Dad, fine.") The Wednesday call had been an aberration. Richard knew his accountant father would still be at work, but his stay-at-home mom had been—true to her profession—at home, and after telling her in a breathless manner about the Decent Proposal, he sat back, enjoying the stunned silence. He could practically hear the gears whirring inside her head.

"You're not actually considering it?" she asked him finally.

"Why not?" he asked, playing dumb for his own amusement.

"Because it isn't safe!" she wailed.

Richard's amusement turned instantly to exasperation: a conjuring trick only his mother was capable of performing. He huffed like a five-year-old. When Richard *was* five, he remembered looking up—literally up—to impossibly tall high schoolers, wondering what it would feel like to be all grown up like them. Somewhere in his junior year he realized his error: *college* was where adulthood truly began. So it was during his graduation ceremony at Amherst that he readjusted his expectations once again, assuring himself that at some point in his twenties it would happen: that magical moment when he would become an *adult.* And now here he was, on the cusp of *thirty fucking years old* and still he felt like a child, especially in moments like this—of involuntary petulance directed toward the loving mother he knew only wanted what was best for him. And yet he could do nothing to stop himself. The phone call had ended unsatisfactorily on both sides, and when his parents had called him a few hours later he wasn't surprised, though the last time they'd gotten on the line together like this was to tell him his grandmother had died.

"Is this an intervention?" he joked.

"We're just concerned, Richie," his mother began. "It's so *odd.* You don't even know this woman—"

"She doesn't know me either."

"If you really need the money," his father cut in, "maybe we can figure something out."

"I'm *fine*," snapped Richard.

"So you always say. You win the lottery or something? Not tell us?"

"Maybe we should fly out there," his mother suggested.

"That's stupid," he said. "You were just here." His parents always visited him in April to bridge the gap between his holiday and summer visits to Massachusetts—visits they paid for, since he was unable to cover the airfare himself. "Stop worrying," he commanded them. "It's not like I made up my mind or anything."

And yet it was only after making this statement that he realized he *had* made up his mind. Because obviously they had to do it. *Obviously.* It was almost too good to be true . . . but only almost. Richard was already imagining the wide eyes and open mouths he'd leave in his wake for the next year and beyond; he'd become the best general meeting in town. Maybe he'd even spin the Decent Proposal into a movie. He had no idea who had chosen him, or why, but he felt certain he'd been chosen wisely and he was eager to reap his reward—not only for the money, but for the *adventure*, for the *story*, in a life that had been stagnant for too long.

WHEN ELIZABETH COULD see again, he was beckoning excitedly with one hand raised high. Some of the people at the tables around him were looking at her too. She guessed they were idly curious to see who belonged to the good-looking stranger. This, then, was what it was like to be one of *those* people, the ones whom others noticed in a crowd. A flair of excitement licked greedily at her insides, nearly causing her to spill her cappuccino. *Calm down,* she urged herself, unwilling to betray her unobserved life, her unmolested freedom. It was the weekend, and for once she didn't have to go into the office; she should have been spending her precious free time on a long skate down the Boardwalk, or surfing in the ocean, or simply lazing, catlike, in her Venice bungalow with the latest obscure Victorian author to catch her fancy (Gissing, at the moment). Contrary to what her coworkers thought, there was a lot to occupy La Máquina's spare time. *It's just coffee,* she reminded herself, not for the first time since responding to Richard Baumbach's e-mail. She'd be back at home in an hour or two at most.

RICHARD WATCHED HER as she walked toward him. She was wearing a loose, collared shirt and calf-length khakis, a curiously formal outfit for the weekend, especially in L.A., where no one other than the aforementioned agents ever *really* dressed up. (This was one of many things Richard loved about the city, and he took great joy in dressing like a slob at all times.) There would be no ogling her breasts today, but he still couldn't help remarking on her ample, curvy shape. *Voluptuous.* Now there was a word he almost never used out here, though as she drew closer he saw it didn't quite fit her either. Voluptuous women invited attention, and even though Elizabeth Santiago was on the tall side (but not *too* tall; he still had a few inches on her), there was a defensive hunch to her shoulders that annulled her height, and a hint of what was commonly known as RBS (Resting Bitchface Syndrome) warping her otherwise amiable features: a high forehead (crinkled), snub nose (nostrils flared), and generous lips (pinched into submission). Her dark hair, which had been up in the lawyer's office, was in a ponytail now, and while it was surprisingly long, almost tickling the small of her back, it was so tight it actually added to the overall severity of her appearance. He never would have chatted her up if she were a stranger, for fear of an icy reception.

She had arrived at his table.

"HEYYYYYYYY," HE SAID, drawing out the syllable nervously, hoping it came across the opposite way.

"Hey," she said, balancing her gargantuan mug on the minuscule table, noticing his iced black coffee was more than halfway gone already. She sat down.

"So . . . ," he began, before realizing he didn't know how to begin at all.

"So." She leaned back, crossing her arms.

"Are you going to repeat everything I say?" he asked her, grinning.

Elizabeth felt a tugging at her lips. His energy was infectious. Already she felt a little overstimulated, and made a mental note to go easy on the cappuccino. There was only one way to answer his question, however:

"Are you going to repeat everything I say?"

He threw his head back—actually *threw* it back, as if his neck were on a spring—and let his laughter rip. *It's wasn't that funny,* she wanted to tell him, glancing uneasily at the tables around them. But his laughter ended as abruptly as it started, and when his head snapped back into place she was surprised to see his handsome features engulfed in red. *He's more nervous than I am,* she realized.

"Honestly I have no idea what to say," he confessed. "This is weird, right?"

She nodded.

"I mean, do you have a boyfriend?"

Elizabeth drew back, as if stung. This was among a handful of questions she dreaded, though usually it was implied rather than asked outright, and almost always by another woman. She couldn't blame him, though. A significant other would complicate the situation. Maybe he was asking because he had one of his own.

"No," she said, doing everything in her power to keep from sounding surly or defensive. "You?"

"A boyfriend? Nah." He snorted. Sometimes people thought he was gay, not that he minded in the least. "No girlfriend either."

Elizabeth wasn't the only stranger he wouldn't dare approach. An instinctive fear of rejection honed during his gawkier years had rendered Richard a bit of a coward when it came to the opposite sex. Like many he relied on alcohol to break down his inhibitions, and when he was drunk he *always* went home with someone, if that was what he wanted to do. But he never particularly cared to see these women again, and over the years he'd acquired a reputation he didn't half mind as king of the one-night stands, which of course led to even *more* one-night stands. He'd had exactly one serious relationship, but that had been in college—ages ago—and he was in no rush to settle down. No one really took him seriously anymore when it came to matters of the heart—including himself.

"Maybe they picked us because they knew we were single," he said. "Personally—"

He edged his chair closer, as if imparting a great confidence.

"—I think it might be a reality show."

"Oh God, do you think?" Elizabeth's eyes widened with horror. The thought had never occurred to her.

"Well," he backpedaled, "I'm not sure how they'd film it unless a crew followed us every week, and it doesn't sound like that's part of the plan. Plus, even if they *did*, they'd have to get our consent before they aired anything. So I wouldn't worry about it."

"Do you work in reality?" she asked politely, lifting her mug with both hands.

"God no," he said. "I do some scripted TV, mainly film."

"Oh, are you an actor?"

She took a longer sip than needed to mask her agitation. *Please don't be an actor*, she begged him inside her head.

"God no," he repeated, flushing again, but with pleasure this time. "I'm a producer."

Could be worse, she thought, while asking, "Oh, really?" in her best cocktail-banter voice.

"Yeah. I have a movie coming out in a few months. *Fight on a Flight*, starring Duke Rifferson?" This was only half-true. The head of the production company Richard and Keith had abandoned was the real producer of the movie, but due to their (infinitesimal) involvement in the selling of the script five years earlier, they'd managed to secure low-rent "associate producer" credits on the screen. Everyone in Hollywood embellished their accomplishments this way; it was helpful to trot out technically accurate, impressive facts like this to keep up the illusion you were flourishing. But Elizabeth Santiago did not seem to be impressed. She was staring at him blankly.

"Duke Rifferson," he said again. "The star of *Bennington Park?*"

She stared, if anything, more blankly.

"The TV show?"

"I don't watch TV," she said.

Ugh, thought Richard. *One of those.* It was his turn to stare. Maybe she was super-religious? She was Latina, wasn't she? He knew there were some crazy Catholics out there. (He'd grown up outside of Boston, after all.) *It doesn't matter*, he reminded himself.

"Okay, I'm just gonna say it," he announced.

Elizabeth put down her cup.

"I think we should do it. I mean, it's crazy, obviously, some stranger wanting us to meet for a year, especially since we're strangers too. But there's probably some random connection we'll figure out eventually. Which reminds me—I looked for you on Facebook to see if we had any friends in common but I couldn't find you. Do you use a nickname or something?"

"I'm not on Facebook," she said.

No TV, no Facebook. Forget Catholic, was she Amish? He moved on quickly:

"Anyway, who knows? But who cares, kinda, right? I mean . . . why not? It's a crapload of money. And if safety's an issue we can always meet in public places."

He grinned again, and so did she, even though she didn't

want to. Wasn't he going to ask her about herself? But it was obvious he didn't really care about her, or whatever connected them. He only cared about the money. . . . Elizabeth stroked the rim of her mug, as if it were a wineglass capable of humming. She didn't need to be reminded of the money. She'd already run up the numbers: if she factored in an extra hour each week for travel and another 25 on top of that for incidental time expenditures like traffic and this coffee, that came out to 181 hours total. According to section 35 of the contract she'd picked up from the floor, the anonymous donor would take care of all gift or income taxes; they would each receive their half a million free and clear. This meant she would be making north of $2,750/ hour for her time, whereas if she divided her base salary and bonus by the number of hours she spent at the firm (billables plus incidentals), her rate came out to less than $150/hour, and that was *before* taxes. The proposal itself was absurd, but the numbers didn't lie. They never did.

This didn't change the fact that the proposal wasn't to be trusted. She remained convinced it was a trap and she refused to fall for it, no matter how much Richard Baumbach might try to sweet-talk her into acting like a greedy fool. Plus, she didn't *need* the money. Her mortgage was on track. Her investments were diverse and thriving. Elizabeth took great pride in her fiscal fortitude; it felt almost like an imposition to be offered such a fantastic sum, like an unwarranted interference with her best-laid plans. No; it was impossible.

But then why had she come? If she were really so immovable, she should have refused him by e-mail. In part it was because she knew someone who could truly use the money: a friend who was struggling, and who would actually accept her charity if she went about bestowing it the right way, or so she hoped. Could she really pass up an opportunity to be an honest-to-goodness savior? But there was another reason too. When she had told

Richard she didn't have a boyfriend, Elizabeth had neglected to add the word *never*. At eighteen, she went through a period she referred to now as her "rough patch," because to call it anything else would be to give it more power over her than it already had. She had emerged from this tumult without a hitch in her academic career or the law career to follow. But throughout her twenties, and now into her thirties, the rough patch became a justification for the black hole—there was nothing else to call it—that was her romantic life. She'd grown used to comforting herself that she was doing so well in every other aspect of her existence, *what with that rough patch and all,* that she could afford to do nothing in this one thorny, difficult-to-navigate area. But it was time, she knew, to address the deficiency, to stop making excuses based on the past and to do better. Elizabeth would rather have died than become one of those women who perpetually bemoaned their singlehood, but lately she'd begun asking herself if this was it, if she was okay not only with being alone for the rest of her life (she felt certain she was, if it came to it), but with not even *trying*?

Thus far she'd managed to visit a few online dating sites, but she could never bring herself to subscribe. Dipping a toe in the dating pool was always *just* horrifying enough to paralyze her at its edge; she couldn't imagine diving in headfirst. Every now and then she made a begrudging effort to meet men the old-fashioned way, in person at organized events like alumni reunions and recreational outings. She'd even forced herself to go to a few bars. These episodes were disasters, all of them, and invariably brought on a wave of reinvigorated contentment with her status quo, because she *did* have a good life—a great life. But then a few weeks or months would go by and she'd begin wondering all over again: was there something better even than "great" out there, some higher state within her reach if only she pushed herself a little harder?

Elizabeth looked directly at the sun. This time she courted it, allowing it to burn a hole in her field of vision. It was a trick of hers acquired during college. Whenever she was on the brink of a momentous decision she forced herself to look at the sun (or a lightbulb if it was nighttime), and wait until the spot faded from view before deciding one way or the other. The idea was that this would prevent her from acting rashly, but the ritual itself was mildly masochistic and she tried not to indulge it too often.

"I have to go to the bathroom," she announced, getting up to stall for time while the spot faded from view.

Richard watched her disappear, his stomach twisting in dismay. For the first time he considered the possibility that this coffee might not go his way. Was she actually going to *refuse*? Why would she do that? His mind began racing, his leg thumping harder to keep up with the thoughts roiling inside him.

ELIZABETH ADJUSTED HER ponytail in the mirror, pulling it a little tighter. She ignored the pulsating sunspot, focusing for a moment on her face instead: nothing to cut herself on in *there*. She looked away quickly, down at the sink, wiggling her fingers beneath the hands-free faucet. She avoided dwelling on her looks, not because she had any particular problem with them, but because such thoughts were restricted and repetitive and ultimately beneath her. She gave up on the faucet, sidestepping to the one beside it. There was nothing wrong with dwelling on *his* looks, though. Would it be so bad, having to look at his face every week for a year?

A thin stream of water trickled from the faucet. The proposal was a risk, it was true, but some risks were worth taking; she was perfectly aware that some rewards couldn't be seen—let alone calculated—in advance. If she refused, would she be throwing away a once-in-a-lifetime opportunity? Wasn't this proposal, ridiculous and idiotic as it was, a better alternative to yet another abortive cycle of dating? She wouldn't actually be *dating* him, but that was exactly the point: it would be like inching into that freezing pool a little more each week, a sort of intensive tutorial—a *paid* intensive tutorial—on relations with the opposite sex. She still believed the proposal was a trap, but wasn't every trap also a sort of *challenge*?

Elizabeth cupped her hands beneath the dryer stuck against the wall. The machine clicked on, the harsh rush of hot air assaulting her ears. It wasn't like her to be indecisive. She consoled herself with the thought that either way, her ordeal today would soon be over. Elizabeth pictured herself leaving Urth Caffe—exiting this floodlit stage and returning to her tiny house three blocks from the vast, unchanging ocean, where no one other than George Gissing awaited her. It would be such a *relief.*

Wouldn't it?

She grew impatient with the dryer, wiping her hands on her pants. The sunspot was gone.

FROM ACROSS THE TERRACE, Elizabeth caught sight of him staring at her. She knew she had to act now, or else lose her nerve. She walked toward him, watching as he averted his eyes guiltily, taking refuge in a long, crackly pull on his straw. She almost laughed. He was harmless, wasn't he? She could easily throw herself into his life for a two-hour lesson each week and then climb back out again, couldn't she?

Elizabeth dropped into her seat, waiting till he finished slurping like a five-year-old.

"Okay, here's the thing," she said.

He nodded eagerly. Now he was a puppy. All he needed were the floppy ears.

"I'm willing, *in theory*, to take some crazy person's money if they want to throw it away."

"Hear, hear." He proffered his iced coffee for a toast.

She stared at him till he lowered it.

"But let's agree right now," she said, "that we're only doing this for the money."

"Of course," he said, cheeks ablaze once again, because *of course* he'd thought about the possibility that the Decent Proposal was some sort of matchmaking scheme. How could he not? Even Mike had been quick to point out that this was exactly the sort of situation in which love was supposed to spring up unexpectedly, a weed between a crack in the cement, a miracle of life where none existed before. But Richard had pointed out that this analogy was both *gay* and *lame*, and then Mike had pointed out that those were both *offensive* and *outdated* words to use, and the conversation had derailed from there.

"Why?" Richard couldn't help himself from adding now, another grin spreading across his face. "Are you worried we're going to fall in love?"

Elizabeth rolled her eyes so quickly, it was more of a flicker. "I'm really not," she said. "I just want to make sure we're on the same page."

"Absolutely," he said. "We are one hundred percent doing it for the money. Roger that. Confirmed."

"Good. Now from what I can see, it's a valid contract. I'm a lawyer," she added by way of explanation.

"Oh, cool!" he exclaimed. "Who do you rep, anyone I might know?"

"Probably not. I do corporate M-and-A."

He was pretty sure that meant mergers and acquisitions, but instead of asking he just nodded.

"I did a little research on Jonathan Hertzfeld and his firm. And I consulted with a colleague who specializes in trusts—redacting our names, of course. It all seems legit."

Richard nodded again. He hadn't checked on anything other

than the payment schedule. And while it sounded like she hadn't told anyone about the proposal, he'd told upwards of a dozen friends and begun adding *#DecentProposal* to as many of his tweets as possible. But she didn't need to know this. He approximated his best businesslike manner:

"So do we have a deal?"

She extended her hand across the table.

"We do."

They parted a few minutes later, Richard eager to leave before she changed her mind, and Elizabeth figuring there would be more than enough time in the year to come to run out of things to say.

THE BEST FRIEND

EARLY ON THE MONDAY after Richard and Elizabeth's coffee, Mike Kim burst out of her Santa Monica apartment building in exercise shorts and a sports bra, pausing at the blue recycling bin on the curb to toss away a letter she'd stopped reading after "Dear Mr. Kim." Like many Asian immigrants, her parents had given her a name—Michaela—that sounded fussy and old-fashioned to cornfed American ears, and from the time she was ten she instructed everyone to shorten it to "Mike." Among those who grasped she was a female, there was *still* some confusion, as there were always a few who assumed her first name was Kim, a sure sign they hadn't grown up around Koreans, since Kim was basically the Korean version of Smith or Jones. Mike's name became a way to differentiate between her inner circle and the rest of the world—her true friends versus all the substitute teachers who called on "Michaela," the work acquaintances who didn't know any better, the spammers who routinely sent "Mr. Kim" e-mails for Viagra and Cialis, to her unflagging amusement.

She slammed the bin shut and darted across the street. A pair of earbuds spilled down the side of her courier-style workbag, slapping against the full length of her naked leg, lean thigh to dainty ankle. She let them hang there, swaying jauntily, while gliding along the sidewalk toward her car. If Mike's name was full of pitfalls, her appearance was straightforward enough. All her life she'd been extremely thin; during puberty she had acquired the slightest curvature to her hips and a decent bust (B-cup easily upgraded to a C if need be): a natural size zero, which—in L.A., especially—made her a perfect ten. Smooth and flawless, her face required no adornment. Her light complexion was the pride of her mother, who despite her daughter's best efforts held fiercely to the antiquated Asian belief that the whiter the skin the better. Mike's natural beauty extended to her hair as well: pin-straight, it was thick and textured enough to hold a natural glow, a burnish that was almost metallic. Even this morning's slapdash ponytail tapering a few inches past her shoulders looked like something out of a shampoo commercial.

She reached her car—a Jeep Wrangler with no windows or roof—pawing blindly for her keys while checking Facebook with her other hand. Richard had already updated his status:

Monday, Bloody Monday

and she dumped her bag on the sidewalk to devote her attention to double-thumbing a reply:

Everyday is Like Monday.

She knew he'd get it, because she'd forced him to listen to Morrissey a few weeks earlier, and this had been one of his favorites. It was an established fact that Richard was hopelessly plebeian when it came to music, and would have been lost without her guidance.

Mike knelt on the ground, unearthing her keys at last. Before starting the ignition she placed two fingers over her lips and transferred them to a plastic St. Christopher statue taped to her dashboard. She did this every time she entered her car, except when her parents were in town. For them, the statue came down. They were evangelical Protestants, and wouldn't have understood why their daughter indulged the Catholic notion of worshipping the saints. But Mike found the saints fascinating, and occasionally inspiring.

She shot eastward on Olympic.

As far as her parents knew, she was still the dutiful daughter whose first move after being dropped off at Amherst was to join the College Community Group affiliated with the nearest Korean Presbyterian Church. At eighteen, Mike had been as picturesque and poised as she was now, at twenty-nine, and she rose to the top of the church's hierarchy with the same queenly insouciance she'd perfected in her old church in New Jersey. Each night she held court in the dining hall among her fellow churchgoers, and for all that her day-to-day existence had changed upon entering college (the communal bathroom was perhaps the biggest hurdle), life felt very much the same. It was only looking back on that first year, now, while turning into the LA Fitness on Bundy, that she could see how unhappy she'd been, how *bored*.

Her discontent came to a head a few weeks before the end of freshman year. It was a simple matter of being late to dinner one night and seeing her usual table from afar. There they all were: her crew, her posse—heads bowed, hands clasped, willfully oblivious to the gawks and stares of everyone around them. Mike didn't want to be one of the ignorant people gawking, but she suddenly didn't want to be one of the earnest people praying, either. She wanted to be free of it, if just for a night; they hadn't seen her yet, so she turned—sharply, on her heel—and carried her tray as far away as she could, to an empty table upon which a discarded textbook lay, making the space feel even emptier, somehow. *Perfect.* She sat down and began leafing mindlessly through the thick pages. It was an introduction to art history, and she was ogling the David when someone cleared his throat above her:

"Uh . . . 'scuse me?"

She looked up. He was holding his tray so uncertainly it looked as though he might drop it. She took in his pocket tee, braided belt, and baggy yet tapered jeans. *Ugh.* When were guys going to learn how to dress? *When?*

"Can I help you?" she asked, not caring that she sounded like a bitch. She wanted to be left alone.

"That's my textbook," he said, casting his eyes downward.

She noticed how long his eyelashes were.

"Oh! Sorry," she said, slamming the book shut and shoving it toward him.

"S'okay," he mumbled, placing his tray beside the book and taking a seat just one chair away from her.

Crap. The last thing she needed was an awkward conversation, but she could hardly ask him to leave, or leave herself. She made a mental determination to eat as quickly as possible.

"So . . . what's wrong with your usual table?" he asked her, busying himself with pouring a glass of milk over a bowl of Lucky Charms.

"My *usual* table?" she demanded.

He took a quick breath, as if steeling himself: "The Asian Christians. Aren't you like their queen bee?"

Mike's jaw dropped in an expression that was half-real, half-mocking, while she watched the boy's face explode in a bloom of red. Later she would learn that Richard had said this because he was desperate to keep the conversation going, but it happened to be the perfect thing to say because it proved he was an *observer*, which made him to some extent an *outsider*, and on this evening, an outsider was precisely what she wanted to be.

"Actually, that's the *Korean Presbyterian* table," she said, tossing her shiny head. "Not to be confused with the Catholic Filipinos, over *there*, or the fake Buddhists—*there*—who still totally celebrate Christmas."

He nodded, grinning widely, a dimple in each cheek.

"Good to know."

"How about you?" she asked. "What's your deal?" And while he fumbled for an answer, she couldn't help adding, "Why the sad solo dinner?"

"Wow, way harsh, Tai," he said, and as Mike approached the cardio machines inside the here and now of the gym (why were half of them always out of order? *why?*), she marked this as the first instance of a special clairvoyance between them, because in the *same exact* moment she'd been thinking about *Clueless*, too.

The Richard of a decade ago was average-looking, maybe even a little on the doughy side, but he was on the cusp of that second stage of male development wherein baby fat melts, chests broaden, necks thicken, and teenage guys hatch from their boy-cocoons as fully fledged, handsome young *men*. The lucky ones, anyway. And despite his eating habits (he followed up the Lucky Charms with a bowl of soft-serve ice cream), she predicted Richard Baumbach was going to be very lucky. He could use a little help getting there, however, and the word had simply popped into her brain: *Project!* Like the hapless Tai, he was itching for a makeover, and she wanted nothing more than to help him.

As it happened, they made each other over, though the process took years and was more of an evolution than a transformation. Mike took a step back from the Korean Presbyterians, and Richard, who confessed soon after their first dinner together that he hadn't made a real connection with anyone at Amherst until meeting her, emerged from the shadows, acquiring by osmosis her natural ability to join, and even somewhat to lead. He became a beloved resident counselor, providing support and guidance to those as lonely and overwhelmed as he had once been. It seemed only natural that he should acquire some of Mike's beauty too, and with the passing of the years he grew into his face and body exactly as she had predicted. Richard and Mike grew together, in both senses of the word: side by side and toward each other, until they became two halves of the same enviable person. Both had an innate fondness for movies (*Clueless* was only the beginning), and with mutual encouragement their predilection became their defining passion. By junior year they were joint presidents of the Film Society, and spent all their time together.

They were young; they were beautiful; they were devoted to each other. It would have been absurd for them not to date or sleep together. They were each other's first, and by senior year they were speaking casually about settling down together after graduation in their own place in L.A.

Mike kicked it up a few notches on the StairMaster to deaden the impact of what came next: *she* was the one who broke it off. Before Richard, her world had been small and confining, and she knew it was thanks partly to him that there was so much now she wanted to do, but this didn't change the fact that he was her first boyfriend, *ever*. As senior year wore on she began to panic. Was this it? Was she really going to move in with him and marry him, eventually have his children? He may as well have been a Korean Presbyterian. She took him out to dinner a few weeks before graduation and got as far as "sow our wild oats" before he cut her off:

"I totally get it," he insisted, draining the bottle of red wine he'd ordered for the two of them. "It's totally cool."

Mike descended from the StairMaster and made her way to the mats for a grueling regimen of abdominal exercises. It was *not* totally cool. He didn't speak to her for two months, and they moved separately to L.A. The first few weeks were torture, alone in the concrete wasteland of a crappy Mar Vista apartment she shouldn't have rented online without seeing in person, and she waited as long as she could before reaching out to him:

"Wanna find the fountain that lights up when Cher realizes she's in love with Josh?"

This was the olive branch she extended to him, delivered over the phone one day with zero preamble, and when he paused she thought he was going to reject it, but he was as alone as she was, and *of course* he wanted to go find the fountain. Afterward they went to Hollywood in search of Angelyne, a living legend who became "famous for being famous" before anyone else. As a struggling actress/singer in the eighties and nineties, Angelyne paid for hundreds of billboards featuring her blond-bombshell, sex-kitten-from-Mars image to be plastered all over the city. Her traditional career never quite took off, and nowadays the billboards were gone, but she still drove around in her custom-made pink Corvette, and seeing her was just as big and L.A.-specific a thrill as spotting one of those mountain lions that occasionally roamed the same area. Even though they didn't find her (and still hadn't, seven years later), by the end of their first day together in L.A. their platonic friendship was sealed, the dynamic duo reunited. And side by side like old times, they rose together through the ranks of the entertainment industry.

Mike became a literary manager—a more interesting, less hated version of an agent—who focused on her screenwriter clients' creative process rather than the business side of things.

A year ago, when she was named one of the *Hollywood Report-er*'s top "35 Under 35" up-and-comers, Richard had framed the article and actually marched into her office with a hammer and nail to hang it behind her desk, much to her coworkers' amusement. *He* had taken the plunge as an independent pro-ducer, leaping off the traditional path like some crazed adren-aline junkie. But Mike respected his audacity, and whenever he needed encouragement (which was more often lately), she told him it was only a matter of time before the risk paid off, even if she didn't feel quite as confident as she sounded. The problem wasn't Richard; she believed in him wholeheartedly; but everyone knew it had never been harder to make movies than it was today. Still, they knew all the same people and went to all the same parties. They were in this thing together, and on the rare occasion Mike ventured out alone, everyone's first question was, "Where's Richard?" When they were to-gether, third parties became superfluous—an automatic fifth wheel—and they loved to have an audience precisely because they didn't need one. Newcomers to their circle always as-sumed they were a couple, and they delighted in trotting out their origin story, complete with an ongoing debate about who had been better in bed (the greater the alcohol, the greater the detail). Lately, Richard had been indulging in an ongoing riff about how Mike was leaving him in the proverbial dust, and joked about moonlighting as a handyman in her office (this coming out of the wall-hanging incident).

She checked her Facebook page, supine on an ab roller. In yet another instance of clairvoyance, Richard had replied to her wall posting a few minutes earlier with a YouTube link to Mor-rissey's "We Hate It When Our Friends Become Successful." She responded with a link to the Verve's "Bitter Sweet Sym-phony" and tried him on his cell. He didn't pick up. It wasn't even nine yet; there was no way he was working, so he was obviously screening her. *Bastard.* She wondered if he was still hungover from the weekend. Saturday had turned into an epic bender to celebrate the commencement of the Decent Proposal. At some point Mike had asked half-seriously if she could sit next to him and his mystery woman on their first date, to watch the farce play out firsthand. There had been an awkward pause and she had been forced to say, "I'm joking!" Afterward, she'd sucked down more shots than usual, and he'd matched her for every one.

Mike switched from the ab roller to an exercise ball. She decided to text him instead, knowing he'd write back immediately:

> y u gotta dis me like that yo?

(They often affected a faux "street" patois in their informal communications, which she found a little exhausting, if not embarrassing. But there was no breaking the pattern now.)

> chill

he wrote back a few seconds later,

> was thinking deep thoughts
> like what
> like y all asians r such bad drivers oops . . . awkwd
> r u DRIVING?!

It was almost a lost cause at this point, but she still tried to get him to put away his phone whenever he was driving.

> . . . maybe . . . dentist appt, woohoo obamcre!! but
>   stopped at light awl good
> going now dumbass have fun singing your little <3 out

She knew he loved singing along to his horrendously cheesy homemade mix CDs. When he was drunk enough, he even did it in front of her.

She headed to the locker room to shower and change.

EVEN WITH TRAFFIC, Mike's commute was gloriously brief, and today she flew down Washington Boulevard. Square Peg Pictures had been in Culver City since 2001, before it was a hip neighborhood. The founding partner loved to tell the story of how the Chamber of Commerce brought cookies to their door, thrilled that a legitimate business had set up shop adjacent to a cockfighting and prostitution ring fronting as a bar on one side, and a leather sweatshop on the other. But a year ago the debut of a swanky restaurant across the street had been written up in the *New York Times*, and now the leather sweatshop was the Pilates Sweatshop. Culver City had its own strip now—a restaurant row of fusion eateries with backlit bars where young professionals sampled fancy grub and drank overpriced cocktails with punny names—and though Mike hated being party to the gentrification process, she had to admit the new Culver City was much more her speed than the old one.

She pulled into the gravel lot and broke sharply, crossing herself with lightning speed while descending from her Jeep. Since college, she'd made amends with the Korean Presbyterians, and come back to them on her own terms. Each Sunday she attended a church service in Koreatown, and if she concentrated hard enough while singing the hymns, eyes on the cross, she could still feel the light of Jesus inside her like when she was a little girl. Mike was grateful for her religious upbringing; now more than ever, she prided herself on not having plunged into the first-generation abyss of resenting her immigrant parents' failure to conform to white American standards. A few months ago, her father had been diagnosed with Parkinson's, and the disease was progressing more rapidly than expected.

Something small and hard burned inside her at the thought

of her quiet and dignified father dying, radiating a pain she knew would consume her if she gave it free rein. She slammed her car door much harder than necessary, and turned resolutely to her office building.

Mike wanted desperately to help him, but while she was capable of supporting herself, she had no money to spare. If she hadn't been able to expense all her social activities (dinner, drinks, movies, books, gas, even valet parking), which were all tangentially related to her job in the entertainment industry, she wouldn't have been able to go anywhere or do much of anything. It was outrageous, but while she maintained a swanky L.A. lifestyle wherein blowing several hundred dollars in a single night at some douchey club was no big deal, she had no way of helping her parents pay for the state-of-the-art surgery (terrifyingly called "deep brain stimulation") that might help keep her father's disease at bay as long as possible. Mike's parents had sacrificed for years to send their only child to Amherst without any student loans, and never once did they press her to become a lawyer, doctor, or engineer as so many other immigrant parents did. She'd reaped all the benefit and now was powerless to share any of the burden—other than the emotional one she placed on herself.

I'm a bad daughter, she thought, physically shaking away the emotion while entering her office, doing her best to force the poison out of her system. No one at Square Peg knew about her father, just as they had no idea about her religiosity. The breezy small talk that made up the bulk of her day was too trifling for such weighty concerns. Richard was the only one who knew, and he knew everything. Whenever they spoke on Sunday afternoons he asked, "How'd church go?" and she always answered, "Fine," or, "It was cool," but they both knew something significant lay beneath the routine exchange. In the last few months he'd taken to adding a follow-up question, "How's your dad?" and she usually answered the same way.

Later that morning, she direct-messaged him on Twitter:

drks/din later?

His reply came almost simultaneously:

pls
rush st?

There was no response, so she wrote again:

i came to u last time . . .
fine

he wrote back a few seconds later.

Mike grinned.

8p don't be late like ujzh

She kept the window open. In the afternoon, while a client complained to her about his studio quote not being high enough, she reached out to him:

been sitting on the f'ing fone for half an hour with this
   whiny SOB.
ugh

he responded, and it truly helped. She felt better, felt heard.

But she wanted more.

In the seven years since college, she had certainly sown her wild oats. Mike was glad for all the experiences whipped up inside her whirlwind twenties, and she had stored each of them away like a wise, industrious ant for the lean times to come.

At this point she had more than enough to feast on: one-night stands for the storybooks, pickup lines so bad they deserved a special section in Ripley's, relationships that ran the gamut from short and disastrous to medium and middling to long with epic proportions, including one man who was delectably French and actually *proposed* to her, thereby forcing her to acknowledge she didn't love him at all. She had zero regrets, but she was tired. The oats had grown; it was time to reap them. Though she could barely admit it to herself, it was such a depressing thought, her father's diagnosis had spurred her to settle down in a way her mother's gentle (sometimes not so gentle) prodding never could: as a reminder both that life *in general* was short and that *his* life was short, and that if he was ever going to witness his only child getting married, ever going to meet at least one of his grandchildren, she'd better get a move on. And as much as she had avoided the issue till now, she knew without the aid of any fountains that the man she wanted to spend the rest of her life with was the same person who watched old *Friends* episodes with her after every breakup (better than any comfort food, plus fewer calories); the boy who had become a handsome man by the end of college exactly as she had predicted, but who had continued to grow better-looking with the passing of each year so that now, on the verge of thirty, his physical beauty at times downright alarmed her; the ex she had so foolishly, idiotically discarded.

There was no question: she was majorly, totally, butt-crazy in love with Richard Baumbach.

True, this love was mixed up with a separate yet similar flavor: the love between best friends. Maybe this was why it had taken so long to recognize. It was like blending two grape varieties into one fine, delicately flavored wine and being expected to taste them both in a single quaff—not impossible, but requiring a mature, sensitive palate. For the greater part of her twenties she'd simply been swilling it, getting drunk off it, and it had been fun, but it was also a mess. Now she was ready to *appreciate* what she had, to do the whole glass-swirl/nose-dip/mouth-swish thing without even laughing, to treat it all as solemnly as it deserved.

But was she too late? Suddenly she found herself trapped inside a real-life *My Best Friend's Wedding*, playing Julia Roberts to his Dermot Mulroney with one key difference. The opening of that movie had always rung false to her—Julia waxing eloquent about some dumb pact she and her best friend had made to marry by a certain age. The audience was supposed to believe that Julia had been determined to marry him *before* she found out he was going to marry somebody else. The real way it would have happened, of course, was that she wouldn't have realized he was the one *until* learning about the other girl. It was an ugly emotion—the same impulse by which a child abandons a toy and wants it back only when her younger sibling shows interest: *you can't have it; it's mine!* Mike could smell the studio note a mile away: "we can't have our heroine be so unlikable." It was a good note. Because it was exactly how she had reacted when Richard told her about the Decent Proposal. And she had been able to experience firsthand what a cheap and ugly feeling it was.

Richard, feckless and freewheeling, incapable of holding down a relationship in all the years since she'd broken up with him—as if he, too, had been waiting till she simply came to her senses and took him back—was suddenly no longer available to her. It was easy to disregard all his one-night stands with whatever pair of tits he happened to be staring at when the bar lights came up (she teased him constantly about his unrepentantly slutty ways). But the Decent Proposal was not so easily dismissed. It was, after all, a *decent* proposal, and the fact that she didn't quite know what to make of it was the reddest flag of all. Her toy was in danger of being snatched away, and she wanted it.

But as unworthy as the impulse was, the emotion behind it was pure; it was true. She loved him with a grown-up, romantic love she could finally taste on its own. There was no other man for her. She was sure of it.

Now she just had to figure out how to tell him all this, how to make him see—no easy matter for two people who knew each other as well as they did. They actually joked sometimes about getting back together someday; she was fairly sure *My Best Friend's Wedding* had even come up, albeit facetiously. Resorting to trickery or an over-the-top gesture was unthinkable, so Mike was, uncharacteristically, at a loss as to how to proceed. For now she would bide her time, and trust herself to recognize when the moment was right—and when it was, to act with the pinpoint precision that moment required.

RUSH STREET WAS a staple of the gentrified Culver City strip, a Chicago-themed restaurant with a bar on one side and a bank of TVs behind it that played whatever Bulls, Bears, Cubs, or White Sox game happened to be on. The vibe was upscale, with high ceilings and muted lighting, but the Chicago expats got rowdy sometimes, and once, Mike actually saw a man pee drunkenly in front of the bar—much to the horror of an elderly patron, who spat out her kielbasa sausage perfectly on cue, as if they were starring in a bawdy sitcom together. At 8 p.m. on the dot Mike stalked past the leggy blonde manning the hostess station and climbed a wide staircase in the back leading to a more intimate bar with twin stripper poles. It was too early for strippers. In fact, there was no one there except a bartender, and in less than a minute she was towing her vodka-soda to a balcony behind the bar where patrons could lounge and perhaps sneak a cigarette or two if they were regulars. Twenty minutes later, a waiter passed by and she ordered a second vodka-soda while her phone buzzed:

walking up
upstairs outsde ur in trub

she wrote back, trying to arrange her mouth into a frown, except that whenever she knew Richard was close she couldn't help grinning like an idiot. Any number of in jokes or funny stories they shared bubbled to the surface. He admitted once that the same thing happened to him, and here he was now, bounding over to her, the same dimpled smile plastered on his face as on that first fateful night in the dining hall.

God, how she loved him.

He sat down.

"Yo." He managed to make the single syllable sound apologetic.

She raised an eyebrow. "You get lost?"

"I know, I know. Sorry! Traffic."

Mike audibly drew in her breath, placing one shapely hand over her chest: "*In L.A.?*"

"Yeah, yeah, suck it. Plus, I was stuck on the phone with the 'rents. Couldn't get them off. They've been calling me literally every fucking day, *begging* me not to go through with the Decent Proposal. But I think they finally get that it's a lost cause."

"First, I'm going to need you to promise me you'll never say 'the 'rents' again. Second, I cannot *wait* to hear more about Dave and Judy's thoughts on the DP."

"DP, ha. Makes me think of director of photography. Are we abbreviating it now?"

"Oh, I think we have to. From this day forth," she lifted her empty glass, "we henceforth refer to this crazy shit of yours as the DP."

He lifted his hand and mimed a glass. "So shall it be."

It had been a while since they'd made up a code word. They used to do it all the time. Some of their favorites arose via autotype

gone awry. When Mike said, "Cute hit, 9 o'clock," she was referring to a guy on her left, since "guy" often came out as "hit"
while texting. On a budget trip to the Greek islands a few years
back when Richard was still gainfully employed, they'd had a lot
of fun with the difference between Greek and English letters and
came to refer to "crepes" by their Greek alphabet spelling, which
looked something like "kpenes." Whenever Mike felt like dessert
after a big meal, she asked Richard if he fancied a "kah-pen-es,"
and they'd break into laughter. (All the better if there were others
present to be bewildered.) The double entendre potential of the
word did not go unrecognized by them either, and many a Saturday or Sunday morning he asked her if she'd "eaten any kpenes"
the night before.

"My mom's crazy worried," he said. "*Of course.*"

"That bitch."

A crash drew their eyes to the fifty-something waiter who'd
been about to deliver her second vodka-soda. He might have
slipped for no good reason, but Mike suspected he was shocked
to hear a dainty Asian woman curse instead of covering her
mouth and giggling like a geisha. For this reason she didn't try
very hard to suppress the laughter she and Richard surrendered
themselves to now. The man hurried off, embarrassed, in search
of a towel and a fresh drink. If either of them had been alone
they never would have laughed so openly, but they couldn't help
it when they were together: their good humor was infectious,
inexorable, and occasionally cruel.

"She thinks whoever's behind it must be a psycho or something," said Richard when he could speak again.

"Well, she's probably right. Only a crazy person would pay
you half a million dollars to sit on your ass and talk to someone."

"Actually, they wanted to know what *you* thought about it."

Richard's parents adored Mike, and insisted on having dinner with her whenever they came to L.A. His presence was optional. Richard's dad in particular was still crushed the two of them had broken up.

"What *I* think?" Mike accepted vodka-soda number two from the returning waiter with an oversize smile by way of apology. She swirled the tiny black straw around the rim, creating a miniature whirlpool before looking up and locking eyes with Richard. "I wish it was me." It was nice to tell the truth occasionally, especially when there were no consequences. "I mean, we already hang out together way more than two hours a week. And we *never* shut up. We'd have it in the bag."

Mike knew exactly what *she* would do with the money, and for a moment she thought of her father, counteracting the image of his tired, lined face with a healthy gulp from her glass. For a split second her eyes lost focus; she was already tipsy. At 105 pounds, her tolerance was terrible.

"That's funny," grinned Richard, "cuz that's exactly what Keith said."

Mike knew Richard considered Keith his *second*-best friend, but she was annoyed he had come up at all.

"I'm sure he's beside himself," she said. "This ruins his plan of turning you gay and making you his *lovah*."

She teased Richard constantly about his gay business partner's alleged attraction to him, but it dawned on her now that her attraction might be just as doomed, their college years notwithstanding. Was she fooling herself?

"So what's the plan?" she said. "Are you gonna take her out for an egg cream with two straws in it and stare into her eyes?"

"Mm, egg cream." He paused. "I dunno. We haven't set the first date yet."

There was that hesitation again. When Mike's star had begun to rise, she worried that Richard would pull away from her, especially since he was having such a hard time with his own career. But he had, if anything, overcompensated for any potential jealousy by tightening their already tight connection. Was it tight enough, however? For the first time this was *his* thing, not hers, and she could already feel the distance growing between them. Or maybe she was just being paranoid.

"What's she like? We didn't really get to talk about it Saturday, we were all so shit-faced."

"Yeah, totally." He took a second to consider. "Honestly? She's kind of . . . severe. I mean, she's a lawyer who doesn't watch TV."

"That's almost as bad as a virgin who can't drive."

"Tell me about it. She's got great boobs, though."

"Well, that's something." Mike decided it was time for vodka-soda number three.

"You'd probably think she was fat."

Better, thought Mike, though she hated herself for thinking it, and hated just as much the way Richard ascribed unkind opinions of the female sex to her, which was his cheap way of expressing what were actually *his* opinions without taking responsibility for them. She craned her neck in search of the clumsy waiter. She was determined to get drunk now, Monday or not.

"I don't think she really sees the fun in it, you know?" He paused. "God, you're so right, could you imagine if it was us? How much fun we'd be having right now?"

Mike's heart expanded, floating upward. Of course he understood how it was with them. Of course he did. She hadn't lost him yet.

"Well, *no one's* as fun as us, right?" She drained the dregs of her drink.

"True dat." He said it ironically, with an emphasis on the *d* to indicate his awareness that a white boy like himself had no business slanging. "Hey, let's go down and get some food. You're gonna get wasted if you don't eat anything."

"I'm already wasted," she said a little forlornly, before pulling herself together and accompanying him to the dining room, where they assumed their rightful place as the most attractive couple in the room.

THE FIRST DATE

"HOW ABOUT IN-N-OUT?"

Richard had asked the question casually, but when Elizabeth paused to consider her answer, he felt like a fallen gladiator waiting to see which way the emperor's thumb would point. She might be a strident vegetarian, or a disciple of the gluten-free regime (when had that become a thing? and why?). Maybe she ate only locally sourced organic foods (blegh), or considered fast food beneath her (bigger blegh). There were a million different reasons, he knew, to deny oneself the simple joy of a burger.

It was Saturday night, one week after their coffee. "Date night!" as he had tweeted (*#DecentProposal* was trending—among his followers, at least). They were at the Universal City-Walk, an outdoor mall adjacent to the Universal Studios theme park, pint-sized cousin to Times Square and the Vegas Strip, a wide promenade cut off from traffic by parking garages named after Universal brands like Woody Woodpecker and Jurassic

Park. Even now, at 7 p.m., there were enough children there to constitute a swarm—limbs flailing, fingers sticky from a day's worth of churros and cotton candy. Every storefront seemed to be shouting (T-SHIRTS SOLD HERE!! BEST MILKSHAKE IN L.A.!!); every light flashed; every color dazzled; it was as though each square foot of the place had its own set of jazz hands. Richard had suggested the CityWalk partly because it was just over the hill from a club in Hollywood where he'd be meeting up with friends afterward, and partly as a joke. If Elizabeth had balked he would have willingly gone elsewhere, but she had agreed without comment, and he was beginning to wonder why, the longer she stood there dithering over In-N-Out versus . . . what? Bubba Gump Shrimp? Panda Express? If she really was a foodie, she was screwed.

"Let's do it!"

Her enthusiasm was overcompensating. In-N-Out was Elizabeth's Friday night ritual, an end-of-the-week treat she devoured in her car, and while she liked to think she couldn't get enough of it, two nights in a row felt a little gluttonous to her. But if she told him, then they'd have to go somewhere else, and In-N-Out was by far their best option in this menagerie of horrors. Why had he chosen this awful place? It was the ideal spot for a couple half their age. *Maybe that's the point*, she told herself. It wasn't a *real* date. She was the one who had insisted on acknowledging they were only going through the motions. The motions were what she had wanted; the motions were supposed to be instructional. Well, here was lesson number one, then: the motions were exhausting. Earlier in the week she'd decided all her nice clothes were daytime-specific, and had squandered several billable hours finding a somewhat slinky, glossy "evening" skirt to wear. The better part of this afternoon had been spent fussing over her hair and nails. She'd endured an hour and fifteen minutes' worth of traffic—the 10 to the 405 to the 101—in getting here. How did people do this night after night, year after year, and maintain the goodwill necessary to search with an open heart for a connection they knew very well they might never find? Maybe it wasn't as difficult for other people. Maybe there was something wrong with her, something essential she lacked, the absence of which made the process of dating such drudgery for her and her alone. Or maybe everybody was miserable.

Stop it, she scolded herself. The venue notwithstanding, she had to admit he'd made an effort too. It was true he was still wearing jeans, but they were *different* jeans: clean(er), with no visible rips. His shirt had an actual collar, and when he held the restaurant door open for her she caught a whiff of something nice—nicer, anyway, than the Axe body spray and Drakkar Noir-ish stuff that clogged the hallways of her firm. The scent vanished a moment later, replaced by fried beef and deeper-fried potatoes—a greasy aroma that greeted her like an old flame she couldn't quit no matter how many times she tried. Elizabeth's spirits lifted. Was it really so bad to be "forced" to eat In-N-Out two nights in a row? True, it had been hellish getting here, but she was out now—out, on a Saturday night—and though she was considerably overdressed for fast food on a tray, he didn't seem to care, so why should she be embarrassed? The whole thing was ridiculous, but the only rational response was to throw up her hands (lavender nail polish included) and relax, to attempt to have some version of what other people called *fun*.

In-N-Out had a fifties aesthetic, all clean lines and hard plastic edges, with a two-toned color scheme of bright red and blinding white, so simple it would have been stark if the place weren't always bursting with people. At the moment a dozen smiling servers were racing behind the counter like natives cheerfully fleeing a volcano. Richard knew from experience his eyes would adjust eventually, as if to the dark, discerning a frenetic sort of assembly line underpinning the chaos. This was the way it had been done at In-N-Out for nearly seventy years, starting with a single burger stand just outside L.A. He loved the chain as much for its association with Southern California as for its mouthwatering cuisine, and hated that in the past decade it had begun expanding eastward, inching across the continent like a pioneer in reverse. For now it was confined to the western United States, but if ever there came a day when those little red palm trees appeared on the awning of some gray New York City block, Richard knew a little part of him would die.

"You've eaten here before, right?" he asked her, as they joined the back of the line.

Little did he know. "I grew up on it," said Elizabeth.

"Oh, no way! So you grew up out here?"

She nodded.

"That's so cool! I don't know anyone who grew up in L.A."

"That's because you're in entertainment." It amazed Elizabeth that this idea—of no one being *from* L.A.—persisted in the zeitgeist. Everyone loved to talk about how "fake" L.A. was; they called it a "dream factory," a place where people came to pretend to be someone else, to escape their pasts and start over, but to the extent that that was even true, it pertained to the entertainment industry only. For most people who lived here, L.A. *was* their past, and their future too. It was their home. There were literally millions of people who'd grown up in Los Angeles, whose families had lived here for generations. Many of them had nothing to do with film, television, or music. But they were as much a part of the city as the flashy transplants who sucked up all the attention. In fact, entertainment made up only a sliver of the city's wealth—a sliver that was shrinking daily due to tax breaks in other states (New Mexico, Michigan, Georgia, New York) for locally sourced film and television productions. Did he know anything about this? Did he ever read a newspaper? Even just online?

"Fair enough," he said. "So where'd you grow up exactly?"

"South Central." Elizabeth watched these two little words go off like a hand grenade. (The man ahead of them glanced backward, as if she'd said something lewd or controversial.) Usually she was vague about where she grew up or, if pressed, became overly specific and said either Westmont (her immediate neighborhood) or South Los Angeles, which was what the area had been renamed in an attempt to wash away the stink of recent history. Upon learning she grew up in South Central, most people were tempted to make a success story out of her, a modern spin on the old Horatio Alger "rags to riches" trope, a pull-herself-up-by-her-bootstraps, Hallmark Hall of Fame narrative that began in the slums of L.A. and ended in the sparkling offices of Slate Drubble & Greer, Elizabeth stationed in her very own office with her very own assistant, business suit stretched modestly over her full Mexican figure: cue triumphant music.

Her story was nowhere near as tidy, but she had no interest in untangling it for strangers, or even for acquaintances. Fortunately most people didn't really care what her story was, and a cursory answer almost always served the purpose. But what else were they going to talk about for 104 hours? (She stole a glance at her watch: 8:06. Make that 103.9 hours.) At the very least, they could talk about the riots a little. She knew from experience it took about three seconds for the riots to come up after referencing South Central. It was like a word association.

"Oh, wow," he said. "So how old were you? During the . . ."

"Riots?"

He nodded.

"Twelve."

She'd been in the sixth grade, immersed in a book report on *The Diary of Anne Frank*. It was embarrassing to remember, but she'd changed topics by the middle of the second day (school had been canceled), opting for a personal essay that likened her situation to Anne's, holed up in her apartment like Anne in her annex. *Except for not getting taken away in the end and murdered by the Nazis,* she thought to herself now. Her English teacher had submitted the essay for a city-wide contest calling for responses to the riots, and she'd actually won. There had been a local news segment, a reading at the Rotary club, a signed letter from the mayor. It had all been pretty exciting.

"That must've been intense," he said.

"It was," she said solemnly.

"So do your parents still live out there?"

Elizabeth's shoulders rose a fraction of an inch. She nodded stiffly. She didn't want to talk about her parents. But it was her own fault. She'd opened the door.

"What do they do?"

"They manage a restaurant together."

"That sounds nice!"

"It's in Studio City," she added, hoping this would dampen his curiosity. He probably didn't get up to the Valley very often.

"Oh, cool, I eat up there a lot." Knocking the Valley was about as wrongheaded and outdated as disparaging Brooklyn had become for New Yorkers. "Lots of great sushi up there."

"Well, it's not a sushi restaurant," she said. "It's Italian, and it's pretty much a dump."

Okay, he thought. *Moving on.* "Well, it must be nice to have them so close."

There was a pause, inside of which Elizabeth scrambled for an answer while at the same time praying: *please don't ask it, please don't ask it, please don't—*

"How often do you see them?"

Crap. She opened her mouth to tell the lie she'd told many times before—*oh, every few weeks or so*—when suddenly she thought: *why bother?* She could have worn a paper bag to this "date" and it wouldn't have mattered, so why lie to him now? He wasn't one of her bosses, who might think twice about making her a partner if he knew that on top of lacking a significant other, she and her parents were estranged. There was no reason to lie to him. He wasn't going anywhere.

"I don't," she said, breathing out, her shoulders descending to their original position.

"You don't see them? Ever?"

"Well, we have dinner on Christmas. And brunch at Easter. And they call me on my birthday. But that's it."

There was another pause, inside of which she watched, amused, while he churned through this information.

"But you live in the same city."

She nodded.

"Why don't you see them more, if you don't mind my asking?"

"To be honest I *do* mind," she said. "It's complicated."

"That's cool," he said, holding up his hands in surrender and taking a step backward. (He nearly collided with a red-aproned worker restocking the ketchup dispenser.) "You're allowed to be mysterious."

Mysterious? "Well, I'm not trying to be," she said.

"If you were, you wouldn't be very mysterious, would you?"

"Fair enough," she said, with the ghost of a smile.

"What about siblings?"

"I have a brother. Two years younger."

He raised an eyebrow. "Do you ever talk to him?"

She shook her head, *no.* He just stared at her.

"What about you?" she asked. "Siblings?"

"Only child," he said. "Much to my chagrin." If *he* had a little brother, he had no doubt they'd talk all the time.

Not a shocker, thought Elizabeth, while gesturing toward the bare-bones menu printed behind the counter: burgers, fries, fountain sodas, shakes. "What do you usually eat?" She was getting a little bored.

"Oh, just a burger," he said. "Protein-style."

As a supplement to its bare-bones menu, there was a "secret" menu at In-N-Out wherein almost any variation on the few items offered was possible, no matter how outlandish or disgusting, such as ordering four—or forty—patties of beef in a single burger, or umpteen slices of cheese. Protein-style meant the hamburger would be wrapped in lettuce instead of a bun.

"Protein-style?" Elizabeth wrinkled her nose. She'd tried protein-style once out of curiosity, and could still recall the way the cool, crisp lettuce contrasted with the hot gooey meat inside. It had reminded her of picking up after a college friend's dog in winter—the soft warmth radiating nastily through the cold plastic bag. "Are you on a diet or something?" The manorexic lawyers at her firm all ordered their burgers protein-style.

"What? No!" he protested. "I just like it that way." The truth was he *had* started ordering protein-style a few years back at Mike's suggestion. But he was so used to it now, it had become his preferred mode.

It was their turn to order. When Elizabeth asked for a double-double (two burger patties and two slices of cheese), Richard whistled softly, but she pretended not to hear him. She insisted on splitting the bill in half, and he agreed immediately. Earlier that morning he'd accidentally glanced at one of his credit card statements, and the image was still burned in his mind like footage from a grisly auto accident or torture-porn horror movie.

"Y'know, we should probably get reimbursed for stuff like this anyway," he said.

"Good point," said Elizabeth.

"By the end of the year we could be out a pretty big chunk of change."

"I'll call the lawyer about it tomorrow."

"Cool."

ELIZABETH TOOK HER time at the beverage station, fussing over the perfect level of ice, squeezing more lemon wedges into her drink than she could possibly want (considering she was drinking lemonade). But as long as she stayed there, the pause in their conversation couldn't turn awkward. She tried reminding herself that pauses—even awkward ones—were nothing to worry about. In the week that had passed since their coffee together, she had scrutinized the rules of the proposal more rigorously than before, and on Friday morning she'd even called Jonathan Hertzfeld to request clarification on the meaning of a "substantially conversational manner." Were pauses allowed? Could they be counted toward the two hours? Yes, as long as their "intent to converse" was "sustained and consistent." She knew she was in danger of violating this intent by standing apart from him now, but she desperately needed the break. While paying, she'd glanced at her watch again and had been horrified to see that it was only 8:17. She'd been sure at least a half hour had passed.

ELIZABETH REJOINED HIM on the bench. They were still waiting for their number to be called.

"Hey," said Richard. "Check it out."

He was holding his cup high in the air, pointing at something on the inside of the bottom lip. She didn't even need to look, and began reciting from memory:

"For God so loved the world that he gave his one and only Son, that whoever believes in him shall not perish but have eternal life."

He stared at her. "I'm guessing that's John 3:16?"

She nodded. "John 3:16" was printed on the bottom of every In-N-Out soda cup. Back in the eighties, one of the owners had printed the book, chapter, and verse of his favorite Bible passages as a means of tempting customers to consult the Good Book. He'd died years ago, but the biblical references remained. It was another "secret" to add to the mythos of the In-N-Out dining experience. Richard had never thought to look up the verse.

"Did you memorize that because of In-N-Out?" he asked.

"I learned it in CCD, actually."

"CCD?"

"Catechism. Sort of like Sunday school, but for Catholics."

Aha. So she *was* religious. Mike was religious too, so it wasn't like there was anything *wrong* with it, but Richard had a secular Jew's distrust for anything that smacked of fundamentalism, and memorizing Bible verses was right up there. *Was* she Latina, though? Religious fervor was less troubling coming from a minority. (See again: Mike.)

"So what *are* you exactly?"

Tired? she wanted to say. *Wondering how we're going to get through a year of this?*

"I take it you're asking me about my ethnicity?"

He nodded, flushing slightly. On a real date he would have fished for this information more artfully, of course.

"Both my parents are Mexican. From Mexico. But don't worry, I was born here. I'm a U.S. citizen. I can bring in my birth certificate next time if you want."

He tittered uneasily.

"One-four-three! Number one forty-three!"

Their order was ready. Richard collected the red tray from the counter while Elizabeth secured them a table. Between bites they exchanged vital statistics. He grew up in a suburb outside Boston ("Braintree: the ugliest compound word in the English language"). She went to Yale for undergrad and NYU for law— full ride for both, with a smorgasbord of grants, work-study programs, and student loans she'd managed to pay off in full several years ago. He went to Amherst, though he failed to mention that both his parents went there, or that the next best school he got into was BU, or that his parents were still paying off a hefty loan he had every intention of paying himself once his credit card debt had been wiped clean. He insisted on naming everyone he knew from both Yale *and* NYU, which was about a dozen people, but she wasn't familiar with any of them. She couldn't think of anyone she knew from Amherst. Whatever it was that connected them, it remained a mystery for now.

By this point it was 8:34.

"So how do you like L.A.?" she asked. "Coming from the East Coast?"

"I love it!" he said, tearing open a salt packet and sprinkling the grains over his fries like seeds across a field.

"Really? I'm surprised," she said. "I know a lot of East Coasters who hate it out here. It's easier to go the other way around, I think."

"So you actually liked New Haven?"

"It's not as bad as everyone says it is. But by senior year I was ready to move to New York."

"I'm assuming you liked New York?"

"I loved it. I never wanted to leave. Especially not for here."

"Oh, so you're one of *those*."

"Who?"

"The L.A. haters."

They were everywhere, and Richard couldn't disagree with them more. The summer after his freshman year he'd gone to L.A. for the first time, for a two-month Hollywood internship. It was like a riot of color punctuating his monochrome existence, the bloom atop a thorny stem. He was instantly hooked. For the rest of college he dreamed of whiling away the afternoon at business drinks on the beach, guzzling beer as bright yellow as the sand between his toes. He pictured himself reading scripts poolside in the courtyard of a Beverly Hills hotel. L.A. was everything Massachusetts wasn't, and it was more than the surface attractions of sunny weather and proximity to celebrities that drew him here. For Richard, the fairer city represented an alternative to the workaday lifestyle of almost everybody who graduated from the East Coast's elite institutions: all the lawyers, doctors, i-bankers, and consultants who endured wintry weather halfway through April and wasted their youth toiling away at jobs that didn't excite them. The morning after graduation, he drove cross-country, fleeing like a refugee for a better existence. And after seven years in the promised land, he cherished even those aspects of the city other people hated: the traffic, the lack of a city center, the way some people thought they had to act like douche bags to get ahead in the entertainment business. These were all imperfections he was more than willing to brook. His love for L.A. was unconditional.

"I don't hate L.A.," said Elizabeth. "I just don't love it. Like New York."

"So why'd you move back? If you loved it so much out there?"

"They needed someone in my department. I got a really good offer."

"An offer you couldn't refuse?"

"Exactly." She smiled.

"Did you have braces when you were younger?"

"No." Had he forgotten about South Central already? Even if she had desperately needed them, her parents could never have afforded braces.

"Well, you have beautiful teeth. You're lucky."

"Thank you," she said, before adding, "You have beautiful eyes."

He looked up, surprised. He got this compliment all the time, but hadn't expected it from her.

"Thanks!"

She waved her double-double dismissively, shedding a slimy onion chunk or two.

"No, no. You *do* have pretty eyes, I'm sure you're well aware of that—"

He flushed crimson.

"—but it's the Arab response whenever anyone gives you a compliment. My roommate in college was from Yemen, and whenever anyone said anything nice to her she'd tell them they have beautiful eyes. The idea is whatever beauty you see is actually coming from you rather than the thing itself. Like the beauty is in the perception, not the thing."

She wondered if he'd get it.

"That's really nice," he said, getting it perfectly, his embarrassment washed away by the pleasure of learning something new.

"It *is* nice, isn't it?" she said. "Best way to throw back a compliment I ever heard. I adopted it for myself, but it sounds weird in English."

"Huh, yeah, but I'm gonna use it now too. So does your roommate still live in New York?"

They fell into a conversational rhythm, like a tennis rally in which the force of the ball going one way could be used to shoot it back over the net. Elizabeth told him about working at Slate Drubble's New York branch for the first six years out of law school, before being transferred to Los Angeles. Richard told her about his early days at Green Trolley, the production company where he and Keith got their start. She described her college and law school friends to him, all of whom still lived in and around New York, and most of whom were either married or in serious relationships. She hadn't seen a single one of them since moving to L.A. two years earlier. But they'd always have e-mail. He told her about Mike:

"Short for Michaela, which no one *ever* calls her. She's my best friend hands down. We're basically the same person. I'd say she was my soul mate if there was a way to say that without sounding like a tool." It was refreshing to be open about Mike. He never would have revealed so much on a real first date. Every girl had seen *When Harry Met Sally.*

"You're sure you're just friends?" Elizabeth asked, shoving a bloody fry—her last—into her mouth.

So predictable, he thought, while admitting aloud: "We *did* go out in college. But that was different. We're just friends now."

She's probably still in love with him, thought Elizabeth, sneaking a peek at her watch. 9:02. *Seriously?* Well, at least they were more than halfway through. *A hundred and three hours and counting . . .*

"So what do you do in your spare time?" he asked, finishing off the last of his hamburger.

"I read a lot," she said. "Fiction mainly. Novels. Anything from Austen to Fitzgerald. And the beach's only a few blocks away. I surf and roller-skate on the weekends."

Did anyone really roller-skate on the Boardwalk anymore? It struck him as a slightly eccentric thing to do. And what about *friends*? Richard knew plenty of people who professed to be "loners." The profession itself was a fairly reliable indicator that they were full of crap. But he was beginning to suspect Elizabeth Santiago was the real thing.

"You surf?" he asked, sucking a mixture of ketchup and "spread" (In-N-Out's special sauce) off his fingers.

"What, you've never seen a Latina surf before?"

He snorted. "I guess not."

"Haven't you seen *Blue Crush*? Michelle Rodriguez was one of the blond girl's best friends, I think." She slurped the last of her lemonade.

Blue Crush? Jesus. She was better off pretending she didn't watch movies either. "So what're your favorite books?"

"*Jane Eyre, Tess of the d'Urbervilles, Howards End, To the Lighthouse*, and *Pride and Prejudice*." She rattled them off without hesitating.

He lifted his eyebrows. "You were ready for that one."

"I read them every year, no matter what."

"I don't think I've read any of them, except *Jane Eyre*, and that was in high school." Ever since college, Richard had pretended there was a choice to be made, books or movies, and he had made his, no turning back, unless he were reading a book that might be turned into a movie, of course.

Elizabeth shrugged her shoulders. She didn't feign superiority about reading. She did it because she liked it, for the same reason others played poker, or softball.

"How 'bout movies?" he asked. "Other than *Blue Crush?*"

She hesitated. "I guess I like the old sixties musicals the best. *The Sound of Music. West Side Story*. Oh, and *Seven Brides for Seven Brothers*. That's a fun one."

Richard was pretty sure *Seven Brides for Seven Brothers* was one of his mother's favorite films. *Yikes.*

"And you? Movies?" Her eyes flicked almost involuntarily to her watch: 9:04. *God help me.*

"*Some Like It Hot, Alien, The Usual Suspects, Driving Miss Daisy, Harold and Maude*, and *Chinatown*."

"Sounds like you were ready for that one too."

"I guess. You get asked it a lot in Hollywood, though. You see any of those?" he ventured.

"I've seen *Harold and Maude*. None of the others. That one's neat," she added conciliatorily.

They stared at each other. The rally was over. It could not be resurrected. They suffered through a long and painful silence, at the end of which Elizabeth stood up.

"I'm getting a milk shake," she announced. "Do you want anything?"

He shook his head.

Elizabeth joined the back of the line. She wasn't proud of herself. There was no question she was violating the intent to converse now. But she couldn't help it; she simply didn't have the knack for banter (hair appointments were always an ordeal for her), and each second she sat across from him in silence felt like fresh evidence of her inadequacy. She imagined for a moment what his conversations must be like with this Mike character, his "soul mate." How in God's name was she ever going to get any better at this whole dating thing? The worst aspect of tonight was that this was the *easy* session, where they had all the introductory stuff like biographical details to fall back on. How were they going to sustain a conversation the next time? And the time after that? And that? And that? What had she gotten herself into?

Richard watched her advance slowly up the line, which was considerably longer than the one they'd waited in before. Well, she certainly wasn't a food snob. If anything, he wished she were a little snobbier, especially when it came to movies. Had she really called *Harold and Maude* "neat"? *Harold and Maude* was many things—inspired, epic, tragic, subversive, even cheesy—but "neat" was not one of them. What would he have said if she had asked him about *Jane Eyre*, though? Would he have had anything meaningful to articulate? He might have said it was "neat" too.

And then, a brilliant idea hit him.

ELIZABETH RETURNED TO the table at 9:28 p.m. with a Neapolitan shake (another item off the secret menu: chocolate, vanilla, and strawberry swirled together). Richard's leg was shaking harder than ever—a habit of his that was already beginning to annoy her.

"Hey!" he said, smiling broadly. "So I have an idea. How

'bout we use our time every week as a sort of book and movie club? Like, we have a certain book we read on our own, in our own time, and then we use our two hours to talk about it? Or we watch a movie and then talk about it for two hours? Your favorite books, my favorite movies. It'll be a fun way to pass the time, and I don't think we'll be violating our contract, s'long we don't use the two hours to read or watch the movie?"

Relief washed over Elizabeth—no, it was more like submerging herself in a bath of warm, fragrant water. She thought about the structure this would bring their dates. It was perfect. This she could handle. *Maybe.* Why hadn't she thought of it?

"Deal!" she said, flashing her perfect teeth. And before she had a chance to think too hard about it, she closed her eyes and counted on one hand to five. She'd never done this in front of another person before, and when she opened her eyes he was staring at her.

"What was that about?" he asked, more amused than curious.

She told him about her habit of taking time out to appreciate the good in an otherwise bad situation.

"So the good thing is my idea, and the bad thing is that we have to see each other every week?"

"I didn't mean it like *that*—"

"It's okay," he said, chuckling. "I get it."

They spent the next twenty minutes debating the best book and movie to kick off the club. In the end they decided to make it easy on themselves and start with what they knew—*Jane Eyre* and *Harold and Maude*. At 9:52, they emerged from In-N-Out into the cool evening air. Even though the temperature had hit 80 during the day, it hovered somewhere around 60 now, the habitually dry Los Angeles air incapable of retaining much heat once the sun went down. At the center of the CityWalk lay a sprawling multiplex playing the blockbuster hits of the day. Richard paused to check out the movies listed on the marquee. He felt an urge for popcorn, which he felt every time he was in the vicinity of a movie theater.

"Man, I'd love some popcorn right now."

"Why don't you go get some?" asked Elizabeth, with the simplicity of a child who wonders why adults don't just make themselves happy.

"Nah, not without a ticket. How'd I get in?"

"Just explain and I'm sure they'll let you. They make all their money off concessions anyway." (*And it'll kill a few more minutes*, she thought. It was 9:54. They were so close!)

She was right. Richard ran into the theater, getting in easily and emerging five minutes later with a big bucket of salty, buttery popcorn. He'd never done this before, gotten a tub of movie popcorn without seeing a movie. It was kind of a revelation.

He walked closer to her, angling the bucket her way. He figured that after a burger, fries, lemonade, and a milk shake she wouldn't want any, but she grabbed a handful and popped it in her mouth.

She saw him watching her, and parted her lips without hesitating, the golden-brown chunks marring her beautiful teeth. She smiled wider, owning it.

"*So* good, isn't it?" he mumbled through his own mouthful.

She nodded, swallowing. "I'll ask Jonathan Hertzfeld if we can add the books and movies to our expenses when I talk to him tomorrow."

"Ooh, good thinking." And then, after a pause: "I wonder if this is what our mysterious benefactor had in mind when he thought this whole thing up."

"Who cares?" said Elizabeth. "He—or she—is obviously insane."

He laughed, and they ambled toward their cars. Before they parted, Elizabeth checked her watch one last time: 10:01. They'd done it.

The first two hours had passed.

THE BOTTLE

ELIZABETH TURNED INTO her driveway, which was always a challenging endeavor since it was so minuscule: exactly the size of her car, maybe even a little smaller. Maneuvering into it was like pouring a sausage into its casing, and required her undivided attention. For this reason it wasn't till she was unbuckling her seat belt that she saw her front door, and froze.

It was open. Her front door was open. Why the hell was her front door open? This seemed impossible, but there it was, swaying in the ocean breeze, welcoming everyone inside as if this were the most natural thing in the world. Which it wasn't. Elizabeth never forgot to lock her door. The importance of looking after her things had been ingrained in her from an early age, and despite its doll-sized proportions, this two-bedroom, one-bathroom bungalow was easily her biggest possession. It had cost her a fortune (Venice was prime real estate these days, especially two blocks from the beach), and sometimes, when she thought about the size of her down payment and the long years of monthly mortgage bills to come, she checked in with her accountant the same way a new mother·consults the family physician: to make sure nothing was amiss, to be reassured it was all going to be okay. Each time she left, she jiggled the locked doorknob exactly eight times, and this afternoon she'd done it sixteen times for good measure, knowing she'd be home late from the CityWalk.

Her heart convulsed like a bird trapped inside her chest, its tiny wings fluttering in a panic. She could have driven straight to the police station at Culver and Centinela, or dialed 911 on her cell and waited for help to come. She could have at least alerted another human being to the fact that there was a potentially dangerous situation at hand. But she did none of these things, because just then she saw something else in the shadow of her door.

It was a wheeled suitcase, the compact carry-on kind flight attendants toted briskly through airports. Once red, it was now brown, or gray, or whatever the color of filth was. Elizabeth's fear gave way to outrage and she left her car, creeping forward, retrieving a tiny can of Mace from the bottom of her purse and brandishing it before her like a gun, right index finger poised over the nozzle.

She stepped inside on tiptoe. It was dark. She couldn't see a thing. A layer of salty grime had coated the threshold, and her shoes squeaked while crossing it. She winced, every one of her senses on high alert. Seconds later her ear discerned a soft, cyclical rising and falling: the sound of deep, untroubled sleep. *Unbelievable!* she thought, flicking on the overhead lights, and letting the can fall harmlessly to her side.

He was sprawled facedown on her white sofa, his right arm spilling off the edge and pointing to the floor, the tips of his fingers brushing against the side of an overturned wine bottle, as if it were a lover. A burgundy pool leaked from the bottle's lip into the creamy white carpet beneath it. Elizabeth swooped down, setting the bottle upright, emitting a raspy sound of surprise and annoyance that came out something like:

"GRAGH!"

The carpet was ruined.

The man stirred, flipping onto his back. He did not wake; he began, in fact, to snore. Elizabeth bent over him, shaking him by the shoulders:

"Orpheus! Wake up! Goddamnit, Orpheus! Wake UP!"

Two crusted eyelids unstuck themselves. A pair of bloodshot eyes opened to the world. He shot up in a sitting position.

They bonked heads like cartoon characters.

"Owwww! Damn it!" she howled, making more of it than it really was, rubbing her forehead ostentatiously. "What the hell?"

He blinked at her, unseeing, but after a second or two his eyes found focus. "Sorry, Lily," he croaked at her, eyes rolling downward to something below. "I fucked up."

She thought he meant the wine, but then she smelled it. His pants were dark around the crotch. Beneath him, a yellow circle with scalloped edges had been etched onto her sofa.

In her adult life, Elizabeth almost never spoke Spanish. Even with her parents, she insisted on speaking English the few times a year they spoke, which was an easy and effective way of maintaining the distance established between them for years now. There were the rare occasions on which people spoke it to her, such as when the waiters at Versailles (a chain of Cuban restaurants) flirted with her, or when recent immigrants (a cashier in a convenience store, an attendant at a valet station) could not speak even rudimentary English, but for the most part she abstained. Now, perhaps as a latent effort by her calmer self—who had already processed what had happened and wanted to shield him from her fury—she unleashed upon his head a torrent of expletives in her first language.

This was what she got for reaching out to people.

Six months earlier she'd noticed him on the Boardwalk, which was only a few minutes from her house. It was a lively scene—a patchwork mess of wacky street performers, aged hippies, young burnouts, yuppie joggers, Euro tourists, and a generous helping of homeless people, such as the one collecting the juiciest cigarette butts from between the cracks in the basketball courts, and stowing them in one of those black plastic bags that came with purchases in small convenience stores. *Is he actually going to smoke them later?* she wondered. *Gross.* His nylon Dodgers jacket had faded to a sickly yellow, the ruined elastic waistband sagging off his sunken frame. Salt-and-pepper dreadlocks sprouted from his head like the fronds of a palm tree or the bloom of a firework; a more modest row ringed his greasy neck, little pod-shaped excrescences that looked as if they harbored some unspeakable pestilence that would burst forth one day, fully winged, and take off into the air. His grizzled beard was thick and puffy; his nose, cheeks, and forehead were so bumpy and discolored, it looked as if his skin had melted and then hardened again. Never before had she seen so much sun damage on a black person's skin; she didn't even know it was possible. *He must have been living out here for years*, she thought. *I wonder how old he is.* It was hard to tell how much of the wear and tear was due to age as opposed to the elements; he could have been anywhere from forty to seventy. He reminded her of Robinson Crusoe, but worse—a castaway trapped inside a crowd, surviving off whatever scraps of human refuse he could find.

He caught her staring. She turned, but it was too late. He extracted a beaten-up coffee cup from his shopping bag and approached her.

"Hey, girl!" he shouted.

Elizabeth pitied the homeless, but as a single woman she made it a rule not to engage with them. You never knew what they were going to do; many of them were mentally ill. She lifted the book she was reading a little higher to cover her face.

"*To the Lighthouse*," he read aloud.

Oh, Lord, thought Elizabeth, eyes glued to the page. *What now?*

"Always liked that Lily Briscoe."

She froze, waiting for more.

"Always had a thing for her. My kinda woman." He emitted a single, staccato burst of a chuckle from somewhere between his chest and throat—a growly, gurgly "huh" that she would come to recognize as his signature noise. "Hey, what's that thing she keeps moving around? On the table? Com'on, you know what I mean. At dinnertime?"

A saltshaker; it was a saltshaker. Lily Briscoe was Elizabeth's favorite too, a confirmed spinster and amateur painter who by the novel's end achieves a measure of artistic greatness, though it will almost certainly go unrecognized and unremembered— like Lily herself. And yet she wasn't a tragic character. She was, by her own reckoning and that of her creator, triumphant. Transcendent.

Despite her rule, Elizabeth put down the book and turned to him.

"You've read *To the Lighthouse*?"

"Whadda *you* think? Huh. Used to teach it," he said, before adding as if it were a natural segue, "Spare change? I gotta get drunk."

Elizabeth refused him the change, but she offered to buy him a coffee at Café Collage on the corner of Pacific and Windward Avenues, just off the Boardwalk. It was a crowded Sunday afternoon; there were people everywhere, and she was too curious to let him go without more of an explanation. She wasn't averse to a little companionship, either. There were plenty of ways to occupy her *time* on the weekends, but every so often she felt unable to occupy her *mind* the way she did at work, and for this reason the weekends were occasionally a trial. It had been easier in New York, where she had friends who were always a subway ride away. In L.A. she had no one, not even the prospect of running into an acquaintance on the street, since everyone was spread so far apart. There was a reason why this anonymous homeless man had reminded her of a castaway: sometimes Los Angeles felt like a string of desert islands—millions of them, stretching to the horizon, and each holding a single exile. You had to take the initiative and affirmatively leave your island if you ever wanted to connect with another human being, or else wait for someone to come to you. And Elizabeth had grown tired of waiting.

The homeless man grumbled, but agreed, retrieving the soiled suitcase she would learn never strayed more than a few feet away from him. As they walked from the courts to the café, a few people gawked, and she allowed herself a glance in their direction, as if to say, *That's right. I'm walking and talking with a homeless man. You got a problem with that?* She hadn't felt so bold in years.

They sat on rusty metal chairs beneath a classical arcade—the kind meant for silent monks contemplating God rather than feverish teens committing videogame atrocities—built over a hundred years ago to evoke the arcades of the Piazza San Marco in the original Venice, in Italy. (When she had been forced to move back to L.A., Elizabeth had decided the only way to make her new reality tolerable was to live as close to the water as possible and become a "beach person." To her surprise, she discovered an affinity for Venice's peculiar atmosphere. Though the neighborhood's interior portions had acquired a sheen of gentrification in recent years, the beachfront was as much of a modern ruins as it had been fifty years ago: the crumbly remains of a century-old amusement park populated largely by outcasts. On Fridays after In-N-Out, she parked in her tiny driveway and tried not to move her car again till Monday morning.) It was January, and even though the sun was shining it was chilly outside. Her companion cupped his hands around his coffee, dipping his grizzled chin into the warm current curling off the top.

"Hard to talk about that book," he said, removing his fuzzy chin from the warmth and jutting it in the direction of her lap, where her copy lay. "Not like other books, where you say what happened, you said it all."

Elizabeth nodded encouragingly. "It doesn't really have a plot," she said. Who *was* this guy?

"That's right. Power's in the words." His voice grew softer. "You talk *about* the words rather'n juss reading 'em, you lose something."

Elizabeth began leafing through her copy for the section at the dinner party, but before she could find it he had jumped out of his chair:

"Yo yo yo, my *man*!" he crowed. It was one of his homeless cohorts, who had wandered nearby. "You got anything on you, make this coffee a l'il more inneresting? Huh."

He made the universal booze sign (thumb pointed mouthward, fingers waggling), punctuating it with a puckish bray of laughter, his wide gray tongue flopping well past his bottom lip. The friend produced a plastic Poland Spring bottle from inside his coat, an amber liquid sparkling inside it.

By this time Elizabeth was already across the street. One homeless man was enough of an adventure; two wasn't happening, especially two who were drinking. When he saw she had left, the man merely shrugged his shoulders and poured the liquid into his coffee.

The next morning, she went to Café Collage before work

and was surprised to see him sitting outside. She took his presence as a sign, and got two coffees that morning instead of one. (It occurred to her later that he might have always sat there in the mornings. It was a popular spot for vagrants, and that Monday was the first time she knew to look for him.) Elizabeth handed him the extra coffee without saying a word, and on Tuesday there he was again. She bought him another coffee, and another one the morning after that. On Thursday she added a bagel with cream cheese, and on Friday she beckoned him to follow her, which he did without hesitation, his wheeled suitcase clattering along behind him.

They went to the basketball courts. It was early, but there were runners and surfers dotting the area, and in her front pocket she had placed the tiny can of Mace that usually lived at the bottom of her purse. She knew it was a risk to lure him away from his group, but she also knew they had to be alone for him to speak plainly. And she had to hear more; she had to know who this Virginia Woolf–loving, cigarette butt–smoking homeless man was. Usually she was not so inquisitive when it came to other people. Elizabeth preferred to learn about humanity by way of books, which could be closed at will and placed upon a shelf. With real people it was only a matter of time before the questions turned the other way— before the questioner was forced to share. But the rule of reciprocity didn't quite apply here. It was an ugly yet undeniable truth that at the root of Elizabeth's eagerness to question this man lay not only a yearning for companionship but the snobbish notion that he wasn't her equal, that she could ask him as many questions as she wanted without feeling an obligation to share anything about herself. If she became uncomfortable, she could press the eject button any time she wanted. For once, she failed to see the downside.

They sat on a bench situated atop the rim of a large concrete bowl inside of which a few early-rising skateboarders whizzed up, down, and around, like fish that had learned to swim in the air.

"Here you go." She handed him another coffee and bagel.

He sniffed the wax paper suspiciously. "This cream cheese?"

She nodded brightly.

"Hate cream cheese," he said. "Tastes like ass." He handed it back to her.

"Oh," she said. "I guess I should've asked."

"Huh."

They stared at each other. Elizabeth wasn't sure how to begin.

"I know what you want," he said.

"Excuse me?" she asked, an imaginary finger already poised over that eject button.

"You wanna hear my sob story."

"Your what?"

"My sob story." He smiled, displaying a set of teeth in surprisingly good shape, other than their yellow hue. They looked as if they'd been dipped in melted cheese, or wax, or gold. "Everyone out here's got one."

"I'm not sure what you mean," she said, even though she knew exactly what he meant, and knew he knew she knew.

"Com'on," he said, "I've seen you out here plenny times." (Elizabeth shifted, feeling through her jacket for the Mace.) "You must've overheard a few of 'em. Always bragging 'bout how bad they have it, trying to one-up each other." He raised his voice, imbuing it with more of a lilt, a swagger: "Man oh man, you think *that's* bad? Wait'll you hear *this*!" When he returned to his regular volume, his accent was closer to hers than it had been before. "I don't tell my story to just anyone. But for you?" He smiled again. "For Lily Briscoe?"

Like Scheherazade, it took him much longer than a day to

tell his story. That first day, they didn't get much further than his name.

"Orpheus?" she repeated dubiously. Was he messing with her? "Why Orpheus?"

"You know the Orpheum? Downtown?"

She nodded. It was an old vaudeville theater, beautifully restored. It even had its own organ.

"Parents met there, back in, I don't know, *long* time ago. Some song 'n' dance show." He took a sip of coffee. "They were so ignorant, they would've named me Orpheum. Huh. But a doctor got ahold of 'em, said Orpheus was more proper. Lucky me, I guess."

He didn't ask her name, and she never told him. On the rare occasion he had to call her anything he called her Lily, and she never corrected him. She grew to love her new name.

She learned he'd grown up not too far from her—in Florence, another neighborhood inside South Central—but at a time when black families had only recently won the right to live there, or anywhere south of Slauson Avenue. This meant he must have grown up in the early fifties, she calculated, putting him in his late sixties now. Elizabeth knew all about racially restrictive covenants from her first-year property law class, but she'd never known anybody who'd actually lived in the shadow of one.

"What was it like?"

He told her about the firebombings—front lawns covered in flames, neighbors (mostly black, a few white) sprinting over with buckets of water, the fire department mysteriously unavailable. He described the "white flight" that within a few years had ceded the neighborhood to the black gangs who had no common enemy anymore, and began fighting among themselves. He explained how the urban decay set in and would not let up, an infectious rot that festered and grew. Elizabeth knew from her own childhood experience a few blocks away, in Westmont, how the story went from there.

They established a pattern: he waited for her by the basketball courts and she brought him coffee and a buttered bagel. Each day he told her a little more, and slowly, like the blooming of a pale and watery flower, his sob story unfolded.

Orpheus was too smart to get caught up in the violence tearing apart his neighborhood. School was his domain, and he ruled it like a king. His first real trial happened when he was nine years old and won his school's spelling bee, beating out thirteen- and fourteen-year-olds. He was preparing to compete in the L.A.-wide regional—the intermediate step before the national competition—when a rule that compelled each school district to contribute to a "spelling bee fund" or else face disqualification prevented him from competing. He wasn't crushed; he was furious. It was on this occasion that his mother first instructed him to defy the expectations of all those who didn't know him. To act on his anger was what those people expected. His duty, she told him, was to do the opposite.

He continued doing the opposite—through high school, college, and graduate school. He became an English professor specializing in the early modernists, Virginia Woolf included. Whenever anyone expressed surprise over his ignorance of Richard Wright or Ralph Ellison, Orpheus thought of his mother. ("No Toni Morrison, no Maya Angelou either. Never read a word of 'em.") On the same principle by which he shunned black authors, he dated *only* black women, refusing to become one of *those* black men who abandoned their race after accruing the benefits of a higher education. And when his girlfriend Rhonda became pregnant he married her immediately, thereby avoiding the biggest stereotype of all: the black man who couldn't commit, who left an unwed mother and fatherless children in his wake.

They had a son and a daughter, Scott and Sherry ("whitest names I could find"), and one summer, when Scott was thirteen and Sherry was ten, they took a family vacation to the Grand Canyon. On the way back they took the scenic route through Utah. It was late, and Scott and Sherry were asleep in the back, Rhonda out cold in the passenger seat. He had coffee and a good night's sleep to keep him up, and he drove straight through the night, wishing he could see the beautiful purple-gray mountains on either side of him. The plan was to get back to their faculty house in Westwood by dawn. The children had music lessons the next day. Traffic, at least, would be a breeze.

A little after 3 a.m., he saw a sea of red each time his car rose over a crest. It turned out to be brake lights: a line of cars at a standstill for what looked like miles. He took his place in that line, his family sound asleep beside him. At least *they* would be well rested. He sat there for a solid half hour reciting poetry from memory, a habit of his whenever he was forced into idleness and unable to read. But he only knew so many poems, and eventually he got out of his car, walking forward to investigate.

A minute later the second boulder of the evening rolled down from the beautiful purple-gray mountains. The first had been the cause of the snarled traffic. It hadn't hit anyone, merely blocked the road in both directions with rubble that took hours to clear away. Orpheus felt the crash behind him before he saw it. He twisted, the reverberation knocking him to his feet. Tiny pebbles showered his body, tearing his shirt, coating him in a film of dust. Suddenly he *knew*, and hobbled back to his family to be proven wrong.

The boulder had flattened half the car in front of his, which thankfully for its driver had been empty in the back. His vehicle, of course, had been crushed flat. An investigation of the accident attributed no cause to the rolling rocks. There was no construction nearby, no evidence of foul play. There were signs posted all over the road, after all, warning of this specific danger. People drove at their own risk. It was just "one of those things." He remembered a policeman on the scene shrugging his brawny shoulders when he thought Orpheus wasn't looking. *But what're you gonna do?* the shrug intimated weakly. The officer was the first in a long line of what Orpheus came to call the "shruggers"—policemen, state officials, lawyers, judges, grief counselors, psychiatrists, friends, family, God—all shruggers. Even if they didn't actually shrug, this was the import of all they said or left unspoken, all they did or failed to do. It was just one of those things.

He felt in his bones that the natural, the *right* course of events was for him to have never left his car, to have memorized just one more poem and whispered its final verse while reaching for his children, the shadow of the boulder closing in around them. He planned to kill himself. He took his time considering the best way to do it, and it was during this time that he discovered alcohol. He had been an occasional drinker before; he enjoyed a beer with friends, wine at dinner sometimes, the rare raucous binge, but he had never truly known the power of this wondrous substance till then. Vodka was his favorite, so potent and yet so smooth and tasteless once he got used to it: like magic water, which was how he came to drink it—all day, every day, from waking till sleeping. He put a handle on his bedside where others put a glass of water. He drank it whenever he felt thirsty, or anything else. It made him forget—a veritable nepenthe—and as long as he kept it up it was as though he'd been underneath that boulder after all. In an epiphany he realized that the drunken oblivion of the here and now was a surer bet than suicide. He had no faith that death would either (1) stamp him out completely, or (2) reunite him with his loved ones, and anything in between was intolerable, an actual hell, no matter what anyone else called it.

Within six months he was fired from UCLA and had lost his housing. His friends tried to help him, but he shunned them, determined to fall and to fall alone. Six months later he was living out of his red rolling suitcase in Venice, among the bums he'd taught his children to pity instead of ridicule.

Had his mother been alive, surely she would have told him that becoming a homeless drunk in the wake of his tragedy was what many people would have expected—and not even particularly imaginative people at that. There was something inevitable, though, about his headlong plummet into obscurity and squalor, as if all along he'd been destined to end up here. Perhaps his mother had known; perhaps her advice to defy expectations had been an attempt to steer him away from the very destiny she thereby assured, like the hapless character in some Greek tragedy, setting him on the path that ended here, on the basketball courts, clutching half a buttered bagel and weeping openly to a wide-eyed woman at least thirty years his junior.

Elizabeth didn't believe him. His sob story was *too* sob-worthy, too awful—especially that boulder. Could boulders even *be* that big? But she shook her head when she was supposed to, and googled "Orpheus Utah accident boulder" the day he told her, not hoping for much. She didn't even know his last name. But there he was: a fatter, smoother-faced, crew-cut "Orpheus Washington" staring back at her from a blurb in the digitized archives of the *Los Angeles Times*, detailing his tragedy twenty-two years earlier. *Twenty-two years*. It was an unthinkable amount of time to spend on the streets, a life sentence in a special kind of prison. It turned Elizabeth's "rough patch" into a bed of roses, except that it didn't, of course. But it was the beginning of a special bond between them. She would never say this to Orpheus because it would require laying herself bare (and perhaps the comparison would insult him), but she understood what it was like to be scarred—mangled even—by the past. She felt guilty she hadn't believed him, and what began as a curiosity grew into something bigger.

"I'M SORRY, LILY, I'm sorry, Lily," he kept muttering over and over, struggling drunkenly to sit up on the urine-stained couch. Eventually she couldn't take it anymore.

"I trusted you, Orpheus," she said, switching to English. "I knew you saw where I kept my key, but I purposely didn't move it because I trusted you." She crossed her arms, staring at him like a mother whose child has deeply disappointed her.

A few months into their routine—when the can of Mace had been returned to the bottom of her purse—Elizabeth had made a deal with him: he could either get drunk on Saturday nights or stay the night on her couch and eat takeout Chinese from Mao's Kitchen down the block. Most Saturdays he took her up on the offer. She'd reminded him twice that morning that she was going to be away that night (she didn't explain and he didn't ask), that there would be no Chinese food or sleepover.

"What the hell happened?" she asked him now.

Orpheus struggled for the words. How could he explain it to her? He saw her now as if from the bottom of a well he couldn't figure out how to climb up to reach her. He was, in fact, terrified that the bottom would fall out and he would plunge deeper into the muck. He didn't know what to do. He was lost.

What Lily couldn't understand was that all this time he'd been spending with her—Saturday night into Sunday morning, and sometimes even Sunday afternoon if he slept long enough— had disturbed the carefully calibrated equilibrium he'd been maintaining for the last however-many years. (L.A.'s steady weather, especially on the coast, lent itself to a timeless mode of living. It was sunny and in the 70s: was it April, August, or December? Who knew? Who cared?) The weekends were when he made most of his money begging for change, and all those bagels and potstickers combined with a meager booze fund had made it harder to maintain his habitual state of drunkenness. There had been no alcohol that night, and no friends willing to share (he'd been seeing less of them, too). He should have been angry with himself for turning his back on the reliable oblivion of the bottle, but it was easier to be angry with her. He convinced himself it was all Lily's fault: the loneliness, the absence of alcohol. He hadn't seen it at first, but she was just another shrugger. Fuck her. She'd done him wrong, and he'd make sure she fixed it. He'd seen her stow the spare key a dozen times underneath the potted bird-of-paradise next to her door.

"Took the spare," he admitted now huskily.

He knew exactly where she kept her wine bottles, the only alcohol she had, a slow accumulation of holiday and incidental gifts from partners or clients after a job well done. He'd counted them: seven total, and not a single one opened. This had angered him too, as if she'd offended friends of his by failing to appreciate their charms.

"Found the wine."

He'd drunk the first bottle in one long glug. Then on to the second, which had taken a little longer. The third he'd downed half over the sink before hauling it to the sofa, where he decided to rest his eyes a few minutes before finishing. She owed him this: a nice drink and a nap. It wasn't asking much. All their babbling had to be worth something. He was forgetting already, about Rhonda, Scott, and Sherry. . . . He knew nothing of the world till she was standing over him.

"And drank it."

"Yeah, thanks, I put that together myself," she snapped. "What I mean is: why?"

Because I needed you and you weren't there. How the fuck had this happened? How had she snuck her way inside his life? He was surprised his life was still a whole enough entity for an inside to exist. It felt more like shattered fragments connected by bits of chicken wire and frayed string, a loose assortment that barely held itself together anymore. One day it would break apart and cease to exist as a single entity, and this, he guessed, was what dying would be. But he saw now that he cared that she was angry with him; he felt remorse at having done her wrong. That he could even see the top of the well was due to the fact that she stood at its lip looking down at him. In the same moment that he needed her more than ever, she never felt farther away. He began to cry.

"You gotta gimme another chance," he heaved between sobs. "You gotta forgive me."

Jesus Christ, thought Elizabeth, handing him a tissue. Could this night get any more ridiculous? She had to get him out of here.

"I forgive you, Orpheus."

He left only after she promised she'd see him the next morning like usual. When he was gone, she grabbed the used sponge from underneath her sink and tried to lift the urine stain from her cushion with hot, soapy water. It didn't work. She put the cushion in a plastic bag and settled for dousing the couch with Febreze to neutralize the smell.

Elizabeth perched on the edge of the puffy white armchair she used for reading, which was now the only seating option in the room. She thought about her night: the two hours she'd spent with Richard, and then coming home to Orpheus passed out on her couch. Was this all really happening to her? Since when had her life become so . . . interesting? It was almost midnight, well past her regular bedtime, and even though she was exhausted she knew it would be hours before she got to sleep. She picked up her phone, scrolling through her contacts. She wanted to talk to someone, to tell at least one person in her life everything that had happened to her, but it was too late to call any of her East Coast friends, and she hardly ever called them anyway, so wrapped up were they in lives demonstrably bigger than hers, encompassing not just a career but a partner—and as the years slipped by, more often than not a child or two as well. For a moment she actually considered calling her parents, who, after getting over the shock of her calling in the first place, would tell her that taking money from a stranger was as ill advised as taking candy. But she guessed that secretly her mother, who was addicted to several telenovelas, would be tickled by the idea of her meeting weekly with an unknown man, and come to terms with the proposal much more quickly than her no-nonsense father . . . especially if they ever met Richard in person. Elizabeth actually laughed—alone, at midnight, like a crazy person—at the thought of her parents meeting Richard. Her mother would *adore* him. And her father would *not*.

She took after her father, for the most part.

THE NEXT DAY Orpheus waited for her by the basketball courts, but she didn't show. He spent the whole day there, and by nightfall was convinced she had abandoned him forever. When he came back the next morning, it was more from habit than any real sense of hope.

But there she was.

"Good morning," she said quietly, handing over his coffee and bagel.

"Morning," he said.

"Beautiful day, isn't it?" The sun was shining.

"Sure is," he nodded. "Looks like June gloom's over."

"No marine layer," she agreed.

Their eyes met. It felt awkward between them, like that first morning when they had still been strangers to each other.

"Lily, I'm sor—"

"It's okay," she said, not wanting to rehash the events of two nights earlier, especially after spending the better part of Sunday on her hands and knees scrubbing the wine stain. It had been no use; the stain had bonded to the very fibers of her carpet, and in the end she'd had to cut it out and order a new swatch. She'd also gotten her locks changed, just in case, and dropped off her cushion at her local dry cleaner, pretending she had a nephew staying with her.

Partly to smooth over the awkwardness, and partly because she was still bursting to tell *someone*, Elizabeth chose this moment to tell Orpheus about the proposal.

She told him everything—from Jonathan Hertzfeld's first phone call, to her date with Richard on Saturday—and when she was done she sat back, waiting for his reaction. Telling Orpheus about the proposal was like introducing one crazy person to another, the Marquis de Sade to Joan of Arc: who knew what might happen? Would they fall in love? Tear each other to pieces? It was anybody's guess.

He didn't like it, not a single thing about it. The anonymous benefactor, the lawyer, the million dollars, it all sounded fishy to him. It was outrageous—preposterous!—like something out of *Great Expectations*. He told her as much, and she smiled:

"I thought the same thing."

Orpheus wanted to tell her she was treating the proposal too lightly: a shiny apple offered up by a leering stranger. She needed to look carefully for the strings that were attached, and surely edged with razors. Life was always finding a way to drag you to hell. If not, then what explanation was there for his calamity? He couldn't merely be unlucky, since that sort of misfortune—gaping, infinite—was in itself a version of cruelty. He used to be fond of telling his children that "anything was possible." It was a means of motivating them to try harder, to do better, and this phrase haunted him now alongside their obliterated faces. It was true. Anything *was* possible. The world was filled with horrors.

"Tell me more about the guy," he said.

She mentioned how Richard had thought the proposal was a reality series, and joked that sometimes she wondered if he was in on it.

"He probably is!" Orpheus latched on to this theory eagerly, but Elizabeth shook her head, smiling again. He shook his own head right back at her, frustrated: "It's too good to be true," he insisted. But he could tell he wasn't getting through to her.

Hmph, thought Elizabeth. She wouldn't mention—not yet, anyway—her idea of giving him at least a portion of the money. She knew he needed help—real help—to get better. She'd love to pay for therapy and rehab, maybe a halfway house of some sort to get him off the streets and off the bottle once and for all. She knew he'd resist, not because he was prideful about charity (he accepted pennies from strangers), but because he wouldn't want the weight of her expectations placed on his shoulders. It really *was* like *Great Expectations*, except she would be Miss Havisham, which, sadly, was a better fit for her than Pip. She smiled at the thought, watching the sun climb higher in the sky, the light growing stronger with the passing of each second.

"Want to go sit on the swings?" she asked.

They did this sometimes, in a small playground abutting the sand at the heart of the Boardwalk.

"Sure," he said.

Elizabeth had never grown out of the simple joy of sitting on a flexible strap of plastic and soaring in the air. She put her coffee on the ground and lowered herself onto the swing in her fancy pantsuit, wrapping her hands around the metal chains on either side.

"Careful!" yelled Orpheus, watching helplessly as her arcs grew larger and she flew farther and farther away. She looked carefree, like a child. He didn't like it. Orpheus preferred her serious; he liked her buttoned-up, determined air, which was the opposite of everything else he encountered on the Boardwalk. Looking at her now was like looking at her from the bottom of the well again, and he realized it was neither her fault nor his; the culprit was this crazy proposal. Without it she never would have gone out on Saturday. He wouldn't have had to break into her house. She wouldn't have missed their breakfast yesterday. Her head wouldn't be filled with some other guy. She was swinging so wildly now she was almost horizontal at the top of each arc. No, he didn't like it. And in this moment he became determined to stop it, however he could. Whatever the cost.

"Huh."

JONATHAN HERTZFELD HUNG up the phone and swiveled to his window. He gripped his tie pin, stroking it rapidly. Earlier that morning Miss Santiago had called him on behalf of herself and Mr. Baumbach, requesting reimbursement for their outings as well as a stipend to pay for certain materials—books and DVDs, she said—that they planned to discuss each week, as if they were in some sort of multimedia club. They had obviously agreed to the scheme in the only spirit rationally possible—a mercenary one—but his client hadn't seemed to mind, and had instructed him to pay whatever bills the duo sent him. He would do as he was told, of course, and be there to suffer the consequences. *Such is the lot of the lawyer,* he thought, grabbing his suit jacket with a sigh.

He went for a walk to clear his head. There was a black-and-white façade among the storefronts of the Century City Mall that had always intrigued him from the window of his office—a zebra grazing inside the colorful jungle of shops on either side of it. On closer inspection it turned out to be a cosmetics shop called Sephora: a women's store. He was disappointed. (Technically, Sephora offered an entire wall of men's cologne, but Jonathan barely realized cologne existed.) While he hesitated on the threshold, a saleswoman swooped down on him and five minutes later she was directing him to sniff a tester strip so as not to get any perfume on him. "For the wife?" she inquired, picking up on his wedding band and surmising he could only be there for her. He nodded, lifting his nose to the paper strip and smelling roses, plus something else. Was it cantaloupe? He wanted to get out of the store; his curiosity had been satisfied and he would never come back. He bought the smallest bottle possible and found he had been fleeced a mere forty-five dollars—not bad. He thought about giving the perfume to Rivka that night. She would think it was stupid. When he returned to his office he felt somewhat refreshed, though, as the experience had forced him to focus on her for a few minutes.

When he went home that night, he presented the smart little bag to Rivka after dinner, much to her consternation. They had decided after their first anniversary, in a bygone era when stockings and hats were still in fashion for ladies and men, that they would never get each other presents. It was silly to waste money on such tokens.

Rivka questioned him sharply: "What gives?"

He told her the story of his morning.

Without commenting she dipped her hand into the bag, through layers of tissue paper. "So fussy! It's why it's so expensive, you know—what a waste," and came up with the bottle of perfume. She sprayed it on her veiny wrist and sniffed.

A great heaving ensued. He had to pound her on the back. "Oh! Jonathan!" she gasped. "So awful! What were you thinking?" The bottle was thrust back into the bag and they moved on to the dishes. But later that night, he watched her take it out of the bag and put it in her special drawer, the one where she kept his old letters and photograph albums of their three children. She locked all this away, he knew, because she did not like to look on the past more than every once in a while.

"Well, well, well," he teased her, as she slipped beneath the covers. He knew he didn't have to specify. He knew she knew exactly what he meant.

"Shut it," she said, laying her head on his arm. It was the only way she could get to sleep. Sometimes he had to lie there for up to an hour, his arm the only part of him capable of joining her as she drifted off. He dreaded the pinpricks to come, but he wouldn't move till he saw she was sleeping. He could always tell by her breathing.

"Wha' wassit you said?" she asked him, ten or so minutes later.

Her voice had acquired the adorable little slur it always had when she was half-asleep. "When?" he asked her softly.

"When you came ba'towork." She paused to let out a little yawn. "After buying that . . . ssstupid perfume. You said you were . . . Wha' wassit again?"

He didn't respond because he honestly didn't know. What *had* he said? She was silent for a long time. Had she fallen asleep? But no: if anything, her breathing was more rapid than before.

She lifted her head from his arm and looked up at him, wide awake. "*Refreshed*, you dolt. You said you were refreshed. Because you thought of me."

She lay back on his arm. A few more minutes passed.

"Thank you," she said finally.

"But I thought you hated it."

"I did."

"So thank you for what?"

"You know."

And he did.

THE BOOK/MOVIE CLUB

THE BOOK/MOVIE CLUB worked. Richard and Elizabeth met for dinner at seven on Saturdays to discuss the book they'd been reading during the week, or at five to stream and then discuss a movie. On book weeks they met in restaurants in Beverly Hills, Century City, or Culver City—all decent halfway points between Venice and Silver Lake. They never went anywhere fancy, their first date at In-N-Out having established a mutual penchant for lowbrow yet quality eating. (Elizabeth never dressed up again.) On movie weeks they braved the traffic and went to her house or his apartment. Neither cooked much, so they always picked up food or ordered delivery. These were different meals from the boozy feasts Richard attended regularly with his industry friends. Elizabeth hardly ever drank, so when he was with her he generally abstained. There was no fuzziness, no loss of inhibition during their time together; they fell into a polite, almost professional rapport, as if they were coworkers striving toward a mutually advantageous goal. They never went over their allotted time—Richard always had plans afterward, and Elizabeth was always eager to return to her routine—but they didn't have any trouble filling the two hours, either.

One week after In-N-Out, Elizabeth hosted their inaugural viewing. She was nervous about having Richard over, but her recent home violation by a homeless man tended to put such qualms in perspective, and despite her obsessive cleaning in the hours leading up to his arrival, she was less nervous than she would have been going to Richard's apartment. She at least knew where all the potential weapons were hiding.

To her surprise, she found she liked *Harold and Maude* less than before. With the movie fresh in her mind and a Campos taquito brandished between her thumb and index finger for emphasis, she was well able to get past "neat." She complained that Maude's suicide at the end ruined it all.

"It's a grand gesture, I get that. She lived her life to the fullest and it was time to move on, but—"

She bit into her taquito and savored it a moment. Richard waited impatiently.

"—you don't just throw away life like that. Isn't that the point? Why is she so determined to die at eighty?"

"Well, eighty was a lot older back then than it is now. Don't forget, the movie came out in '71."

"Yeah, but even so. Who knows what she might've done at eighty-one? Or ninety-two? Even if she had one more second, she didn't have any business giving it away. And she of all people would've known that. It feels like whoever made the film—"

"Colin Higgins and Hal Ashby. Writer and director."

"—right. It feels like they just wanted to wrap things up neatly. I can see what they were going for, the irony of an actual suicide after all of Harold's fake attempts. It's elegant, but it isn't real."

In his eagerness to respond with what struck him as an insightful rejoinder (*who says reality should be valued over elegance when telling a story?*), Richard dripped hot sauce all over her carpet.

"Oh, crap, sorry."

He gazed at the cluster of red dots with a dismay that struck Elizabeth as far too complacent. "It's okay," she insisted unconvincingly, rushing to her linen closet for some spray-on cleaner. *Unbelievable.* It had been only two days since the new piece of carpet was installed.

While she was thus occupied, Richard looked around a little more intently than he'd been able to do upon entering. Her place was tiny, not much larger than his one-bedroom apartment, but nevertheless it was a freaking stand-alone *house* and he was duly impressed. The décor was spare, which he supposed made sense for such a limited space, but why had she chosen to make everything white? Carpet, couch, armchair, coffee table, even the TV stand shoved into a corner like an afterthought: all aseptically white, as though her living room were a hospital lobby. Two large (white) bookcases took up most of the wall space; he saw an entire shelf dedicated to Dickens, his eye catching on titles like *Hard Times* and *Bleak House* (he half expected to see one called *Life Sucks*) before landing on the only piece of artwork in the room, a pale print modestly framed, of a painting even he could name: *Christina's World*, by Andrew Wyeth.

Richard felt instinctively that every space in this spartan little fortress—every closet, cabinet, shelf, container—held the bare minimum of impeccably ordered items, and while she was still on her hands and knees he made a quick visit to the bathroom to test his theory. He peeked underneath her sink. *Bingo.* She had none of the paraphernalia he was accustomed to seeing in other ladies' lavatories—just extra toilet paper and a few cleaning supplies. He opened her medicine cabinet. *Yup.* She had the same amount of toiletries he did, which wasn't many, with one exception: a little plastic doohickey clamped over the middle of her half-used tube of toothpaste. *What the . . . ?* It looked to be some sort of toothpaste squeezer, for those OCD enough to insist on eking out every last drop. *Yikes*, he thought, shutting the cabinet door more forcefully than he intended, banging it loudly against the frame.

When he returned to the living room, the chemical reek of carpet cleaner hung heavy in the air, though it looked as if she'd lifted out the stain successfully. (He was too scared to ask.) She was staring at him oddly, and he wondered if she'd heard the cabinet door.

"You know," he said, "when I was sixteen my best friend died."

He'd had no intention of telling her this story, but in the context of their earlier conversation it was the first thing that popped into his head. He sat down and grabbed a forkful of car-nitas, shoving it into his mouth to prolong the moment. He was enjoying the shocked expression he saw now on her habitually impassive face: brown eyes wide, dark brows raised.

"It was a car accident. Drunk driving. Not him, the other guy. I actually had to testify at the trial, about what Kyle was like—that was my friend, Kyle—what he said he wanted to do when he grew up, stuff like that, to show what a tragedy it was. Which was really weird. But it must've worked, cuz the driver ended up getting a really heavy sentence—"

"Good," she said.

"I know. It was definitely worth it—to testify, I mean, even though my parents didn't want me to. But I felt like I had to, because of what happened at the funeral, which is why I'm even bringing the whole thing up." The meat was a lit-tle dry; he took a sip of water, swishing it like mouthwash. "Kyle's family was Catholic, so it was an open-casket wake.

It's still the only time I've ever seen a dead body, and it was so crazy how totally disconnected this—this embalmed corpse was from Kyle, you know? And you'd think I would've felt this overwhelming sadness standing next to him, and part of me *was* sad, obviously, but I also felt . . . *giddy*. And *joyful*. Because I was alive. I was the furthest thing possible from this, dead meat—I know that's awful, but those're the words that came into my head, I'll never forget it—and I had to cover my mouth with my hand because I was *smiling*—actually smiling at my dead best friend whose mother was standing, like, five feet away from me. It was awful."

"Well, you shouldn't—"

"Oh, I know. I was in shock, and I was only sixteen. It's not like I have any *guilt* about it or anything. But ever since then, when I think about the *joy* of being alive, it's always felt a little . . ."

"Heartless? Rapacious?"

"Uh, I was going to say 'harsh,' but sure? I guess that's why I like it when Maude offs herself. It's like—this's been great and all, but now it's your turn. Which is clearly stupid—obviously they can *both* enjoy life at the same time, the world's plenty big enough. But in a way . . ."

He trailed off again. Elizabeth regarded him thoughtfully.

"I never thought about it like that," she said finally.

For weeks they tackled *Jane Eyre*. Upon a more mature reading, Richard decided he hated Mr. Rochester.

"He tried to marry her under false pretenses, then propositioned her to become his mistress!" he exclaimed, perhaps a little too loudly for the Mormon family seated next to them at Islands.

"But only because that was the best he could do under the circumstances."

"Yeah, because he was married!"

"But he wasn't *married* married."

Elizabeth could easily forgive Rochester his (many) faults, because he alone had recognized the value of that little, plain, and above all *weird* Jane Eyre. There were many dashing men of literature upon whom she could have pinned her heart, but she would always prefer the man who was as flawed and fiery as his mate—missing eye, stumpy arm, and all.

"Oh right, because he was stupid enough to get tricked into marrying a crazy woman. And what, we're supposed to think it was Bertha's fault she went insane? It was passed down in her family, right? So how could she help it? Or are we supposed to think she got syphilis by sleeping around too much?"

"It's never really explained," Elizabeth admitted, toying with her Hawaiian burger. "Maybe it's a combination of the two?"

"Bertha gets totally hosed," retorted Richard between gulps of Dr Pepper.

"You should read *Wide Sargasso Sea*."

"Why sarcastic see?"

"No: *Wide, Sargasso, Sea*. It's a prequel, basically. About Bertha—her life in the Caribbean, meeting Mr. Rochester, being brought to England. This woman Jean Rhys wrote it in the sixties. It's like a postcolonial response. I don't think it's very good, but if you want more Bertha in your life, you should give it a try."

At their next session, at Sugarfish in Beverly Hills, Richard told her he'd only been able to get through a quarter of Rhys's book.

"I mean, it's a great idea, telling everything from her point of view. But it felt like a different story. With different characters."

"Agreed," said Elizabeth, chopsticks poised over a particularly delectable-looking piece of salmon sashimi. "Besides, Bertha isn't the point. It's not her story anyway." While the salmon melted on her tongue, she reflected on how strange it was that the brown girl was instructing the white boy to ignore the minority and focus on the white people as the more interesting characters. She felt the need to qualify her statement:

"It's a subversive element in the book, that the fascinating, passionate character is the plain one, not the exotic one. I wrote a paper about it in college, how the book's a reaction to all the romances written in the century before it. The heroines in those romances were always noble and upright but *so* boring."

"How so?" Richard shoved a spicy tuna roll in his mouth, tilting one ear ever so slightly toward her.

"Like in *Ivanhoe*," she said, "where the woman he eventually ends up with, Rowena—"

"Spoiler alert!" he mumbled, mouth still full.

"Oh, it's really long and I don't even think it's worth reading if you're not a teenager. Anyway Rowena's basically like Maid Marian—noble but *so* two-dimensional compared to this Jewish girl Rebecca, who's a healer and gets tried for witchcraft and is *so* interesting, and who everyone *knows* Ivanhoe should've ended up with. But in *Jane Eyre* the upstanding one is also the weird one, the one everything happens to *and* who gets the guy. Eventually anyway. You know?"

She was actually panting a little by the time she stopped.

"Wait, Rowena? Like my street?" Richard lived on Rowena Avenue in Silver Lake.

"Yeah, exactly like your street," she said, spilling some soy sauce over the lip of the ceramic dish next to her plate. Richard watched it spread out in a dark circle over the tablecloth. "You know all of Silver Lake used to be called Ivanhoe?"

"I didn't, but there's a school there called Ivanhoe. And part of the reservoir."

"Correct," said Elizabeth, "and back in the day the whole neighborhood was called Ivanhoe, after the book. That's why some of the streets are named after the characters. You can thank my fourth-grade social studies textbook for that fun little fact."

"Huh!" he said, genuine pleasure inflected in the syllable. He loved learning factoids like this, especially about his beloved L.A. "Learn something new every day."

As the weeks became months, they both learned a lot. They had no codes to rely on as Richard had with Mike, no underlying connection like what Elizabeth had with Orpheus. They were forced to spell out what they meant, and this required a general hammering, a tacit agreement to let come what may. They were like miners who chipped away at great slabs of rock during each session and went home to discover leftover slivers collected in their pockets or on the inside of their shirts. They picked these pieces off and stored them away, because even though they hadn't meant to acquire them, they were still the by-product of hard work, as precious as the larger chunks— maybe more.

For their second movie night they went to Richard's place in Silver Lake. Elizabeth rarely ventured out to what she now thought of as "east L.A.," though her teenage self would have been mystified by this designation. Since returning from New York and settling in Venice, her reference point for what separated the "west side" of the city from everything else had shifted about ten miles, from the 110 freeway to the 405, which meant that anything east of La Brea could now properly be termed "east." Silver Lake and its surrounding neighborhoods (Echo Park, Los Feliz) were in fact so far east now, they were practically a different city, and as she searched for a parking spot in and around Rowena Avenue, Elizabeth was surprised by how much the area reminded her of New York. In particular, it made her think of Brooklyn—Fort Greene, or maybe Carroll Gardens— with its cool yet cozy vibe. Dark dive bars and ancient-looking restaurants lined the ramrod-straight boulevards, and at night, enough of these storefronts had iron railings over them to keep the area looking sufficiently edgy. Between the boulevards meandered curvy residential streets like tranquil rivers, carving quiet, domestic spaces into the gently sloping hills. For all its neighborhoody vibe, she reflected, cozy was one thing Venice would never be.

The main door of Richard's building was open, so she went directly up to his apartment and knocked.

He opened the door. Shirtless.

"Am I early?" she said, averting her eyes, but not before noticing he had a healthy amount of chest hair. It was embarrassing to admit it, but she found this au naturel look appealing, though it was surprisingly rare among the myriad surfers, swimmers, and sun worshippers whose bare chests she couldn't help observing on the beach year-round. She didn't understand why so many guys shaved themselves these days.

"Not at all, I'm just running late," he said, turning around and padding away from the door. His back, on the other hand, was perfectly smooth—and surprisingly muscular. She forced herself to stare at his naked feet. They were nice too. *Lord.* Was every single part of him pleasing to the eye? A burst of heat prickled at her hairline, a momentary flare due to where this innocent query had transported her, unawares. Elizabeth felt a rapid throbbing in the space behind her navel, accompanied by a hunger she tried to neutralize by voicing it without delay:

"I'm starving!"

He whirled around, the flat of his hand rubbing against two of the eight abdominal muscles carved into his lower torso in obscenely high relief. "Me too." He grinned.

It was the grin that did it. He was too pleased with his own beauty, she decided, too gleeful of her admiration. His vanity counteracted his pulchritude, shrinking it to within an acceptable range. *Show's over*, she wanted to say. *Go put a shirt on.* And somehow, this thought must have communicated itself, because his grin faltered and he held up one finger, disappearing into what she guessed was his bedroom.

"Food came already, it's on the table!" he shouted through the wall. "Soda's in the fridge!"

Elizabeth did a quick survey of his kitchen and living room. He had all the right appliances and furniture (his TV was *enormous*), and it was obvious he'd neatened up in preparation for her visit, but it was equally obvious he hadn't given the place a thorough cleaning in a long time, if ever. There was dust everywhere, and the poor carpet in the living room looked as if it had leprosy or smallpox, there were so many scars and stains on its mottled gray surface. A thin layer of green mold circumvented the drain in his kitchen sink, and she would have scrubbed it away right then and there if any dishwashing liquid were in the vicinity. She slipped some Purell out of her purse and doused a knife and fork with it, setting them aside for herself. She was debating whether to clean another set for him when he reentered—with a shirt on, and white athletic socks covering his shapely feet.

"I cannot *wait* for you to see this movie," he announced, resurrecting his trusty grin.

THE POINT AT which the titular alien burst out of the guy's chest was actually the *third* time Elizabeth would have stopped watching, had it been up to her. The first was when that same guy and two of his crew members (idiotically) entered the spooky alien spacecraft, and the second was when the "facehugger," as Richard called it—assuring her this was the official term—attached itself to the guy's face.

"Wait, so it basically laid an egg *down his throat?*" she asked. "Which then hatched and burst out of him?"

"Exactly." Richard helped himself to a little more chicken tikka masala. "And notice it's the *guy* who's getting forcibly impregnated, and the *woman* who leads the action and survives. Totally subversive, especially for its time."

"So it's a horror movie."

"A hundred percent."

Which explained why she hated it. "I always thought it was an action movie."

"A lot of people do, cuz the second one *is* an action movie. Pretty good one too, although the third one's shit even if it *is* Fincher, and the fourth one's got issues even though it's not as bad as everyone says it is. Do *not*, however, get me started on the alleged prequel."

"How old were you when you first saw it?" she asked, more than a little concerned that getting started on the alleged prequel was exactly what he was about to do.

"Ten."

"There's no way I could've watched that when I was ten."

"Well, I wasn't supposed to," he said. "I was at sleepaway camp—which by the way was the only Jewy thing my very *un*-Jewy Jewish parents did for me while I was growing up—but anyway, we had this counselor, Paul, and even though in my memory he was a full-on adult he couldn't've been more than seventeen. And Paul was having this *epic* love affair with one of the girl counselors, Sara. And we all thought it was disgusting, or at least I did cuz I was immature for my age—you're shocked, I know—but by the end of the summer Paul would do whatever he had to to get rid of us and spend time with Sara, since he lived in Connecticut and she lived in Virginia and that was like living on *opposite ends of the earth*, and they needed to make the most of *what little time they had left*, like one of them had cancer or something. So one night he announced we'd be watching *Ferris Bueller's Day Off* for the eighteenth time before lights-out, except he was in such a rush to get out of there he put in the wrong VHS tape—God, that makes me feel old to say 'VHS tape'—and by the time *Alien* started, he was already gone."

"Oops," said Elizabeth, spooning her second helping of chana masala onto a hunk of garlic naan.

"I was totally hooked. When I got home I begged my mom to buy the sequel, and it took her about ten minutes to figure out what happened. Paul didn't get asked back the next summer, but Sara did, and she of course immediately started hooking up with this other counselor, Barry. There were always guys named Barry at camp, but *only* at camp, you ever notice that?"

"I never went to camp," she said.

"Anyway you'll be relieved to know it all turned out okay in the end, cuz a few months ago I got *aggressively* bored and looked up Paul on Facebook and guess what? He and Sara got married! They have two kids now. I was so relieved. Thank God for Facebook, right?"

Elizabeth opened her mouth—

"I know, I know," he said. "You're not on Facebook, and you're very proud of that."

She shot him a look of crinkle-eyed annoyance she couldn't remember giving anyone since high school. Was that the last time anyone had openly teased her? He chattered on:

"I think I can honestly say watching *Alien* for the first time is my best memory from childhood, hands-down. Wow, that's kind of sad, isn't it?"

Elizabeth shrugged. "I don't see why. You love movies, right? You even made a career out of them."

"If you can call it a career."

She knew he wanted her to give him a pep talk now, to say something like: *You'll get there!* or *Look how far you've come already!* But this was not her style. She allowed the pause to lengthen, broken only by their respective munching.

"Okay, your turn," he said finally.

She looked at him questioningly.

"Favorite memory from childhood?"

His mouth was coiled, as if on a spring, and his expression was more impish than usual thanks to a reddish tinge around his lips (a remnant of the masala sauce). There was no mistaking the challenge inherent in the question. She guessed this was payback for not propping up his ego, an attempt to throw her off balance by asking her a personal question. For this reason (and this reason only), Elizabeth took great satisfaction in replying:

"That's easy. When I was eight I had to stay home from school one day, which was really unusual for me. Most years I had perfect attendance—"

"Of course you did," he interjected.

"—but I threw up at breakfast that morning, so there was no way I was going to make it through the day. By the afternoon, though, I was feeling better enough to go with my mother to the laundromat. It was just down the street, and I used to love it there, all the women laughing and talking at the top of their voices, the clanking machinery. . . . It was like going to a party. At that age anyway. My mother gave me this Ziploc bag of pretzels—the ones shaped like little nuggets?—to help keep my stomach settled, and I laid them down on one of the washing machines we were using."

Elizabeth closed her eyes. Richard noticed for the first time that her eyelids were darker than the rest of her face, with little smudges on them that looked like makeup. But he knew her well enough by this point to guess it was a natural effect.

"Whenever I picture them I'm still this tiny eight-year-old who can barely see over the top of the washer. And they're rattling inside the bag like they're alive, and they're all I can see. Even the salt grains are huge—these enormous squares glittering in the sunlight like they're diamonds or something. . . . They fill up everything. Not just my field of vision, but *everything*."

She opened her eyes.

"I felt completely . . . *safe*. But it was more than that. You have to know what it's like to feel *unsafe* before you know what *safe* feels like, you know? And I hadn't experienced that yet. It's stupid, but the only thing I can think to compare it to is a baby in the womb. With the vibrations from the washer, and my mother right there, and all these other women who loved me and would protect me if they had to. . . . It's like I was able to re-create that feeling of total security for a few minutes—or maybe it was hours, or seconds, I don't know—and preserve it in a memory."

She paused. Richard wanted to say something, but he maintained his silence so as not to spook her, as though she were an exotic bird that might fly away at a moment's notice. This was by far the most personal thing she had ever told him.

"If I ever have trouble sleeping, all I have to do is picture the pretzels shaking in rhythm with the washer, and I drift right off. It's like my personal sleeping pill."

There was another, much longer pause, at the end of which she jumped up:

"I'm going to do the dishes," she announced, making her way to the kitchen sink and waving away his protests. "Where do you keep your dishwashing soap?"

"Oh," he said, "I ran out." *Three weeks ago*, he added to himself. "Here"—he ran into the bathroom and emerged with a liquid hand soap dispenser—"you can use this. It's the same stuff. But seriously, you don't have to."

"I want to," she said, which was half-true. What she really wanted to do was eradicate that ring of mold around his drain.

With a guilty pang, he thought back to dinner at her place the night of *Harold and Maude*. He hadn't even offered to clean up. His mother would have been ashamed of him. There were moments—such as now, as he watched her roll up her sleeves and get down to business—when Elizabeth actually reminded him of his mother, and as Richard stacked the plates on the counter, he thought back to the most remarkable instance of this phenomenon, that same night in Venice.

They had walked to Campos before the movie, since the restaurant didn't deliver and was only one block away. Elizabeth's bungalow was near the "Canals" section of Venice, which was the final vestige of the neighborhood's glory days a century earlier, when there had been canals crisscrossing a much larger area, with gondolas manned by authentic gondoliers imported from the motherland. These Italian strongmen transported coat-tailed men and corseted women in search of a day of pleasure, who were meant to feel as if they were traversing the canals of Venezia, except that it all ended in a big amusement park on the Pacific Ocean. Since then, all the canals had been drained and filled in except for a small, three-block grid that had essentially become an oddly shaped pond. In the spring and summer, all that standing water in an urban neighborhood filled with tourists and trash created a haven for ducks—lots of them. They were like stray cats: dirty, battered, and distrustful of humans, especially when caring for their duckling broods.

While Elizabeth was fiddling with her lock, a bedraggled mother duck waddled in front of them onto her tiny square of lawn, a teenage brood of four in tow. Richard and Elizabeth froze, as humans generally do when nonthreatening animals approach, to see how close they might come. Richard raised his eyebrows, murmured, "what the duck," and after a few seconds looked away, but Elizabeth clasped her hands in silent jubilation. She watched them waddle; she listened, delighted, to the mother's perturbed quacking. The last duckling was too slow and lost his family around a corner. He quacked—high-pitched, panicked—and Elizabeth looked to the corner, concerned on his behalf. The mother came speeding back, snapping at him and nipping his neck, and the little duckling hung his head as he scrambled after her.

Elizabeth laughed aloud, clapping her hands. Richard gaped at her. *This* was what made her laugh? A few dirty ducks? It was exactly how his mother would have reacted, and as much as he loved his mother, the comparison was in no way comforting. He liked to think his brand of humor went deeper, plumbed murkier depths. It was one of the many attributes he'd fine-tuned during college, with Mike, and he'd always pointed to a shared sense of humor as the number-one characteristic he required in a mate (as opposed to a mother). This incident made him feel disconnected from Elizabeth, and he despised feeling disconnected from people while he was still with them. The alienation born of the failure to connect was the worst sort of loneliness there was, much uglier than simply lamenting a person's absence. Had they been on a regular date, he would have felt more than justified from this single experience in never calling her again.

He would have been surprised to know that a few weeks later, Elizabeth felt the same way. As Richard grew more comfortable with her, in addition to stories about his childhood he began relating tales of his various barroom encounters. Even though his money problems had been temporarily solved with the infusion of cash from their first monthly payment, Richard's career prospects continued to falter, and often these drunken liaisons were the sole highlight of an otherwise dreary week, the only events he felt like recounting when she politely asked him how he'd been. Many of these stories ended with him "hooking up" with women he had no intention of calling afterward.

The tastelessness of his overshares was repellent enough, but in these moments Elizabeth felt as if she'd made a mistake by agreeing to the proposal. What was she learning? How would she be more equipped to meet someone who was right for her when their year was over? Why were guys so *gross*? It all felt so pointless. She knew she should have confronted him, told him she didn't want to hear his sex stories ever again, but she also knew he'd think she was a prude at best, or jealous at worst. So she kept her mouth shut and endured his blathering. *At least I'm getting paid*, she reminded herself whenever it got really bad. At the end of every month Jonathan Hertzfeld wired her earnings into a new account she'd nicknamed "Orpheus Funds" in her online banking profile. She almost had enough to cover the first few months of some sort of assisted living situation, though she hadn't yet raised the issue with Orpheus himself, which was easier said than done. In the meantime she would keep attending her weekly sessions, dutifully and diligently. But had she been at liberty to avoid Richard after any one of these interactions, she unquestionably would have done so.

If it had been up to Elizabeth, she would have avoided discussing politics as well, but it wasn't long before Richard pressed the issue. A dyed-in-the-wool Boston Democrat whose views were reaffirmed daily among the liberal denizens of Hollywood, there was no doubt in Richard's mind that the Democrats were the good guys and the Republicans the bad guys, and it pained him not to know where Elizabeth stood. It was at Sugarfish, during their final discussion of *Jane Eyre*, that he took the opportunity to find out. Richard theorized that the novel had a socialist message in Jane's refusal to hold on to her hard-won inheritance, in her insistence on sharing it with her impoverished relatives.

"I disagree," said Elizabeth. "If she was really a revolutionary she would've taken up St. John's offer and gone to India. And that's kind of the point. She wants the traditional path. She wants to fit in. And eventually she does so without compromising who she is. That's the wish fulfillment of the story."

"Well, it's not like you have to be a *revolutionary* to be in favor of socialism," he said.

"Actually, you do. Especially in nineteenth-century England. But now too," she added, immediately regretting it.

"Oh God, you're not one of those people who hate socialism, are you? Who think it's like a dirty word?"

"I don't *hate* it, I just—"

"Are you a Republican?" he asked impulsively, with a breathless intonation. He may as well have asked: *Are you a pedophile?*

"No."

He drew his hand across his brow, flashing her his signature grin.

"I'm more of a libertarian," she said.

"Ugh," he groaned, the grin vanishing, "Please don't tell me you're one of those people who believe in fiscal conservatism even though they claim to be socially liberal? Like the Tea Party? You're not in the Tea Party, are you?" he asked, anxious all over again.

"I don't belong to any party," she said. "I'm a registered Independent. But when you came as far as I did to get to where you are and have to watch half your salary go to taxes that're mostly a waste, maybe it's more frustrating for me than it is for you."

He refrained from groaning again—but just barely. She'd brought up class, which was one of her two trump cards, the other being race, of course.

"So you *are* pro-choice?"

"I am," she admitted reluctantly, annoyed that he couldn't fathom an intelligent person thinking otherwise. Until she was eighteen she'd been unquestioningly Catholic, hence staunchly pro-life, but her "rough patch" had included a wholesale rejection of the notion of organized religion. Still, this didn't mean she couldn't respect people who felt otherwise.

"And you *are* pro–gay marriage?"

"Of course!" she said, a little too emphatically for his taste, before forcibly moving on to another topic.

Back in his apartment on the night of *Alien*, Richard clicked out of iMovie and happened to see the YouTube logo among the options displayed on his AppleTV screen.

"Hey," he shouted over the din of running water, "there's this spoof of *Alien* I saw once, where the alien is Sarah Palin and the crew are like all these prominent Republicans and Democrats, and she's just *eviscerating* them. Except for Hillary. Hillary is Ripley, of course. I'll bet I can find it on YouTube."

"Oh, goodie!" Elizabeth shouted, managing to convey tartness at a high volume.

She didn't turn around, but he shot her a look anyway. And because she couldn't see him, he allowed his eyes to linger on her backside, which shook in rhythm to her scrubbing. *Just like those pretzels*, he thought, amused by his irreverence. At least her story proved she'd been close to her family once. It was the first time she'd mentioned her parents since telling him she never spoke to them, and he still had no idea why. And of course they were both as clueless as ever about what—if anything—connected them. Every now and then Richard would mention a person or place from his past—most of which had been supplied to him by Mike, whose curiosity about the connection between him and Elizabeth had never abated. But nothing ever clicked. The connection eluded them.

He let himself stare a little longer while she scrubbed away, oblivious. Now that she had relaxed around him—on this night she had literally let her hair down, which was much wavier than when she tied it back—she was officially pretty. But he never would have pronounced her "hot" if he saw her walk into a bar. And yet she wasn't the type to walk into very many bars, and while he wished he could label her a "prude" and be done with it, this word was as ineffective as "voluptuous" had been in his first attempt to define her. She was too unpredictable for such categorizations: the way, for instance, she'd gotten dressed up for their first date like some tween girl playing dress-up in her mother's clothes, which proved how touchingly inexperienced she was when it came to matters of self-presentation outside the professional sphere. She was an odd one, and it had become a favorite game of Richard's to contrast Elizabeth with Mike, whose self-presentation, for instance, was professional-grade. Mike's beauty was natural but by no means effortless, requiring at least an hour at the gym each day, a biweekly facial, and no fewer than five skin creams and emollients (he'd counted them once himself), applied as religiously as her prayers before bed each night. He wondered now: what did Elizabeth do before getting into bed? Probably just washed her face, maybe brushed her hair? He imagined her lifting the dark waves off her back, letting them cascade onto those stupendous breasts, which wouldn't have a bra reining them in. . . . Maybe she was the kind of girl who wore only boxers to bed, nothing else? He could see that. . . .

To his surprise, he felt a telltale throb down below, and looked away from her, as if she could feel it too. This was a first. But wait: was it only a coincidence that he was fantasizing about her while she was *doing his dishes*? In the wake of this horrifying thought (he couldn't wait to share it with Mike, she'd get such a kick out of it), all activity below his waist subsided harmlessly.

He walked into the kitchen, leaning against the wall behind her.

"You know, we never talked about what we're going to do with our money," he said.

She glanced back at him, startled by how close he was.

"I'll be paying off my mortgage," she said, turning back to the sink.

Of course, he thought. *How sensible.*

"What about you?" she asked.

"Pay off my credit card debt for sure. And some student loans from college. But I'll still have a lot left over after that." He hesitated. "You know my friend Mike?"

"Your soul mate? Sure."

"Ha, right. Well, her dad has Parkinson's, and they're really struggling to give him the best treatment they can. So I'd like to help with that."

Elizabeth turned off the water and faced him, wiping her hands on a dish towel.

"Richard, that's really great," she said.

He basked in the rare warmth of her tone, even though he knew he didn't deserve it. He had every intention of helping out Mike, but he'd promised never to tell another person about her father, and the only reason he'd told Elizabeth now was to make him look better in her eyes. *I'm an asshole*, he thought.

"It's not a big deal," he mumbled.

"Yes it is!" she insisted, stepping toward him.

Now he could add false modesty to his growing list of crimes.

"You know," said Elizabeth, "I actually have a—"

"You think we put in our two hours yet?" he asked, retreating to the living room in search of his phone. Suddenly he was ready for the night to be over.

She didn't answer him, but he found his phone quickly enough.

"Oh yeah, wow, we're good. It's almost ten."

When he turned around she was already at the door.

"Remember to get *Pride and Prejudice* this week," she said, reverting to her default monotone. "Make sure you read the first few chapters."

She was gone before he could respond. Richard sighed. Sometimes he felt like he was getting to know her, but other times she was as much of a mystery as the first day they'd met. He poured himself a generous gin-and-tonic. He was supposed to meet up with a bunch of people that night, the usual crew, but he texted Mike now to say he wasn't feeling well. When she texted back asking if it was another herpes flare-up, and then suggesting a different STD every few minutes (gonorrhea? chlamydia? HPV? etc.—she must have started drinking hours earlier), he didn't even bother to respond.

PRIDE AND PREJUDICE was less successful for purposes of the book/movie club, because there wasn't much to debate. It was, plain and simple, a delight. Richard was shocked by what an easy read it was, how light, how pleasurable, how *funny*, and on their third and final week of the book he erred on the side of effusiveness to make sure she knew just how much he'd enjoyed it.

"Mr. and Mrs. Bennet are so hilarious together! They should have their own sitcom, you know what I mean?"

"I guess," said Elizabeth. Austen wasn't *all* fun and games, and she wondered if he understood this. She still couldn't quite believe he'd never read *Pride and Prejudice* before.

"Are you *sure* it wasn't required reading in high school?" she asked, watching him dump half a saltshaker into his matzoh-ball soup. They were at Factor's, a Jewish deli—and L.A. institution—a few blocks south of Beverly Hills.

"Oh, it was," he said airily. "And I read every page . . . of the Cliff Notes."

CliffsNotes, she corrected him inside her head.

"Maybe we should watch the movie," he suggested. "I remember hearing good things about Joe Wright's version when it came out a few years back—"

"Is that the one with the skinny actress? With the underbite?" Elizabeth stuck out her jaw as far as it would go.

"Keira Knightley, yeah."

"Don't waste your time," she said, cracking a bagel chip in two. "If you're going to watch anything, it should be the BBC miniseries with Colin Firth and Jennifer Ehle."

"So you *do* watch television."

"On occasion. If period British dramas count."

"Oh, they count."

Sometimes she wanted nothing more than to smack that self-satisfied, smug little grin off his face.

"Want to split a black-and-white cookie with me?" she asked, looking for an excuse to leave the table.

"Duh."

"HEY, CHECK IT OUT," he said, when she returned from the deli counter with a Saran-wrapped disk so massive it looked like a miniature Frisbee. His eyes were trained on a table a few booths down. On one side sat a young black woman with a little blond boy who looked to be about three years old sprawled in her lap. Opposite her sat a white woman at least twice her age holding a baby that was bawling so loudly, the younger woman—who was obviously the nanny—had to reach across the table and retrieve it, at which point it settled down immediately. The older woman then tried to coax the boy to come to her, but he cowered where he was, refusing to leave the nanny's side. Richard chortled through his nose, so as not to make too much noise.

"Amazing," he said. "I *won't* have what she's having."

What's so funny about it? thought Elizabeth. The mother, who was trying to put a good face on the situation, glanced around the restaurant uneasily, and for one horrible second she and Elizabeth made eye contact. Elizabeth looked away guiltily, annoyed that Richard had drawn her into witnessing this painful scene. She took no delight in making fun of the woman. It was almost mean-spirited, she decided, the way Richard insisted on extracting comedy from every situation he encountered. Everything was "amazing" or "fascinating." He loved talking about "awkward" encounters during which someone had behaved inappropriately. He did it to himself, too: after making a stupid or inappropriate joke he would self-critique, "See what I did there?" or, "Too soon?" All these catchphrases were supposed to indicate an appreciation, but from a distance only—an ironic detachment. *Haven't we gotten past irony yet?* she thought a little desperately. There was a fine line between self-deprecation and self-obsession, after all.

Richard sensed she was taking the whole thing too seriously, which was typical of her. He'd simply been looking for an excuse to make the "I'll have what she's having" joke, which he always felt the urge to make inside big diner-y restaurants. The actual people at the other table were beside the point. If Mike were there she would have *bah-dum-dum*'ed, or pretended to sock him in the jaw, and they would have moved on immediately. Elizabeth's failure to *get it* was an unwelcome reminder of their incompatibility when it came to their senses of humor, like the episode with the ducks . . . except this time there was something else at play, something unpleasant he could no more than dimly acknowledge. She would *never* enjoy a joke at someone else's expense, no matter how clever it might be, because she was too thoughtful, too empathetic. "Too boring," he could hear Mike sniping inside his head. But was that really true? Annoyed that she'd made him feel like a bad person for what should have been a blip of a joke, his tone grew peevish:

"I'm just kidding, jeez. It's from *When Harry Met Sally*, in the diner—"

"I know. I've seen *When Harry Met Sally*. I get it," she said with her habitually wooden cadence, which he had never found so maddening as in this moment.

"Anyway I don't ever want to become one of those parents who need a nanny," he said.

And I'm sure you'll pitch in just as much as your wife, thought Elizabeth.

"There's something so depressing about the idea of paying someone to raise your kids, you know?"

"I *don't* know," said Elizabeth, slicing the black-and-white cookie crosswise into four perfect quadrants. "And I can't really judge anyone for it. I don't want kids."

"None?"

"Nada." She cut her chocolate quarter down the middle, into eighths, popping one of the miniature pie slices into her mouth.

"Let me guess. You're one of those people who think the world's too shitty to bring kids into."

"No," she replied, swallowing. "I just don't think I'm cut out to be a parent."

What the hell was *that* supposed to mean? "Well, even if *you* don't want kids, you have to admit it made a difference for your mom to stay at home, right?"

She didn't answer him.

"I mean otherwise that pretzel story never would've happened."

She regretted ever telling him that story. "My mother never stayed at home," she said, enunciating slowly, so that the words came out sharp and pointed, lethal little shards of ice. "Both my parents worked once we were old enough to go to school. My mother lost a day's pay that day, taking the day off."

"Ah," he said, for once looking properly humbled. But she wasn't done with him.

"We had to go without milk for two days because my father got the same virus I did, and had to take a day off too. And when we did our big shopping trip at the end of the week, my mother wouldn't let us get a treat. There wasn't enough money. My brother cried the whole way home."

"That must've been a pretty painful ride back home," he said, attempting to lighten the mood.

"You mean in our car?" she asked. "Sitting in the backseat?"

"Exactly," he said, his unflappable grin returning.

"We didn't have a car!" she yelled, loudly enough for the mother and nanny to glance over at them. She watched Richard's grin fade; it was impossible to keep the triumph out of her voice as she continued, not as loudly as before, but higher than her usual volume:

"You really think if we couldn't buy *milk* we had enough money for a car? I know you think everyone in L.A. drives, but have you ever actually gotten off the 10 at Crenshaw? Or Normandie? Instead of just driving past it on your way downtown? Have you ever even seen that half of the city? Believe me, not everyone who lives here is rich enough to own a car, even if you barely realize those people exist."

She shoved the other chocolate slice in her mouth, chewing her way through the stunned silence. Already she felt the urge to apologize, but she forced herself to keep chewing. If she said she was sorry she might as well have never said it in the first place.

"I never said everyone drives." Richard's voice sounded small now, pinched with hurt and surprise. "You should see this area"—he waved his hand a little shakily toward the window—"on Friday at sundown. The Jews are out in full force. You can barely drive without hitting them."

She suspected this was an oblique reminder that he too was a minority, if nominally—a pathetic attempt to level the playing field.

Their eyes met, bouncing off each other, and the silence grew longer, expanding slowly, painfully, like a rubber band pulled tighter. The longer they waited, the harder it was to end it. So they just sat there, waiting for the rubber band to snap.

I'm done, thought Richard, resolving not to say another word. He was reminded of those couples he saw sometimes in restaurants—glum old pairs who don't have anything left to say to each other. If there were no books or movies to discuss, he realized, he and Elizabeth would be another one of these couples. *What a nightmare*, he thought. *I honestly can't wait for this year to be over.*

The silence ended, but only when they said their goodbyes.

They did not complete their two hours that week.

THE DANCE

SOME PARTS OF L.A. are exactly what they seem: neighborhoods within a larger city. Others are independent municipalities with their own government and police force. It's impossible to tell one of these miniature kingdoms from a regular neighborhood; Santa Monica, Culver City, and Beverly Hills are technically cities separate from the City of Los Angeles, whereas Venice, Century City, and Silver Lake are neighborhoods inside of L.A. It makes no sense and those who know better don't bother looking for sense in the first place. To love L.A. is to love a mess: a jumble of sand, concrete, sunsets, and strip malls; a snake's nest of highways on top of which the full emotional spectrum, from rage to carelessness, may be witnessed inside every single hour of the day; suburban sprawl punctuated randomly by urban markers—museums, hotels, nightclubs—that in other cities would exist in one concentrated area; a metropolis associated persistently with the darkness of literary noir despite the starched-white sunlight that drenches it most every day, and the pink polluted sky that lasts into the dead of night; a city so expansive it encompasses a little bit of everything, *but only a little bit.* L.A. is all breadth and no depth—most of the buildings here don't even rise higher than a story or two—and there are many who believe this shallowness to be its fatal flaw. But shallow waters run clear and are easier to tread, and if L.A. sometimes feels like a million desert islands, the water between these islands isn't very deep at all—a folly more easily crossed than it would appear to be from a distance, which is why that old chestnut about L.A., like a palm tree or an aging starlet, actually looking *better* from a distance has little truth to it. The chestnut perseveres because, to those who merely visit, this city doesn't look like *anything* up close, doesn't look like a city at all. It's up to those who live here to imbue it with whatever character they like—or don't like—which is why Los Angeles has that singular, precious ability to accommodate each and every person who chooses to make a life here.

West Hollywood is another one of these miniature cities masquerading as a neighborhood, and just west of its City Hall on Santa Monica Boulevard lies its greatest treasure: a walkable strip of bars from San Vicente to Robertson. It's possible to hop from bar to bar and make a debauched night of it without ever getting in a car. Many cities are full of areas like this, but in L.A. there are only a handful, and most are tourist traps. The WeHo strip, however, does not cater to tourists. It belongs to the gay men and women who live there and those who wish to party with them, and all the bars and clubs along it—Trunks, Revolver, Rage, Motherlode, Here (to name only a few)—are a reliably good time.

At the end of August, Richard's business partner Keith was celebrating his thirtieth birthday at the Factory on the western end of the strip, during a Friday-night dance party called "Pop-starz." Mike was returning to L.A. the same day from a week-long vacation with her parents, and before she left she extracted a promise from Richard to bring "the DP" to Keith's party. (Over time, the code word "DP" had shifted from referring to the proposal to Elizabeth herself.) After two months, Mike and Elizabeth still hadn't met.

Richard had intended to invite Elizabeth the previous Saturday, at Factor's, but the evening had gone so badly he'd abandoned his plan. He hoped Mike would forget about it too. It wasn't that he was angry with Elizabeth; he was constitutionally incapable of holding a grudge, and had more than enough white man's guilt to blame himself for his perceived insensitivity to her challenged upbringing. Still, he was by no means eager to see her again. Saturdays were more than enough.

It was with a sinking heart, then, that he read Mike's Facebook message the Monday after Factor's, five days before Keith's party:

> Ugh so bored up here going nuts. 1 week + 2 parents = HELL. Yesterday my mom asked me when I was getting married, Jesus H. . . . My dad is good thx for asking. Anyhoo you'd better make sure the DP comes Fri I'm counting on it you PROMISED. It's all I have to look fwd to mwah.

Fuck, thought Richard. He was still in bed, and his leg shook so violently the mattress began to squeak. Mike affected an amused curiosity about "the DP" that allowed her to ask as many questions as she wanted, but Richard knew perfectly well she hated this weekly standing engagement that had nothing to do with her. She was a jealous friend, and had been ever since breaking up with him. It was almost as if her possessiveness was meant to make up for her pushing him away, and in a way it *did*, because he'd never had a problem with any of the men who'd come in and out of her life over the years—never felt as though he might be toppled from his privileged perch as "the best friend" by any of them. It was funny to him, yet unsurprising, that Mike should feel threatened now, and he knew that if he didn't introduce them soon there would be hell to pay. He clicked over to his inbox. Elizabeth wasn't even on IM, so the only way he could contact her besides texting was old-fashioned e-mail. (Calling her was unthinkable.) This message was a bit too substantial for text, so he gathered his courage and clicked the "new mail" button:

Hi Elizabeth,

Happy Monday!! Hope your doing well and work isn't too crazy?? Looking fwd to Sat (movie night!!), but wanted to invite you to a party this Fri also. It's Keith's bday and alot of my friends want to meet you (they've heard good things!!) esp Mike. Do you think you could make it?! Would be great to see you let me know and I'll send you all the details.

He pressed SEND before he could read it over. The mouse arrow swirled over his inbox in tiny, agitated circles: *what have you done?* it asked him in a language only he could understand. He'd taken Elizabeth's acceptance for granted when he promised Mike she'd be there, but after their last session and this horrendous e-mail (he read it over now—what was with all that double punctuation?!), he wasn't so sure.

He refreshed his inbox: no answer.

RICHARD'S MESSAGE ARRIVED at Slate Drubble & Greer in the midst of an electronic war. One corporation was selling off the shares it held in another, and long-simmering resentments were frothing to the surface via rapid-fire e-mails. It was up to Elizabeth to get the two sides to calm down. Richard's lone message with a distinct subject heading (*Fri Night?!*) appeared in her inbox like an innocent child teleported magically, and horribly, onto the battlefield. His e-mails were always off-putting to her anyway; she knew it could have been much worse, but she wished he were a *slightly* better writer. Why, for example, did he have to abbreviate so many words? All she wanted to do was get it out and away. What's more, it was obviously an overture, and she felt duty-bound to reciprocate:

> R,
>
> Of course! Would love to come, thanks for asking. Work indeed crazy today so that's all for now—
>
> E

Her response popped up on the fifth refresh. Something burst behind Richard's eyes, and he actually went dizzy for a moment from the relief. Crisis averted. He rewarded himself by watching six episodes of *Family Guy* back-to-back off his DVR.

HOURS LATER, WHEN the battle (not the war) was over and Elizabeth was concentrating on nothing more engrossing than preventing turkey-club bread crumbs from falling between the letters of her keyboard (she imagined that once trapped there, they would remain forever imprisoned in an eternal bread crumb hell), she allowed herself to wonder for a few minutes what meeting Richard's friends would be like. She assumed he entertained them weekly with updates on their time together, which they pronounced "amazing" and "fascinating." *They must be itching to get a glimpse firsthand*, she thought, dropping guard over her keyboard long enough to allow a dollop of mayonnaise to lodge between the *l* and *o* keys. *Great*. Now she'd have to get a replacement board from the misanthropic IT guy with body odor issues, who'd yell at her—again—for eating at her desk.

RICHARD AND MIKE made plans to meet up for a drink before the main event. They chose the Abbey, which was the only gay bar on the strip that straight people patronized regularly, since it happened to be a great bar—though Richard, who relished the ample and obvious admiration gay men routinely bestowed on him, would have been comfortable in any gay bar. Arriving a few minutes before Mike, he ordered two gin-and-tonics and took a double-fisted turn around the place, feasting his eyes on its considerable amenities while pretending to ignore the side-long glances he inspired. There were four separate bars (three indoor, one al fresco), a kitchen, a café, two patios (one covered, one open), a six-foot-high fireplace, a dance floor, and a faux-cathedral tableau including an altar to Elizabeth Taylor. (In her final days, the Abbey was the only place she ever went; there was even a glossy painting signed by the dearly departed legend herself.) Beyond the iron palings separating the outer patio from the sidewalk, he caught sight of Mike flashing her driver's license at a bouncer, pleased to have been carded.

"Gibler!" he shouted, sucking down the remnants of his first drink and depositing it on a table.

This was another one of their codes: when the umpteenth person had mistaken her first name for Kim, he suggested she change it to "Kimmy Gibler" (the hyper next-door neighbor on *Full House*) and be done with it.

"Dick!" she shouted back. This one was more obvious, and it was usually what she shouted at him in gay bars, uttered in enough of a monotone that it sounded as though she were yelling for penis. They hugged fiercely, and he asked after her parents (they both knew he meant her dad). "They're good," she said. "They say hi. So how's the DP? Ready to meet her maker?"

He raised an eyebrow.

"Yeah, I have no idea what that meant either," she said.

He laughed. He'd missed her, even in a week.

"She's good. Word on the street, and by 'street' I mean the e-mail she sent me, is she's excited to come, so that's good."

"Sweet," Mike replied evenly, motioning to the bartender for a vodka-soda. She watched him plunge a tall glass into the ice well, his tanned shoulders bulging outside his regulation Abbey tank top. It was always a bit of a shock to come back to the beautiful people after spending time away from L.A. Even if you happened to be one of the beautiful people yourself.

"What? You want a piece? I think that one might actually be G-A-Y, unfortunately," he whispered, spelling out "gay" as if it were a dirty word. He looked down; somehow he was already halfway done with his second gin-and-tonic. "He was giving me the eye before. Looks like he could put away a mean kpenes if you know what I mean, and I think you do." He elbowed her ironically.

Oh, Richard. She'd missed him too. Mike studied her best friend over the rim of her glass. He was looking particularly good tonight, in a tight-fitting polo and snug pair of Diesel jeans she'd never seen on him before. She guessed he'd bought them with his newfound income. A pair of aviator sunglasses were perched on top of his head like fashionable Mickey Mouse ears, rendering him both cool and adorable. *How does he do that?* she wondered. Pulling off the "man tiara" was no small feat.

"I cannot *wait* to meet this girl," she said.

Richard gulped down the rest of his drink, leering in response. Mike could sense he was too buzzed for so early in the night, but there was nothing to be done about it now. If she called him out on it he'd deny it, and this would only make it harder to persuade him to slow down in the hours to come.

"I see you're not losing any time," she said. "Lemme chug this and we'll get the show on the road."

A little before ten, Richard and Mike made their entrance to Keith's birthday party. Richard sailed through the Factory's lobby, bounding up a metal staircase two steps at a time and practically leaping into the front room on the second floor. (Mike plodded behind him, placating the bouncer at the top—who had eyed Richard an unheeded warning—with a head shake and a beseeching look heavenward.) He scanned the early birds for the birthday boy, spotting him soon enough at the bar. But Keith seemed to be the only one there as of yet. Richard felt a pang of apprehension. Were he and his "business" partner such losers that no one was going to show up? How embarrassing would that be—oh, God, especially with Elizabeth on the way? Was there time to call her, tell her it was canceled—

Keith saw him and Richard ran over, throwing his arms around his neck and shouting "happy birthday!" with the perfect blend of irony and sincerity. While they were ordering the first round of drinks, five more guests arrived, and by the second round (Richard stuck to gin-and-tonics despite Mike's subtle efforts to downgrade him to beer) there were at least thirty people there for Keith in addition to the club's regular patrons. By the *third* round, the room was packed, and Richard saluted his business partner across a sea of friends, friends-of-friends, frenemies, and strangers, *cheers!*-ing the air. He turned and saw Mike talking to a loathsome D-girl (a catchall term for the army of women who worked on the *development* of film projects in their nascent stages, rarely—if ever—getting to actual film production). They both saw him looking and waved. He waved back, pulling down the corners of his mouth into a "yikes!" expression when the D-girl wasn't looking. Mike's eyes flashed, but she kept the conversation going without missing a beat. Next to him, a tall woman laughed, another friend of Richard's who'd observed the exchange. He began bantering with her, the party sounds swelling around his ears, the climax of the first movement of a magnum opus that would last for hours and hours: the sustained ecstasy of a successful party, filling him, as it always did, with a febrile joy he didn't dare articulate for fear that others would make fun of him for it.

He felt a tap on his shoulder. He whirled around.

If Elizabeth had known how appalling the parking would be in West Hollywood, she wouldn't have come. It had taken her nearly an hour to find a space (she refused to park in one of the overpriced lots), and by the time she'd paid the twenty-five-dollar cover fee (which Richard had failed to mention), trudged up the metal staircase, marched into the knot of party-goers, and tapped him on the shoulder, it was well past 10:45. She glanced at the blonde by his side, guessing she was Ally, a minor yet regular member of his crew. *But really*, thought Elizabeth, *she could be anyone*. It was her own fault she didn't know what any of his friends looked like, since—as Richard reminded her constantly—there were photos of all 658 of them perfectly accessible on his Facebook page.

Richard stared at her. Somehow, in the last hour, he'd forgotten she was coming. *How much have I had to drink?* he wondered, dismissing the thought before he could answer it. She was dressed too formally, in the same black skirt she'd worn to their first date, which ended well below the knee and made her look heavier than she was. Her starched white blouse accentuated her breasts, but paired with the skirt she looked like a maid without the apron, and her hair was pulled back in a librarianish bun. Richard glanced at Mike—beautiful, brilliant

Mike—who was still engaged with the D-girl and who looked so effortlessly glamorous by comparison. His stomach bottomed out at the thought of having to introduce them finally, but there was no getting out of it now. He felt a twinge of embarrassment on Elizabeth's behalf, his drunken mind racing to the "What's Wrong with this Picture?" section of *Highlights* magazine, and causing him to actually giggle before saying hello.

"Hey," he cried, swooping in for a hug.

Elizabeth took a half step backward before accepting his embrace. They'd never hugged before. He was obviously drunk, and she didn't think she was going to much like the drunken version of Richard Baumbach.

"I'll be *right* back," he said, hurrying away without explanation.

Elizabeth and the tall blonde were left staring at each other. He hadn't even introduced them.

"You must be Ally." Elizabeth held out her hand.

"I am!" Ally shook her hand, but Elizabeth could see the panic in her eyes. She had no idea who Elizabeth was.

"I'm Elizabeth."

Ally blinked.

"Richard's friend?"

"Ohhhh, nice to meet you!"

But it was obvious she still didn't have a clue.

This was Elizabeth's first inkling that in the two months since Richard had told his friends about the Decent Proposal, he hadn't mentioned her to anyone other than Mike, and occasionally to Keith. Mike hadn't told anyone because she wanted to minimize the DP's impact, and Keith hadn't said a word because he wasn't one to gossip. People like Ally, on the outer rim of Richard's inner circle of acquaintances, had either forgotten about the Decent Proposal or grown tired of asking about it and being shut down. They'd moved on. *#DecentProposal* had gone dark a long time ago.

The crowd parted, and Richard reappeared with a figure behind him. He stepped aside like a magician unveiling his final trick:

"Elizabeth, this is Mike. Mike, this is Elizabeth. There." He mimed wiping his hands, "That's over with."

Elizabeth knew Mike was Korean-American and from New Jersey, but to her she looked like a Mongolian princess: beautiful, proud, and fierce—all flint and bone. Mike radiated a hardness, not just of body but of spirit too, an iron will that rivaled even the steely reserve of La Máquina. Elizabeth would have been impressed if the poor girl weren't so obviously filled with hatred. Her nostrils were quivering.

"It's so nice to meet you finally," said Elizabeth, extending her hand and smiling.

"Likewise." Mike squeezed back, *hard*, matching her smile. She'd already cataloged the DP's physical attributes, and aside from her impressive rack (which was a matter of taste), her teeth were the one area where it could be argued she beat her. *Argued*. Otherwise, she was nothing special. And her clothes were fucking horrible. She could do so much better, capitalize on those natural curves, take out that stupid bun. . . . Mike felt the old "Project!" urge well up inside her, but promptly stomped it down. She wasn't going to do this girl any favors.

Richard flicked his head from one to the other, as if they were playing tennis, but after a few seconds he looked over their heads, too drunk to concentrate on them any longer. He began flapping his hand wildly:

"Keith! Get over here!"

Elizabeth watched as a tall man extracted himself from a circle of guests and loped across the room on long, elegant legs. He was skinny except for a little paunch hanging over his belt, and was already sticking out his hand when Richard barked, "This is Elizabeth!"

The shake became luxurious, two-handed. Keith stepped back and viewed her at arm's length, like a work of art in a museum.

"Elizabeth!"

He emphasized the "beth" in a way she immediately loved.

"You're not what I pictured at all," said Elizabeth.

He was dirty-blond, freckled, and had none of Richard's beauty, though from the way he let his smile spread slowly across his face—into the very crinkles around his eyes—Elizabeth found him attractive in a manner that struck her as belonging to an earlier era, when men relied on charm and charisma rather than appearance. Already she could feel his good humor infiltrating her via an osmosis that had nothing to do with the brightness of his eyes or the fullness of his lips.

"Oh, really? And what did you picture?" Keith dropped her hand, crossed his arms over his chest, and shifted his weight onto one foot: a rakish, sassy pose.

"Glasses?" She paused. "Definitely not so handsome."

Keith scooted behind her, grasped both her shoulders, and wheeled her around so that she was facing Richard. "Ooh, I *like* her already!"

He pronounced "like" as "lock" and drew it out with the luxurious drawl Mike was convinced he affected, or at least greatly exaggerated. He was from Florida, for fuck's sake, and though he claimed it was a small enough town and close enough to the state's northern border to count as the Deep South, she still wondered. (Behind his back she called it his "Tennessee Williams *thang*," and Richard tried not to laugh.) Mike resisted the urge to sneer now, and instead joined in loudest of all as the little group laughed merrily.

"So tell me 'bout this book and movie appreciation club you guys have goin' on," Keith said. "I just think that's the greatest thing. Y'know I'm in a book club myself, don' know if Richard told you."

"He didn't!" said Elizabeth. "What're you guys reading?"

He mentioned a novel published recently that had polarized readers, and they were delighted to discover they both hated it. The next few minutes were spent tearing it apart and desecrating its corpse. By this point Ally had wandered away, and Mike decided they were all in need of a drink. It took a gargantuan effort not to roll her eyes when the DP asked for ice water, since it was "a long drive back to Venice." *Bo-ring!* she wanted to say, and it pained her that instead of exchanging a surreptitious "yikes!" with Richard, she had to avoid looking at him altogether. An ancient sadness washed over her, like the loss of a loved one, but she could *not* afford to go there right now, so she grabbed Richard's hand to counteract it, leading him to the bar, where it was too noisy to carry on a conversation but where they would at least be alone together inside a sea of people. She decided to order him another gin-and-tonic without even asking. She didn't care how much he drank anymore.

When they returned, Keith and Elizabeth were laughing.

"Whasso funny?" Richard demanded.

Elizabeth waved her hand dismissively. "It'd take too long to explain," she said, shooting Keith a mischievous look.

Well, they're a lovefest, thought Richard. This should have made him happy. He'd suspected Elizabeth was a touch homophobic (her Catholic upbringing, her hurried affirmation of gay marriage, as if it were something she'd rather not think about), and he'd taken a sadistic pleasure in inviting her to a gay club. He'd expected her to feel out of her element, to be a little wowed by the experience. At the very least, he'd expected Keith to throw her off a little, but here they were, heads tilted together like old friends. Richard watched as Keith grabbed her hand, and when Elizabeth not only let it rest there but squeezed it harder to emphasize a point, some brutish, animal instinct unleashed itself inside him and he had to check the impulse to pull Keith—*Keith*, his friend and business partner, *gay* Keith—away from her. *Am I actually—whatever*, he told himself, except that it wasn't so easy to throw this thought away. Instead, he had an unwelcome moment of clarity amid his fuzzy, drunken state. Usually he loved these instances, like a shaft of sunlight breaking through the clouds of inebriation and illuminating an insight by way of contrast—one that never would have been visible in a clearer, sober state of mind—but this time he shied away from the brightness and waited for the clouds to return. The light, however, remained. It had to be confronted.

Why had there been no spark, no instant connection between him and Elizabeth like the one he was currently witnessing between her and Keith? Why was it so *difficult* for him to draw her out? Why didn't she ever squeeze his hand, or touch his shoulder? He knew why. There was no denying that Keith was the smart one between the two of them. Whenever they had to give notes on a script, Keith always took the lead; he read something like five magazines and one book a week. He'd gone to *Harvard*, the prick. *Of course* they loved each other. They were the smartest people he knew. And what did he have to offer, really, besides good looks (an unearned gift) and enthusiasm? He remembered suddenly his stupid joke at Factor's: *I won't* have what she's having! The shame of this moment crackled through him like an electric shock, practically knocking him off his feet. She must have been so *bored* having to talk about books with him; it was probably like a remedial version of the animated conversation she was having now.

Richard's cheeks flushed with embarrassment, or maybe it was just the alcohol. *Whatever.* Suddenly the aforementioned sea of revelers wasn't buoying him up but pulling him down, smothering him in its depths, and he looked toward Mike, flailing for her like a lifesaver except that she too was focused on Elizabeth and Keith, jackhammering her silky head in a manic attempt to show that she was following along. For all her glamorous appeal, Mike looked agitated, *desperate* even, beside the perfectly composed Elizabeth. Richard threw his head back and gulped down the remnants of his latest gin-and-tonic, rattling the ice cubes to shake away the whole scene.

Without meaning to, Mike and Elizabeth exchanged glances. They'd both been thinking the same thing: he'd had too much to drink.

"I think the dancing just started," announced Richard, shaking his leg. He needed to move. Everything would be okay again if he could just *move.*

"Yeah, let's book it to the back room." Mike cocked her head like a delicate bird poised to take flight in the direction of the loud, thumping music leaking from beyond. "We can burn off some of that alcohol with our dance moves. That bouncer's going to lose it if we don't move some of the party out of here anyway. I smell 'roid rage."

Keith began herding his guests. Mike grabbed Richard's hand again to lead him away, and Elizabeth followed a few steps behind.

THE DJS AT POPSTARZ blasted the sort of music people listened to with their windows rolled up or their headphones at half volume to prevent the world from finding out how unsophisticated and sentimental they really were. Mariah and Madonna, Britney and Beyoncé, Katy and Kelly, Gaga and Rihanna all crashed onto the dance floor in a tidal wave of unapologetic pop, and the crowd let it wash over them; they wallowed in it; they splashed about; they drank it down with their alcohol. Popstarz was a place for revisiting middle school roots, except this time no one was embarrassed by their inability to dance, or pining away for their dance partner—other than in a carnal way that only enhanced the experience. As soon as the dance floor came into view, Richard dropped Mike's hand and took a running leap into the middle of the crowd already gathered there. Whitney Houston's "I Wanna Dance with Somebody" had just come on.

Richard took pride in being an exception to the rule that white guys couldn't dance. He liked to point out that it usually took some form of minority to be a good dancer: you had to be female, or black, or gay, or *something*. He was technically Jewish, of course, but according to him this was the one minority that didn't count when it came to moving your body. And while he may have overestimated his prowess, he wasn't bad. His enthusiasm counted for a lot.

Mike tolerated Popstarz. She could dance if need be, but she didn't get any joy out of it. She hated the rhythmic pelvic gyrations that had come to be accepted by her generation as recreational dancing, the puerile lewdness of it all. She preferred the restrained head-nodding of music-loving crowds drinking in live bands arrayed on a stage, and if she had to dance at all, the practiced steps of ballroom, while admittedly dorktastic, were more her sort of thing: civilized, recognizable moves requiring at least some basic skill. She would need a few more drinks in her before she could join Richard, so she sidled over to the nearest wall and watched helplessly as Elizabeth followed her.

Keith was busy playing host; most of his guests were still in the other room. There wasn't anyone handy she could use as a buffer. Mike had been needling Richard to introduce her to the DP for months, and now that the DP was here she would have given anything to get away from her.

They stood side by side, two wallflowers.

"So *he's* wasted." Mike nodded toward Richard, who by now was riding an invisible pogo stick, a tiny crowd heckling him from the sidelines, egging on his ass-hattery.

Elizabeth smiled her annoyingly beautiful smile.

"I think it's our fault. He was nervous about introducing us."

"Well, can you blame him?" Mike had meant this to be funny, but it came out wrong: antagonistic, bitchy.

"I've never seen him like this actually," said Elizabeth. "We don't really drink together."

"*Really?* That surprises me." It felt as though she were a suitor marking out her territory, proving to the interloper how much better she knew the belle of the ball. Mike hated what she was doing, but she was powerless to stop herself. "Well, you're in for a real treat. He's a messy drunk, I'm warning you now."

"You just came back from vacation, right?"

Mike nodded. "A week with my parents. Sort of hellish, but what're you gonna do?"

"How's your father?" Elizabeth asked. "Is he doing okay?"

When Richard had told Elizabeth a month earlier about Mike's father, he had failed to mention it was a secret. At the time, Elizabeth was an isolated acquaintance, and when he invited her to the party he forgot to tell her not to say anything to Mike. Richard danced on, twenty feet away, "raising the roof" with ironical intensity.

"He's fine," Mike snapped. How dare he tell this bitch about her father? The flimsy buttress of goodwill that had been barely supporting her self-restraint snapped in two, and her ability to put a good face on this night and the Decent Proposal in general came crashing down around her. She opened her mouth to say something—anything—unpleasant or hurtful, but Richard chose this moment to bounce in their direction.

The song wasn't over, but he was feeling self-conscious. He had reached that stage of drunkenness wherein he was *very* drunk but acutely aware of it, and overcompensating by pretending to be sober. His dancing had gotten too wild; he needed to rein it in a little.

"Whatchoo guys talkinabout?" he said.

"What do you think?" said Mike. "You, of course. What else?" She didn't give a shit about sounding like a bitch now. *Fuck them both*, she thought.

Elizabeth felt sorry for her, though she knew the last thing Mike wanted was her pity.

Richard didn't feel sorry for Mike. He had expected *her*, not Elizabeth, to rise to the occasion tonight. He associated Mike's failure with his own, and his revelation from earlier returned to him. He fumbled for something to say.

"You know whass funnybout this song?"

"What?" asked Elizabeth.

Mike stared daggers at them both.

"Th'lyrics make you think she's like desperate, ya know? I wanna dance wi' somebody—like she juss wants t'dance with somebody, anybody." He paused in the effort not to slur. "Like anybody who's willing. But then you get the full verse, and she says she wants t'dance wi' somebody who loves her."

"Deep," Mike deadpanned.

Richard stared at his best friend. He should've known she wouldn't get it. This was typical, in fact, of the reaction he got from Mike whenever he tried to say anything that wasn't either clever or flippant. She was so scared of falling into the cliché of having a "deep" conversation that she was often afraid of saying anything at all. Somehow his shorthand with her, which was supposed to be a code for something deeper, had begun to supersede rather than abbreviate whatever used to lie beneath it. He realized he would never be able to have the sort of open, earnest exchange with Mike that he achieved every week with Elizabeth.

This was why he hated bringing his friends together. He acted one way around Mike and another way around Elizabeth, and there was no way to be both people at once. He couldn't help alienating one of them. The awkwardness of the situation helped sober him up a little, and he was able to speak more clearly while answering:

"No, really. The lyrics're good! 'I want to take a chance on a man whose love will burn hot enough to last.' Good stuff."

"I can't believe you know the lyrics that well," said Mike. She turned to Elizabeth: "Richard has terrible taste in music. I don't know if you've learned that yet in all your 'sessions.'" She lifted her drink in one hand and used air quotes in the other.

There was a lull as the song ended, hence no need for Elizabeth to raise her voice when she said, "In grade school I convinced a group of girls to lip-synch to that song, and we each had a big cardboard cutout of a heart with flames around it that we waved back and forth whenever that line came around. It's my favorite part too." She smiled above her straw.

Cunt, thought Mike, even as somewhere, some part of her was urging her to *calm the fuck down* and stop playing the harpy. *You're better than this.*

"I'm gonna go pee," she announced, pivoting on her heel and heading for the bathroom.

Richard turned to Elizabeth.

"I'm sorry," he said. "She's coming on strong, but once you get to know her she's really amazing. I promise."

"I don't doubt that," said Elizabeth. "She obviously cares a lot about you." It was as close as she would ever come to telling him what she knew with certainty now, that Mike was in love with Richard.

She took a longer-than-necessary sip of her ice water.

Richard looked all around him, his discomfort over Mike and Elizabeth, Elizabeth and Keith, him and Elizabeth, any and all of this intimate interpersonal crap melting away as the alcohol kicked into overdrive and the euphoria of the successful party took over again. Who cared about individual grievances? What were they compared to the spirit of camaraderie he gave himself over to now among all these lovely, wonderful people? *His* people? He was beaming so wide, it felt as if his face might crack in two.

Elizabeth eyed him over her glass, a fainter version of his expression playing about her face.

"Collective effervescence," she said.

"Huh?"

"The energy you get from a group of people. That magic you feel around them. Like a sum greater than its parts."

He stared at her.

"I can't take credit for it," she said hastily. "It was Émile Durkheim who came up with it."

"You'resso smart!" he exclaimed, without a trace of sarcasm. The alcohol was raging through him now; he no longer had the mental wherewithal to despair over her superiority. He was too drunk, too astonished by her intelligence and perspicacity. How did she do it? He just stood there, gazing at her with naked admiration.

A rare blush spread over Elizabeth's features, which she hid behind her glass.

Just then Leona Lewis's "Bleeding Love" came up. It was an unusual selection, as Popstarz favored poppier, boppier songs, but sometimes the DJ liked to throw in a slow ballad early in the night and work his way up from there. They both froze a moment, inhaling, and then turned to each other, surprised.

"D'you love thisong as much as I do?" If he'd been sober he never would have asked the question, at least not so artlessly. It was embarrassing to like "Bleeding Love," especially as a guy.

She nodded.

He took the glass away from her and replaced it with his hand, leading her onto the dance floor.

Something surged inside Elizabeth's chest, constricting her throat and blurring her vision—a feeling as painful as it was pleasurable. She dropped his hand and he turned, extending his arm for her to take again. She looked at him and waited a few seconds longer to identify the feeling. It was *happiness*, but not the muted kind she felt when she did a good job at work or had a new book she was excited to read. This was a giddy, untamed emotion she hadn't felt since childhood. Elizabeth knew instinctively that Richard was about to make a scene on the dance floor and that it was probably going to be a disaster, and that by dragging her out here he was implicating her in his drunken antics, his carelessness, his idiocy. But instead of dreading all this she actually *couldn't wait*, because even though she let loose to the radio inside her house more often than anyone would have guessed, and allowed herself on occasion to be drawn into the impromptu group dance parties that ended almost every (drunken) social gathering sponsored by her firm, it had been a long time since anyone had asked her—properly asked her—to dance.

She took his hand.

THERE WEREN'T MANY on the dance floor, and as the lights dimmed and Leona's voice swelled in the first tortured, tenuous notes of this wantonly sentimental song, everyone looked to them instinctively. They struck the traditional pose, his right hand on her left shoulder, his left supporting her right. The beat kicked in, and they turned together as the lyrics began, *Closed off from love, I didn't need the pain.* . . . Slowly at first, then faster as the music picked up speed. Elizabeth's skirt flared out, giving her a traditional dancer's silhouette.

In two months of sharing the intricacies of their personalities, they had never talked about music. Richard wished he was like Mike, or even his hipster neighbors, who knew as if by intuition about every cool indie band to grace the sweaty bars dotted across Silver Lake and Echo Park—the mustached men and tattooed women who climbed onto dark stages and wailed away for two hours at a time. But he didn't care. Elizabeth was no stranger to iTunes, yet her tastes hadn't changed much since she was nine years old and dancing onstage with a cardboard heart. The secret behind her love of roller skating was that it provided an excuse to blast this kind of music in her ears on a regular basis, and, for his part, Richard couldn't go too long without singing along to one of his cheesy mix CDs inside his car. They both loved pop music for the same reason so many do: because it made them feel good. And while this focus on the *effect* of the music rather than the music itself rendered their taste somewhat indiscriminate, it was a preference by no means careless. They both deeply loved the way certain pop songs could within seconds make everything okay—a picture frame tilted askew but righted easily enough—as if all the change the world required were to be found inside a key shift. After two months of chipping away at each other's personalities, of collecting meager specks and slivers, they had hit upon something solid, something they shared, and while it was a small find—commonplace even, in no way a point of pride for either of them—it felt significant because in the very moment of discovery they were able to pool it between them and watch it grow, a sum greater than its parts.

At the top of the second verse he led her in a box step around the perimeter of the floor: *But something happened for the very first time with you.* A few people hooted, catcalling from the sidelines. When they got to the chorus he let go of her, and they each did a revolution around their half of the dance floor before reuniting in the center. They switched to freestyle. Richard allowed the slow beat to undulate across his body, left to right, top to bottom, each sequence ending with a gentle version of the pelvic thrust Mike hated so much. He knew from years of practice that most guys messed up by trying too hard. All you needed was a little rhythmic motion from the body's core; the rest was attitude. Elizabeth swayed, shimmied, and spun; she'd never thought about how she looked while dancing, and it showed in the native elegance of her movements.

The heart of the chorus kicked in, *You cut me open and I keep bleeding, keep keep bleeding love. . . .* Mike watched from the sidelines, her arms crossed tightly over her chest. From beside her, Keith snaked an arm around her waist, inviting her wordlessly to lean against him. For a few prideful seconds she resisted, and then she rested her head on his shoulder, swearing never again to make fun of Richard's business partner and second-best friend, as together they watched the couple reunite in the center of the dance floor.

At the second verse's bridge, *You cut me open and it's draining off of me,* Richard spun her. Growing up, his mother had dragged him to the Boston opera regularly, and the only exception to the abject pain of these experiences was the laughter that sprang from the singers whenever it was called for in the course of a story. These baritone belly laughs and soprano titters ringing out across the stage always sounded so ridiculous to him—as obscene as farts—so it was a shock to hear one escape from him now. It turned out those stage laughs weren't so false after all, when the source of the laughter was joy instead of amusement: so routine in opera, so rare in real life.

There was a long, standout note less than a minute from the end of the song. It happened on the word *I*, and Richard was waiting for it. On the words *Ooh, you cut me open and*— he stepped back from Elizabeth and rushed toward her, catching her up in a massive spin, rotating on a tighter and tighter axis as their bodies drew together, ever closer, spinning faster, then faster still: impossibly fast. He could feel her heart beating against his chest as they whirled in a cocoon of their making, shielded from the rest of the world by their motion. The crowd roared. They were going so fast!

Maybe a little *too* fast?

They began listing dangerously to one side, like a spin-top before it falls over. Richard overcompensated by wrenching their bodies in the opposite direction, which succeeded in keeping them on their feet, but at the expense of the glorious spin, which was brought to an ignominious end. Elizabeth opened her eyes. The song had at least half a minute to go, but Richard was obviously finished. He was crouching over, hands on his knees, panting from the exertion. He looked up into her face.

She had no idea what would happen next, so she simply waited, breathless.

His eyes clouded over. He jerked his head back down toward the floor, but it was too late. He spewed six gin-and-tonics and three-quarters of a pesto-chicken wrap onto the bottom half of her skirt, her ankles, her shoes.

"Aw, sick! Fucking gross! Get him out of here!" came the general cry, as he toppled to the ground. Heedless of the state (not to mention the smell) of her clothes and the puddle of vomit quickly forming around her, Elizabeth bent over him, alarmed to see that he'd actually passed out, though before she could do anything about it his eyelids began to flutter, and by the time the muscled bouncer reached them, Richard was looking up at her in a dazed, supplicating manner that was nonetheless conscious. The bouncer forcibly lifted him to his feet, ignoring Elizabeth's protestations, and hustled him away, screeching "Eighty-six!" into a walkie-talkie. He pushed Richard through the front room, down the flight of stairs, and out the door in less time than the spin that had caused all the trouble. Elizabeth and Keith followed behind him, with Mike bringing up a distant rear.

"I'M TAKING HIM to the hospital," announced Elizabeth, beelining for a cab that by some miracle was standing empty on the curb. She folded Richard into the backseat and opened the front passenger door.

"I'm coming with you," said Keith.

Elizabeth turned, shaking her head. "All these people came here to see you," she said. "I'll take care of him. Cedars-Sinai's just around the corner."

"You guys, this is total overkill." Mike strode toward them. "Believe me, this isn't the first time he's puked from drinking too much."

"I saw him pass out," said Elizabeth.

"What, for like a second? Yeah, that wouldn't be the first time that's happened either," said Mike. "He just needs to go to bed. Give the driver his address. I'm telling you, he'll be asleep and dreaming in half an hour."

"Give me your number and I'll update you," Elizabeth told Keith, ignoring Mike even as she turned to her. "You too."

"Don't bother. Have fun," Mike said, retreating to the club. She stopped, tossing Elizabeth a scorching glare over one bony shoulder:

"I told you he was a messy drunk."

ONE IV DRIP and a few routine tests later, Richard managed to sign himself out of the hospital. The attending doctor had recommended he stay overnight, since technically he'd sustained a head injury (a tiny bump on the back of his head where he'd fallen), but there was no way that was going to happen. Since his monthly payments started coming in, Richard had been meaning to purchase a better health insurance plan than the cheap one he'd signed up for on the open exchange, but he still hadn't gotten around to it, and he was eager to keep his hospital bills from the evening's festivities to a minimum. He had no memory of the ride to the hospital, but was relieved to discover he'd come in a cab and not an ambulance.

He didn't know who he would find when he reached the lobby, and was surprised to see Elizabeth there alone, embarrassed more than hurt that Mike wasn't there with her. He'd talked up their epic friendship, but neither he nor Mike had quite followed through on it this evening. And then, of course, there was the more obvious source of his humiliation. He glanced at Elizabeth's skirt, which was conspicuously wet, the black fabric glistening in the fluorescent light of the lobby.

"Was that . . . me?" he said, gesturing.

Elizabeth nodded. She'd more or less washed away the vomit in the bathroom, which had been nothing compared to Orpheus's mess on the couch. Without warning she flashed back now to the wonder she'd experienced that night, two months earlier: about life getting messy, and the messiness actually being somewhat pleasurable.

"I'm so, so sorry," he said. "I'll obviously pay for the skirt—"

"Don't worry about it," she said, in as soothing a tone as she could muster. A mess was still a mess, and it was almost 2 a.m.; she still had to drive all the way back to Venice. She wasn't used to staying up so late. "It's fine. It was pretty much all gin any-way."

"Ugh! Don't even say that word to me!"

Keith picked them up outside. He insisted on dropping Eliz-abeth off at her car and driving Richard home. She was parked on San Vicente, between Melrose and Santa Monica, and when she got out of Keith's car Richard followed her.

The Pacific Design Center loomed above them: a glittering glass behemoth that looked as if it were plucked from another city's skyline and plopped into the relatively flat landscape of West Hollywood. It had a neon trim that changed color every few seconds.

"Sorry about your skirt," he said. Again. Like a doofus. But it was all he could think to say.

"Don't worry about it!" she scolded him gently, unlocking her car remotely. The beep echoed north past the Strip, into the leafy green hills south of Sunset. She stared at him. Did he have anything else to say? She was tired. She wanted to go home.

Richard stood there like an idiot, trying to figure out what to say to her. His industry friends were already buzzing about his disgrace. When he'd checked his phone in the hospital park-ing lot he'd had twenty-five e-mails, some genuinely solicitous, others gloating. He'd almost changed his Facebook status to "D'oh!" but decided this might encourage people to post com-ments on his wall, thereby alerting even more people to his shame than necessary. He didn't need his parents or high school friends knowing what had happened. He already had enough damage control to do in the days to come.

In the end, he settled for hugging her. It was about as awk-ward as their first hug a few hours earlier, but he felt he had to make some sort of overture.

"Thank you," he said. "For coming with me to the hospital, and waiting. You didn't have to do that."

"No problem," she said evenly. The neon trim turned from red to blue, and his eyes took on a deeper hue as they reflected the color. *Beautiful eyes*, she thought.

There was a pause. The trim turned green. She got into her car.

Richard watched her spotless Honda Accord grow smaller, until finally it disappeared from view.

THE SLEEPOVER

THEY WERE SUPPOSED to meet at Elizabeth's house the next day. She half expected him not to show; they'd never done two days in a row before, and when she woke up (much later than usual), it felt like the day after a raucous office party—the aftermath to an evening of workplace transgressions. If there were a lesson to be taken from her ongoing "tutorial" in dating, it was that meeting your date's friends en masse was to be avoided, especially in a setting as volatile as an alcohol-fueled party. She would have been better off meeting each of Richard's friends—Mike in particular—in a more intimate setting, at dinner, or a night at the movies. All day long—at coffee with Orpheus (she chattered nervously for much of it about Richard's impending visit that evening), in the ocean on her surfboard (the waves were puny, so she spent most of her time watching the pelicans skim the water with their long, scissor-like beaks), and in her armchair, staring at (instead of reading)

Gaskell's *Wives and Daughters*—she felt an anxiety akin but not quite identical to dread. *She* had nothing to be embarrassed about, after all, and while she was by no means eager to see Richard so soon after their night together, she *was* curious to see how he would handle the unexpected turn events had taken less than twenty-four hours earlier. (She counted to five on one hand a total of five times that day—squaring the number like this pleased her.)

At 5 p.m. exactly she heard a knock on the door, and there he stood with a gift-wrapped package in one hand and a bottle in the other. He offered up the bottle first:

"Nonalcoholic." He grinned sheepishly.

Elizabeth walked inside to place the bottle on the kitchen counter, and he followed her, thrusting the box forward with both hands, as if it were a bowl and he, Oliver Twist asking for more:

"Here. To help make up for last night."

What could it possibly be? Elizabeth tore off the wrapping. It was from Saks Fifth Avenue. She lifted the lid, tossed it aside, and pawed through multiple tiers of tissue paper.

It was a skirt.

She lifted it out of the box. It was black, like the one she'd worn the night before, but the material was denser, with an intrinsic shine, like the glow of an animal's pelt. It was obviously very expensive—much more expensive than the one sitting in a crumpled ball in her "to be dry-cleaned" hamper.

"You really didn't—"

"Yeah, I did. I still feel so bad about last night."

Why was he harping on the stupid skirt? It felt to her as if he didn't want to owe her anything, as though he wouldn't be comfortable till he'd repaid her. She saw the size on the inside of the waistline: 12.

"I'm actually a ten," she said. "And sometimes I'm even an eight—"

"Mike said this designer runs small. I called her while I was in the store. She's good with stuff like that."

It had been a truncated call, during which Mike had coined the phrase "the Retch Heard 'Round the World" and Richard had pretended to find this amusing, while failing to tell her how hurt he had been by her coldness toward Elizabeth, and her failure to come to the hospital.

He watched Elizabeth fold up the skirt and return it to the box. When she placed the cardboard lid on top of it, it felt as though she were sealing off a tomb. Was she mad because of the size?

"Marilyn Monroe was a sixteen, you know."

"That's actually a myth." She was thrilled to be able to contradict him. "She was more like a ten, and that was in British sizes, which's more like a six or even a four here. She had an unusual figure anyway, a bigger bust and hips but a really tiny waist."

She didn't need him to console her about her dress size.

"I did not know that," he said—slowly, carefully, as if she were a maniac recently escaped from the local asylum whom he'd happened upon during a solitary walk in the woods. It had only been a week since her outburst at Factor's, and he didn't think he could handle another verbal lashing, at least not tonight. He'd been doing damage control all day, abasing himself before an assemblage of smirks (mostly electronic), and he was trying hard not to hate everyone—not to resent them for their very existence, for being there to witness his folly. He moved instinctively toward a savory smell wafting from the kitchen, so strong he could practically see it in wavy lines. He hadn't eaten a proper meal all day, thanks to his hangover, and suddenly he was starving, ready to bury his troubles in food like a boy who's skinned his knee and requires nothing more than an edible treat to make it better.

Elizabeth was relieved he didn't question her source of information regarding Marilyn Monroe's figure, which was an article on the website Jezebel. She'd been researching *Some Like It Hot* online, since he'd said it was one of his favorites, and she figured they'd be watching it eventually. It hadn't taken long to fall down an Internet rabbit hole on Marilyn herself.

They each got a slice of pizza and sat on either end of the sofa. Elizabeth reached for the remote. They had to watch *Driving Miss Daisy* (which she had also researched, and was not much looking forward to—it sounded depressing) and discuss it for two hours. They might as well get on with it. This was what the next ten months would be like, she supposed. The dance had been a momentary deviation with no lasting effects, a wrong turn easily corrected. The straight and narrow stretched before them, all the way to the vanishing point in the far—but not quite as far as it once had been—distance, nothing mysterious or unknowable about it.

The Warner Bros. logo shimmered into view.

There was a knock at the door.

Elizabeth paused the movie, jumping up from the sofa.

"Who could that be?" she asked, though she knew perfectly well it could only be one person. She opened the door.

Nothing could have prepared her for what stood on the other side.

He was unrecognizable: his dreads lopped off and replaced by a smooth, silver crown of (somewhat receding) hair. His Robinson Crusoe beard was gone too, revealing a chin and jawline several shades lighter than the upper two-thirds of his face. His clothes were clean, but had obviously been bought secondhand, lending him a frayed, business-casual look. He was wearing a wrinkled, plaid button-down tucked into pleated khakis, the threadbare edges of which ended a few inches too soon; she could see his naked ankles sticking out of preppy "deck shoes," their tips worn to a shine.

It was certainly an improvement. For the first time in their acquaintance, he wasn't accompanied by a smell. But he had never looked more out of place or uncomfortable than he did now, fidgeting on her doorstep.

"Orpheus!" she exclaimed. He'd looked like his old self this morning. What had he been up to?

Orpheus craned his neck, peering inside. He had to see him. He had to meet the boy who'd started all the trouble.

Two months earlier, he made the first stumbling attempts at climbing up the well and reaching Lily. He needed the trappings of a sane, reasonable man again if he was ever going to wield enough influence to persuade her to reject the proposal, and for that he needed new clothes and a haircut. For that, he needed money. And for that, he needed to give up the bottle. This was the only crack or fissure he could find among the dark walls surrounding him—the only makeshift handhold he could use to hoist himself toward her.

A clear path, but easier traced than trod. If his life were a movie, the two months between the morning Lily told him about the proposal and this moment, now, on her doorstep would have been edited into an extended montage set to soulful music with jaunty interludes, as he slowly but surely progressed. The real thing was much slower, and never sure.

It was physical torture to stop drinking. After twelve hours without a drink, his brain, used to producing stimulants to counteract the depressant effect of the alcohol, was like a tiger that's strained against the confines of a steel cage all its life and suddenly finds itself free to roam the wild. But it was less like the cage door had been thrown open and more like the cage had disappeared before the startled animal's eyes—a liberation terrifying rather than exhilarating. Orpheus experienced the worst of withdrawal: his hands shook, he saw stars, he was sick to his stomach, and once he hallucinated an army of cockroaches swarming over his body when really there had only been one. All he had to do to end this pain was get a drink, and he did this time and time again. Why wouldn't he? He'd lived for years on a philosophy of instant gratification grounded on the notion that life was cruel and capricious. The only sort of return he could be guaranteed was an instant one.

Each time he drank, however, he woke from the aftermath determined to try harder. He continued to meet Lily each morning per their routine, but every morsel of food she gave him stuck in his throat now; every word of kindness and encouragement turned dismissive and patronizing the instant it met his ears. He did not tell her about his plan. This secret quest to reach her as her equal became his personal obsession, lending shape to his shapeless days. After two weeks of failed attempts he destroyed all his alcohol. (He always kept a stash in his carry-on, plus several more buried in the sand.) It was easy enough in the moment; he was still half-drunk when he smashed the bottles and threw the shards into the ocean. But twelve hours later, he cursed himself as he suffered through the withdrawal symptoms one last time.

"Good evening, Lily." He stuck his pinkie inside his collar to keep it from chafing against his neck. "I hope I'm not interrupting?"

Oh, Jesus. How was she going to explain the "Lily" thing to Richard? Or the "Elizabeth" thing to Orpheus? She was in no way prepared for the two of them to meet. But inside this squashed moment of panic, Elizabeth was surprised to find room for a speck of gratitude: there was no way to really prepare for such a meeting, so if it was going to happen she was glad not to have known about it beforehand. There was simply no time for the wringing of hands.

"Good evening, Orpheus," she said, mirroring his formal address. "You look good."

"Thank you."

She stepped back, gesturing for him to come inside. A figure bounded off the sofa. Orpheus's heart drummed in his breast. The moment was here; it was finally happening.

Three days after his last bout of withdrawal, he came out the other side as dry as the discarded chicken bones lying in a Styrofoam box next to his head. He sucked on them anyway; he didn't think he'd ever been so hungry. A little girl walked up to him, staring at his greasy dreads with an innocent fascination until her mother caught up to her and jerked her away—so forcefully, she dropped her half-eaten cup of ice cream. It sailed the three feet from her soft little hands to his grimy paws in slow motion: graceful, in an arc, like manna from heaven. Orpheus knocked aside the pink plastic spoon with his nose and lowered his mouth to the cup, taking bites as if it were a watermelon slice, his slurps drowning out the child's cries. From the corner of his eye he watched the mother cart the girl away and approach a uniformed cop. When she pointed at him, he tossed the cup, scurrying farther down the Boardwalk.

It was the day before the Fourth of July and the summertime revelers were out in full force. A fat man whizzed by on a skateboard, his round, hairy belly hanging over violet corduroy cutoffs. Yellow sunlight danced inside a tangled heap of blue-glass pendants being sorted by three older women with witchy hair and flowing skirts. A perfect, heart-shaped female ass clad in bright orange nylon strutted past him, and he followed it toward the green, foamy shore, then farther still into the smooth, indigo ocean where skin of all shades, whitest alabaster to blackest ebony, grew redder in the heat of a barbecue sun that made everything go wavy.

This place had been Orpheus's prison for countless years, the site of his misery and degradation. He hated it. But for a moment he saw how beautiful it was, like a postcard brought to life. He shut his eyes and shook his head from side to side because it was too much, and he wanted—he *needed*—for it to go away. When he opened his eyes again, he felt as if his bluff had been called because everything had indeed been replaced by a single object: a fist, its thumb pointed sideways in a gesture Orpheus knew all too well, *move along*. The cop had found him.

Richard stuck out his hand.

Orpheus gripped it, shaking as hard as he could. He almost whistled in appreciation. Now here was a good-looking man in the prime of his life.

"Richard, this is my friend Orpheus. He's a—a professor of English literature." Elizabeth flashed him an apology; she hoped he wouldn't mind the fib.

By nightfall that first day, on July Fourth, Orpheus celebrated his first twenty-four hours of sobriety with a bag of peanuts, which was the cheapest thing he could buy to fill his stomach. He'd spent all day begging sober, which was a new experience for him, and had discovered he was much better at it than when intoxicated. His trick was to assume a pathetic posture, legs in a pretzel, elbows jutting out on the pavement, head bowed into his crotch. People assumed he was crippled, and it was remarkable how much more loot he accumulated in this position. He'd never been able to hold the pose for more than an hour, but this time he lasted almost four.

He watched the red, white, and blue colors explode above him. He'd bought a pack of cigarettes too, a luxury he never allowed himself before, since every penny had to be devoted to alcohol. Having his own pack made him feel like a squire among knaves, and the pleasant sensation of satisfying his appetite and having a smoke afterward encouraged him to keep going in the face of the emotional torture that came with a clear head and functioning memory. His son Scott had loved fireworks. The Fourth of July had been his favorite holiday.

"A professor, cool!" said Richard. "Where?"

"UCLA." He and Elizabeth exchanged another glance; he was happy to keep up the fiction. He needed to fit in if his plan was going to work. But he also *wanted* to fit in, and it was this realization—that Orpheus Washington, the erstwhile contrarian, the onetime proud defier of expectations and blazer of his own trail, had been reduced to this adolescent yearning to belong—that laid him lower in this moment than all the years of vagrancy preceding it.

In the last two months he had become a pariah who no longer belonged among his fellow pariahs. Most of his homeless cohorts were drunks or junkies, and it was no fun being the only sober one. Orpheus lost the dazed docility integral to his previous popularity. His old self resurfaced—quick-witted, ambitious—and he grew dissatisfied with his lot. For the first time he noticed how the homeless population swelled in the summer months, like bugs swarming. He saw people sniff the air when they passed him, or go out of their way not to pass him at all. The pokes and prods, the offhand interrogations from police officers began to anger instead of frighten him. Begging became intolerable, so he scored the lowest of low-rent jobs standing in the middle of the Boardwalk with a sign that read "Frozen Lemonade 99¢" on one side and "Giant Slice Pizza $1.99 (cheese)" on the other. (His "interview" had consisted of a patdown and a Breathalyzer.) With a mixture of amusement and anger, his homeless brethren decided he was putting on airs and taunted him from the sidelines: "Big man! Got a *sign*! Got a *job*!" Sometimes they ran up behind him and knocked the board out of his hands. In this regard, his new job was more humiliating than begging for change, but he was allowed to eat as much leftover pizza as he could stomach, and together with

Lily's breakfasts and Saturday dinners, this meant he didn't have to spend any money on food. The few bucks he earned each day accumulated slowly. Every time he checked it, the bulge in the zippered compartment at the bottom of his wheeled suitcase had grown a tiny bit bigger.

"I was just in the neighborhood. . . ." He faltered, staring at them helplessly.

It sounded like the sort of outdated phrase a foreigner would use, something acquired in a language course—an elegant yet empty address that hung there, helpless and lost. What did he think he was going to do anyway? Why was he so intent on banishing this beautiful boy beaming in front of him? That would be like dumping a precious painting among the trash heaps he used sometimes as bedding, or lobbing a priceless sculpture into the fathomless ocean.

"I'm glad you stopped by," said Elizabeth a little too brightly, as if she were projecting for the benefit of the cheap seats. "We were just eating pizza and watching a movie. Do you want to join us?" She glanced at Richard. Allowing a third person in on one of their sessions was technically forbidden.

"Yeah, join us!" he said. "It's so rare I get to meet one of Elizabeth's friends." He paused. "And by 'rare,' I mean never."

Elizabeth? Orpheus looked at her, but she refused to meet his eye. "Elizabeth" was obviously her real name. So why had he been calling her Lily all this time?

"*Elizabeth* likes to keep herself to herself, doesn't she?" replied Orpheus, switching allegiances to the boy with an ease he didn't know he was capable of till after it happened.

Richard grinned. "You can say that again."

Orpheus clapped him on the back. "I just might. Huh."

THE LAST THING he wanted was more pizza, but Orpheus stuffed himself dutifully while they sat in a snug little row on the sofa watching *Driving Miss Daisy*. He had to will himself not to fall asleep; it seemed outrageous to be expected to sit for two hours on a soft surface indoors without talking, and to stay awake. The movie didn't help either. The old Orpheus Washington would never have made it all the way through such sentimental garbage, and when they got to the final scene, Morgan Freeman feeding little bites of pie to a senile Jessica Tandy, Orpheus leaned toward Richard to make a crack, an observation—*something* to cut through this offensively tender scene—when he saw an unmistakable dampness, a flurry of blinking. Was the boy . . . was he *crying*?

"Gets me every time," said Richard matter-of-factly, or perhaps even a little defiantly, wiping away his tears with the heel of one hand.

"Huh," responded Orpheus, surprised that anyone could be moved by a story so obviously constructed to do just that. He supposed there was still a bit of the contrarian in him yet. Now that he knew what *real* heartbreak was, it felt not only cheap but disrespectful to fabricate such emotions, only to resolve them a mere hour or so later. He looked at Lily, whose eyes were as dry as his, and as she stood up from the couch another flash of understanding registered between them. How could he not have seen it before? She too knew real tragedy; she had a calamity all her own. It was so obvious. But why had she never told him about it? He looked at the boy again, who was sipping a fizzy drink contentedly, and a shiver of something akin to jealousy ran through him, bursting like a geyser on the crown of his newly shorn head. Did *he* know, this boy who just as obviously didn't have a care in the world? Had she told *him*?

"Did you guys eat *all* the pizza?" cried Elizabeth.

Both Richard and Orpheus whipped their heads toward her. She was standing at the counter, staring in horror at the empty pizza box.

"I only had one slice!"

The two men looked at each other like children caught with their hands in the cookie jar, and laughed.

Elizabeth forced them to carry the conversation to the kitchen, where she announced her intention of making spaghetti for herself. "And you guys can't have any!" Richard and Orpheus leaned on the counter while she retrieved a pot and colander from her well-ordered cabinets. In the harsh fluorescent light, Richard couldn't help noticing the finer points of Orpheus's ruined face, and Orpheus couldn't help noticing Richard's fascination; it reminded him of the little girl on the Boardwalk with the ice cream, and he raised a hand to shield himself from view.

It was only earlier that afternoon, after Lily had told him Richard would be coming to Venice that evening, that he took a bath in the ocean with a bar of soap purchased in a liquor store on the corner of Venice and Pacific. Afterward he headed to a hippified secondhand clothing store next to Café Collage. The woman behind the counter was a former flower child—faded, but still sharp enough to ask to see his money before letting him touch any of her merchandise. *So much for free love*, he thought, struggling to contain his ire. He desperately needed the clothes.

Fifteen minutes later he was wearing his new outfit out of the store, just as his daughter, Sherry, used to do, so excited was she to acquire new clothes. Down the street was a hair salon called Rock Paper Scissors. He hoped that in his new outfit he'd pass for a dirty hippie and not quite a homeless man. The receptionist was sorting receipts, and didn't look up as she greeted him:

"Hullo, you have appointment?"

She sounded Russian. He shook his head, *no*.

She glanced up at him and her eyes froze, and then her smile after it, as if a frost were racing down her face. Orpheus's heart sank; she was going to ask him to leave. Another memory bubbled to the surface, this one from long, long ago: his mother dragging him at seven years old on some errand that took them out of their way, and stopping off at an unfamiliar grocery store, not their usual place. He remembered there was no one there except an old white woman with puffy blue hair and a cigarette hanging from the corner of her mouth. She looked up at them from her cash register where she was sorting receipts, and immediately looked down again. "Out." This was all she said: the single syllable, pointed toward the floor. It didn't even seem as if she was addressing them. His mother faltered—confused, disoriented—and the woman repeated herself, "out," her voice raised slightly, though she still refused to look at them. He remembered his mother pulling him away, and sensing more from her mood than a true understanding of the situation that he wasn't to ask her any questions.

Looking at the Russian girl now, he waited to hear that same syllable again, but instead she gestured to the swivel chair farthest from the window:

"I take care of you, yes? Am in training. Reduced rate. Here, please."

When she wrapped the black plastic cape around him, her hand brushed against the tiny dreads stuck to his neck and she jumped back, as if they'd pricked or burned her skin. Their eyes met in the mirror—hers startled, his accusing.

"What do you like?" she asked, tying her long brown hair into a ponytail.

"A buzz cut." He imitated a razor scraping across his scalp. "Short as you can get it. And a shave too."

She nodded, relieved.

Fifteen minutes later she announced: "All done!" and swiveled the chair to face the mirror.

He was balder than he realized under all those dreads: his hairline had retreated at least an inch or two. He'd been steeling himself for the resurrection of the old Orpheus—the husband, father, and professor—and for the fresh batch of painful memories this image would bring to the fore. But the old, shrunken man who stared back at him was like one of those age-progressed photos of a lost child printed on milk cartons, not so much a reminder of who he was as evidence of what he had become. He saw now that the Orpheus of years ago was gone, as dead as his wife and children but still separated from them. Forever.

"You look good," the woman beamed.

He sprang out of the chair and handed her all the cash he had, which amounted to a 50 percent tip. She called out to him—gratified, amazed—but he was already out the door, head down, eyes averted, and he assumed this posture now in the tiny kitchen, staring at the fake tiles on the linoleum floor. He must have looked so old, so hideous to this beautiful boy.

"Gotta wear sunscreen," he mumbled, massaging a large red lump—the worst offender, though it had plenty of competition—beneath his left eye.

"For real," said Richard, "Especially for a pasty white guy like me, ha. But I'm *so* bad about it. I know I should wear it every day but I hate that greasy feeling, you know? And even when I go to the beach I never put on as much as I should. I got the *worst* burn of my life, a while back, in Greece? My stomach was seriously *purple*. It was insane."

Elizabeth asked him which islands he'd visited, which led to an improbable discussion of Greek mythology, and before any of them realized it three hours had passed. It was nearly ten when Orpheus succumbed finally, falling asleep with his head propped up on the back of the couch. Richard raised his eyebrows and made a "sh!" gesture with his index finger over his lips.

"I'm going to let him sleep here," Elizabeth whispered. "He lives alone, just around the corner, and he looks so peaceful, doesn't he?"

Richard nodded, watching enviously as the old man's concave chest rose and fell. He was dreading the ride home, which would bring him that much closer to another day of confronting the Retch Heard 'Round the World. It was easy to pretend it had never happened while he was here, even though this made no sense, since Elizabeth was the only person besides him who had been physically affected by the incident.

The pause between them lengthened. Richard kept staring at Orpheus to avoid the inevitable goodbye. It was childish, but he had an idea that if he stared long enough, eventually she'd ask him to spend the night.

"Do—do you want to spend the night too?"

He swung his head toward her, nodding vigorously.

"Let me go get my AeroBed," she said. "I'll blow it up in my room so I don't wake him up. Be right back."

She reappeared a few minutes later, lugging the mattress behind her. Richard jogged over to help her push it into the middle of the floor.

"Thanks," she said. "There're towels and an extra toothbrush in the bathroom." She placed sheets, a blanket, and a pillow on top of the AeroBed, and draped a blanket over Orpheus, who by this point had managed to assume a somewhat horizontal position. She retreated to her bedroom.

"Elizabeth?"

She turned around, framed by the open doorway.

Richard hesitated.

She waited.

If she had been anyone else, he would have begun singing "Thank You for Being a Friend" from *The Golden Girls*, to simultaneously acknowledge and mock the sentiment he was feeling. But there was a good chance Elizabeth had never watched *The Golden Girls*, and he was well aware by this point that mockery was not her style. And yet he still wanted to convey the emotion somehow, because she *had* been a good friend to him last night. And tonight. She was, in fact, a friend. When had that happened? It didn't really matter.

"Thank you," he said finally.

Elizabeth paused. "You're welcome," she said, turning away, and closing the door firmly behind her.

SECONDS LATER ELIZABETH locked the doorknob, unwilling to take any chances while trying on the skirt she'd vowed hours earlier never to touch again. It fit perfectly, of course, and was even more beautiful on her hips than it had been in her hands. She shifted her weight from one foot to the other, watching it sway gently, back and forth: *swish-swish, swish-swish, swish-swish* . . . By the time she roused herself from this skirt-induced reverie, she was unwilling to risk waking or otherwise encountering Richard on the way to the bathroom. She was too tired to brush her teeth anyway. She was exhausted, actually—more tired than she'd been in ages, deliciously spent after the prolonged adrenaline rush of an evening spent with her boys. *Her boys?* Now there was a ridiculous phrase. But she was too tired even to laugh, so instead she simply climbed into bed, skirt and all, and slipped beneath the covers, repeating the ridiculous phrase to herself over and over, sleepily, like a mantra:

My boys . . . my boys . . . my boys . . .

THE BINGE

EARLY ON THE MONDAY MORNING following this Saturday night, Orpheus began pacing the basketball courts. Upon waking twenty-four hours earlier, it had been obvious that whatever gossamer spirit of camaraderie had settled over Li—no, *Elizabeth's*—house during the night had been dissolved by the arrival of the sun. The boy had gone home almost immediately, and when Orpheus had said (after buttered toast and coffee) that he guessed he should get going too, Elizabeth hadn't stopped him. He'd felt hungover the entire day, as though he were coming down from an epic binge of conversation instead of liquor, and all he wanted was more of it, the old hair-of-the-dog trick to make himself feel better. He whipped his head from side to side. Where *was* she?

Orpheus thought back to the one day she'd stood him up, the day after he broke into her house and ruined her couch. He hadn't been invited to sleep over again after that night—not until yesterday. But had barging in on her movie night been an infraction of equal, or even greater, value? Maybe she hadn't wanted to say anything in front of the boy. Maybe this time she'd sworn him off for good. Maybe all his efforts to keep her close had backfired. Maybe the sleepover had been his final treat, a monster's ball for a man condemned to ostracism and oblivion. Maybe he'd never feel like a real human being again.

Suddenly she appeared, two cups trailing steam behind her like a locomotive train, the familiar wax-paper parcel tucked underneath one arm. Orpheus let out a breath, and then he did something he hadn't done in years: he laughed at himself. *A monster's ball? Ostracism and oblivion?* He needed to take it down a notch.

"You look tired," she said, handing him his buttered bagel.

He puffed out his cheeks, expelling his breath through puckered lips. He *was* tired. He'd spent the last twenty-four hours roaming, reliving his magical Saturday night like some lovesick girl in the delirious afterglow of her very first date. He'd passed out on the sand in the small hours of the morning. He was lucky no one had picked his pockets, or worse. His new clothes were already beginning to smell.

They sat shoulder-to-shoulder on the bleachers overlooking the racquetball courts. He couldn't wait to tell her how much he liked the boy he'd been set against for so long, albeit in the privacy of his addled mind. But she was staring moodily at the ocean, and he knew instinctively she didn't want to talk just yet.

He blew through the sipping slit of his coffee lid with his top lip protruding, as if he were playing a wind instrument. He took a sip: still too hot. He stuck his pinkie inside his ear, coming away with a mixture of sand and wax he flicked into the air. He ran his free hand over his new, bristly buzz cut, releasing a few dozen more grains of sand. He heard the words spill out of his mouth: "I cheated on her," as if they came of their own volition, but of course this was bullshit. He had meant to say them. He couldn't keep them in any longer.

Elizabeth turned. "What?" She was confused. "What did you say?"

"I cheated on her," he said again.

"What do you mean?"

"She was another professor. In the English department. I was gonna leave Rhonda for her."

He remembered reassuring himself that a generous alimony and partial custody would preserve him from the cliché of becoming a deadbeat dad. After the accident, this other woman had refused to talk to him despite several attempts on his part. Orpheus supposed his tragedy had been as toxic to her as it had been to everyone else, him included. He heard himself tell Elizabeth now that rising above it had never been an option, as long as he believed he didn't deserve to be redeemed. But secretly, he knew this facile sort of pop psychology was beside the point. He was not a jigsaw puzzle to be solved, piece by jagged piece. He was more interested in what Elizabeth had to say to him. He could sense she wanted to tell him about the tragedy from her past, the calamity that, once shared, would connect them even closer than before— and he rushed through his confession to let her speak.

But when he finished, she hesitated.

He held his breath—waiting, willing her to join him.

Elizabeth looked away from the ocean, toward the sun rising in the East, until it burned a tiny disk in her field of vision. It was true; she'd been on the verge of telling him why she hardly ever saw her parents, why she wasn't even sure her brother was alive: the dreaded "rough patch." *What a stupid phrase.* She knew it would comfort him to see what she saw months ago— that they were the same, both haunted by events from the past they could never change. But even though it would help him to know, it wouldn't help her to tell. It was simply too much to go through the hell of bringing it to the surface again, even for Orpheus.

The sunspot was gone.

"That must've been really hard for you," she said, turning back to the ocean.

Her rejection felt like a kick in the groin, a jab between the eyes. Orpheus tried to shake it off. She wasn't ready; he should have known this. She hadn't even told him her damn *name* till two days earlier.

"Guess I'll have to get used to calling you Elizabeth now."

She shrugged. "It doesn't really matter. You can still call me Lily if you want."

She could tell he wanted a *moment* with her, some intimate, tender scene. And it pleased her in a juvenile way to withhold this satisfaction from him. She made a great show of stifling a yawn while checking her watch.

"He's a great guy," Orpheus blurted out of nowhere. "Great looking too, huh."

"Yeah, he's a real catch," she said acidly.

"When're you gonna see him again?"

"On Saturday obviously."

She stood up to go, but his expression arrested her. Other than the first time they met, Elizabeth had managed to avoid seeing Orpheus beg, and she wondered now if this was how he looked while carrying out the act. If it wasn't, it should have been, because the abject misery etched on his features forced her to sit down again, to repent for her petulance by fumbling for something else to say:

"Actually, I need to tell him what book we're reading next. Today. So we can do a few chapters by Saturday. I was all set on *Howards End* but now I'm thinking *Tess of the d'Urbervilles*. What do you think?"

They spent the rest of their time comparing the merits of one book to the other. It was a frenetic banter, plugging up a silence they both knew could have been more poignantly yet painfully spent. Every time Elizabeth tried to leave, Orpheus thought up a reason to detain her. He even followed her to her car, loitering beside her window in the middle of Pacific Boulevard until finally she had to say:

"I have to go, Orpheus. I'm going to be late for work."

Her elbow was hanging out the window. He nudged it with his fist. It was the first time he had ever voluntarily made physical contact with her.

"Go with *Tess*," he urged her.

Elizabeth nodded, *okay*, and gave him a little wave. She drove off, leaving him in the middle of the street.

Orpheus still couldn't lose her. But he realized now the only way to make sure he didn't was to have *her* come to *him*. On this morning, he vowed to help her however he could. Respecting her privacy would be a good start: about her past, and everything else. He would have to learn to content himself with paying close attention to whatever information she volunteered, and sifting through these pieces on his own. Somehow, he promised himself, he would be of use to her, and he was convinced it would have something to do with the proposal. He still didn't trust this anonymous benefactor, this lawyer, these outrageous sums of money. He would get to the bottom of it, because for the first time in forever he was no longer at the bottom of his own life, and while he'd done it all by himself, he had *her* to thank for his exaltation, his newfound strength. Somehow he would prove his worth to her as a friend for life—one she would never want to leave.

But he would not pry.

MIKE, ON THE OTHER HAND, had decided that prying was exactly what she needed to do. Her abandonment of Richard the night of Keith's birthday party did not sit any better with her in the days to follow than it had minutes afterward, when she'd sashayed back inside the Factory and pretended not to feel the giant pit of regret settling firmly in her stomach. Over time the pit only grew larger, demanding further attention. It laid down roots; shoots sprouted from the top of it, filling up her stomach cavity and ruining her appetite. The shoots lengthened, vinelike, wrapping themselves around her vital organs, and she knew she had to rip it out before it did even greater damage.

In the real world, she and Richard spoke the next morning while he was buying the DP a new skirt (she purposely steered him toward a designer with larger sizes), and a few days later they patched it up more thoroughly over drinks at Chaya Brasserie:

"Sorry I hurled like that," he said. "Hope I didn't embarrass you."

"Eh, not really. You pretty much just made an ass of yourself."

"Ha!" It was one of his single, staccato bursts of laughter, just as easily an exclamation of pain as of pleasure. "True. Anyway, just wanted to say sorry."

Mike toyed with her straw. She still hadn't told him about the DP asking about her father. She decided she was over it. Everyone knew Richard couldn't keep his mouth shut. He hadn't meant to hurt her.

"I'm sorry too," she said, and she meant it.

"For what?" It came out garbled through his drink.

"For being a bitch."

He spat his ice back into his glass. "But you're *always* a bitch."

"Shut up you know what I mean. I came on pretty strong with the DP, and I feel bad about not going to the hospital with you guys. I was thinking about you the whole night. I called Keith afterward to make sure you were okay."

"I know," he said. And then, after a pause: "It's not your fault."

What does that mean? Mike thought. *It's not my fault he got drunk? Well, duh. Or it's not my fault I was a bitch because he knows she asked about my dad? Or it's not my fault everything went to shit because he knows she's ruining everything and he can't wait till she's gone too?* She wanted to grab him by the shoulders and scream, "Explain yourself!" But instead she just motioned for the check. It seemed impossible to her that they had arrived at a place in their relationship wherein she was afraid to speak her mind for fear of rocking the boat more than she already had. Was this really *them*? Wasn't their relationship, in all its messy, fuzzy glory, stronger than this? Better than this? The pit remained. Mike frowned. She tried again:

"So how were things the day after with the DP?"

"Oh, fine. We just hung out at her place. And apparently we're reading *Tess of the d'Urbervilles* now instead of *Howards End.* You ever read that?"

She knew he wasn't telling her everything, but it was impossible not to allow the conversation to veer into a discussion of the book instead of the girl. Over the next few weeks, this dodge became an ongoing pattern. Every time Mike tried to bring up the DP, Richard found a way to shift the conversation. It would have taken an outright statement on her part to steer it back, and she refused to do so. In fact, as soon as she realized what he was doing, she went out of her way *not* to mention her rival. The DP became the elephant in the room, and without saying a word, they both worked to shrink her to the size of a pea. But they couldn't make her disappear. She lingered on the edge of every conversation, and if she had to be there at all, Mike concluded, it would have been better if she were in plain sight rather than some dark corner where she was always felt, but never observed, a ghostly presence that haunted their every word and gesture.

The DP was supposed to be the one tested at Keith's birthday party, but somehow Mike was the one who had failed. By abandoning Richard she had lost the privilege of *certainty* with him, the notion that she could say or do anything and he'd always stick by her. She hadn't fulfilled her end of the bargain; she hadn't stuck by *him*. She and Richard used to thrive on violating boundaries; they loved to analyze when a joke or pronouncement "crossed the line." The fun of it was that, for them, there *was* no line. Except now there was, and it didn't matter that she'd only been able to see it once she found herself on the other side. Mike was terrified that if she asked him to choose, he would do the unthinkable and choose the interloper. It was as if she had willingly stepped aside and allowed the DP to take her place. It was enough to make her scream.

All this came to a head about two weeks after their supposed reconciliation. Checking her calendar one morning, Mike realized she had a "premiere" that evening for a client whose animated children's movie would be released direct-to-DVD later that week in Targets and Walmarts, as well as being made available for downloading through various online platforms. She stood to make more money off this single movie than all her fancier clients' art-house dramas combined, and she had no problem celebrating its success, but she had no desire to actually *watch* the stupid thing. Richard's presence would make this trial a thousand times better, so she forwarded him the invite with a subject heading that read:

ugh pls be my date.

But she heard nothing from him.

By the time she got to work a few hours later, she had texted him, hey check your email lemme know

but there was still no response. Midmorning she IMed him,

I'm not gonna be ignored, Dan

and by noon she was truly irritated. On her way back from lunch, she became convinced that something terrible had happened and made the unprecedented move of calling Keith, who informed her that Richard was, on the contrary, alive and functioning and reachable on his cell. Mike called him, muttering "fucker" when she got his voice mail. She and Richard almost never left each other messages, but this time she waited for the beep.

"Emergency," she breathed into the phone. "Call me back immediately."

It wasn't an outright lie. It *was* an emergency—to her, at least. Ten minutes later he called her back.

"Hey, what's wrong?"

His obvious concern eased the tightness in her chest a little, but she filled the extra space with a forceful intake of air:

"Where the hell've you been all day?"

"What? I don't know, I've been . . . reading. For work. Wait, was *that* the emergency? That I didn't IM you? Seriously?"

"Whatever like you didn't have two seconds to write me back? Since you're so busy? With *work*?" She could hear his squeaky mattress; she was almost certain he hadn't gotten dressed yet for the day. Mike had never unironically disparaged Richard's work habits before because she knew how vulnerable he was to any criticism on the subject, but this was precisely why she couldn't help herself now. "I'm sorry for interrupting your *Simpsons* marathon. So what about tonight?"

"Can't," he said flatly. "I'm swamped. And yes, with *work*."

"That's cool," she said, hanging up immediately so that he would know it was most definitely *not* cool. And he didn't call her back. This was their sole interaction for the day.

She was losing him. In the two weeks following this incident, she saw him a total of three times, and never one-on-one. The torrent of texts and IMs between them had dried up to a trickle. She was no longer his partner in crime. Instead she was becoming one of those tedious women too frightened of alienating the object of their affections to speak plainly to them, a mealymouthed malcontent whose primary motivations were possessiveness and jealousy. She couldn't blame Richard for avoiding her; she was beginning to hate herself too.

Mike was determined to find a way out of this mess. And the more she thought about it, the more convinced she became that she had to locate the person who had orchestrated the Decent Proposal, the one who had brought on all these troubles in the first place. For starters, her curiosity had never diminished; she wanted to know *how* and *why* Richard had been chosen, and what this supposed benefactor's endgame was. She told herself she was doing Richard a favor. *He* couldn't investigate without jeopardizing the money he was getting, but what was the harm in *her* doing a little sleuthing? If she uncovered something bad, something that would bring the proposal to an end while restoring her to Richard's good graces, it would be a double win, two points for Mike. And even if by meddling she ruined a perfectly decent proposal, it would still be *over*. Richard would be angry; if he lost some or—God forbid—all the money coming to him, he would be furious. But he wouldn't starve. Eventually, he'd move on. He'd get past it. And she'd be there for him when he did.

But how? All she knew was that a lawyer named Jonathan Hertzfeld had made the proposal on behalf of an anonymous client. When she googled him, she easily found the name of his firm—Heaney Schechter—but it was shocking how little else she discovered. What she needed was his client list, but as she soon learned, this was like saying she needed the *Mona Lisa* or the Hope Diamond. The identities of a lawyer's clients—especially clients as rich as Jonathan Hertzfeld's—were closely guarded secrets. How could she possibly get her hands on such a thing?

For a week and a half Mike didn't do much of anything other than to go about her life. She didn't see Richard at all during this period, and the pit stuck around like a houseguest incapable of taking a hint. But then she got the query letter.

Mike got query letters all the time, of course. Wannabe screenwriters bombarded her inbox as often as ten times a day. Nine hundred ninety-nine out of a thousand of these fell somewhere on the spectrum from boring to nonsensical to downright cockamamie, and the query that changed everything was no different:

A pro-life thriller where the fetus fights back!

she read.

It's *Alien* meets *The Hand That Rocks the Cradle*!

Mike lunged for the DELETE button, but on her way there she caught sight of the e-mail address:

asingh@heaney-schechter.com.

She paused. *Hm.*

Two days later she was sitting with Anand Singh at the Conservatory for Coffee, Tea & Cocoa, a tiny café across from the Sony lot, a few minutes away from her office:

"I'm surprised it was *Fetal Attraction* that finally got your attention," he said, slurping the triple espresso she'd bought for him.

"Finally?" asked Mike. He had the typically famished look of a struggling screenwriter, which was something akin to hyperthyroidism: skinny frame, bulging eyes, a constant tremor running through his extremities—a combination of existentialist anxiety and caffeine.

"*Fetal* is my fourteenth screenplay," he told her proudly. "I've sent you queries for all of them. My favorite is this fantasy script that's sort of *Harry Potter* in reverse—"

"Why don't you tell me a little about yourself?"

"Sure, sure. Lawyer by day, screenwriter by night. Kind of like a superhero." (She watched with moderate alarm as he dumped a 5-hour Energy shot into his cup.) "Which reminds me, I actually created an online comic deconstructing the superhero genre and I really think there's a TV show in it, I can send you the URL—"

"Anand. Listen. I can tell you're a go-getter."

"I will do *anything*," he said, his bulgy eyes shining with a zealot's lunatic devotion, "*Anything*, to be represented by you."

Mike paused. Had it really come to this? What would her parents have said? She pushed away this horrible thought. *Desperate times . . .*

"I need you to get me Jonathan Hertzfeld's client list, no questions asked."

"Done!" he exclaimed, gulping the dregs of his drink triumphantly.

Apparently there was no overestimating the commensurate desperation of the unrepresented screenwriter.

The next day she received thirteen screenplays, four television pilots, two novels, a music video, a stand-up routine recorded on an iPhone, the aforementioned online comic strip, and a rundown of Jonathan Hertzfeld's clientele. That same day she cross-referenced the list against anyone unusually rich and/or illustrious using a pinch of Google, a dash of Ancestry. com, and a heaping spoonful of Wikipedia.

There was one candidate far richer than the others. Mike managed to find an address: it was a historical landmark, one of the oldest mansions in the Hollywood Hills. And the very next day, on a slow Wednesday in the middle of October, she ducked out of work early to make the trek north from Culver City.

Mike hated the Hills. She could never understand why so many people wanted to live there. It was a wild, mountainous region full of cliffs and ravines tailor-made for death, albeit of the spectacular variety. The roads were steep and narrow. The air was thinner and colder than the rest of L.A. Cell reception consistently failed. It was the perfect setting for a horror movie. She had to admit that once the ordeal of getting into one of these houses was over, the view on either side—the L.A. basin to the south, the Valley to the north—was sublime. But who could enjoy it, knowing they had to take their life into their hands every time they went somewhere? She approached a hairpin turn on a 45-degree incline, the pebbles kicked up by her tires hurtling past the edge and plummeting to their fallen comrades fifty feet below. A Range Rover careering downhill almost sideswiped her, and she jerked to a stop to offer it the finger. *Probably some idiot actor.* Celebrities loved the Hills, of course.

Mike paused a moment to look down on Los Angeles in all its flat, metallic glory, glinting in the afternoon sun. It was a literally breathtaking view, and it was hard for her to believe she was really *here* and not down there, chatting away on her phone while texting, IM'ing, Facebooking, *whatever*-ing with Richard. She felt like an astronaut looking down on Earth, except hers was a voyage fueled by desperation. Was it really possible that *love* had led her to this point in space and time? She could still go back. There were little lookout points all along the road, ideal for turning around. . . .

Mike pressed her sunglasses firmly into the bridge of her nose and continued the upward climb. The maze of concrete eventually led to a maze of gravel, and slowly an iron gate materialized in the distance. She lowered her sunglasses, squinting.

A call box had been hammered onto a giant eucalyptus tree standing beside the gate. She approached it slowly, the gravel crackling beneath her tires. She leaned halfway out the window, pawing at the box uselessly. Nothing happened; there was no button to press. What was she supposed to do? She pictured herself making a three-point turn and descending the hill after all, returning to the pile of unread scripts by Anand Singh that were sitting on her Kindle. The pit in her stomach throbbed a little, as if anticipating a hearty feeding.

The call box let out an ear-piercing screech.

"Who there?"

Fob, thought Mike. The voice undoubtedly belonged to an old Asian lady who at some point in her life had been "fresh off the boat" from somewhere across the Pacific. Mike could sniff them out a mile away. She leaned out the window again, her head tipped toward the box, as if she were about to order a burger and fries, supersize.

"I'd like to speak with the owner."

"What for?!"

Mike hesitated. *Screw it.* "I want to talk about Richard Baumbach and"—she hated saying the DP's name; it pained her to say it aloud—"Elizabeth Santiago." The pit in her stomach throbbed again and she imagined the shoots traveling another centimeter up her chest, its leaves rustling against her exposed blood vessels and mucous membranes.

There was a long pause on the other end, which she took as a promising sign. A camera on top of the gate angled downward like an owl tipping its head, eyeing her unnervingly. The pit was pulsating now, and when the gate cracked open it gave a sick little quiver.

There was another long stretch of gravel to cross before a sharp corner revealed the house as suddenly as if a curtain had been lifted. Mike knew what to expect from the photos she'd seen online, but it was even more impressive in person. The house itself wasn't much, just a big three-story rectangle: solid, well made, with large windows and simple moldings. All the ostentation had been reserved for the landscaping. The front lawn was a wonderland of palm trees and bright, tropical flora: orange-and-blue birds of paradise; a rainbow's worth of begonias and other flowers she couldn't even begin to name; dark green, dangerous-looking plants that looked as though they belonged in *Jurassic Park*, with their humongous leaves and hairy tendrils trailing on the ground. *How much water did this place use up in a day?* Blood-red bougainvillea exploded in a majestic arch over the double-wide front doors. Pressed against the floor-to-ceiling windows lining the ground floor were snow-white trellises dripping ivy and an assortment of softer, paler-colored flowers. Mike spied a lagoon-like pool peeking out from behind the house, and beyond that a lush, multitiered garden where half a dozen laborers were toiling in the orangey afternoon sun. But she almost missed these details because her eye had been drawn immediately to the HOLLYWOOD sign towering over the property. Like any iconic landmark, it looked a little unreal to the naked eye, especially up close, and as she approached the half flight of stairs leading up to the front door, her eyes roved over the tall, white letters hungrily, though she must have seen them a thousand times before.

The door flew open. In its place appeared the fob. She was an old Vietnamese woman with a salt-and-pepper bob and loose, sallow cheeks. She motioned impatiently with one flabby arm: *come on!*

Mike flushed. She could already feel the woman's hot, toxic disapproval tumbling toward her, and she began climbing the stairs as slowly as possible to spite this old Asian biddy with her pidgin English, who probably wore surgical masks in public and walked in the sun with an umbrella to keep her precious skin as light as possible—something even her somewhat fobby mother would never do. She guessed that to this woman, her oversize features—the big eyes, full lips, and jutting cheekbones so coveted by white people—were disgusting. Even though she was Korean and looked nothing like her, Mike was often compared to the Chinese-American actress Lucy Liu, usually by her parents' church friends and never in a complimentary way, since Liu had larger, "Western" features too. Mike always pretended to be flattered, and rhapsodized about the actress's beauty, knowing full well this made her seem more "whitewashed" than these reverse racists already thought she was. Behind their backs she joked that it was people like them who destroyed all the "hard work" she did boozing and slutting it up in the clubs, teaching white people that not all Asians were good at math and obeyed their parents to the letter. There was something real behind the joke. What was the point of leaving a place if you were going to spend the rest of your life pretending you never left? She resented being judged for fitting in. When Mike reached the top of the stairs, the woman offered neither a smile nor a word of welcome, pressing herself against the door to let Mike pass, as if she were afraid of contracting a disease.

Mike found herself inside a tiled courtyard. The roof was sky-high and made of glass. A big fountain gurgled contentedly in the middle, an assortment of ferns and palm trees around it housing what sounded like a flock of chirping birds. Here and there she caught a flash of primary color as one of them moved. The air was steamy and smelled of wet earth. She barely had time to take this in before the woman stalked over to another door and flung it open.

"In here," she barked, pointing.

Mike stepped through. The door slammed shut behind her, the noise from the birds and fountain ceasing instantly, as if someone had flicked a switch and muted them. She paused, bewildered. She'd been transported from the tropics to a European salon.

The room was long and narrow, with fluffy white furniture everywhere. The trellises in the bay windows filtered the afternoon sunlight flawlessly, rendering the space both bright and comforting. Fans high up in the ceiling maintained a soft breeze that blew gently on her face. Every inch of the wall opposite the windows was crammed with books, but there were no leather-bound "great books" here, no stuffy encyclopedias. Most of them were paperbacks, their bindings worn and stained, and from what Mike could see they were all popular fiction from the last two hundred years or so. On a little side table lay *The Bell Jar*, its waterlogged pages curled and separated from each other, no doubt the casualty of some aquatic mishap, probably in the pool outside. Beside it, the cover of *Vanity Fair* looked as if it had been chewed on by a baby or mauled by someone's dog. Mike guessed that every book in the room had been read in its entirety, that it was a hard-and-fast rule of the house: *you don't get to stay if you haven't been read.* Many of them had probably been consumed in this very room. It was the perfect spot for reading. She imagined curling up with a careworn volume on one of these white couches while the sun slowly set, bathing her in its soft and gentle glow. . . .

"Igggh-ack!"

It came from the far end of the room. Mike's childhood piano teacher had smoked three packs a day; she would have recognized the phlegmy hack of a smoker's cough anywhere. She walked toward it blindly.

BEVERLY BUFFUM CHAMBERS stared, transfixed, as the lovely vision grew closer, like a shimmering oasis drawing slowly into focus. It was rare to see such beauty up close these days. There had been a time when it surrounded her, when her instinct was to disdain it because the problem with pulchritude, of course, was that it often came laden with vanity and other tedious qualities. It was boredom that Beverly abhorred above all things, so it was a surprise to discover now that the exquisite face before her was in and of itself a source of novelty. *How strange.* When she was seventeen and attending that ridiculous finishing school her father had insisted on sending her to instead of a real college ("Am I finished yet?" she asked at the end of every lesson), she wouldn't have blinked an eye at the girl who stopped short a few feet in front of her now, except to remark on her Oriental features. *Asian,* she reminded herself. *Oriental* had gone out of fashion long ago.

Her ethnicity notwithstanding, this beauty would have fit right in at all the tennis tournaments, the pool parties, the dishwater-dull banquets followed by endless rounds of cocktails, dancing, and dope during Bev's later teens and twenties, when even *she* had her own measure of beauty—on a good day any-way. (If she raised her right eyebrow and curled her top lip *just so*, some man was bound to tell her she looked like a young Bette Davis, to which she always replied, "Was Bette Davis ever really young, though?" The originality of the man's response was a fair test of his wit, or lack thereof.) She took another drag on her cigarette. It was no good avoiding the truth. She was an ugly old woman now. When had that happened? *Decades ago,* was what Charlotte would have said if she were there, and as usual Charlotte would have been right. *I should be used to this by now,* she chided herself. Old age had never quite cottoned to her mind the way it had to her body, though, and there was something merciless about the contrast between herself and this exquisite girl, who had let her slender hands with their tapered, candlelike fingers fall to her sides, her dainty feet planted apart, as if she were about to draw a gun and shoot. What on earth was she doing here? Bev had half expected someone to turn up eventually, but she had no idea who this person was, or how she was connected to the names provided at the gate like a secret password: *open sesame.* She decided not to say a word. The intruder would have to be the first to speak. This was only fair. But she couldn't help giving her a smile of encouragement.

MIKE HAD TO resist the urge to jump back when the old woman leered at her with yellow, pointed teeth, like a witch from a fairy tale. She knew that Beverly Chambers was the heiress to a container-shipping empire with a net worth believed to be several hundred million dollars. She also knew that this woman, along with one of her socialite friends, had become renowned over the last few decades for devoting herself to the California-specific problem of prison overcrowding. Mike's eyes had glazed over while she read online about the hundreds of hours they'd spent interviewing guards, administrators, and prisoners, making the case to anyone who would listen for better conditions and more serious rehabilitative efforts. *Whatever.* She had sounded exactly like the sort of rich, meddlesome old woman who would have concocted the Decent Proposal for her own idiosyncratic reasons.

Mike knew from Wikipedia that this woman was only in her early eighties, but the wizened mass of flesh in front of her looked closer to a hundred, with its sagging face, speckling of liver spots, and strawlike, thinning hair. She could have been a valuable asset for the antismoking movement simply by placing herself in front of a camera: *The Marlboro Hag.* Mike watched her take a surprisingly long drag on her cigarette (it was in fact a Parliament), exhaling the smoke in a steady stream through her ruined nostrils. She was perched on a poofy white mushroom of a chair, and Mike revised her impression of a fairy-tale witch, likening her instead to Little Miss Muffet, aged into Old Miss Muffet the chain-smoking spinster, still sitting on her tuffet after all these years.

"My name is Michaela Kim." Her full name sounded strange to her ears, as if it weren't quite hers, but she was out of her depth and wanted to sound as impressive as possible.

Beverly sensed her discomfort. Eight decades' worth of good manners (perhaps the finishing school wasn't such a waste after all?) took over:

"Come closer, dear, and sit down," she said, affecting the grandmotherly tone she reserved for those occasions on which she was forced to interact with the minor members of her extended family. She had no interest in children (especially the pampered variety), but assuming the role of the doting auntie, speaking softly and using phrases like "my darling" and "my dear" was the only way she could think to make it through these exchanges without losing her mind.

Mike took a seat opposite the mushroom, on what she believed was called a fainting couch. Her reference point shifted yet again: now she was Alice sitting down to tea with the Mad Hatter.

"Would you like something to drink?" Beverly held up a tiny silver bell.

Mike could have used some water, but she dreaded the return of the grumpy fob. She shook her head *no*.

"I'm a friend of Richard Baumbach's," she said. "His *best* friend."

"Ah," said Beverly, and there was a twinkle in her birdlike eye, which was sharp and piercing, the only part of her to have been seasoned rather than spoiled by the passage of time.

Mike caught the twinkle. *There it is*, she thought. *Took her about one second to figure the whole thing out.* Tears gathered in her eyes—of sadness and frustration, but humiliation too, for being so easy to read and, in a feedback loop of self-pity, for being weak enough to cry in front of a stranger. To her horror, the tears accumulated and began to flow. *This is a disaster!* she thought, struggling to stem the tide, except that in her agitation her thoughts strayed as if by some perverted, masochistic instinct to her father, who would be gone soon, whether a year from now, or five years, or ten years, but whatever the case it would be sooner than she could bear and why couldn't she just *get it together* if not for her then for *him?* But she couldn't. The tears flowed on and on.

Beverly rang the bell after all. The old Asian woman appeared—so quickly she must have been standing outside the door.

"Get us some tissues, Peaches, will you?"

Peaches? Somehow Mike found enough mental space inside her breakdown to gawk at this revolting Anglicization. *Seriously?*

Peaches stomped out of the room. By the time she returned, Mike had recovered and was in the middle of explaining how she'd managed to find Beverly.

"'Fetal Attraction,' *oh dear*," Bev mumbled.

Mike smiled faintly, despite her wretchedness. One of the lesser tragedies resulting from her immoral (and potentially illegal) actions was that she hadn't been able, in what little good conscience she had left, to share this screenplay title with Richard. He would have laughed about it for a week. Maybe longer.

"No one knows I'm here. I did this all on my own. Please don't tell your lawyer," she pleaded. "I don't want to get anyone in trouble."

"Of course not, my dear. I won't say a single word." *No, it will take much more than a single word,* she thought, looking forward to torturing Jonathan Hertzfeld with news of a traitor in his ranks.

Bev wouldn't tell him the junior lawyer's name, though; she would make him figure it out on his own. *Serves him right*, she thought. *For how much I pay him.*

Mike didn't trust those shiny, mocking eyes for a second. She realized suddenly that she was at this woman's mercy, that if Beverly Chambers wanted to she could destroy Mike's career, her relationship with Richard (whatever *that* was at this point), pretty much her entire life. The woman named Peaches deposited the tissue box on the coffee table and looked at her for a moment with something approaching motherly concern. Beverly waved her away with a flick of the wrist, and Mike felt a bubbling of resentment toward this rich old white lady with her grand manner and her Vietnamese maid, her team of gardeners and her meddling ways. She lorded it over all of them with such ease. Mike was yet another plebe whose life she held so carelessly in her scabby claws. Why couldn't she leave well enough alone? Why was she doing this?

"Why are you doing this?"

Bev took the last possible drag of her cigarette—little more than the filter—and stubbed it out in an ashtray. She gave Mike the tiniest of nods, as if to say, *Well done. Straight to the heart of the matter.* But she didn't answer until her next cigarette was lit.

"I'm afraid I can't tell you that," she exhaled. "We don't know each other nearly well enough."

Mike nodded miserably. What was she doing here? She began calculating how quickly she could leave with a modicum of self-respect.

"But perhaps we can remedy that. You say you're Richard Baumbach's best friend. How did you meet?"

For the next half hour, Mike told her everything about herself. She even told her about her father's illness. It was a relief to be one hundred percent honest with a stranger. For the first time, she understood the draw of therapy.

"When did you suspect they were attached to each other?" Bev asked when they got around to the Decent Proposal again.

"Well . . . Richard started out saying *we're not going to fall in love*, so obviously I worried that was exactly what was going to happen."

"Of course." Bev grinned behind a wall of smoke, more Cheshire Cat than Mad Hatter now. "I assume that sometime later you had a better indication?"

"At the party, this birthday party," said Mike. "When they danced together. To this awful song. But it didn't matter. There was chemistry, everyone could see it."

Just as I can see how much you love him too, thought Bev, feasting on the girl's perfect, pain-filled face. But could her lovesick impressions be trusted? Could it really have happened so quickly . . . ? Bev realized that Mike was still speaking, and with great effort she refocused her attention:

" . . . and it's just not the same anymore. Basically, I'm fucked."

Mike looked up to see if her language had shocked the old woman.

"Would you like a drink, my dear?" Bev asked. "A *real* drink, I mean?"

"Hell yes," said Mike without thinking. She searched again for a sign of disapproval, but Beverly Chambers laughed, a much younger laugh than Mike expected: like water rippling over stones, or the soft tinkle of bracelets on a wrist. It seemed impossible for such a pleasing sound to have come from such a body.

"Didn't have to ask *you* twice."

Mike shrugged her shoulders, offering up a tiny smile.

Bev seized the bell again and gave it three short rings, followed by three long rings, then three more short.

"Did you just SOS?" Mike asked incredulously.

"I most certainly did," said Bev. "That's my prearranged call for alcohol. Unless specified otherwise, Peaches will bring in a tray of gimlets in a moment. You like gimlets, I hope?" she asked anxiously.

"I've never had one," said Mike, and at long last the shock and disapproval she'd been waiting for leapt onto Beverly's face.

"Oh, Michaela!" Bev's hideous grimace morphed into a hideous grin. "You're in for a treat."

Peaches burst in with a silver tray that held a bottle of Tanqueray No. Ten, Rose's lime juice, an empty crystal decanter, two cocktail glasses, a metal stirrer, a bowl of freshly cut lime wedges, and a bucket of ice. She banged the tray onto the coffee table and knelt on the floor to mix the drinks. Her servile posture made Mike uncomfortable, and she suspected the woman was taking as long as possible to maximize her discomfort.

"For God's sake, Peaches," Bev huffed after a few minutes of this, "you're not making a bomb. Stir the damn thing and pour!"

Peaches grunted. She gave the first glass to Beverly, but left Mike's drink on the table, refusing to hand it to her. With a disapproving shake of her flat-haired bob that conjured the fringes on a flapper dress shimmying from side to side, Peaches took away the tray and everything on it except for the ice bucket and the decanter, nearly full, and stalked away, slamming the door behind her.

They eyed each other, frozen, before bursting into laughter. Mike felt suddenly as if she were at a slumber party and the adults had just gone to bed.

"Peaches is a treasure," said Bev. "Don't let her stormy exterior fool you. I don't know what I'd do without her."

Mike took a sip of her drink. She shuddered; it was strong—*really* strong. She was surprised Peaches hadn't watered it down, but then she imagined Beverly Chambers (who was sucking on hers contentedly) wouldn't stand for a weak cocktail. Mike had eaten only half a salad at lunch, and the alcohol rushed straight to her head.

"Well, if everyone called me Peaches I'd probably be pretty pissy too," she said. "Why doesn't she use her real Vietnamese name? Is she afraid you won't be able to pronounce it?"

"I like you, Michaela," said Bev, refusing to take the bait.

"Call me Mike. *No one* calls me Michaela."

"Then why did you introduce yourself that way?"

Mike shrugged her shoulders again, more aggressively this time.

"Well, *Mike*, now that I know you a little better, it's only fair I tell you something about myself in return."

Deep inside her stomach, Mike felt the pit rustle ominously. *Here we go.* Somehow she was already at the end of her first drink. She leaned over the coffee table to pour herself another, and Bev held hers out for a top-off.

"I happen to know a thing or two about best friends," said Bev, drawing back her glass. "Mine was named Charlotte." She took a healthy gulp to keep from spilling. "Our mothers were best friends too. There used to be a photo. We lost it years ago, but it was the two of them arm-in-arm, both about to burst. This was in the days before women paraded their pregnant bellies in public every chance they got. It was an unusual picture, practically scandalous, and we used to say it proved our friendship started before birth. And if we had enough of these—"

She tapped her glass with one crooked finger.

"—we'd say it was going to extend beyond the grave as well."

She paused to take another sip.

"We forced everyone to call us 'CharBev,' if you can believe it. *That's* how much we were together."

"Like 'Brangelina'?" asked Mike, more saucily than she would have if she hadn't just downed a buttload of gin.

Bev laughed. "Yes, exactly, a portmanteau. We did it first. In any case the day came, as I always knew it would, when Charlotte announced she was getting married."

"Uh-oh. CharBev was splitsville," Mike volunteered, and she had to make an effort to keep from giggling.

"Do I need to cut you off?" Bev asked, but there was only humor in the question. "Stop interrupting. I didn't like her fiancé much." She stamped out her latest cigarette. "He was a bore, not the sort of man *I'd* have chosen to spend my life with. But I pretended to like him for her sake, and I helped her get ready for the wedding. And when they went away on their honeymoon, *God*, how I missed her." She put down her drink, picked up her lighter, and stuck a fresh Parlie in her mouth. When she spoke, the cigarette dangled from her bottom lip, waggling with each syllable: "Those were the longest three months of my life."

Mike crinkled her brow. Bev paused to light her cigarette. "Yes, three whole months." She exhaled. "Back then honeymoons lasted *months*, not weeks, at least for rich people like us. Nowadays no one goes away for very long, not even the ones who can. It's a shame." She began coughing, but managed to stave off a full-blown fit with judiciously timed gulps from her glass. "The whole time Char was away," she continued eventually, "I fretted. I knew things would never be the same. How could they be? She had a new best friend now." Bev flicked away a crown of ash with her talon of a thumb. "She'd always been the straight man of the act—the Abbott to my Costello, if that means anything to you."

"I know who Abbott and Costello are," Mike said, staring at her nearly empty glass.

"I'm glad. So you can appreciate how the straight man is just as crucial to the act as the show-off is. I felt lost without her. Suddenly there was no more fun to be had. I became convinced I was destined to live the rest of my days alone, starved for companionship. And worst of all, I would always have more than enough of the false kind: *people, people, everywhere, and not a one to talk to.*" She took another drag. "To really talk to, I mean."

"I get it," said Mike.

"I'm sure you do. So imagine me, at the tender age of twenty—I know it's hard, but try—in this very house, on Valentine's Day, all the way back in 1952. Well over fifty years ago. *God,* that makes me feel old. I went to bed early that night. Alone, of course. Valentine's Day was our special day, you see. As girls we made valentines for each other, and insisted that for us it would always be a celebration of the love between best friends, nothing drippy or romantic about it. And this was my first Valentine's without her. She and her husband were due back any day, but in those days it was difficult to pin down a return. And I hadn't heard a peep. I couldn't blame her, of course. It was her honeymoon! I told myself our tradition was childish, it was only natural for her to move on. But secretly, I was heartbroken."

Mike wondered if the story was about to take a lesbian turn.

"My thoughts were so disturbed that night, I couldn't fall asleep. I tossed and turned for almost an hour. And then suddenly I saw her face. She was floating above me."

Bev paused, unwilling to even attempt to describe what seeing Charlotte's face had been like. It was her most dearly cherished memory.

"I thought it was a dream," she said finally. "And I was glad, because it meant I'd fallen asleep. I've always been a sound sleeper, and I have no tolerance for insomnia. So I closed my eyes. But then something splashed my face so I opened them again, irritated as hell. She was still there, but this time she'd come down to earth and was sitting on the side of the bed, dipping her fingers in a glass and flicking them at me. I licked my lips and tasted gin, and then I realized it couldn't be a dream. I've always loved gin"—she took a long draught, as if to prove her point—"but not *that* much. So I bolted up, and she dropped the whole drink right there on the sheets!"

Bev snickered at the memory.

"Guess you had to be there," observed Mike.

"I guess so." Bev downed the rest of her gimlet, poured herself another, and refilled Mike's glass. She continued:

"It was eleven fifty-three. We only had seven minutes of Valentine's Day that year, but we talked past midnight, there in my bed with a towel sopping up the alcohol. And we never missed a Valentine's Day after that. Those three months were the longest time we spent apart."

Bev's eyes went soft. She sipped her drink, staring off into the middle distance.

And?? Mike wanted to say. But apparently story time was over. What the hell was she supposed to get from *that*? Even if Richard married the DP he'd still be her best friend forever? That she should content herself with being the fifth wheel the rest of her life? *Screw that.*

"How did her husband feel about you two spending all that time together, after they were married?" Mike asked, tossing back a good portion of gimlet number three, which she was beginning to realize from the telltale swaying of the room was more like gimlet numbers seven, eight, and nine.

"Oh, he died a year later." Bev waved her hand through a shaft of cigarette smoke, scattering it to the heavens. "In Korea. Didn't even get a chance to knock her up. Idiotic."

It was unclear whether she was referring to the man or the war. Mike suspected it was both. *So I just have to make sure the DP dies,* she thought, suppressing a burp. *Check.*

"At first people pitied us," Bev continued, "the widow and the spinster, confined to a dull life together." She smiled wickedly. "It was far from the truth, but we were happy to keep up the façade. Then the sixties happened, and let me tell you, Mike, that was a good time to be young but an even *better* time to be middle-aged. Especially for two rich single women like us. We went crazy, it was *superb*. We stopped wearing makeup, screwed lots of men—"

Mike choked theatrically on her gimlet, but Bev pretended not to notice.

"—and we didn't hide a thing. I was the black sheep for years." She released another long stream of smoke through her nostrils, and Mike watched the cloud trail lazily toward the ceiling, where the fans laid waste to it. "But that sort of hedonism can only last so long, you know, before it becomes boring too. I've always been an all-or-nothing person, Our Lady of Extremes, as Charlotte used to call me, the cow. So when we decided it was time to leave the jet set I insisted we go in the opposite direction."

"I read all about that," said Mike. "Your work in prisons."

"Did you?"

Bev tried to downplay it, but Mike could hear the delight in the old woman's voice.

"You've been very generous," said Mike. *Too generous*, she wanted to add.

"We did more than throw our money around. We spent years inside those hellholes, interviewing people, recording their stories. The conditions were *unthinkable*. One of our cases went all the way to the Supreme Court."

Mike nodded politely. *I don't fucking care.*

"And do you know the funniest thing?" Bev paused to sip her drink. "The whole time we were in those prisons, we were the widow and the spinster no more. Everyone—the lawyers, the wardens, the guards, the prisoners themselves—assumed we were queer. Can you imagine it?"

Mike shook her head, maintaining her best poker face.

"It was far from the truth, but we were happy to keep up the façade."

Bev went back to contemplating the middle distance. Mike was left with the same refrain: *And??* She wanted—no, she *needed*—more: a twist ending, a life lesson, some measure of profundity to apply to herself. What about the Decent Proposal? Wasn't she going to tell her why she'd chosen Richard and the DP? What she had planned for them? If there even *was* a plan? Mike was beginning to feel like an idiot for thinking Beverly Chambers had any answers at all.

"Can I have one?" Mike motioned to the pack of Parliaments resting beside the old woman.

Bev hesitated, but they were just cigarettes, after all, and she reminded herself that Mike Kim was a grown woman, not a girl.

Mike took one and lit it expertly. She rarely smoked, but whenever she did it was a sure sign she was drunk. She touched her cheek: yup, red-hot; the "Asian flush" had officially set in. *No more gimlets for me*, she thought. *Wouldn't want to pull a Richard.* The pit in her stomach flexed a little at the thought of him, and she decided she didn't care anymore, that the time had come to throw caution to the proverbial wind she was three sheets to at this point anyway:

"So that's it?" she said. "That's all I get? No explanation for this stupid experiment or whatever the hell it is you're doing?" She took a quick, impatient drag, and everything in the room tilted on its axis, though she was reasonably sure she hadn't moved. "How about an apology for ruining my fucking life?"

Bev put down her glass and stubbed out her cigarette with a purposeful air.

"I will *not* apologize, Mike. Because your life isn't ruined, even if you think it is."

Mike snorted; suddenly she needed to blow her nose, and she dropped her cigarette among the ice cubes in her otherwise empty glass to free up her hand.

Bev watched sadly as this gorgeous girl lunged unsteadily for the tissue box on the coffee table. "Do you know what my biggest regret in life is, Mike?" she asked her softly.

Mike shook her head, setting off a minor earthquake in the room.

"Underwear."

Mike managed to subdue the shuddering long enough to meet the old woman's eye. "What?"

"It's true," Bev nodded. "I spent half my life wearing a girdle, which is essentially a corset except with garter belts to keep up your stockings. Good God, *stockings!* I won't even get started on *those*. It was the one thing I did because everyone else was doing it. I should've invented my own garments. Or worn nothing at all."

Bev paused, searching for the words.

"For all your courage, Mike, you act as if you—"

Mike honked into her tissue. Bev waited impatiently for her to finish.

"As I was saying, for all your courage, you act as if you aren't in control of your own life."

"I know, I know. It's not his story." Mike let the dirty tissue fall to the floor. "It's mine."

"*That's* where you're wrong." Bev poured herself another gimlet, declining to offer any to her lightweight of a companion. (The pitcher was almost empty anyway.)

"It's *not* your story. It's no one's story. It isn't a story at all."

They lapsed into silence. Mike turned sideways, leaning back against the fainting couch's headboard. The extra support helped steady her, and she swiveled her head toward Beverly while the rest of her body remained perfectly still.

"So what should I do now?"

Bev paused to light another cigarette. "I'm not going to lie to you." She took a long drag, shaking her head at the end of it. "I have no idea what you should do."

Mike closed her eyes before nodding, to minimize the dizziness. At least the old woman was being honest.

"But I know you'll figure it out. And do what needs to be done."

Mike nodded again, more slowly this time, drawing her legs up onto the couch. She had an instant of perfect, panicked clarity in which she wondered if this was really happening, if she was really passing out in a drunken stupor inside a strange old lady's mansion. But seconds later she was snoring.

Bev finished her cigarette, staring at the sleeping beauty splayed before her. She rang for Peaches, ignoring the uncharacteristic gasp that escaped her housekeeper's lips upon entering the room. Bev took great delight in antagonizing Peaches, and gestured carelessly to the girl in an offhand manner she knew would infuriate her:

"Let her sleep it off for as long as she needs."

Peaches cleared away the mess quietly, which did not prevent her from shaking her piebald head of hair more fiercely than before. After she left, Bev stepped through one of the French windows Peaches had cracked open earlier to vent the cigarette smoke, and walked onto the lawn.

The sky was yellow-red with pink around the edges, like the petals of one of the hundreds—if not thousands—of exotic flowers strewn over the grounds. The sun had dipped below the highest peak, and its warmth would linger no more than ten or fifteen minutes longer in the bone-dry air blown in from the desert by the Santa Ana winds. It was no wonder people still believed the city was built on a desert—especially these days, with California's protracted droughts lasting years at a time. Los Angeles actually had a classic Mediterranean climate with relatively rainy winters; the desert myth was an old lie dating back to the Water Wars of a century ago—the basis for the movie *Chinatown*. Bev was old enough to remember her father, the shipping magnate "Big Stan" Chambers, arguing with his fellow business titans over whether William Mulholland was a villain or a hero. She could still see him gesticulating wildly with the tumbler of Scotch practically glued inside his giant, hairy-gorilla hand for the duration of every evening.

She threaded her way among the colorful obstacles on the lawn with a slow but steady gait. When she reached the middle she turned around, facing northeast, where she knew she would see the HOLLYWOOD sign. When she was a little girl, the sign had still read HOLLYWOODLAND, and there had been lightbulbs surrounding each fifty-foot letter. In those days it had lit up in three discrete chunks: HOLLY, WOOD, and LAND, before flashing in its entirety. What would she do if, one day, she turned and it wasn't there? *Die, I suppose.*

Hollywood had been different back then: the hills and canyons were wild, filled with oaks and hollies and natural springs. There were foxes and coyotes everywhere—a great deal more than there were today. Playing in the farthest reaches of the estate, it had been easy for her to imagine she was a princess in an enchanted forest far, far away. But all she had to do was look up at that sign—*her* sign—and she knew she was home. When she went to sleep she always saw the big white letters on the insides of her eyes. They played a starring role in her favorite dream, in which she would climb to the top of the H and soar over the city, which even back then was spreading into the basin below like an electric patchwork quilt.

Of course, when at age ten her big brother Tom told her that the very same year she was born, a struggling actress named Peg Entwistle had climbed to the top of the H and plunged to her death in the ravine below, Bev's favorite dream turned into a recurring nightmare that lasted for weeks. But she refused to give her brother the satisfaction of knowing he'd gotten to her, and never cried out from her bed. No one other than Charlotte ever knew.

Charlotte, always Charlotte. Beverly had left out one important detail in her recital of the life and times of CharBev that afternoon. CharBev was dead. "Beat you," had been Char's final words six months earlier, as Bev watched her slip away.

The sky turned purple. A chill invaded the air.

It hadn't taken long for Bev to hurtle over the precipice— into the abyss of excess from which her best friend had rescued her time and time again. It started with the smoking. Charlotte had quit in the early seventies like any reasonable person, when it became clear how harmful cigarettes really were. Bev, of course, had refused. Out of respect for Char, however, she refrained from smoking in her presence, which limited her to half a pack a day at most. Now that Char was gone, Bev took a grim joy in smoking almost every waking minute. She was averaging four packs a day. Her doctor was beside himself; he said it was a miracle she had no ailments other than an intermittent cough, and guessed that without the smoking she could easily live to a hundred, but that if she continued on her current course she wouldn't make it past ninety. "Good," she'd told him, and when he'd recommended that she see a psychiatrist, she'd laughed in the poor man's face.

This business with the prisons: this, too, had originated in Beverly's love of excess. She chose this particular social dilemma precisely because it meant immersing herself in such an unpleasant, such an *unlikely* world. Bev delighted in upending the expectations of all her friends and family, and it was only to deny them the satisfaction of her failure that she stuck with the plan after her first few horrified visits behind the clanging prison doors. (If she had a nickel for every time she'd been called the C-word . . . she would have at least a dollar, maybe two.) Here as well Charlotte saved the day, remaining by her side, her steady partner, and in truth, though Beverly was the one who had started it, Charlotte became the more passionate advocate—as evidenced by Beverly's failure to visit more than one prison since her best friend's demise.

Char always had a knack for seeing the two of them more clearly than Bev ever could, but for once, on this night, Bev forced herself to look at CharBev without the obfuscating haze of self-regard. She had claimed this afternoon that she and Char were more than a spinster and a widow, and while it was true they'd been an unusually fun-loving variation on the theme, this didn't change the fact that for half a century it was exactly what they were. And now the widow was dead, and the spinster was alone.

Bev let out a sigh that no one other than the HOLLYWOOD sign could hear. She thought back to the version of herself she'd conjured earlier: the dewy twenty-year-old, to whom spinsterhood was never truly an option. She hadn't married, but it wasn't from lack of opportunity. She racked up no fewer than fifteen proposals in her day (and one of them from a young William Holden). She was simply too rich not to receive offers, even if she had been stupid and ugly, and she had been neither. Her serial refusals first amused, then baffled, and ultimately alarmed her friends and relatives. But her reasoning was simple: she refused to marry without love. "The one" hadn't gotten away; she'd simply never found him.

It was one thing for Beverly not to realize the dream she'd dreamt like every other human on the planet—to fall in love, to find the one person who was more special to her than all the others—but it was another not to attain that which she had always expected to achieve—to eventually marry *someone*, to have children, to make a life together with a man. It hurt more keenly than she could have imagined, especially since she thought she'd gotten over the "marriage issue"

decades ago. Her biggest regret was *underwear*? What a joke.
What a lie.

She began shivering, and moved farther across the lawn to
ward off the cold. If her biggest tragedy was something that hadn't
happened to fulfill her emotionally, she knew she should take
comfort in having snagged a choice spot on Fortuna's Wheel.
Besides, her charmed life *had* been filled with love, though it was
a friend's and not a lover's. She'd even had plenty of sex, much
of it good, some of it *great*; it's just that the love and the sex had
never matched up. It was a shame, but it wasn't a tragedy.

And yet Bev imagined that girl now: here, on the lawn, underneath the indigo sky, wearing nothing but the nightshirt she
wore to bed that Valentine's Day in 1952, too young, too angry
to feel the cold.

"What have you *done*, you old hag?" the girl demanded.
"You failed me. What do you have to say for yourself?"

Beverly opened her withered mouth to speak, but she faltered, croaking helplessly. There was nothing to say. It *was* a
tragedy. It was *her* tragedy. Better to have loved and lost, etc.—as
Charlotte had. For all of Arnold's doltishness, Char truly loved
him, and was married for so little time she never had the chance
to grow to despise him, not even a little bit. Charlotte never re-
married because no one could measure up, whereas Beverly had
never loved at all. Suddenly she remembered a heated argument
(one of many) with her brother Tom, who'd married a year out
of Stanford and was constantly setting her up with his awful
friends, desperate to secure both the family's wealth (which was
more precarious back then) and their elevated social standing.
All these years later, his words returned to her, cutting, precise:
"You don't even know what love *is*."

Was this why she had done it—this stupid, impulsive proposal? There was no mystery (to *her*, in any case) about how
she'd found Elizabeth Santiago and Richard Baumbach. But un-

til tonight she had never asked herself *why* exactly she wanted so badly to bring them together, why she had been so obsessed by the idea of their falling in love. Charlotte would have simply waved her hands in the air as though she were swatting a fly, and told her to stop being an idiot, and that would have been the end of it. But Charlotte was gone, and there had been no one to stop her.

It wasn't *really* about proving her dead brother wrong; Tom didn't deserve so much credit. But he deserved a little, because deep down a part of her had always believed him. It was about proving to herself, she supposed, that she *did* know a thing or two about love. And now, if the gorgeous girl passed out in the library was to be believed (and Bev was convinced she was), it was within her power to answer the question definitively. Had she actually known what she was doing when she brought together Richard Baumbach and Elizabeth Santiago? Did they actually love each other?

She would have to see for herself.

The girl in the nightshirt raised a full and luscious brow, as if to say, "get to it then," and before Bev could tell her she really *did* look like a young Bette Davis, she faded away into the night, which was black now, and freezing (which was to say, somewhere in the upper 50s).

It wasn't part of the plan, but screw the plan. There had barely *been* a plan. Bev hurried back inside the house.

BEFORE MIKE KIM had so much as twitched an eyelid from her perch on the fainting couch, the e-mail went out from the law offices of Heaney Schechter in Century City:

Dear Mr. Baumbach and Miss Santiago:

Your benefactor requests the pleasure of your company one week from today, at a family estate in Death Valley, which I have been assured will be of particular interest to you both. You will be responsible for getting yourselves there (I will provide directions) no later than noon, to avoid the midday heat. Please note that this trip will qualify as your required session for the week.

I look forward to your prompt confirmation by return of e-mail.

Yours sincerely,

Jonathan Hertzfeld, Esq.

THE MAKEOVER

RICHARD HAPPENED TO BE scanning his inbox when the e-mail *pinged* into sight. He opened it immediately.

"Holy *shit*," he breathed, failing to notice when the traffic light ahead of him turned green. The car behind him honked. He looked up, catching the driver's operatic gesture inside his rearview mirror: *move!*

He dialed Elizabeth with one hand while maneuvering through the intersection with the other.

"Hi, Richard."

"Did you see it?"

"*Hello*, Richard."

"You didn't see it yet, did you?"

She sighed. "See what?"

"The e-mail!"

"I've been reviewing tax codes for the last four hours. So, no."

"I think you might be the only person I know who doesn't check their e-mail every two seconds in their office. What's the Internet *for* other than shameless workplace procrastination? Is this the pharmaceutical thing?"

"Yes, actually." She sounded surprised.

"Don't sound so surprised. I listen. Anyway, sorry to tear you away from tax codes, but I'm going to need you to check your e-mail. Right now." There was a pause. "I think I can actually hear you rolling your eyes."

"Hold on, I'm checking."

He let a few seconds go by, thumping his leg against the floorboard of his car. "Oh, by the way, you'll be so proud of me, I read another whole page of *Tess* today!"

Tess of the d'Urbervilles had become something of a joke between them; they'd been reading it for over a month and a half. More specifically, Elizabeth had read it all the way through, twice, but Richard still had about a hundred pages to go. For him, wading through Hardy's muddy prose felt like a pointless exercise. Tess had been raped and then blamed for becoming a "fallen woman" by pretty much everyone she knew. This was bad—very bad—but how many ways did it need to be said? Quite a few, apparently, and each of them via run-on sentences.

"I'm done," said Elizabeth a minute later, more quietly than before.

"Can you believe it?!"

"I can't."

"We're gonna meet the man behind the curtain! Finally!"

She hesitated. "If we go."

"Why wouldn't we?"

"Well, it's on Wednesday."

"Yeah, a week from today. So? You can get off work, right?"

"Probably. But . . . isn't that the day after your premiere?"

"Oh, *crap*, you're right."

Fight on a Flight would be premiering that coming Tuesday, and since Richard was technically a credited producer, he would be walking the red carpet, a first for him. Per an arrangement made months ago, Mike was his plus one, but he had a second, optional invitation, and a few weeks earlier he'd asked Elizabeth, who was the only one of his friends who'd never been to a premiere. Keith would be there too, of course. All this fanfare for a movie he hadn't actually produced felt a little silly to him, which was why he hadn't invited his parents (it would have been ridiculous for them to fly out), but opportunities to show off in Hollywood were not to be missed. Celebrating oneself was practically a duty, and Richard couldn't afford to shirk it. He was sure to be massively sleep-deprived on Wednesday, if not hungover.

"Well, *you'll* still get a good night's sleep, right?"

"Right." Elizabeth had already told him she'd be going straight home after the movie.

"If you can drive us there in the morning, I promise to go easy. I'm not as much of a lush these days anyway, I swear. And then I'll definitely be okay to drive us back at night, cool?"

"I guess so."

"Hey, I'll skip the stupid premiere if I have to. There's *no way* we're not going."

At this point in the conversation, Elizabeth had moved from her office to the tiny kitchen down the hall. She opened the freezer, blindly grabbing two Smart Ones from among the handful of frozen dinners she kept there for late nights. She had at least a few more hours of work ahead of her, especially if she was going to take off a day in one week's time.

"It's not that. I just want to make sure nothing's changed." She slammed the freezer door shut. "With the payment schedule and everything."

"Oh, sure. Good point. Well, do you want to write back? For both of us?"

"I talked to him last time," she reminded him, peeling the plastic back on one of the dinner trays and tossing it in the microwave. "About reimbursement for the books and movies." She set it on high, the metal box humming to life.

"Exactly, and look how well that went. You two just get each other. It must be a lawyer thing." He paused, but she didn't respond. "Unless it goes deeper than that? I always thought I saw a spark between you two that afternoon. Have things gotten . . . uncomfortable? Did you say things that can't be unsaid? Has he—"

"Fine," said Elizabeth, ignoring the sound of what she wouldn't have thought was possible before getting to know Richard: a grown man actually *giggling*. "I'll write him back later tonight. Go read *Tess*." She clicked off.

RICHARD SHOVED HIS phone into his glove compartment, grinning. He glanced around him; how the hell had he gotten onto Hollywood Boulevard? He drove north to avoid the tourist mess surrounding the Hollywood & Highland complex like a stink cloud. It wasn't uncommon for him to get turned around like this while talking on the phone; Mike would have given him *such shit* if she were in the car with him. He made a right, heading east on Franklin. *What was she doing tonight?* he wondered idly. *Probably a work dinner, maybe a screening.* Everyone agreed that Mike was "killing it," though lately Richard had begun wondering whether "it" deserved such a violent end. He had nothing to do, not a single thing, but it was still early enough—a little after seven—to feel as if anything might happen tonight, though he was fairly certain nothing would.

The Magic Castle loomed into view on his left, a kitschy

mansion made of turrets and gables where magicians performed nightly in several different theaters. The venue was restricted to members and their guests, and it was one of the few places in L.A. with an actual dress code, but he could have ferreted out an invitation with a few phone calls, and dashed home for the lone suit collecting dust at the back of his closet. Nor was there anything stopping him from buying a last-minute ticket to a sketch comedy show at the Upright Citizens Brigade a little farther east, or driving north to the Griffith Park Observatory and checking out the moon through the big telescope there. Tonight, it was enough simply to have these options, so he stayed the course on Franklin, heading toward a quiet night at home.

What's happening to me? he asked himself. The question was only half-serious. Like many, Richard was accustomed to sudden, sporadic bouts of introversion: "alone time," as it was commonly known, though these days he found himself opting for it a bit more than sporadically. In truth, "these days" was an unnecessarily vague time frame; he knew exactly when things had begun changing for him—six weeks earlier, after Keith's birthday party. (He drove onto the Shakespeare Bridge, which traversed a dry and rather unimpressive ravine among the Franklin Hills. Because of the bridge's name, the tiny pointed cupolas on either end always reminded him of those peaked hats—like dunce caps—that women wore in *Romeo and Juliet* and other Renaissance-era plays.) For a few weeks, he gave up drinking entirely. His lean physique got leaner, the pounds sloughing off him so easily it was "offensive," according to Mike, at least. Even after falling off the wagon—because was there anything more dispiriting (*literally!*) than marking time in a bar or club without drinking?—he went easier than usual, calling himself out on his own vanity by joking that he needed to keep his "new figure." (While making a left onto St. George

Street, his stomach rumbled. What was he going to do for dinner?) Usually in September he made a point of growing out his annual "summer buzz cut," but this year he didn't feel like bothering with his hair and kept it short, thereby accentuating the deeper hollows of his concave cheeks, the newfound prominence of his already oversize eyes. His friends began calling him "Hot Monk," which was partly a putdown for his relative withdrawal from the social scene. It wasn't like he *never* went out, but when he did there was a reticence to him that had subtly yet unmistakably altered his standing within the group. Richard had always been the life of the party, the one who galvanized everyone else into action, but now he was merely a participant, and at times a halfhearted one at that. Mike, in particular, was beside herself, though she hadn't said anything to him yet. He hadn't even hooked up with anyone since August. Which was crazy.

He pulled into the Trader Joe's on Hyperion to pick up a prepackaged dinner. The parking lot, as usual, was totally backed up, and he eased into the line of cars waiting for a spot. There was no question the Retch Heard 'Round the World had been the watershed moment, not that this made much sense. The vomiting incident itself was already ancient history, and besides, it was exactly the sort of funny, self-deprecating story he normally would have loved to tell everyone who was willing to listen (except his parents), now that he was safely ensconced on the other side of it.

A topknotted hipster ambled toward a car parked a few feet ahead. Richard turned on his blinker. His newfound reserve was beginning to hurt his friends' feelings, and in the case of Keith it was beginning to damage their business relationship too. Richard had always been the one to urge them to meet new people, to read *just one more* script, even to attend those horrible "pitchfests" wherein crazy writers pitched their crazy ideas.

But his new Zen-like state (apparently Hot Monk was a Buddhist) extended to his career as well. (The hipster was just *sitting* in his car, probably Instagramming his groceries or something. Richard honked, giving him the same spread-armed "move!" gesture he himself had gotten earlier in the evening.) He'd lost the hustle that used to come so naturally to him, and up till now Keith had been too considerate to do more than inquire gently whether everything was "okay," but the winds of a serious talk were in the air; Richard could feel them. And he had no idea what he was going to say.

Mike, of course, had been more forceful—though less direct—in voicing her discontent with the new Richard. At the thought of her, Richard's stomach jerked in rhythm with the parking brake he yanked upward now (he'd finally parked, *hallelujah*). He had no idea what to do about Mike. There was no question he'd been avoiding her, and he felt terrible about it. But their friendship had been built on the notion that they were practically the same person, two halves of a whole, and it was disorienting to spend time with her now, they were so out of synch. It actually made him *uncomfortable* to see her. Richard sighed, whipping his phone out of his pocket to avoid eye contact with the do-gooder brandishing a clipboard outside the store. It was as though he'd reverted to the pre-Mike version of himself, a shy, quiet kid who was content to play video games with his equally shy and quiet best friend all afternoon until said best friend *died* and he spent most of his free time (as a senior in high school!) on long, silent nature walks with his mom. He couldn't believe he was turning into that kid again— and he wasn't, not by a long shot—yet something about reacquiring the elements of that teenage reticence felt *right* to him, like returning to his true self. But how could he ever explain any of this to Mike without hurting her? He didn't even fully understand it himself.

Richard checked his e-mail: nothing yet from Elizabeth. It was funny how these weekly sessions of theirs, which had begun as such an oddity, were now his only angst-free social engagement. Was that ironic? He was always scared to use that word, in case he was using it incorrectly. Elizabeth would know. It was actually a relief to focus on the continuing mystery of the Decent Proposal, especially now that they were finally going to get some answers. He didn't even mind pondering the enigma of Elizabeth herself anymore. They were friends now, it was true, but there was still a great deal he didn't understand about her, such as her estrangement from her family (old mystery), and her sweet yet bizarre friendship with that old black guy he'd met at her place (newer mystery). *What was her deal?* he asked himself, for what seemed like the thousandth time while drifting down the frozen food aisle. It had become an almost comforting question.

BEFORE FINISHING HER first Smart Ones, Elizabeth had e-mailed Amber Hudson, the partner in charge of the pharmaceuticals merger occupying most of her time, to ask about taking a personal day a week from today. She hated asking for time off; it always felt as if she were asking for a favor, even though the personal days were hers to use and she had weeks upon weeks of them accumulated from over the years.

She watched the second plastic tray rotate slowly inside the microwave's chemical-yellow glow. Her next e-mail would have to be to Jonathan Hertzfeld. She had told Richard she wanted to be sure the rules of the proposal hadn't changed, but she was reasonably sure the lawyer would have brought up any proposed amendments in his e-mail. Besides, they already had a signed contract. No; she couldn't pretend—to herself at least—that money was the source of her anxiety. The microwave beeped. She took out the tray, peeling back the plastic cover. It had taken almost two months since the action-packed weekend of the dance and the sleepover, but finally, *finally*, they'd fallen into a comfortable routine. The two hours that used to gape before them like a chasm were no longer so difficult to fill. Elizabeth scolded Richard about not reading *Tess*, but secretly it pleased her that they didn't need a book or movie to prolong their conversations anymore.

She broke through the tray's remaining layer of frost with a fork, stirring the gloopy contents underneath with a savagery the task did not require. Why did everything always have to *change*? It wasn't just the trip to the desert. She had no desire to attend this stupid premiere, either. *Fight on a Flight* was obviously the sort of brainless action movie she detested, but more important, the premiere on Tuesday would be another aberration, another opportunity to disturb the delicate balance they'd struck. Saying no would have been just as bad, though. She would have hurt his feelings. So she decided the best way to handle it would be to show up as late as possible and leave immediately after the movie. Plus, she had no desire to meet Drunk Richard again, or to say more than a few words to Mike, who surely hated her. Elizabeth noticed that Richard had stopped mentioning Mike after their meeting at Keith's birthday party, and guessed that Mike had voiced her displeasure with Elizabeth, and did so often, and loudly.

Elizabeth threw the dinner back in the microwave, setting it spinning once again. What was she going to wear to this premiere? Here was another source of anxiety; she knew she'd dressed too formally for Keith's birthday party, but people *had* to kick it up a notch for a premiere, didn't they? Even in L.A.? When she'd asked Richard, his eyes had gone vague and he'd said, "it doesn't really matter," which was about as helpful as she'd expected him to be. Her current plan was to wear the skirt he'd given her, but she'd already returned two tops to go with it. The whole thing was exhausting.

The microwave beeped again. Elizabeth used a wad of paper towels to remove the tray and cantered with the steaming, gooey mess back down the hallway. Shutting her door, she took a deep breath. As usual, she needed to calm down.

When she got behind her desk, she saw that Amber had e-mailed her back:

Pop into my office pls? Thx!

"Ugh!" Her assistant was gone for the day; no one else could hear her through the door. Why did everything always have to be so *difficult*? There was nothing she wanted less right now than a face-to-face chat, but there was no getting around it, so she rose from her desk and marched back down the hallway, past the kitchen, toward one of the plush corner offices on the other side of the elevator bank. This Band-Aid was getting ripped off. Now.

The door was open. She tapped a fingernail against its frame, jumping slightly when a child-sized woman in a tailored suit popped up behind an oversize computer monitor, like an impeccably dressed jack-in-the-box.

"Elizabeth! That was quick! Come in!"

Amber Hudson gestured frantically for Elizabeth to take a seat, the fortysomething partner's blond bob shimmering in the custom recessed lighting overhead. Elizabeth stepped inside, captivated for a moment by the view on high of Wilshire Boulevard's "Miracle Mile" captured behind Amber's desk. From here Los Angeles almost looked citylike, with high-rises leading toward the skyscrapers of downtown far, far in the distance. The partners' offices had all the best views.

Elizabeth sat on the edge of the hardest chair she could find, trying to convey without being rude whatever the opposite was of "settling in." A studio portrait of Amber with her husband and two small children stared her in the face. In the *highly* unlikely scenario that Elizabeth were ever to put a photo on her desk, she would at least have turned it inward so that she could see it from her desk. Wasn't that the point? But it made sense that Amber would turn hers outward; she loved to tell the story of how she met "the one" at thirty-eight and had two children with him by forty-two—all of this narrated as though by the survivor of some great peril narrowly escaped. Elizabeth didn't like Amber very much, but had to admit she was an excellent lawyer, who used her perky demeanor to her advantage against anyone foolish enough to patronize or underestimate her.

"I am *so glad* you reached out because I've been meaning to talk to you!" chirped Amber, collapsing into her big, comfy desk chair with an affected sigh and, to Elizabeth's horror, kicking off her heels and drawing up her little birdlike legs in one fluid motion. "*What* a day! So. First thing's first. *Of course* you can have your day off! You've been doing *such* great work, and *not* just for me. Everyone's always saying what a *rock star* you are!"

"Thank you," said Elizabeth uneasily. She was waiting for the "but."

"But I *did* want to bring up something with you. Something we noticed."

Elizabeth knew without asking that "we" meant the partners. She stiffened, as if in expectation of a blow.

Amber licked her cherry-painted lips, which were already quite moist, her tongue catching slightly on a sticky patch.

"Like I said, your work is *top-notch*, Elizabeth, as always, but we just did our third-quarter breakdowns and noticed your billables were *way* down from the same period last year."

A tight little wave of nausea shot through Elizabeth like a bullet. She had to restrain herself from visibly shuddering. She remembered this feeling from the handful of Bs she'd received over the course of a quarter century of school: a lethal little mixture of anger and shame poking at the lining of her stomach.

"By how much?" This came out more sharply than she intended.

"Twenty-nine percent." Amber shot this figure back without consulting so much as a piece of paper.

Elizabeth's stomach churned again; this was what she got for being an overachiever. Even now, at this reduced rate, she still had to be one of the top-billing associates in the firm.

Amber reached a tiny, infant-sized hand across the table. "You're *fine*, Elizabeth. It's not like you're in trouble or anything. We just wanted to make sure"—she offered up what was ostensibly a concerned smile—"everything was okay?"

How could she not have realized she was slipping? Elizabeth wished she could refute it, but now that she forced herself to think about it, *of course* her billables had plummeted. Between Orpheus and Richard, she hardly ever came in on Saturdays anymore, and her concentration when she *was* here had become undeniably less . . . concentrated.

What could she say? She had to say something. Amber could tell her she was "fine" all she wanted, but they both knew she wasn't by virtue of this conversation's existence.

"I recently started a new relationship," she said. Because it was true, wasn't it? Twice over.

"Oh!" Amber's wispy eyebrows lifted, and her red smile widened, turning jubilant. "How wonderful! *Well*, I'm not such an old married woman I can't still remember *those* days. You don't have to tell me!"

Elizabeth decided to take her at her word, and just stared at her.

"So what does he do?" asked Amber.

"Who?"

"Your boyfriend!"

Elizabeth paused while considering how to extricate herself from this mess in the quickest and cleanest way possible.

"Or girlfriend!" Amber squeaked, suddenly panicked. "Don't want to be heteronormative!"

"He's a film producer," Elizabeth said finally, not bothering to hide her annoyance.

"Ooh, *fun!*" Amber was relieved. "Anything I might know?"

"No," said Elizabeth. Surely this was almost over?

"What's his name?"

"Orpheus," she said, perhaps because she liked the idea of merging the two men who together were responsible for her inferior work product, or perhaps because it was less humiliating to make up someone who didn't exist than to pretend she was dating someone who did. Either way, she had forgotten what a crazy name "Orpheus" was.

"Oh, wow!" Amber's eyes widened disbelievingly. "*Love* that name!" she overcompensated.

At the very least, the weird name put a pall over Amber's enthusiasm, ending their conference sooner than it would have otherwise. Elizabeth promised to improve her time management skills, and Amber kept insisting everything was *fine*.

Elizabeth returned to her office. She closed her door again. Her Smart Ones was waiting for her where she'd left it on her desk, lukewarm and congealed. Behind it glared not-Rosie, the "We Can Do It!" woman. Elizabeth gave her the finger and sat down heavily, like a much older person. Hadn't she just been lamenting the way everything changed? Well, now she was going to have to embrace that change. And it wasn't just a simple matter of reverting to the singularly focused La Máquina; she had other obligations now, to Orpheus in particular, which couldn't be ignored. And yet she refused to let her career founder; she would not, could not fail. Why was it that when people like Amber talked about "having it all," they assumed everyone *wanted* it all in the first place? In this moment, as she shoved a forkful of whatever the hell it was she was eating past her lips, she wanted none of it.

MIKE NEVER REMEMBERED her dreams. She had read somewhere this was a common effect among those who enjoyed deep, untroubled sleep, which is why it made sense that in the few seconds before she woke from her neck-cramping doze on the fainting couch, she found herself inside a surprisingly lifelike vision.

She was in the church she attended every Sunday in Koreatown. Richard was there too, which made no sense, but then, it was a dream; sense wasn't really part of the deal. Even though she couldn't picture the individual faces, she knew everyone important to her was there, including her parents. Richard was looking out at the crowd, and when he turned to her, he smiled, and all her problems—her current physical discomfort, the pit that even as she slept pulsated steadily inside her like a second heart, the ever-present anxiety she felt over her father's failing health—all this *crap* lifted away from her, magically, like a stain in some dumb commercial for laundry detergent. Richard crooked his arm for her to take, and even though he was wearing the same jeans-and-polo outfit he'd worn to Keith's birthday party, Mike knew suddenly what this was. *No.* She couldn't say the word, not even to herself, and all the hurt and anxiety, the shame and pain seeped back inside her, staining her indelibly. She opened her mouth to protest, and from out of the hole spilled everything that had been growing inside her, everything that had sprouted from that hideous pit, except now it was growing ten or maybe a hundred times faster—uncontrollably, relentlessly, like Jack's beanstalk, assuming a life of its own and twisting, plaguelike, to the vaulted ceiling, blotting out the light from the multicolored windows and scattering the panicked crowd like extras in a disaster movie. Swept up by their movement, Richard threw out his arm for her, his delight transformed to horror as the tide of human flesh carried him away . . . until he became no more than a pinprick of light at the edge of her vision. Moments later he disappeared altogether. And then there was nothing but darkness.

Mike struggled to open her eyes, but it was impossible to move her eyelids or any other part of her body. For what felt like ages she remained pinned to the couch, an insect in its case, the agony of this claustrophobic sensation silently consuming her. Finally, with a superhuman effort, she managed to jerk one of her legs, thereby freeing the rest of her body like a spring releasing a lock.

Her eyes snapped open. She nearly screamed. Peaches was peering over her, inches from her face, and from below all Mike could see was the salt-and-pepper bob and a single, narrowed eye, like one of those hairy ghost-monsters in a Japanese horror movie. It was the perfect epilogue to Mike's fever-dream-turned-nightmare.

"Keys!" the monster screeched.

Mike dug her hand into her pocket without getting up, forking over the entire set. She watched Peaches painstakingly extricate the Jeep Wrangler fob from the larger ring, and when the phrase *one good fob deserves another* popped into her head, she heard laughter, unaware until after the fact that it was hers. *I'm still drunk*, Mike realized. *Very drunk.*

Peaches thrust the rest of the keys back into her hand and gestured, glaring, for Mike to get up, which somehow she did, following the old woman back through the tropical courtyard, down the front path, and out toward a taxi idling next to her car.

Mike tumbled into the cab, slumping against the far window. She supposed she must have given the driver her address, but she didn't remember a thing about the ride home except for when she tried to pay, realizing she'd left her wallet—her whole bag, in fact—inside her car. As it turned out, it didn't matter. The driver had already been paid in advance.

The next morning was torture, but Mike told herself she deserved every thwack on the side of her head (she imagined a giant spoon prizing open her skull like a hard-boiled egg), every fiery burst of pain shooting through her ruined gut (she pictured the fires of Mordor bubbling inside her). She pulled on gym shorts and an old T-shirt, dreading the inevitable return to the scene of the crime. But she had to get her car back.

A tiny gray envelope lay on the floor, just inside her front door. She stared at it, puzzled. All the units in her building had mail slots rendered vestigial years ago by mailboxes installed in the lobby. One of her neighbors must have left her a note. Had she made too much noise coming in last night? This portion of the evening was hazy at best.

It took a good half minute to retrieve the envelope from the floor. Inside it was her car fob and nothing else—not even a slip of paper. *The hell?* Mike shambled outside, nearly vomiting up the few gulps of water she'd managed thus far to keep down.

There it was on the curb: her locked and lovely car, everything exactly as she'd left it except for her driver's license, which had been removed from her wallet and placed on her dashboard, no doubt for the purpose of finding her address. It was a little creepy, but it was also the best possible thing that could have happened to her in this moment.

Mike would never know that it was Peaches who had acted alone, without Beverly's consent or even her knowledge. Bev was feeling the effects of their binge that morning too, and for an eighty-something heiress a hangover was an all-encompassing debilitation.

Mike hobbled back inside, e-mailed her boss and assistant a message titled

Mike Sick Today ☹

and arranged a moist towel, a bottle of Excedrin, and a jug of water within arm's reach of her sofa. She drew down the blinds and assumed a horizontal position, pulling a throw blanket to her waist. It was time to commence channel surfing, which for her was the best hangover cure, and an excellent form of meditation.

Her adventure with Beverly Chambers had been a genuine adventure, but there was no takeaway (she zoomed past an episode of *Oprah's Master Class*), no "aha" moment to use as her mantra moving forward. She still didn't even know why Richard and the DP had been chosen. *What a waste of time,* she thought, spending a few minutes on an old episode of *Sex and the City,* the one where Miranda learns the power of the phrase *he's just not that into you.* Mike grunted; now *there* was a mantra. She flipped the channel, astonished to land on *He's Just Not That Into You* the movie, and grunted again—at the notion of the universe sending her a message cloaked in such cheap and shoddy garments. Could it really be true that all her issues with Richard were reducible to this trite little saying? It was a depressing thought, and she was happy to let go of it by drifting into a deeper sleep than she'd been able to achieve the night before.

When she woke up, it was early afternoon and her head

and stomach were still throbbing, but less so than in the morning. (The pit, of course, maintained its presence unabated.)
She took three Excedrin, drank half the jug of water, and had
no trouble keeping it all down. With the towel draped over
her forehead, she lay back again and picked up where she had
left off. If he just wasn't that into her, if he wanted nothing to
do with her anymore, she would be devastated, she would be
heartbroken, but she would at least *know*. As unthinkable as
life without Richard was, Mike still had enough self-regard
to imagine herself moving forward, to long for an end to her
present, painful uncertainty no matter the consequences. It
wasn't as if she didn't have any other friends. And even though
many of them were friends she held in common with Richard,
she was confident they'd choose her if it came down to it, especially after Richard's gradual disappearing act over the last
few months. Ally, for example, had recently announced she
was "over Richard" in general.

Through the fog of drunken memory, Beverly Chambers
resounded inside her head: *I know you'll figure it out. And do what
needs to be done.*

There was only one thing to do. There had really only ever
been one thing to do, as awful as it was guaranteed to be. But
how? And when?

By the time Mike peeled the towel from her forehead and
padded into the kitchen to make herself some toast, she'd
formed a plan, and for the next six days she conducted her
affairs with a machinelike efficiency. Almost every free minute was spent at church or the gym, both of which involved
the same rhythm of emotions for her: a reluctance beforehand brought on by a sense of duty rather than pleasure com-
pelling her to go, the realization when she was there that it
wasn't as bad as she'd been dreading—that she actually sort
of enjoyed it—and the glorious feeling afterward of accom-

plishment, of having done something good for herself at no one else's expense. These were the only two places she could go and be certain she wouldn't regret it. And Mike was done with regrets.

A few days before the premiere, she texted Richard to ask him if he wanted a ride to the theater.

Hellz yes

he wrote back. She had been counting on his eagerness to avoid driving on what would surely be an inebriated evening, but what he didn't realize was that he would be her captive for the time it took to get from his apartment to the theater. He would also be nervous, hence vulnerable, and more easily trapped into having what others (not her, never her) would have called a "heart-to-heart."

A little after seven on Tuesday night, Mike turned onto Rowena Avenue, dressed in jeans and a blazer—a more informal outfit than she normally would have worn to her (alleged) best friend's (technical) first premiere, but there was a good chance that fifteen minutes from now she would no longer be attending said premiere, and it had felt like jinxing herself to fully commit to dressing for the event. It had been more than three weeks since she'd last seen Richard, on a crowded Friday night at the Griffin in Atwater Village, to celebrate a mutual friend's promotion. Before the DP, three weeks apart from Richard would have been inconceivable. Mike's hands began to shake as she pulled up to the curb outside his building. She placed them on the St. Christopher statue to steady herself and recited a quick prayer.

He came out wearing a new suit. It was charcoal gray: sleek and stylish. He'd never looked so handsome, and her stomach lurched at the sight of him, the pit's leafy offshoots growing another inch. When he got into the car she detected a hint of the cologne she knew he wore only on special occasions.

"Hey, stranger," he said, halfway apologetically, and she nearly abandoned her plan while pulling wordlessly into the street. In this moment she could have easily vomited all over the car. She remembered suddenly a skydiving excursion with a handful of her church friends a month into college: it had been her idea, an attempt to prove she'd hatched from her parents' protective cocoon, though in hindsight this fruitless gesture was proof of her ongoing immaturity. She remembered peering outside the Plexiglas window of the airplane and looking down, down, down to the grassy field below. It was absurd to think she was about to jump, to hurtle to the ground, and yet she *knew* she was going to do it because she was no wuss. *No guts, no glory*, she told herself then. And when it was over and she was high-fiving her friends in the grassy field below, she was glad she'd done it. Would she feel the same way a few minutes from now?

The pit mushroomed inside her. She imagined an exploratory tendril curling up the back of her throat, tickling the roof of her mouth. She had to swallow to keep from gagging. *Enough*, she thought. *No guts, no glory.*

And she dove.

"So I have something to say and you have to just let me say it all at once."

"Okay?"

He sounded amused, and curious, with an edge of faux fear. It was vintage Richard, and she had to resist the urge to look at him one last time before passing the point of no return. Her eyes remained glued to the road.

"I'm in love with you. I've been in love with you for years, probably ever since college, even though I didn't realize it till the DP showed up."

She glanced at him, unable to help herself. His eyes were clouded over with what looked like a mixture of confusion and alarm. The pit rocked her stomach and she imagined it sprouting babies, a hundred little tumors feasting on her insides. She felt dizzy, and realized the one flaw in her plan was that she had to keep driving throughout this ordeal. She considered pulling over, but decided this would only make the whole episode more humiliating. Some foolish, girlish part of her had hoped that her confession would inspire an immediate and corresponding profession of love from him. *Just finish it, you idiot.*

She made a right on Fountain.

"I just felt like—like I needed to tell you how I felt. I just—I guess—I needed to clear the air or whatever, as your, your friend"—she had wanted to say "best friend" but she wasn't even sure this was true anymore—"since the air's been pretty . . . muggy? Between us lately?"

You sound like a moron. But she was almost done. The grassy field was rising to meet her; she could practically feel the blades tickling her palms.

"I still feel really bad about Keith's party. I should've gone with you to the hospital, but I was pissed at you because the DP, Elizabeth, asked about my dad when we were alone for a second. So I know you told her about him, and it's fine, it's fine, I'm not angry about it anymore. But I sort of went crazy when I found out, because it felt like—maybe this sounds stupid, but—it felt like you *betrayed* me or something, and like maybe we weren't as close as I thought we were? And that feeling's only gotten worse and I just—I guess I thought it was important to tell you how I was feeling, no matter what *you* might be feeling."

This was his cue to jump in, but he didn't say a word.

"So, that's all."

He was just sitting there: motionless, staring through the windshield.

"I'm sorry I sprang this on you tonight, I just—I had to get it off my chest." *Wanna use another cliché, dipshit?* "It's probably better if I just drop you off at the theater."

Mike lapsed into a wounded silence. Was he really not going to say anything? Or even look at her? She managed to endure half a block's worth of tedious start-and-stop traffic before giving in to the tears she could no longer hold back. She realized this was the second time inside of a week she was crying in front of another person, and that this had never happened to her before, excepting of course her parents. At the thought of *them* she cried even harder, the salt water dribbling down her nose and pooling with the snot bubbling from her nostrils. She had to pull over after all, at Fountain and La Brea.

She began fumbling miserably for a tissue in the pocket of her door.

"Why did you break up with me?"

His voice startled her; it was strained, and small, and utterly unlike him—not vintage Richard at all, but a Richard she'd never heard before. She turned to him. He still wasn't looking at her, but at least he was talking.

"What?" she asked, even though she'd heard him perfectly.

"At the end of college. Why did you break up with me?"

"Because I was an idiot?" She shrugged helplessly. "I was twenty-one, I didn't realize what we had. I regret it now. Obviously."

He nodded slowly. "I should've been honest with you back then," he said, "like you were with me just now. But I didn't have the guts."

He turned to her:

"When you broke up with me, I thought my life was over."

Mike's stomach flipped, pit and all, and her throat constricted and her diaphragm spasmed in what would have been another sob if she had let it out because, against all odds, the hope returned: *he's about to say he loves me.*

"I thought I loved you."

Hm, not quite.

"And when we moved to L.A. I tried to stay away from you. Which lasted about two seconds. And at first when we started hanging out again, I still felt the same way, I just didn't tell you. But after a while . . ."

He let out a sigh, and Mike knew this tiny sound was the death knell of all her hopes.

"I moved on."

So this was her reward for pressing the issue: forcing the love of her life to tell her he was over her. *You stupid bitch,* she thought. *Now can you get it through your fucking head? He's just not that into you.* She could feel the snot hardening above her lip; it felt exactly like the one time she'd had her mustache waxed.

"Mike, you did the right thing breaking up with me—"

"Do you love her?" she asked. Because why not? She might as well get it all out. This car-ride confessional had officially become a shitshow.

"What . . . Elizabeth? No! Of course not, don't be crazy."

Was he lying to her? Or to himself? *It doesn't matter,* she thought wearily, unearthing the soft-packet of tissues at last. *He doesn't love me.*

"Do you want to know why I told her about your dad?"

Mike shrugged her shoulders, tending to her viscous mouth and nose area. *Sure. Whatever.*

"I was telling her what I want to do with the rest of the money, after I pay off all my stupid bills."

"Huh?" (This came out more like *Mmph?* behind the tissue.)

"I know you're still trying to figure out a way to pay your dad's medical bills, and make sure he gets the best care. I want to help you."

Mike's hand shot out, palm to the sky, in a *WTF?* gesture she was about to make explicit, but before she could find the words his fingers closed over hers and he wrenched her toward him:

"You're family, Mike. You're my best friend. And that will never, *ever* change."

And then, Richard did something Mike knew she would never forget. Silly, sloppy, sarcastic, self-conscious Richard Baumbach cupped her face with both his hands and placed his thumbs underneath her eyes to catch the fresh tears that had begun falling there, yet again. He tilted his face toward hers, no more than an inch or two away so that it was all she could see, and said:

"I love you."

It wasn't everything she wanted—not even close. But the *pit*, that pulsating putrescence, its roots, its shoots, its leafy outgrowths: suddenly, it was gone. Banished. Excised. Obliterated. It was a miracle, except that it wasn't, because everything was simply back to where it used to be. She and Richard were best friends, and nothing would ever part them. The word came to her like a memory from long ago, though she'd only known it for a week: *CharBev.*

Mike dried her eyes, pulling into the street and zooming west on Fountain.

"You're crazy if you think I'm taking your money like that," she said, weaving between lanes, provoking more than a few honks and gestures from the vehicles around them. "But we'll discuss it later."

And then it happened. The honks and gestures, as it turned out, were *not* due to her bad driving, but to Angelyne, who pulled up next to them at the next light in her pink Corvette. Richard and Mike looked over in unison, as if they were starring together in a music video, and Angelyne—who was significantly older than in her billboard days but still unmistakably herself—winked at them before taking off up Fairfax with a flash of metal and a screech of rubber.

They looked at each other, delighted. It had felt like a benediction.

THERE WAS A spacious patio in front of the DGA Theater on Sunset ideal for the flamboyant celebration required of a film premiere, especially if this flamboyance had to be obtained at bargain rates. Much grander, more classic venues lay to the north on Hollywood Boulevard (the Egyptian, the Chinese, the El Capitan), but for a movie like *Fight on a Flight*, whose budget had been cobbled together from "independent," nonstudio entities and the sale of distribution rights in foreign territories, the DGA offered a smaller, cheaper, yet perfectly respectable alternative for the U.S. distributor footing the bill. By the time Richard and Mike arrived, a crowd had gathered on the terrace of the Coffee Bean across the street and on the sidewalk behind a velvet rope. In the center of the patio a half-scale jet dominated the space, the words FIGHT ON A FLIGHT! stamped across its nose in big block letters. Mike led the way toward the will-call table, which had been done up to look like an airline counter. Behind it, a busty woman dressed as the platonic ideal of a flight attendant (tight skirt, perky cap, scarf tied tightly round her throat) checked their names and handed them two laminated "boarding passes" to the show. A second flight attendant told them to enjoy their *fight*, while indicating the way past the rope with her thumb and two fingers.

"Wow, they really went all out on the airplane theme, huh?" said Mike, accepting a tiny pair of plastic wings from a man she guessed was supposed to be a pilot, though his bushy mustache, skimpy costume, and sultry demeanor made him look more like a pilot in a porno.

"Want me to pin you?" he asked her huskily.

"Uh, I'm good," she said, thrusting the wings in Richard's direction. "He'll do it."

The pilot slunk away, while Richard fumbled with her lapel.

"Now isn't this *romantic*," purred Keith, who had glided behind them without a noise.

"Oh, Keith, you have *no* idea," Mike purred back, before taking pity on Richard, who was getting nowhere with the plastic button. "Here, let me do it."

She pinned it herself.

"Sorry," said Richard.

"No worries. I'm pretty sure I already asked enough of you for one night."

Keith looked from one to the other, intrigued. "What on earth did I miss?"

"You don't want to know, Keith," said Mike. "Well, you do. But we aren't going to tell you."

Richard shook his head at her, but he was smiling.

"I know, I know," said Mike. "I'm incorrigible."

Just then the crowd erupted in a cheer. A hulking figure had emerged from a stretch SUV: Duke Rifferson, the star of the show! He answered the screaming multitudes with a low, rumbling growl. (In the TV promos that had been airing for a week or two, he made the same noise while squaring off with the lead terrorist in the cargo hold, and then delivered the film's tagline: *You're gonna feel a little turbulence.*)

"OMG, he's so effing hot."

Richard turned: it was Keith's plus one, Raoul, who Richard knew from prior meddling was only a friend. In fact, Keith confessed once to Richard that they weren't even *real* friends, merely *social* friends who relied on each other for company at bars and clubs, where the hypersexualized jargon and exaggeratedly effeminate mannerisms Raoul apparently felt were required to maintain his good standing as a gay man were less jarring than in moments like this. Richard threw Keith a commiserating glance, wondering for the hundredth time why his business partner didn't have a boyfriend.

Raoul tore open a miniature packet of peanuts acquired from another "flight attendant" wandering the area. He watched, practically drooling, as Duke bent over to shake a child's hand, visibly straining the seat of his tuxedo pants.

"That's right," he stage-whispered, shoving a handful of peanuts into his mouth. "Put on a show."

"All right," said Keith, wresting the peanuts from him. "Ah'm cuttin' you off."

"Well, from what I hear, Raoul," said Richard, "you might have a shot with him. Not that I have any *real* insider information."

"Nah, I'm pretty sure he's not smart enough to be gay *and* pretend he isn't," said Mike.

"Mike, I think that's the *nah*-cest thing you ever said." Keith beamed at her.

"What can I say? I'm simply overflowing with love tonight, right, Dick?"

Mike batted her eyelashes at Richard, who shook his head again. A few minutes later, he and Keith joined a separate line for those walking the red carpet, which was at the far end of the patio. Much to Raoul's dismay, they couldn't bring their plus ones with them. The procession was reserved for those directly involved in the film, as well as those celebrities whose presence added to the fanfare. A publicity assistant with a headset jammed over her frizzy hair herded them into a corral-like staging area bounded by low metal barriers. Richard felt like a bucking bronco about to be released into the rodeo, and looked nervously ahead of him at what lay in store.

As it turned out, the red carpet was neither red nor a carpet: it was more of a gray tarp meant to look like a runway, with a dotted white line running down the middle. Enormous white lights had been installed on temporary posts running the length of the gauntlet, and they were so bright—even from a distance—as to nearly blind him. It reminded him of a construction site lit up at nighttime, and he realized that all the cracks and crags, the minute imperfections that existed inside regular human faces, would be washed away in any photos snapped under such bright lights. But in person, it made for a garish rather than a glamorous effect.

Behind the carpet stood a canvas wall he knew was called the "step-and-repeat," adorned by logos for a beer company and discount clothing store that had nothing to do with the movie, but must have helped pay for the premiere and after party. Richard had to admit that these corporate symbols took something away from the supposed stateliness of the elegantly dressed figures parading in front of them, though he couldn't blame the step-and-repeat entirely: from what he could hear while inching closer to the front of the line, it was pure chaos out there. *Fight on a Flight* featured a number of cameos from action stars young and . . . less young, and the fans who had shown up to see them were apparently the rabid kind who rent their hair and shrieked when their idols came into view.

"Sounds like the Beatles out there," he muttered to Keith, who smiled sickly in response. The photographers weren't making things any better: they kept screaming out celebrities' names for a head turn or a better angle ("Bruce!" "Jackie!" "Over here!" "Com'on, Sly!" "Gimme a smile, Arnold!" etc.). Before he had time to really process all this—he wasn't ready, he wished they'd warned him!—he was pushed into the light, Keith stumbling after him.

The photographers closest to them rested their cameras on their shoulders, assuming a posture of indifference it was impossible not to take personally. Then Richard made the mistake of looking directly into one of the lights, and for the next few seconds he couldn't see a thing. Someone grabbed his hand and pulled him farther down the tarp. He blinked, and heard a few photographers ask, "Who are *they*?" And then he heard Mike shouting from the great beyond, "They're producers on the movie! Rising stars! Get a shot while you still can! Woot!"

The photographers chuckled, and snapped a few photos out of goodwill. "Do a pose!" Mike shouted. He and Keith did an ill-coordinated fist bump, which got a few more flashes. The hand, which Richard could now see belonged to the harried publicity assistant, pulled him farther down the line until they reached a bottleneck caused by the three Chrises (Pratt, Evans, and Pine) monkeying around at the end of the carpet. The photographers all scrambled to get a better shot of these hunky hijinks, and instead of waiting, Richard casually jumped the barrier between the carpet and the patio, where no photographers were blocking his way. He helped Keith over after him.

His first red carpet experience was over. *And probably my last*, he thought. Richard knew that if he said this aloud, Keith would protest and tell him not to be such a pessimist, but was the notion of his Hollywood "career" coming to an end even all that depressing to him anymore?

Mike and Raoul joined them.

"So that happened," Mike said.

"Yup," said Richard. "Somehow it managed not to live up

to even my extremely low expectations." He glanced around him. All these trappings that had enticed him from afar looked downright dingy, now that he could see them properly. Rocky himself was standing not quite twenty feet away, but he was disconcertingly short and old in person. Richard found to his surprise that he had no desire to go up to him. What would be the point? There was no way to have anything approaching a substantive conversation in this environment. It was all so *stupid*, so *unimportant*. He still loved movies, but what he really loved was *watching* them, dissecting them, discussing them, not—it was time to face the fact—making them. And yet what the hell else would he do if not this? He was about to suggest they find the bar when he happened to glance back at the red carpet.

A new figure had appeared.

Elizabeth was the harried publicity assistant's one mistake. After collecting her ticket, she had stood at the entrance, uncertain where to go, when a sweaty hand grabbed her by the elbow and guided her to the red carpet queue. "Wait here, it won't be long," the curly-haired woman had told her, turning away and barking into her headset before Elizabeth could say a word.

The assistant thought she was an actress who had RSVP'd, but as it turned out, the actress never showed. Elizabeth thought she was lining up to get into the theater, and when she saw where the line led, she figured everyone had to cross the red carpet. For someone who had never been to a premiere before, this made perfect sense.

Richard caught sight of her the exact moment she stepped into the lights. She was dressed in pale purple—violet, or maybe lilac—in a gown made of the thinnest material, and cinched by a belt that obviously hadn't come with the dress, but which was the perfect accessory to showcase her figure. The dress was strapless, and cascaded inward from the bust, underneath the belt, and out again over her hips in a perfect hourglass, with a modest train trailing elegantly on the floor. Her hair had been professionally treated to lie flatter than usual, and it tumbled down one side of her face in gentle, undulating waves: the Latina version of Venus on the half shell, Sophia Loren by way of Veronica Lake. A small white orchid peeked from behind her left ear. She smiled nervously. Bright red lipstick highlighted her perfect teeth, and bold black eyeliner brought out her soft brown eyes.

The only person behind her was Duke Rifferson, the grand finale of the procession, who made no attempt to hide his appreciation of her backside despite the waifish model hanging off his arm. The photographers, who were done with the Chrises by this point, all jockeyed for position around her. One of them whistled.

"Who you wearing, darling?"

Elizabeth blinked. She couldn't see a thing, and wasn't even sure the comment had been meant for her.

"In the purple! Miss Vavavavoom. Who you wearing?" the photographer repeated.

"I don't know," she replied to the abyss. And this was true. The dress was a vintage purchase at a Beverly Hills boutique; there was no name on the label. The photographers laughed, snapping hundreds of useless photos, yelling "Babe!" and "Angel!" because they had no idea who she was, though they had no doubt she was someone special.

Before long they moved on to Duke Rifferson and his girlfriend, with whom they would be occupied for a while. There was plenty of time for Elizabeth to join the others before going into the theater. She saw Richard first, waiting with Mike, and Keith, and some other man—Keith's boyfriend, she guessed—and even though she sensed she'd overdressed for the occasion *yet again* (was Mike wearing *jeans?*), she knew that this time she'd made a good impression.

"How did you get on the red carpet?" Raoul hissed at her by way of introduction.

"Oh! I thought everyone . . . I don't know. They just put me there, I guess."

He almost spat at her.

"Well, I'm not surprised. You look amazing, Eliza*beth*," said Keith, looking her up and down.

"You look awesome," Richard supplemented, even though he wasn't so sure. She sort of looked like she was wearing a costume; she looked nothing like herself. And yet he had to admit she was pulling it off.

Elizabeth smiled at them gratefully. "Well, don't tell *me*," she said, gesturing to Mike, who was looking at the ground.

"What do you mean?" said Keith.

"You didn't tell them?" asked Elizabeth.

Mike shook her head, fascinated by her shoes.

"Mike put all this together." Elizabeth pointed to her head, and Richard watched her finger trail downward, past her breasts and waist, coming to a rest on her hip. "She called me up a few days ago and took me out on Sunday. She put together the whole thing: the dress, the shoes, the makeup. She even booked an appointment with a hairstylist. Who was great, by the way," she added to Mike.

"He did me proud," said Mike, whose distressingly awkward Sunday afternoon with Elizabeth was the one chunk of time in the last six days she hadn't devoted to work, sleep, church, or the gym. It had come to her while she was praying. She'd quelled the "Project!" urge for too long. It had been time to start thinking about someone other than herself.

Mike caught Keith staring at her. He looked away, smirking. She turned instinctively to Richard to share a *can you believe this shit?* look with him, knowing full well he wouldn't be looking at her, except—and forget that whole thumbs-under-the-eyes thing from earlier in the car, forget Angelyne, because *this* was the moment she would never forget, one of the greatest of her life—he *was* looking at her, he was looking *directly* at her, and never had she felt so recognized, appreciated, beautiful.

God, how she loved him.

"Let's go inside," Keith said finally to the group.

"I'll meet up with you guys," said Mike.

MIKE LINGERED THERE, alone, and for all purposes bereft, except that she felt too joyous to shut herself inside a dark theater just yet. She wished her parents could have been there to witness the events of the previous hour. They would have been so proud. . . . Mike saw stars; her ears rang; she felt dizzy but she steadied herself because she didn't want to miss a moment of this. She felt it now too—this glorious pride—and not the bad kind, which was just another form of vanity, but the earned kind, the ennobling kind—the ultimate reward for a job well done, so much better than the tit-for-tat of karmic retribution. She felt that if her father were to die tomorrow it would still be too soon, it would *always* be too soon, but she could at least look him in the eye and tell him with an honest heart that she was happy, she was complete.

There was still one thing left to do. Mike had promised herself she would do it if everything worked out for her on this day, and though things hadn't gone exactly according to plan, she felt she owed it to the universe—why hide it now? to God, to *Jesus*—to follow through on her intentions to the last possible degree.

Mike sank to one knee in the middle of the pavement and bowed her head in prayer: a full-on bout of Tebowing that was the furthest thing from the spontaneous gesture it was meant to be. She was actually thankful when the harried publicity assistant hurried over to her, headset askew, reaching out the same sweaty hand that had been maneuvering celebrities all night.

"Please tell me you're okay," the assistant pleaded, towering over her.

"I'm fine," said Mike, crossing herself before accepting the proffered hand.

"What happened, did you faint?"

"I just tripped, and fell for a second," she said, pulling herself to her feet. "But see? I'm up again."

Mike brushed off her knees and headed into the theater.

THE CASTLE

SCOTTY'S CASTLE WAS not a castle, and the Scotty in question did not design, build, or even own it. Scotty was a con man who convinced millionaires to buy land in Death Valley on the promise that it was teeming with gold. Mines were dug at great expense, but no gold appeared; nothing piled up except the years, during which something unexpected happened: Scotty made a friend. Unlike all the other dupes who talked of suing him—or worse—the Chicago insurance millionaire Albert Johnson continued stubbornly to believe in Scotty, and together they continued exploring the land for gold. Over time, their outings became less about searching for a precious metal they would never find, and more about appreciating each other's company and the natural wonders around them.

Death Valley was much the same then as it is today. A vast valley of flat plains, it lies so low on the surface of the Earth that it constitutes the lowest point in all of North America: almost

300 feet below sea level. Enclosing these plains are gray and purple mountains that trap the sun-warmed air and send it rolling back to the plains to be heated over, and over, and over again. In summer, the temperature routinely hits 115 degrees. No one who visits Death Valley wonders how it acquired its name. And yet it is no wasteland: it has a meandering creek in which pupfish populations leftover from the last ice age have adapted and survived; a crusty white salt basin that occasionally becomes a saltwater lake in rainy winters; golden sand dunes; fields of yellow flowers that bloom in spring; abstract rock formations carved into mountain faces and painted with mineral splotches of color; and many other natural phenomena.

In the 1920s, Johnson built a Spanish Colonial villa so that his wife could join him in comfort and style. It was made to look like a desert castle, with Anglo-Saxon architectural motifs adapted to the American Southwest. Instead of guards in suits of armor, two giant cacti flanked a wooden portcullis painted red, with curling iron flourishes fixed inside each latticed square. The walls and towers were the color of sand, and made of stucco. From a notched battlement flew an American flag in place of a knight's pennant. Red Mission tiles created specially to withstand the sizzling desert heat capped off this ridiculous yet impressive monstrosity. There was even supposed to be a pool (the Jazz Age equivalent to a moat), but before he could install it, Johnson discovered that the government owned the land the house had been built on. Scotty had either made a mistake or purposely misled him; his tract lay farther north. It took years for Johnson to legally acquire the land in question, and by then the Great Depression had bankrupted his insurance company like all the others. The pool was not to be. Most people dismissed the millionaire as a fool for continuing to associate with a known huckster, but by then the friendship was sealed, and Johnson let Scotty live in the castle for the remainder of his life.

The Chambers family owned a desert estate near Johnson's. As a girl, Beverly was forced to spend extended weekends there, and while she relished the extreme heat—as she did all extreme things—the desert held few other distractions for her. Even with Charlotte there it took only a few hours for her and her brother Tom to begin fighting. Their father, "Big Stan," was constantly taking them out on neighborly visits as a way of forcing them to behave (they knew better than to act out in front of strangers), and they spent many an afternoon at Scotty's Castle this way. Stan grew fond of the place, and at some point in the fifties he got it into his head to build a replica. Beverly, who was a young woman by then, convinced him to at least build this embarrassment where no one could see it from the public road, and never tell anyone about it. She said every great family should have a secret, and Stan was tickled by the idea of a hideaway.

The only difference between Scotty's Castle and its secret twin, Stan's Castle, was the tiled swimming pool Beverly Chambers stood staring at now from a window on the second-story landing. It was gorgeous, less a watery oasis than a second sun, as bright and glittering as its skyward companion but with the added attraction of refreshment. Bev had inherited the house from her father, and for decades "that vulgar castle" (as CharBev always referred to it) had lain unused. But in her old age, Bev discovered she had a measure of affection for it, as she did for anything that had managed to survive from long ago, and she spent at least a few weeks there each year, usually between the months of October and April.

The sun's glare began to overwhelm her. She looked away, puffing on her latest Parlie. A dirt road stretched from the entrance through a series of rolling hills to the public roadway, scores of miles in the shimmering distance. *Shimmering, and not even noon yet.* The desert heat still fascinated her. As a girl, she loved how the sweat under her arms would evaporate before it even had a chance to settle. Out here, it was as if the Earth's atmosphere didn't exist—as if there were nothing between her and the heavens above. If she were religious (as Albert Johnson had been), this might have made her feel closer to God, but instead it always made her think about alien abductions, how easy it would be for a vessel to materialize out of the endless sky and snatch her from this desolate landscape. It was no coincidence, she always thought, that both Roswell and Area 51 were located in the American Southwest. The desert revealed how empty the world really was. In more reasonable climates, nature at least gave the illusion of providing cover, and in towns and cities people could crowd together and pretend they weren't powerless. But there was no pretense out here, no semblance of comfort, or false impression of safety. There was simply . . . nothing.

A distant noise intruded on her reverie. Bev's consciousness returned to the world like a swimmer rising to the surface of the pool outside—breaching the liquid coolness of interiority for the dry, blazing heat of shared reality. What *was* that noise? Of course: it was the faraway whirring of a car engine. She couldn't see them yet, but they were close. This was always how it was in Death Valley; sound traveled unimpeded over the flat land and through the crystalline air, over distances greater than the eye could see. In the desert, hearing was the more reliable sense.

They were early, which surprised her. What happened to young people being fashionably late? In their day CharBev were never on time for anything. There were a few things she still had to do. Bev turned to Peaches, who was brushing up her latest trail of ashes inches from her feet:

"Stop fussing, Peaches, and help me down the stairs."

She stuck out her arm and wiggled her fingers impatiently. It was absurd, but at some point in the last week, during the aftermath of her hangover from her binge with Mike Kim, Bev had lost the ability to go up or down the stairs without assistance.

Peaches had tried to convince her to use a cane, but she refused. Decrepitude was officially a bore.

IT WAS RICHARD, not Elizabeth, who was responsible for the early start. As it turned out he celebrated well into the night of the premiere with a number of friends, but no one more so than Mike. They did a series of shots (he lost count somewhere around six or seven) in honor of "Mikard," a word that became funnier to them the more they said it, which happened to coincide with the more they drank. They both had to Uber it home, and it wasn't till well past 2 a.m. when a Lincoln Town Car ambled down Rowena, stopped a moment, and ejected a stumbling Richard onto the curb like a garbage truck emptying itself into a landfill. He was just sober enough to remember Elizabeth was picking him up at seven sharp. His head ached already; he knew he would be massively hungover in the morning and threw himself into bed in the desperate attempt to get a few hours of sleep. This desperation, of course, ensured that he got none. Two hours later he gave up, and on an impulse he texted her:

u up yet

She texted back almost immediately:

Yes. You?

Elizabeth had forced herself to wake up at five on Tuesday for a rare weekday roller skate. This had ensured she would be tired enough to go to sleep immediately upon returning home from the premiere the night before, at eleven. When she woke at five again on Wednesday morning, she was reasonably refreshed and ready to go.

A few texts later, they agreed they might as well get started.

It took Elizabeth only thirty minutes to get to Silver Lake so early in the morning. When Richard tumbled into the front passenger seat it was still dark outside, not quite 6 a.m.

He looked across at her. She was back to her normal self: loose clothing, ponytail, face devoid of makeup. He was glad. It was nice to have the old Elizabeth back. But she wasn't *quite* back, was she? Somehow she looked different; he couldn't put his finger on it. But it bothered him, and as she fiddled with what looked to be a picnic basket shoved between their seats (what the hell did she have in there?), he stared at her, trying to figure out what it was.

She caught him staring. Their eyes met, bouncing off each other in opposite directions. Elizabeth made a big show of re-arranging the objects inside her basket. She removed a thermos and unscrewed the cap. The car filled with the aroma of fresh coffee.

"Do you want some?"

She had time to make coffee? he thought, declining with a shake of his head. The smell was actually making him sick, and when she opened the basket to put back the thermos, he leaned over to take a peek, the sight of a homemade PB&J smeared against a Ziploc bag nearly making him heave. He swallowed thickly. Nausea and exhaustion were descending on him, fast, and he wasn't sure which would win out. He hoped it was the latter, though the saliva pooling in the bottom of his mouth portended otherwise. *Not again*, he begged silently. Richard was angry with himself for being hungover after promising he'd drink less—especially after being so good the last few weeks. But then he thought of Mike, and everything that had happened yesterday. He didn't regret a thing. He couldn't tell Elizabeth, though. He'd betrayed his best friend to her once before, and he was determined not to do it again.

Elizabeth pulled into the street. There were no other cars on the road except for a lone Prius behind them. It was 6 a.m., a full hour earlier than they'd planned on leaving.

"So how was the rest of last night?" she asked, once they'd gotten on the 101.

"Eh. You didn't miss much at the after party, or the after–after party. Nothing to report."

"How're you feeling?"

"Not too bad," he lied. "I'm not really much of a morning person anyway. Unlike you, apparently."

"It's true. I am a morning person," she said, with her uniquely flat intonation, devoid of inflection or innuendo. Richard remembered how he used to rail against her peculiar manner of speaking. He even had a "DP robot voice" he used to do for Mike in the early days, when he and Elizabeth were just getting to know each other. His eyelids began to droop.

"Feel free to lie down in the back if you want to."

"Really?" he asked gratefully. "You sure you don't mind?"

Elizabeth shook her head. "Go for it," she said, swapping out the 101 for the 10. There was still hardly anyone on the road, and even though by the time she got to the 15 there were plenty of vehicles in her rearview mirror, the traffic remained light. Elizabeth did a quick five-count with "Mississippis" in between, while from the backseat Richard snored steadily. Soon, their suspense would be over.

Elizabeth thought about Orpheus, who was so often on her mind these days. He was doing so much better. She realized it was only a matter of time before she told him everything, rough patch included, because how could she not? They'd grown so close, especially over the last month or two. Suddenly she wished she could have conjured him there now, by some magic spell, and talked to him for as long as he would listen. She wouldn't have held back a thing.

————————

ORPHEUS DID NOT appear magically in Elizabeth's front seat, but by a more minor miracle he was only fifty yards behind her, in one of the many Priuses dotting the road—the same Prius, in fact, that had been following her all the way from Silver Lake.

Since showing up on Elizabeth's doorstep in the guise of a new man almost two months earlier, Orpheus had made significant progress up the side of the well. It became easier once Elizabeth knew what he was doing; it was as if she threw him down a rope, beckoning excitedly from the top. He continued his job hawking pizza on the Boardwalk, and each week they went to the supermarket together (he had his own shelf in her kitchen now). He slept over almost every night, and when she wasn't there, he had permission to loiter on her back porch as much as he wanted. (She made sure her neighbors knew he was her guest.) They'd even done a little "house hunting," which consisted of trawling through Craigslist and Westside Rentals listings for something dirt cheap yet otherwise dirt-free, which turned out not to be such an easy find. They were in touch with Phoenix House and the St. Joseph Center, two local charities that helped the homeless with housing, both temporary and permanent. Elizabeth had told him finally about her "Orpheus account" and her intention to use the money she received each month from the lawyer to help him however she could, as long as he kept in mind that the ultimate goal was his financial independence. She was so businesslike about it, there was little opportunity for emotion, and he had to settle for a simple "thank you," which he found himself repeating thereafter almost every day.

Elizabeth had told him about the lawyer's e-mail the night she received it. He didn't say a word; the "do not pry" strategy had been working well for him. But he wanted desperately to go with her. Partly, he wanted to protect her, but mainly he was curious: his ability to keep inching up the well and eventually over its lip and onto solid ground was now tied directly to this anonymous benefactor. There was, however, another reason. The idea of getting back inside a car and hurtling down the highways of greater Southern California scared him—deeply—but he was drawn to this fear the same way a child insists on seeing the goriest horror movie in the theater or riding the biggest roller coaster in the park. Wouldn't this prove how far he'd come? That he had acquired more than the trappings of progress and secured real, lasting change for himself? In a flash of inspiration he realized it would be even *better* if he weren't just a passenger, but actually *driving* the vehicle in question.

He became determined to follow them.

But how was he going to acquire a car? Renting one was impossible; he hadn't had a driver's license or credit card for twenty-two years. (He'd consulted a calendar recently, more baffled than shocked by the hemorrhaging of time.) For days he wasted his energy on wishful thinking. If Elizabeth had an anonymous benefactor, why couldn't he? Someone who dropped a pair of keys in his lap and pointed to a shiny, waxed car waiting on the curb just for him. (This did not happen.) He knew a few people who lived out of their cars, and even though most of these vehicles were ancient RVs or oversize vans—dubiously mobile shanties that hadn't gone east of Lincoln in years—he asked each of these homeless car owners if he could borrow their car for a day. They all told him some version of "fuck off." And then suddenly it was Tuesday morning, and he and Elizabeth were sitting at the kitchen counter eating omelets (his new specialty). She reminded him about the premiere that night and the trip the next day. She said she'd be getting home late and waking up early, so he might as well take her spare key to let himself in and out.

She placed it gently in the palm of his hand: the same hand

he'd used only a few months earlier to break into the house he more or less lived in now.

"Orpheus, I'm so proud of you," she said, before making a hasty exit, leaving him staring in her wake. He hadn't even been able to say his usual "thank you."

How could he possibly *not* follow her? He had to restrain himself from running out to her in the driveway and proclaiming his intention never to let her out of his sight from this moment on, not even for work. There was *no way* she was going to the desert without him.

But how?

He left his rolling suitcase in the house that morning. Walking without it felt strange, like he was missing both a load *and* a limb, his step lighter but also less steady. He headed toward the Boardwalk, sidestepping a young family whose paraphernalia cascaded from their car onto the sidewalk: T-shirts, caps, sunglasses, bottles of water, sunscreen, a half-empty box of donuts, the trappings of a stroller. The harried father glanced up at him from a pile of toys, shrugging his shoulders apologetically. In the last few weeks, Orpheus had bought some more outfits, and he now regularly availed himself of Elizabeth's washer and dryer. He'd taken to wearing a baseball cap to keep out of the sun, and to hide the worst of his ravaged face from view. Pleased to have been mistaken for a regular functioning human being, he saluted the man, "huh," without breaking his stride.

It was busy on the Boardwalk for a Tuesday in October. Orpheus watched a performer jump in his bare feet from a chair onto a pile of broken glass. (He managed, as always, not to cut himself.) A Jimi Hendrix look-alike on roller skates nearly crashed into him while playing "The Star-Spangled Banner." A bald, red-faced woman in a sundress banged her fists on an upright piano, failing to make much noise since the instrument was missing most of its keys. Orpheus yearned suddenly to be back inside Elizabeth's house and away from the madness of the world. He turned to walk back, and saw the tourist family from a few minutes earlier taking in the Boardwalk for the first time—overwhelmed, mesmerized. Something dropped from the father's back pocket, traveling the short distance to a nest of palm husks lying on the ground. The husks, which had been blown off the tops of the surrounding palm trees by coastal winds, must have broken the object's fall. The father didn't hear a thing, and was already running after his young son, who was eagerly inspecting the glass walker's pile of broken bottles. Orpheus walked over—all it took was a few steps—and reached down among the hairy brown husks, plucking out the object easily. A large plastic holder said "Enterprise Rental." It was as he had suspected, but hadn't dared to hope: they were the keys to the car a few short blocks away, a *fully functioning* car guaranteed to be empty and unattended for hours to come.

Orpheus pocketed the keys, striding off at a brisk-but-not-too-brisk pace.

It was only when he was inside the car that Orpheus realized how odd these supposed keys were. They weren't keys at all. Where was the slender, notched, metallic protrusion to be inserted into a matching hole? This was nothing other than a black rectangular cube. *The hell?* His eyes darted around the dashboard for the ignition. How the fuck was the car supposed to start without a *key*? What had happened to cars in the last two decades? Was he so out of touch he couldn't even start a *car* anymore?

He heard a police siren, his heart rate spiking, hands sweating as he surveyed the dash more urgently. The siren couldn't be for him. Could it? No; he'd be long gone by the time anyone knew. *If* he could figure out how to start the damn thing.

He saw a START button, which looked promising. He pressed

it: nothing. He punched it with his fist: still nothing. What was happening? What was he doing? The old, proud Orpheus would never have stooped so low. No, for that man, the means always justified the end, which was how he'd ended up marrying a woman he didn't love and betraying his family for another woman who wasn't worth his spit. *Fuck it.* For once, the end would have to justify the means.

He took a deep breath and pressed the START button again: nothing.

He tried again: still nothing.

He began pressing the button over and over, without hope, pressing harder each time, until he was practically punching it with an index finger he was in grave danger of breaking.

Orpheus kicked at the floor in anger, letting loose a furious, animal yell.

Later, he realized his foot must have hit the brake pad just as he was pressing down the button. The headlights and all the interior controls flickered to life, and a little screen in the middle of the dashboard showed him the view from the back of the car. This thing had *cameras* too? It didn't sound like the engine was running, however, and without hoping for much, he put the car in drive and stepped on the gas.

To his amazement, it moved.

Over the course of the previous week, Orpheus had asked Elizabeth a series of nonchalantly phrased, cunningly disconnected questions to confirm the logistics of the desert trip. (So much for not prying, but at least he did it artfully.) This was how he knew she would be picking up the boy at 7 a.m. from his apartment in Silver Lake. One day, he asked her to show him how her phone worked. (He didn't have to pretend to be mystified by this device.) Since the Internet meant very little to him, he focused his wonderment on the fact that it was both a phone and a Rolodex.

"So everyone you know, all their numbers and addresses are right there? Stored *in* the phone?"

"It'd be more impressive if I knew more people, but yes, that's right," said Elizabeth.

"So if you wanted to look up, say, Richard, huh—"

She gave him the tiniest flicker of side-eye.

"—say if you forgot his address. What would you do?"

Elizabeth clicked on her contacts, pulling up Richard's card. "Here, look." She handed him the phone.

"*Outstanding,*" he crowed, committing the address to memory.

He wished he had a Thomas Guide to help him find his way to Silver Lake, but he was surprised how much he remembered once he was back on the streets as a driver instead of a vagrant. Too vast from the pedestrian point of view, L.A. came alive inside a moving vehicle. As he turned onto Washington—his namesake—Orpheus felt himself become a part of the hatched pattern of boulevards and avenues stretching eastward. Not even twenty-two years of deprivation and neglect could induce him, as a native Angeleno, to forget that after Lincoln came Sepulveda, and then La Cienega, followed by La Brea, Crenshaw, and Western. They were all still here, exactly as he'd left them (except for what looked to be an elevated rail—*the hell?*—just west of La Cienega). He'd forgotten how many billboards there were in L.A., adorning the space where the streets met the sky. Many of them were digital now and changed every ten seconds or so, reminding him of futuristic cityscapes in movies like *Blade Runner.*

"The future is now," he whispered, gazing out his window. "Huh."

Orpheus made a left onto Vermont, heading north: Venice, Pico, Olympic, Wilshire, all the numbered streets in between. It was like visiting old friends. If anything, the city looked better than he remembered it, though maybe that was because *he* looked so much worse.

He went east again on Beverly Boulevard, knowing it would turn into Silver Lake Boulevard eventually. From there he got a little lost; the grid went wavy, like straight layers of sedimentary rock turned groovily metamorphic, the parallel lines melting into curves, the perpendicular intersections swirling into spirals. It wasn't until close to sunset that he found a suitably inconspicuous spot on Richard's block from which to keep watch.

His plan was to stay up all night. He spent the first two hours reading the manual he found covered in crumbs in the glove compartment, learning about hybrid energy and (most important) how to turn the damn car on and off. Close to 3 a.m. he saw Richard stumble into his building. Somewhere around 4 a.m. he fell asleep, despite his best intentions, succumbing to the inevitable crash that followed the adrenaline rush of his day.

Orpheus had no idea why he woke up two hours later, but he suspected it was the noise of Elizabeth's ignition turning over (at least *her* car still operated the old-fashioned way), because almost immediately he saw the familiar Honda Accord begin to move. He was still wiping sleep from his eyes when he started the Prius like a pro and took off behind her. If he had woken up even thirty seconds later, he would have waited another hour before realizing they were gone. He would have missed them entirely.

It was still dark when he followed Elizabeth onto the 101 and the 10. Orpheus had thought that driving—especially on the highway at night—would bring back the memory of his calamity like never before, but he was so intent on negotiating the delicate balance between not letting Elizabeth's car get too far away and not getting too close to it that the eastern sky went from black to navy to cerulean to bright Dodger blue before he realized the night was over. It was only when the sun's rays began poking him in the eye that he recognized the beginning of a new day.

Orpheus pulled down his visor. A photo fluttered to his lap. It was a studio portrait of the tourist family: father, mother, son, and even their baby daughter in matching khakis and Christmas sweaters. He squirmed, casting it off him as if it were an insect he couldn't bear to touch. He looked around him. In the light of this supposedly glorious new day all he could see was the flat suburban sprawl of the Inland Empire extending endlessly on either side of him. Orpheus released a long sigh. He was tired, so tired. Every bone ached; every joint creaked.

There would be no ghostly visions of his lost family, no painful yet revelatory resurrection of the past, no real demarcation between that past and however many days were yet to come. He had no idea what he'd say to Elizabeth if she saw him following her, no way of justifying his actions. What the hell was he doing out here? He'd already ruined one family's vacation; what more could he accomplish?

He had no answer, but he continued following the spotless Honda Accord, maintaining a carefully calibrated distance several car lengths behind.

BY THE TIME Richard woke up, Elizabeth had moved on from the 15 to CA 127, also known as "Death Valley Road." They were getting close. His head popped up in the rearview mirror.

"How long was I out?"

She looked away from the road for a split second to glance at him. He was rubbing his eyes with his fists, and even though he had only a half inch or so of hair, somehow it was still sticking up in the back of his head. It was a rare moment in which he had no idea how adorable he looked, which enhanced his adorableness by about a thousand.

"A little over three hours," she said, training her eyes on the road again.

"Yikes, really?" he yawned. The sleep hadn't been refreshing, but it had helped. He at least didn't feel like vomiting anymore. He climbed into the front seat, his denim backside brushing against her shoulder. "Sorry," he muttered.

She caught a whiff of his unique scent: Right Guard deodorant, Head & Shoulders shampoo, and the tiniest tang underneath it—an earthy, animal something that refused to be contained by artificial fragrances.

"You still okay to drive?" he asked. "Not too tired?"

"I'm good."

"D'you have any water?" He yawned again.

Elizabeth cocked her head in the direction of the basket. Richard opened it and saw a veritable cornucopia of edibles: the aforementioned PB&Js, which looked slightly less revolting now; two baggies stuffed with baby carrots, celery sticks, cherry tomatoes, and cucumber slices; two Balance Bars (mocha chip and yogurt honey peanut); two apples; two pears; a netted bag of clementines; and two individual-sized bottles of water. He grabbed one, draining it in three long gulps.

"Wow, you really went all out, huh?" he said, wiping his mouth on his sleeve.

She shrugged her shoulders. "I like to be prepared. Could you actually hand me one of those sandwiches?"

They were already in the desert. Growing up in Massachusetts, Richard had pictured bumpy sand dunes as far as the eye could see, like in *Star Wars*, whenever he imagined "the desert." But on his way through the American Southwest seven years earlier, and on countless road trips to Las Vegas since, the real thing consistently failed to live up to the fantasy. For one, there was no sand. It was all brown, crumbly dirt and dusty, low-lying plants. This desert scrub spread out in all directions over gently rolling hills. Every time he saw it, he couldn't help feeling a little disappointed.

"Where're the cacti?" he asked suddenly.

Elizabeth took a moment to swallow the last of her PB&J, which she had scarfed as quickly as if she were on one of her lunch breaks. "What do you mean? There are tons of them out here."

"Yeah, but, you know, the big ones, with the arms?" He stuck both hands in the air, as if he were making two solemn oaths at once, dragging one shoulder down as far as it would go. "Like in the cartoons? With a sombrero hanging off one arm?"

"Oh, that's the saguaro cactus. They're in the Sonoran Desert, which is farther south and east, mainly in Arizona. We're in the Mojave Desert now."

"God, how do you *know* all this stuff?"

"Well, we had these regional geography quizzes in fifth grade—"

"Yeah, that's what you always say—'oh, I learned it when I was twelve, or eight, or four,' but I don't know anyone else who actually *remembers* everything like you do."

"I guess I don't forget things easily."

"It's impressive. And kind of scary."

She smiled.

Richard began shaking his leg against the floorboard. "Are we there yet?"

She smiled again.

Two in a row, he congratulated himself.

"I think we still have a little over an hour."

He retrieved his iPod from the floor, where he'd dropped it when he first entered the car. This had been his sole preparatory measure for the trip.

"Do you have a USB port in here?"

She jerked her head toward the basket again. He lifted it, spotting the port with a white connector sticking out of it.

Richard started with a playlist labeled "Cool/Not Embarrassing Music," which he had crafted for a party at his apartment a year ago. By the end of the party, a wasted Mike had hijacked his iPod from its stereo cradle while he was in the bathroom and switched over to his "Top 25 Most Played" list, which included such humiliating gems as Miley Cyrus's "Party in the USA" and "Slide" by the Goo Goo Dolls. He smiled at the memory, realizing there was no need to play "cool" music for Elizabeth. He already knew what she liked. Currently the topmost track on his "Top 25 Most Played" list was Mariah Carey's "Always Be My Baby"—his favorite song, though he didn't advertise it. He began playing it now.

Elizabeth made a noise. He turned to her.

"This is my favorite song," she explained.

Come on. "Mine too," he said, a little reluctantly. But how could he not tell her?

She took her eyes off the road again.

"Really?"

"Really."

They lapsed into silence, accompanied by Mariah's silky crooning. Richard was reminded of their dinner at Factor's, when he vowed never to be a part of those couples who sat in silence, the ones who had nothing to say to each other. But he saw now that he'd gotten it wrong, that sometimes there was nothing better than sitting next to another person and thinking your own thoughts alongside them—nothing more intimate than being alone together. Maybe this was, in fact, the very definition of intimacy: acting with another person the way you did when you were alone.

The song ended. Neither of them spoke. Richard couldn't imagine sitting in perfect silence like this with anyone else in the world. He and Mike, certainly, were incapable of shutting up for more than a few seconds at a time, and he wouldn't have it any other way. But he wouldn't change this, either. Wasn't it funny, he thought, that the one person he was being paid to talk to was also the one person he could *not* talk to? Maybe this was why he'd been withdrawing incrementally from his old social scene (though it had been a mistake to lump Mike together with all his other friends; Mike was special, and after last night he would never forget it). When you had someone you could *calm down* with in this way, didn't it feel a little pointless to keep expending all that energy?

"D'you have any Selena in there?" Elizabeth asked him, breaking the silence at last.

"Selena Gomez? Nah, she's too Disney, even for me."

"No, *Selena* Selena."

"What other Selena?"

He was scanning his iPod for his next selection, and for this reason he failed to see her exaggerated double take.

"Do you seriously not know who Selena is?!"

Richard looked up. This was the most animated he'd ever heard her.

"Selena was like the Mexican Madonna," she told him breathlessly. "She was Tejana, actually, meaning she was a Latina from Texas, and had hit songs in Spanish and then later in English too, pretty much every year from '85 to '95, which was when she was shot to death by this crazy woman who used to be the president of her fan club and was caught embezzling money from her. She wasn't even twenty-four yet."

It hit him without warning, like a slap in the face: he wanted nothing more than to kiss her. But lunging for the face of a driver currently operating a motor vehicle hurtling over sixty miles an hour was not the most prudent course of action, and also: *what??* Richard scanned his iPod blindly. What was happening? He didn't even want to have sex with her (he couldn't bring himself to say "fuck her," even though this was the phrase he had always used up till now, for both its pithiness and bite). He just really, really, *really* wanted to kiss her.

"That's terrible," he mumbled, refusing to look up.

"It really was. Whenever people talk about remembering where they were when JFK was shot, I think about the day Selena died. I remember I was in math class, and I was bored, and then there was all this commotion in the hallway and people started turning on radios and televisions and . . . I know it sounds melodramatic, but it was like the world ended."

They were silent for a few moments.

"Look in my glove compartment," she instructed him.

In among a pile of Balance Bars, he found a CD labeled *S* and handed it to her. She slid it in.

They listened to "Dreaming of You" first. Richard loved it. Even though it was a wistful song, he could hear Selena's smile in every note; it was as though she could barely contain her joy in singing. After that, Elizabeth played him "I Could Fall in Love," which he liked too, and then "Como La Flor" and some of her other Spanish-language hits, which he liked less, but pretended to love just as much as the others.

A road sign came into view.

"Look!" he pointed. "That's Big Stan Way coming up, isn't it?"

Jonathan Hertzfeld's directions had been simple: they were to ignore the no-trespassing signs posted at the turnoff for "Big Stan Way" and take the road all the way to what he simply called "the estate." They were due at noon, but they hadn't hit a bit of traffic, and they'd never had to take a bathroom break. Elizabeth drank only a single cup of coffee, and even with his bottle of water, Richard was still dehydrated from his hangover. It was a little past eleven.

They turned onto the one-lane road, which went from well paved to badly paved to not paved at all. They passed a range of low-lying hills. "The estate" came into view.

Elizabeth jammed on her brakes. Richard bolted upright, inadvertently ripping the iPod from its socket, cutting off Selena in the middle of "Bidi Bidi Bom Bom."

It was like a limited-edition "Hacienda" version of the Lego castle he'd been obsessed with when he was nine. Richard clicked the camera app on his iPod. He *had* to get a picture of this.

"Holy *shit*," he said. "It's a fucking castle."

Elizabeth nodded. "It's a fucking castle."

The portcullis split in two with an electric hum, opening like a regular gate instead of rising upward as Richard had been hoping it would. Even so, he imagined two little Lego knights in Zorro masks and gaucho hats on either side of it, pulling on a rope, their pencil-thin mustaches quivering with the effort. He was about to share this flight of fancy with Elizabeth when he wondered if she would find it racist.

They passed through the gate into the bright light of the courtyard.

BEVERLY HAD CONSIDERED wearing an elaborate getup for the "Summit of Love," as she'd been calling it to herself for a week. She toyed with the idea of impersonating a character halfway between Katharine Hepburn and Norma Desmond—brash yet grandiose, the eccentric old bat with a fortune to spare on her kooky whims—and as recently as that morning the plan had been to greet them in the middle of the courtyard in a turban, brandishing a cigarette holder, arms raised to the heavens. In the end, she decided a simpler approach would do. Stan's Castle was impressive enough on its own.

It was Peaches, therefore, who greeted them in the middle of the courtyard, staring glumly through her silver-flecked bangs. Above her was a miniature footbridge connecting the two wings of the castle. Below her Crocs-clad feet were red ceramic tiles, miniature cacti, and succulents arranged in garden beds against the two long walls of the rectangular space. There were at least six iron-studded doors leading inside, and three times as many thick-paned windows. A hill overlooking them provided the promise if not the guarantee of shade at some point in the day. The effect produced was contradictory: snugly grand; kitschily enchanting; as if the architect hadn't been able to decide whether the building was meant to be a joke or not and had settled for somewhere in between.

Richard got out first, turning in a circle to take in the view. Peaches got a full, 360-degree look at him, a rare smile lighting up her sullen visage. But the smile collapsed on itself when she saw Elizabeth staring at her.

"In here," she said, gesturing to one of the doors.

They entered a cathedral-like space soaring two stories in the air, an upper gallery running the perimeter. A dual-tiered chandelier hung from the wooden-raftered ceiling, two great rings of iron with electric candles sticking out of them. If they had been real candles, it would have been easy to believe this massive fixture had been lifted straight from a medieval banquet hall. Tapestries hung on the white plaster walls and over the balcony of the upper gallery. A great stone fireplace at one end of the room descended from the ceiling all the way to the ornately tiled floor. Across from it stood *another* fireplace, this one merely a story high, hiding the staircase leading to the gallery above.

It took some time for Richard and Elizabeth to observe these details, since despite the numerous windows, the space was dark and gloomy. Thick, leathery drapes had been drawn against every pane of glass, blocking out the sun, and their eyes needed a minute to adjust. The air smelled smoky, and what with this, the gloom, and the churchlike proportions, Elizabeth looked instinctively for the font of holy water and tiers of votive candles beside the door. (They weren't there.)

Placed in the center of the room, directly beneath the chandelier, was a high-backed, circular couch made of dark, button-tufted leather. It seated up to fifteen people, and was the sort of thing that belonged in a posh train station or glittering hotel lobby rather than a private home. And yet it fit the grandiose space perfectly.

Upon it sat an old woman, like a lone traveler, an unlit cigarette hanging off her bottom lip.

Richard saw raw, red scalp and sagging, papery skin; he still retained a vestige of that knee-jerk abhorrence of old age that belongs to children—an aversion to infirmity by the young and healthy who cling instinctively to each other. He glanced away, choosing to survey the furniture instead. It was all dark leather and even darker wood; it struck him as a little creepy. The only object that looked out of place was a glass plaque propped up on a slim, marble pedestal. He squinted, reading: *To CharBev, in grateful recognition of years and years of love and devotion, from the California State Prison, Los Angeles County, Lancaster, CA.* He guessed the old woman was the "CharBev" in question, but what the hell kind of a name was that?

Beverly had wanted to light her cigarette in front of them as a means of drawing out the moment—to observe them, to put them off their guard—but she was having a hard time igniting the lighter. She flicked it helplessly. Inside her ear, Char's voice taunted her: *Serves you right.*

Elizabeth stepped forward:

"Can I help you with that?"

Elizabeth hated cigarettes; she thought smoking was idiotic, but she couldn't just stand there watching the old woman fumble. Besides, the damage was already done. That much was obvious.

"I'll manage," Bev replied coolly, her eagle eyes blazing a warning. Elizabeth stumbled backward, as if singed. It was this infinitesimal victory that gave Bev the burst of confidence she needed to light the damn Parlie at last. She drew in a deep breath, which of course brought on a coughing fit. Peaches, who had been hovering in the back of the room, stepped forward, but Beverly waved her away.

When she could speak again, there was a flush on Bev's cheeks that made her appear livelier than before. "Thank you for coming. My name is Beverly Chambers, and it's such a pleasure to meet you both in person."

Elizabeth just stared at her.

"You too," muttered Richard.

The stupidity of the "Summit of Love" broke upon Bev like an icy wave socking her in the gut. What the hell was she doing? She'd been like a crazy person for the last six months. Suddenly she wanted to stamp out her cigarette, throw the two of them out, and take to her bed like a normal octogenarian. But she merely paused.

"Peaches, let's have some refreshment," she said finally. "Some tea and sandwiches, maybe? Something lunchy." She looked at Richard, a half smile curling one side of her mouth. "And, Mr. Baumbach—may I call you Richard?"

Richard nodded his head uneasily.

"Richard, then. Please help Peaches with the dishes and things."

Richard's eyes widened with surprise, and Peaches turned her head for what would have been the mother of all head shakes if Beverly hadn't dismissed them both with an imperious wave of her Parlie-free hand. Richard followed Peaches to the door, glancing backward in hopes of catching Elizabeth's eye. But Elizabeth only had eyes for Beverly Chambers, who was offering her a seat with a birdlike bob of the head.

Elizabeth sat, never breaking eye contact with her host. The footfalls of their companions faded away on the hard ceramic tile. They were alone.

"RICHARD AND ELIZABETH," Bev singsonged. "Tell me, did you ever acknowledge the happy coincidence of your names?"

"I don't know what you mean," said Elizabeth.

Beverly tsked. "Don't you?"

"No."

"Richard and Elizabeth? Surely you've heard of the famous pair . . . ?"

"I haven't."

Bev sighed dramatically. "Richard Burton and Elizabeth Taylor? Only the most popular love story of the twentieth century." She took another drag of her cigarette, careful not to breathe in too much. "Although I suppose it's been fifty years since the world was incapable of gossiping about anyone else. The twentieth century was a long time ago, wasn't it?"

Elizabeth decided this was a rhetorical question and did not respond.

"It's what first gave me the idea," Bev continued, "though there were other, more substantial considerations, of course."

"Such as?"

Bev sighed again. She couldn't help comparing Elizabeth Santiago to Mike Kim, and there was no question whom *she* would have preferred. But then, her tête-à-tête with the latter had begun in exactly the same sort of no-frills, antagonistic manner. (If these two were any indication, women had certainly mastered the art of candid and plainspoken communication: an

improvement from her day.) Perhaps she wasn't giving Miss Santiago enough of an opportunity. On a perverse impulse, she held
out her pack of cigarettes, waving them temptingly.

"No thank you," said Elizabeth firmly. "I've never smoked."

"How wonderful for you," said Bev, ashing on the floor even
though there was an ashtray beside her. "I hate to disappoint
you—"

No you don't, thought Elizabeth.

"—but I didn't bring you here to tell you why I chose you for
my little, *ahem*, experiment."

"So then why did you? Bring us here."

"For the pleasure of your conversation," Bev said tartly. "And
to see how you two were getting on. So tell me," she smirked,
"what do you think of him?"

"Why ask, since you obviously think you already know the
answer?"

Tiresome. And insolent. "Has anyone ever told you it's rude,
my dear, to answer a question with a question?"

"Is it?"

Bev smirked again, nodding, as if they'd been fencing and
she was bound by honor to acknowledge a hit.

"It doesn't matter what I think anyway," said Elizabeth,
breaking eye contact for the first time, and glancing backward
to confirm they were still alone.

Bev raised what was left of her eyebrows, in what was meant
to come across as a question.

"It's not going to work," said Elizabeth, a slight tremor to
her voice.

Interesting. "No?" asked Bev softly.

"No. But I'll keep putting in my time like I've been doing.
I'll get to the end of the year and I'll get my money. All of it.
You owe me that, for—for—"

"For what, my dear?"

Elizabeth couldn't finish the sentence, so Beverly did it for her:

"For making you hope?"

Elizabeth stared at the tiles on the floor. They were big—about the size of the plates on a baseball diamond—and every so often there was a glass mosaic inside one of them depicting a mythological creature: a hydra, a basilisk, a mermaid. Elizabeth was staring at a centaur when she heard Beverly's voice again, so soft it was almost a whisper:

"You have to tell him."

The hairs rose on the back of Elizabeth's neck; the centaur took on a new association of horror she knew it would retain for the rest of her life. She looked up at Beverly Chambers. There was no way this harpy could know about *that*. What she meant, what she *had* to have meant, was that Elizabeth needed to tell Richard how she felt about him. She looked down again at the centaur, forcing herself to think about this other secret—the blameless one, the one of much more recent vintage.

It wasn't love at first sight; Elizabeth didn't believe such a thing existed. Love at first sight always sounded like revisionist history to her, more like love in hindsight, a good story at the expense of the truth. The problem was that love didn't creep up on a person the way it did in so many books and movies. It didn't advance in fixed increments; it wasn't an accumulation of tiny affections and kindnesses; there was no internal scale to be tipped in the eleventh hour by some shared quirk, unlikely remembrance, or grandiose gesture. Like every other miracle, it came all at once, fully formed, and once seen, it was impossible to *un*see. It was only natural, yet erroneous, to assume it had always been there, even in the very beginning.

She hadn't loved Richard that first moment in the lawyer's office—not even close. But she'd been attracted to him; she'd been intrigued by him; and from that first encounter she'd been launched down a path that led irrefutably to love. She supposed that for others the path was meandering, a maze with false turns and dead ends, any number of riddles and obstacles to be overcome before the end came suddenly into view. But for her it had been a straight path; it was so obvious, so inevitable, now that it was there, try as hard as she might to ignore it or look elsewhere. It was love *from* first sight and it couldn't be denied, as much as she wished it could.

"My best friend and I used to play a game sometimes," Bev said, after a long break in the conversation—occupied on her end by the arduous business of lighting another cigarette. "We'd divide everyone we knew into two categories based on the way they related to a single qualifying factor. It was a way to make sweeping generalizations that were wildly inaccurate, but invariably amusing to pronounce. For instance, people fall into two categories, those who listen to music to *put* them in a certain mood, and those who listen to music because they're already *in* a certain mood. Do you see what I mean?"

Elizabeth nodded dumbly.

"And when I learned about you two—even though I won't tell you why it was I sought you out—I thought of a new one, maybe the best one *ever*. Can you guess what it was?"

Make her stop, Elizabeth pleaded silently, even while shaking her head in the negative.

"People fall into two categories!" Bev trumpeted. "Those who need to *be* loved by someone, and those who need to *love* someone. Here, I said to myself, are two people who belong in opposite categories, what a perfect pair! And you see," she stamped out her half-smoked cigarette with a flourish as the sound of footfalls returned to them, "I was right."

Richard and Peaches were carrying two heavy, overburdened trays. Back in the kitchen, Peaches had insisted on displaying every variety of fruit, vegetable, cold cut, cheese, and condiment available and asking Richard which ones he liked, and he had been too polite to say he didn't like any of them. It had helped that by this point he was truly ravenous; the last thing he'd eaten were a few hors d'oeuvres at the premiere after party the evening before. Apparently a well-behaved, handsome young man with a healthy appetite was on the extremely short list of things Peaches approved of, and she had been happy to transport nearly every foodstuff out of the kitchen. Bev was astonished to see what appeared to be the first smile on that sallow, sour face in ages:

"Well, well, Peaches is in love!" she cried. "Wonders never cease."

Peaches shook her head, but for once there was no violence in the gesture, and when Richard leaned down to deposit his tray on the table she actually patted him on the head. Beverly laughed to see his cheeks burn, but the sound was nothing like the pretty jangle Mike had remarked on a week earlier. Her smoker's cough had worsened, warping her girlish laughter into a throaty cackle.

"There's no question which category *she* belongs to," Bev said, winking at Elizabeth.

Elizabeth resented the wink. She felt no intimacy with this horrible crone, but did her best to keep up with the conversation while Peaches began serving them lunch.

"Have either of you been to Death Valley before?" Bev asked.

"No," said Elizabeth, accepting a cup from Peaches and lifting it to her lips.

"But I've been meaning to go for a while," added Richard.

"Oh, well then, you'll have to look around! There's so much to see here: Artist's Palette, Badwater Basin, Devil's Golf Course, the Red Cathedral, Scotty's Castle—but then, you'll hardly need to go there."

Bev explained about the replica. "And of course there are the Mesquite Sand Dunes—"

"Sand dunes?" echoed Richard.

"Oh, yes. They were the ones used in the filming of *Star Wars*."

Richard almost choked on his sandwich. He turned to Elizabeth.

"We *have* to go there," he garbled through a mouth half full of ham-on-rye.

Elizabeth nodded at him vaguely.

Beverly beamed at them both. "Of course you do. I'll give you directions."

She made Peaches print out directions. The sand dunes were only an hour away.

"Pardon my rudeness," said Bev as they were finishing their meal, "but I'm an old woman and I tire easily these days." She wiped her shriveled mouth daintily with a napkin. "Take your time exploring the desert, but please know that your obligation to me is over. I'll be resting for the rest of the day. You're free to return to Los Angeles whenever you like."

Her implication was clear enough: their time at the castle was up. *We drove five hours for this?* thought Richard. *What the hell?* He glanced at Elizabeth, who nodded at him ever so slightly, and somehow he understood her immediately: *don't say anything, let's just go.* Had Beverly Chambers already told her everything when they were alone? Did she know what it was that connected them?

"You won't be disappointed!" were Bev's final words as she waved them out the door. She was overcompensating. The problem wasn't the boy; she had noticed immediately how he deferred to the girl; it was subtle (as most meaningful relations between two people were) but wonderfully clear that he'd already grown to depend on her. Even so, Bev worried that disappointment was exactly what lay in store for them both, if that unpleasant girl didn't learn to speak up.

"WHAT DID SHE SAY to you when I was gone?" Richard asked the second they got back in the car.

Elizabeth paused to crank up the air conditioner. It was boiling inside the Honda—the kind of trapped, greenhouse heat that imperiled unattended pets and children.

"She told me she wasn't going to say why she picked us," said Elizabeth, passing through the gate and starting down Big Stan Way. "She said she just wanted to get a look at us. Together." Her eyes flicked toward him before returning to the road. "I'm sorry. It was a total waste of time."

"Unbelievable!" Richard threw his back against the seat in a tantrumlike gesture. "Well, we are *absolutely* seeing those dunes. Maybe we should see some of that other stuff she mentioned too. We've got to make this trip worth *something*, right?"

"Sure," replied Elizabeth, turning from Big Stan Way onto Death Valley Road again, too preoccupied to take more than passing note of the silver Prius parked by the side of the road. "Might as well."

THE DUNES

MESQUITE IS A PESKY PLANT, with long thorns prone to puncturing car tires and poking the soft parts of children playing on the ground. It prefers semiarid climates like the southwestern United States, where its ability to suck up water has alarmed more than one rancher trying to maintain a steady water table. Its roots grow deep; it's nearly ineradicable, and many consider it a pest, the rabbit of the plant species. It is perhaps not a small consolation that mesquite wood burns slow, hot, and flavorful, adding a distinctive twang to barbecue grills across the region where it thrives.

Thousands of years ago, the Mesquite Sand Dunes were a muddy lakebed teeming with mesquite. When the bed dried out, conditions became less than perfect for the plant but, true to form, it refused to vacate the premises. Over time, the desiccated area acquired bits of feldspar and quartz swirling in from the surrounding mountains. The sandy debris piled up—in some places as high as 150 feet—and spread out over fourteen square miles. The sand dunes were born. And yet the mesquite hung on.

"Wow, can you believe plants actually live out here?" Richard trotted up the first sandy hill, which was about fifty feet from where they'd parked on the side of the road. He marveled at the low-lying clumps of vegetation dotting the shallower, outlying hills. Farther in, there was nothing but sand.

He already loved the dunes. They were just sitting there on top of the boring, scraggly, southwestern desert, a bit of Tunisia grafted onto California: a beach with no ocean, or a beach where the ocean *was* the sand, each individual dune like a giant wave frozen in place, its surface rippled by a wind that must have gone elsewhere for the day. The air was perfectly still.

They were the only ones there. This was no surprise, since it was the middle of the week and well past noon, though fortunately for them the weather was mild, the air temperature hovering somewhere in the 80s. Elizabeth joined him, carrying a backpack retrieved from the trunk of her car. He watched her walk up to a plant at the edge of the sand. There were two shriveled, yellow flowers on one side of it, but as far as he could see it wasn't much to look at—unremarkable, other than for its existence.

"Those flowers look pretty rough," he said. "The Beverly Chambers of flowers." He was still annoyed they hadn't learned anything useful at the castle, and on the ride over he'd made several other clunkers at the old woman's expense. Elizabeth nodded mechanically. He could tell she wasn't listening. *What's her deal?* he thought, his eternal refrain. She'd been quiet on the ride over—quiet even for her. "What's that smell?" he asked, mainly to say something, sniffing at the air like a bloodhound on the trail. "Must be coming from the plant. Smells sort of . . . smoky?" He had an inspired thought: "I guess it's mesquite! Mesquite Dunes, right? And the smoky smell makes sense. Mesquite grill."

Elizabeth gave an infinitesimal shrug of her shoulders. If she'd been paying attention, she could have told him he was wrong, that the plant was creosote, not mesquite, and that the odor it emitted was responsible for its name since it smelled similar to the creosote leftover from burnt coal or wood. All this information lay in her brain somewhere, buried yet accessible. But she was too lost inside her head to recall it now.

Richard gave up on her, racing up the face of a much steeper dune. When he reached the crest and got a better look at the vast expanse of sand stretching before him, he turned around, exclaiming, "It really *does* look like Tatooine!"

He wished Elizabeth would catch up with him so that he could tell her about the Skywalkers' home planet, with its dual suns and endless deserts. But she was too slow, so he bounded ahead again, eyes trained on the largest hilltop in the center.

Elizabeth's calves began to ache as she slogged her way through the dry, shifting sand. She paused, scanning the dunes for Richard. He was already far in the distance, and the perfect, pristine silence closed around her like a physical presence, a massive swaddling blanket she found either comforting or constricting, she wasn't sure which. She watched as Richard scaled another dune without hesitating, his knees practically touching his chest with each deep stride he took, arms pumping, head thrust nearly straight up in the air. *I love you, I love you, I love you,* she thought, certain now that the silence was, in fact, intolerable. She wished desperately for something to break it—the distant whir of a motor, the caw of a bird overhead, the devastating crack of an earthquake. Maybe then she could have whispered the words aloud instead of just thinking them. And if she could have whispered them, she could have spoken them, and if she could have spoken them, she could have run over and shouted them directly into that stupidly perfect, pink beach shell of an ear of his. But the silence was impregnable, and the words remained stuck inside of her.

Richard reached the crest of the center dune and put his hands on his hips to catch his breath. He turned in a full circle. The valley floor stretched well beyond the dunes in every direction, ending in a continuous mountain range that encircled them like a giant, purple-and-silver-fingered hand, the dunes the golden treasure cupped in the middle of its palm.

He peered down, looking for Elizabeth, and experienced a rush of vertigo. In an effort to regain his balance, he focused on the dune directly beneath him. It had two distinct sides, he realized: a gentle one, up which the wind coaxed individual grains of sand, and a much steeper face, down which the sand tumbled. He saw now that he'd made things harder for himself by going up the steep face of the dune: *against the grain . . . s*, he thought, relishing even this pathetic little wordplay. The two sides met in a long, peaked ridge upon which he now stood, venturing another glance down the steeper side to check on Elizabeth's progress, or lack thereof.

A portion of the topmost layer of sand shifted, in a cascade that began with the grains directly under his sneakers and ended about five feet down the slope. Elizabeth was another fifteen feet below this and didn't notice a thing. Richard ran to an untouched section of the ridge, and did it again.

It was cool to see a miniature avalanche of sand, but this spectacle was not the source of his fascination. When all those grains moved together, they made a magnified version of the sound of pouring sand, and even though it was magnified, it was a sound so gentle, so delicate, that hearing it was like an affirmation of the silence that reigned before and after. It was like a negative sound, Richard decided, highlighting the otherworldly quiet upon which it intruded for a moment. Somehow it left things more peaceful than they were before—like a shushing, as if the sand were telling him to hush, to listen, to appreciate the stillness of the world in this untouched, magical place.

His leg shook as he watched Elizabeth trudge up the last few feet. When she reached the top, she put her hands on her knees, panting slightly. She was in good shape, but she never climbed hills. Venice was unvaryingly flat.

"Slowpoke," he teased her.

Elizabeth lifted her head without moving, shooting him a glare that would have been icy if they hadn't been enveloped by sun, sand, and heat.

"Okay, I have to show you something," he said.

She dumped her backpack on the ground, producing two Poland Spring bottles from inside it. Richard took one without opening it, waiting impatiently as she took a long swig from the other. To his annoyance, she insisted on returning it to her bag, from which she then produced a gargantuan tube of SPF-85 sunscreen, offering it to him.

"Do you want any?"

"Nah, I'm good."

"You should at least put some on your face."

"I'm fine!" he exclaimed, a little shortly, because he knew she was right. He was without a doubt in the process of getting a burn. Out here in this unembellished landscape, the sun showed its true character—like a veiled woman with tempting eyes who, when she removed the shroud from the lower half of her face, revealed nostrils flared with hatred and a leering mouth full of needlelike teeth chomping hungrily: *I will destroy you.* But there was no room to worry about the sun.

"Okay, so you have to be *really* quiet for this."

Not a problem, thought Elizabeth, rubbing the thick, pastelike cream into her arm.

"You have to look!"

She sighed, but good-naturedly, looking up. Richard was crouched over the peaked ridge, and he was almost too beautiful to behold. It would have been easier to look at the sun.

He put up a finger. "Now, listen!"

He pushed down with one foot: another plain of sand fell away, accompanied by the soft, low *shhhhhhhhhhhhhhhhhhhhhhh* sound he had already grown to love. He looked up at her, grinning.

"Isn't that the coolest thing ever?!"

Elizabeth clenched her eyes shut, pressing her temples with the thumb and middle finger of her right hand. It looked as though she had a sudden and catastrophic headache. Richard stood up.

"What's wrong?"

She shook her head, and her right hand along with it, while with her left hand she made a fist at her side. Richard regarded her uncertainly, relieved when a few seconds later she dropped both hands and opened her eyes, a more collected expression on her face than he expected.

She pointed to the ground:

"Sit."

He obeyed her immediately.

She took the spot next to him, on the peak of the dune. This time she did look at the sun, allowing it to burn a hole in her vision. She closed her eyes. Against the black backdrop of her eyelids, the spot pulsated an electric silver-green. She opened her eyes again. The spot turned red against the boundless blue sky, and over the next few minutes it lost its radiance more quickly than she wanted it to, fading to a bruised-looking purple that marred the otherwise spotless firmament more faintly as each precious second fell away. She held on to this stain as long as she could, but at last it disappeared completely. There was nothing left.

And yet, she still delayed. *Just pretend it's Orpheus,* she told herself, and the thought of him strengthened her just enough to bridge this terrible pause. She cleared her throat.

It was time.

"I was the perfect child. I know that sounds obnoxious, but it's true. I was like a poor Chicana version of Hermione Granger. I did everything right and I always followed the rules. By the time I was a senior in high school, I was number one in my class, the editor of the school yearbook, and captain of the girls' soccer team. I taught CCD after school at my local church. I was a National Merit Scholar. I represented my school district in the Young Republicans of California.

"I was offered full scholarships to a lot of colleges. *A lot.* I was leaning toward UCLA because I wanted to stay close to my neighborhood. I wanted to stick around there during college. That way I could become a congressional representative for my district as soon as possible. I had my career all mapped out. I was going to become the first Latina president of the United States.

"My brother Hugo was smart too. But he was shy. He was two years younger than me and he leaned on me a lot. My parents worked long hours, so a lot of the time it was just him and me. He looked up to me. He asked my advice on everything. I was like his second mother, and I liked it that way. I encouraged it.

"He came to me in April. I could tell something was wrong, but it took a while to get it out of him because I was the first person he told. He said he was gay. He said he'd been attracted to boys since he was twelve, and he couldn't stop thinking about this one boy in his class, who he was pretty sure had feelings for him too. He said he didn't know what to do.

"I told him his impulses were wrong. That the church and community he belonged to condemned them for a reason. I said he had to figure out a way to stop having these thoughts, not just for his family's sake but for his own sake too, for the sake of his soul. I lectured him about how we couldn't as human beings give in to our baser impulses, how showing restraint was what separated us from animals.

"He listened to every word. Like he always did. And when we were done I told him I wouldn't tell our parents if he promised not to act on his desires. I said he had to try as hard as he could to improve himself. I said I was willing to help him, but only if he helped himself. I made an analogy to how hard it was for me to get a perfect eight hundred on my SAT math, since verbal came so much easier, but how I studied hard and made it happen. He said he would try. He promised.

"A few days later I came home early from soccer practice. My parents still weren't home. I called out to Hugo and he yelled to me from his room. He said he was doing homework, but something was off, I could tell.

"There were no locks on our bedroom doors, but we always knocked—we were always respectful of each other's privacy. I figured it was worth barging in just this once to make sure everything was okay. Given what he'd told me before.

"They were on the bed together. With their shirts off. I threw the other boy out without saying anything to him, not even a word. Then I marched back to Hugo's room and told him I was going to have to tell our parents everything, because he hadn't kept up his end of the deal. He looked at me, and he was crying and he said, 'I can't help it, Lola. I love him.' And I told him, 'You don't even know what love is. That's not love. It's disgusting.'

"He started to cry even harder, so I left. An hour later I was done with my homework and I went looking for him. But he wasn't in his bedroom. He wasn't in the bathroom either. He wasn't anywhere.

"He ran away. So I did end up telling my parents everything. They weren't even angry with me, at first. They just wanted to find him. So they filed a police report, but the thing is, even though my brother and I were born here, my parents weren't. They came here illegally, and if they were deported it would only make things worse. So there wasn't much they could say when the LAPD told them they were 'working on it,' but didn't seem to be doing much of anything.

"Our neighbors did what they could. They helped us look, and pray, and wait. But we never found him. He just disappeared. As soon as I had some real money of my own, the first thing I did was to hire a private investigator. I've hired three of them, actually, the last one a year or two ago. I'm pretty sure he's dead. I know that's what my parents think."

There was a pause. She knew without looking that her face had acquired the pained, squinty-eyed expression she'd seen on her mother's face so many times before, and which usually meant there were tears on the way. But she also knew she would not cry.

She heard his lips part before he spoke. They sounded dry. She wondered dully why he wasn't drinking any of the water she'd given him.

"Did he have a mole on his forehead?" he asked her. "Above his left eyebrow?"

"Yes," she said, turning to him, the dread rising inside her. "How did you know that?"

Richard winced. "I think—"

He cut himself off. Elizabeth watched dumbly as he took a few sips from the neglected water bottle before speaking again.

"I think your brother was responsible for Kyle's death," he said finally. "My best friend from high school. Remember?"

Elizabeth stared at him: petrified, uncomprehending. Eventually Richard took the opportunity of filling the silence with a monologue of his own.

"Kyle was visiting his aunt and uncle in San Diego over spring break. It happened on the Five, and even though he was killed instantly, the driver only had minor injuries. They arrested him at the hospital. He had no license or ID, and he wouldn't tell anyone his name. I remember they guessed he was around nineteen, so it must've been a few years after he ran away. The car he was driving was stolen, too. He was . . . he obviously wasn't in a good place. I guess they never matched him with any missing person cases. The one your parents made was probably long gone by then, or maybe the police never even bothered to make one.

"I told you how I testified at the trial, right? To help put the driver away for as long as possible? He got twenty years to life. Which was a lot, considering he didn't have a record. But I remember the judge making a lot out of the fact that he wouldn't identify himself. She said she was going to have to assume there were prior convictions under his real name. I think it was meant to call his bluff, because that was pretty much a worst-case scenario. But he still wouldn't say who he was. So he got sentenced like he had all these prior felonies, no chance of parole for at least nineteen years. That was thirteen years ago. I can still remember him staring at me as they read out his sentence, before they took him away. I'm pretty sure he hated me. I know I hated him.

"There was a plaque at the castle today. I think she put it out as a clue. It was for charity work at a prison, and it made me think of him because he's the only person I know, not that I really *know* him, obviously, who went to jail. That's why when you said he ran away—" Richard hesitated. "I mean, maybe it's not him—"

"It's him," said Elizabeth flatly. It was all so awful, it had the unmistakable ring of truth to it. She supposed she should have been elated that her brother was still alive, but all she could think about was that she'd been responsible for another person's death. She'd always known this, somehow. Even though her lawyer's brain was already arguing that this accident was in no way foreseeable, that her actions were nowhere near proximate enough for legal guilt—she thought of *Palsgraf v. LIRR*, plunging all the way back to first-year torts—there was no question according to her personal code of ethics that she was 100 percent guilty.

"You're probably right. That birthmark would be too much of a coincidence. The only reason I remembered it is cuz I mentioned it in the first sentence of my college essay: *The man who killed my best friend had a large, round, black birthmark approximately one inch above his left eyebrow.*" He paused. "He must've told her about us. About both of us. But I still don't know why she'd go and do all this. There's no way *he* would've wanted it."

I know why, thought Elizabeth. Her parents believed their only son was dead, and all that old witch could think about was playing matchmaker. But she guessed Hugo had told Beverly Chambers not to tell his family where he was. If he'd gone this long without contacting them, he probably never wanted to see them again.

Elizabeth had an overwhelming desire to be alone, like an animal that retreats to some dark, solitary place to lick its wounds in peace. "Thank you for telling me," she said. Her tone was formal, distant. "It'll help my parents to know, no matter what's happened to him since. So—thank you. For that."

There. Done. Over. Mystery solved, duty discharged. She'd said what she needed to say.

But this wasn't true. There was a great deal she'd left unsaid. And it was more than the three words that had been repeating themselves in her head over and over again like some ancient, muttered curse ever since they'd left Stan's Castle.

She wanted to tell him she knew what he was thinking: that her teenage views were archaic—backward even—but that there was nothing backward about treating homosexuality as a mortal sin in the L.A. she knew growing up. All their neighbors were Catholic (at least the ones they talked to), and everybody took their faith seriously; her parents proudly gave ten percent of their paltry income to the church, and believed whatever the pope told them to believe. Elizabeth read constantly as a child, but avoided any books the church told her not to read, anything that would have opened her up to a different perspective. The biggest scandal to have touched her till Hugo's disappearance was her parents having only two children. As an addendum to the "birds and bees" talk, her mother explained that after Hugo was born, she'd had a hysterectomy for medical reasons. But people still whispered about them going to hell for interfering with God's plan, and sometimes her schoolmates made her cry about it. She did not know a single self-identifying gay person growing up.

And yet blaming her environment only went so far. Why didn't her sisterly love overpower everything she was taught? Why didn't she embrace Hugo and tell him they'd figure it out together? Why weren't her prejudices and misconceptions washed away, as they were for the heroes and heroines of the stories she loved?

She wanted to explain to Richard that she gave up asking why—that she went to Yale instead of UCLA to get as far away as she could, and that she stopped going to church. That she let her membership in the Young Republicans lapse. That like so many people, she grew up during college. That she read every book the church told her not to read, and that she evolved, her worldview expanded. That she did all she could to separate herself from the girl who bought into the groupthink of religion and politics, which included separating herself from her parents, who were far from bad people—who had in many ways been wonderful parents, but who were so broken from losing one child they actually, in their grief and weakness, allowed their second child to drift away. That when she emerged from this dark period of her life, her "rough patch," with the help of antidepressants and twice-a-week therapy—both of which she eliminated from her life as soon as she could do so responsibly—she forced herself to move on, because wallowing in the past helped no one. That it took Orpheus entering her life to realize she'd been conflating thinking solely *for* herself with thinking solely *about* herself, and that she was working on this, too. That she would never be done improving herself.

But most of all she wished she had the courage to tell Richard that it wasn't until she got to know him—*really* know him—that she knew what it was to truly desire another person. That even before the incident with Hugo, she worried secretly she was asexual. That she told all her school friends who teased her for being such a good girl that she was too focused on her studies to entertain the notion of a silly teenage "romance," and that every time her mother thought she was comforting her by saying that crushes were "normal," and "nothing to be ashamed about" as long as she didn't do anything about them, Elizabeth felt both abnormal and ashamed because she never had an adolescent crush, not even one. That she realized only after it was too late there was an element of jealousy, of covetousness in her condemnation of Hugo, in her disgust at seeing him with another boy. She wanted to tell Richard that this failure, this lack only deepened in all her years at Yale and NYU—that it took hold of her and became a part of who she was. That it was the same at the firm. That the few men she dated she never saw more than two or three times, and only ever kissed, nothing more. That when she turned thirty she panicked about still being a virgin and picked up—in some sleazy bar—a guy whose name she purposely didn't learn, and used him to deflower herself, except that the process was so mechanical that afterward she felt, outrageously, as if she were *still* a virgin, that she had concluded she would *always* feel like a virgin, and that she had tried to make her peace with this condition by committing to the role of La Máquina, sturdy and implacable. . . . Until him.

She wanted to tell Richard that in the beginning she used to think she'd have her fill of him eventually, that there would come a time when his presence failed to thrill her. And it did; the thrill *did* fade. But it was only because she'd grown used to having him around—not just each week for dinner and conversation, but each second in her thoughts—and if it wasn't a thrill to picture him every time, it was because she could no longer imagine her life without him.

It was fear of losing him that held her back from saying all this, though she knew instinctively this was the time to let it all out, to not lose courage and stop halfway, to tell him *everything* or risk losing him anyway at the end of their year together. The seven months they still had might as well have been seven seconds compared to the eternity she craved. She would gladly have paid back the half a million dollars to ensure their weekly sessions continued for as long as they both were breathing. She would have read any book, watched any movie.

But she couldn't do it. She couldn't say any of it. Maybe she would find the courage tomorrow, or the next day, though her instincts were telling her it was now or never. . . . *No.* She was done. She looked out at the purple-gray mountains and waited to see what he had to say, if anything. Who knew? It was entirely possible he wanted nothing to do with her now.

RICHARD DIDN'T KNOW what to say. He knew she'd been keeping something from him about her family, but never would he have guessed it was linked to the one event in his life he could reasonably term a tragedy. He had a million questions for her, but held off. Now was not the time.

He turned, regarding her silently. She was staring at the mountains, and the sunlight was pouring down her back, unlocking the rich, chestnut hue that remained hidden inside her dark brown hair in every other type of light. Sitting there on top of this lonely dune, she looked like the last woman on Earth—or maybe the first. Either way, she was the only woman in the world who undoubtedly belonged here with him, in this unreal landscape, on this unreal day. It seemed impossible to him now that he had ever wanted or looked forward to being free of her, and this made him think of *Tess of the d'Urbervilles*, of all things. During his two sleepless hours in bed that morning, he had actually finished the damn thing, in the hope it would have its usual soporific effect. But *Tess* had moved along in the last hundred pages, and he'd stopped reading only once, to look up a phrase Hardy had quoted from Shakespeare: "love is not love which alters when it alteration finds." It was meant to be a description of the inferior love of Tess's fickle, unworthy husband, who rejects her when she confesses she isn't a virgin, but at the time Richard hadn't understood it. If someone changed, why wouldn't your feelings about that person change too? *Because it was the perception, not the thing that mattered*, he answered himself now, and the phrase came back to him with unexpected clarity all the way from their first date at In-N-Out: *you have beautiful eyes.*

Richard turned away from her, flashing back to a series of moments radiating outward from that first date: Elizabeth slurping on her milk shake, Elizabeth spilling soy sauce in the excitement of explaining *Ivanhoe* to him, Elizabeth spinning on the dance floor in his arms, Elizabeth asking him to sleep over, Elizabeth in that slightly ridiculous yet undeniably sexy purple dress, Elizabeth checking him out in the rearview mirror while he pretended not to notice, at the tail end of his nap. It was like piecing together clues at the end of a movie with a big twist—*The Usual Suspects, The Sixth Sense*—in support of a seemingly impossible conclusion, except that he was cherry-picking because there were other memories too: Elizabeth checking her watch a million times at In-N-Out when she thought he wasn't looking, Elizabeth berating his myopic worldview at Factor's, Elizabeth wanting desperately to go home after being pelted with his *vomit* (this still humiliated him, this would always humiliate him), Elizabeth hating his gift of the size-12 skirt, Elizabeth leaving the premiere immediately after *Fight on a Flight* ended exactly as she said she would, despite his desperate pleas (masked in cowardly irony) for her to reconsider.

Richard tried to picture what she had looked like the first time they met—less than five months ago, and yet a different era—in the lawyer's office in June. The image he managed to conjure actually confused him, because she looked nothing like that to him anymore. *Perception*, he thought. *All perception.*

And then—and this was strange, but it was Mike's face, not Elizabeth's, that came to him. Beautiful, brilliant, *brave* Mike, who shone in his mind's eye like a lightbulb over his head. What was it she had said? *I thought it was important to tell you how I was feeling, no matter what you might be feeling.* Mike had known before he did. Of course she had; this really shouldn't have surprised him. He still couldn't quite see how the hell he'd gotten here, but somehow he had.

Richard paused. Deep underground, the roots of a mesquite bush at the edge of the dunes sucked up a bit of subterranean moisture. He turned to her. He opened his mouth. Was he actually going to say it? He was.

"Elizabeth, I love you."

THE END

BEVERLY CHAMBERS DRAINED her drink to the dregs and let the glass fall from her hand. The smash wasn't nearly as dramatic as she had hoped. It didn't matter. She reminded herself that the time for playing a part was over. She was neither Katharine Hepburn nor Norma Desmond now. She was nothing more or less than herself.

As before, she was sitting on the preposterous couch Char-Bev had airlifted, giggling, from their favorite Vegas hotel. It looked as though she hadn't moved in the half hour since lunchtime, but she had in fact been busy. She'd made the climb up to her room, and transferred all the sleeping pills from a recent prescription into her pocket. Two had gone into the tea she'd insisted that Peaches drink, and in this way her killjoy of a housekeeper had been safely put away for the rest of the day. She hadn't planned it this way, but as usual there hadn't been much of a plan at all.

Bev slipped into a languid sort of reverie, which was, after all, the best way of riding out a desert afternoon. . . . So it *had* been an inspired bit of thinking to play matchmaker, she mused lazily, even if she doubted whether Hugo Santiago would appreciate her interpretation of his instructions to "check on" his sister and the boy who testified at his trial, to "help them" however she could. His only stipulation had been never to tell them on whose behalf she was acting, and she hadn't violated it. Jonathan Hertzfeld had been a paragon of discretion, even if his underlings had not. She hoped that upon greater reflection, Hugo would be pleased with her efforts, not that she would ever know one way or the other. She would never see him, or anyone, again.

He had been Charlotte's project anyway. Her favorite. How many sessions did they spend with him? She couldn't remember, but many, many more than with anyone else. Charlotte had been touched by his story; she'd urged him up to the very end to make contact with his family, to stop being so stubborn and to let them know he was alive, to let them see him. He was so *extreme.* "He reminds me of *you*," Char said more than once, joking that she wanted to fix him the way she'd fixed Bev. But she had been getting through to him, she really had—the same way she'd gotten through to so many others.

And then, of course, she died. And when Hugo made his request, Beverly granted it without delay. But for Charlotte, not for him.

Even so, thought Bev now, wasn't she just as forlorn and bereft, as lost and abandoned as Hugo Santiago? No one ever looked hard enough to see the connection between the spinster and the jailbird, but it was there; it was real. And when she argued that society as a whole was at least a *little* responsible for the failings of such fallen individuals, she knew that deep down what she was really saying was that it wasn't—it couldn't—be her fault entirely that she was going to die alone.

After what she'd seen this afternoon, she couldn't help wondering if *any* two people could be made to fall in love, given time and the requisite motivation. Wasn't this the principle upon which arranged marriage worked for half the world? It was hardly an earth-shattering proposition—quite the opposite: earth-defining—and it made Bev wonder if her brother Tom had been right all along to barrage her with those blind dates. If she'd just picked *someone*, could they have been happy together? It was a shame no man would cross her door again. She had half a mind to fall in love with the next one who did.

A man crossed her door.

HAD ORPHEUS BEEN warned ahead of time what he was about to see, he couldn't have predicted the effect of Stan's Castle when it came into view because it neither astonished nor intimidated him as he would have expected it to do. He felt immediately that he belonged inside this edifice of absurdity, that his road trip to the middle of nowhere had finally led to the somewhere he was meant to be. Orpheus parked outside the open gate and wandered, slack-jawed, into a kitchen filled with more copper and porcelain than he'd ever seen, through a music room that featured its own built-in organ, and into a great room that held at its center, like a pearl in an oyster, the someone inside the somewhere he knew without a doubt he'd been destined to meet.

He stared at her from the doorway, frozen.

The only way to make sense of what it felt like to look at her was by means of a comparison he never imagined would be possible. He had felt this way exactly twice before. First when presented with his newborn son minutes after he was born and, second, when meeting his daughter through the glass of a hospital nursery.

Oh, he thought, *it's you. You're here.*

Beverly gestured toward the same chair Elizabeth had occupied a half hour earlier. When he sat, she smelled the sharp tang of cheap, sporty deodorant, which was how her male tennis partners always smelled after freshening up at the end of a session. It was a manly smell, and it made her feel young; it made her feel—it was absurd, but it was true—*bashful.* When was the last time she had felt *that*? Beverly averted her eyes, enjoying the sensation.

Orpheus didn't know what to say, and it was primarily to break the silence that he asked, "Did you drop something?" gesturing to the broken glass at her feet.

Beverly followed the direction of his hand. *Ah, yes.* The other eighteen sleeping pills she had swallowed moments earlier, convinced she was done with life—that nothing interesting or notable other than the persistent ache of Charlotte's absence could possibly happen to her during whatever little time she had left. *Oops.* She had to suppress the urge to laugh, because this was exactly what the young version of herself—the girl running across the lawn in her nightshirt—had been waiting for. It was all too idiotically romantic, like some grotesque, geriatric parody of *Romeo and Juliet.*

"I'm afraid I've taken something," she said.

"How long?" Orpheus asked softly.

"An hour?" she said. "Maybe less."

"Huh." He shook his head. "What a world."

"That's what the Wicked Witch of the West says while she's dying. At the end of *The Wizard of Oz.* Did you know I went to the original Hollywood premiere? At Grauman's Chinese. Or Mann's, or whatever they're calling it these days. I can still remember seeing Judy Garland in the flesh. She was so pretty.

Of course she was probably on drugs, even then." Bev paused. "I'm old."

"Makes two of us," said Orpheus. "Huh."

"You have some time," said Bev, pulling off a final, farewell twinkle with her birdlike eyes before they began fading away. This stuff she took was working faster than she expected. "You know, you could have come an hour later. Or not at all. We could never have met."

Orpheus nodded. "Anything is possible," he said, softer than before. And the phrase shone for him again, burnished brand-new and hopeful, like when he told it to his children.

"I believe I am going to pass out soon," Bev announced, staggering up from her seat. "And since you're here, I'd like you to help me upstairs and into my bed. I hope you're not too shocked. But better you know now, I'm not much of a lady of virtue."

BEV'S ONLY REGRET was that she would die out here in the desert and not in Los Angeles, where she belonged. But when she closed her eyes she saw the big white letters of the HOLLYWOODLAND sign, and she was home again. Even though she couldn't see him anymore, she could still feel him, her gentleman caller sitting beside her, and before she could help it she thought of *Driving Miss Daisy*, which she'd watched a few weeks after Richard and Elizabeth. (Jonathan Hertzfeld still sent her all their receipts.) This time she didn't have to suppress her laughter because she was too weak to produce it, but she knew others would compare them to the rich old white woman and her elderly black driver if ever they saw them together. She was glad no one ever would.

She couldn't allow *Driving Miss Daisy* to be her last thought on earth, so Bev tried to think of something more profound. The girl in the nightshirt would be angry with her for ruining this moment, though it was silly to continue indulging this mental trick of hers, of treating the girl as someone separate. And why stop there? Bev thought about all the other people who were really a part of her: Charlotte, of course, and Big Stan her father, and her bossy brother Tom. Her new friend Mike Kim, and that charming boy Richard Baumbach. The *not* charming Elizabeth Santiago, too. The darkness behind her eyelids grew darker still, and she realized she could go further: Jonathan Hertzfeld, and Orpheus Washington—but who was that? It was he, of course: the man at her side. His name was *Orpheus*? Oh, that was almost too good to be true. . . . But how did she know that? And suddenly there were so many more: Charlotte's husband, Arnold; Jonathan's wife, Rivka; Orpheus's wife, Rhonda; his children, Sherry and Scott; Peaches, Keith, Ally, and Raoul; Albert Johnson and Death Valley Scotty; Colin Higgins and Hal Ashby; Peg Entwistle and Amber Hudson; Kyle, Selena, Tess, and Angelyne—more names than it seemed possible to know at once.

Bev's body went slack, and she thought about how they were all a part of her, but not in a way that made her any less the Beverly Chambers she'd been all her life. How was this possible? How could she be all people and one person at the same time? The answer was just out of her reach, but it was *there*, and she saw that the world was made up of neither individuals nor a single, coherent entity. It was an amalgamation, a sum greater than its parts. It was a mess. It was love.

The throbbing in her joints, the burning in her lungs, all this pain disappeared and Bev realized with a thrill that this was a vision of the world she could get behind, because it had nothing to do with balance or restraint. She saw now that there was no true opposite to love. People thought it was hatred, or fear, or indifference, but these were all so trivial in comparison to the Great Emotion—a force so powerful, a God with so many faces that if its true opposite existed the world would cease to be. There was no need to strive for moderation anymore, no reason to control her impulses; she was going to a place where good intentions were enough, where what she wanted to do and what she ought to do would always be the same. Bev brought her hands together and actually rubbed them in anticipation, and as she did so she felt a pair of hands above hers. Annoyed that the drug hadn't worked yet, she opened her eyes to tell Orpheus Washington to sit back and give her some room, when in his place, just like Valentine's Day 1952, she saw Charlotte. Always Charlotte.

"Get up, you old cow." Char grinned: young, vibrant, as she was back then.

Bev smiled.

Bev frowned.

"Wait," she said. "How do I know this is real? That it's not made up? Some stupid dream or something?"

"I guess you don't," Char said a little impatiently. "But was it a dream last time? In 1952?"

"Good point," said Bev, springing out of her bed. It took her a moment to realize she had *sprung*, that she too was young, that she was the girl in the nightshirt again, folding her beloved best friend in her arms.

"You know," Char whispered in her ear, "we actually saw *Driving Miss Daisy* when it came out in the theater. In '89."

"Absolutely not," said Bev, stepping back from her and shaking her head. "I would have remembered that."

"*No*, you *wouldn't*, because you have an atrocious memory."

"Ah, yes, because yours is *photographic*." Bev used air quotes.

"Eidetic, not photographic, and don't use air quotes, Beverly," said Char, in that authoritative, schoolmarmish voice Bev always conveniently forgot in her fond remembrances of her best friend. "They're tacky."

"Well, now I'm *sure* this isn't a dream," said Bev, "unless it's a nightmare. Rest assured if I dreamt *you* up, you'd be a mute."

Even as CharBev continued to bicker, Beverly could feel herself drifting away. It was as if she were ascending: the greater the height, the more she could see, except that her field of vision was not only space but also time, allowing her to catch glimpses of the future as it played out in the aftermath of her demise.

She saw Orpheus Washington return to Los Angeles under the cover of night, abandoning his stolen Prius off the 10 in West Covina in the effort to keep himself from getting arrested.

She saw a bleary-eyed Peaches discover her body. She had expected Peaches to scream, perhaps even to clutch and tear at her salt-and-pepper bob, but Peaches surprised her. She lifted the bedsheet over Bev's head, bid her employer a simple adieu, and left as soon as the ambulance arrived, headed straight for her sister in Rosemead.

She saw a tired-looking Jonathan Hertzfeld in Century City giving Richard and Elizabeth the rest of their half-million-dollar reward, informing them that Beverly Chambers was dead and they were free never to speak to each other again.

She saw Richard in bed at his apartment in Silver Lake, leg thumping, a wrinkle appearing where none had appeared before on his marblelike brow as an unfamiliar emotion coursed through his body. How was he going to handle this weight, this worry, this *burden* for the rest of his life? How could a happiness this perfect, this profound, possibly last? He couldn't shake the feeling that something awful was going to happen. And then Bev saw him lift the sheet beside him, uncovering a perfectly sleeping (and perfectly naked) Elizabeth, and she saw him curl up beside her and match his breathing to hers.

She saw Rivka in Hancock Park worry her children by refusing to cry when Jonathan Hertzfeld died, much earlier than either of them expected. "What's the point?" she protested. "What's done is done." But she couldn't sleep properly, not without that arm, till one night she rustled furtively in her special drawer looking for something, anything to make her feel better, and she found the horrible little bottle of perfume, as full as the day he gave it to her. And Beverly saw her take it, and slip it under her pillow, and find the sleep she desired.

She saw Elizabeth in her brand-new partner's office in Beverly Hills, hosting a crowded little cocktail party foisted upon her by her coworkers, during which Richard made a point of introducing himself to everyone as quickly and loudly as possible, since Elizabeth still knew hardly anyone's name. And in one corner she saw Elizabeth's parents, shy yet proud—and behind them, shyer and a little prouder too, she saw Orpheus Washington, taking it all in.

She saw Mike walk down a red carpet of her own, arm-in-arm not with Richard but with Keith, who became a frequent collaborator and real friend in Richard's absence—an absence that was limited to the professional sphere only, because she also saw Richard and Mike arm-in-arm on another carpet, which was white and ran the length of a church in Koreatown, at an event for which Mike's father was absent without qualification, despite the best medicine and rehabilitative efforts several hundred thousand dollars could buy. And she watched as Richard walked Mike slowly down the aisle, toward the man waiting so eagerly for her at the end of it.

Many years later she saw Hugo Santiago make a home for himself in Glendale upon his release. And though he spoke regularly to his parents and sister, and even, incredibly, to the brother-in-law who played a role in putting him away, she saw that he kept mainly to himself. He was, however, unable to deny the combined chorus of his three nieces whenever they demanded he make the trek to Venice for a family dinner, which they did from time to time.

She saw Richard and Mike at countless restaurants all over the city, though the frequency of these mealtime dates ebbed and flowed with the times, and the lulls in between weren't punctuated by nearly as much talking, or texting, or digital chatter as during what Richard insisted on referring to as his "salad daze," that period of his life before he threw in the towel on his Hollywood career and reverted to being an aficionado and much later, after his girls were grown, a professor of film.

She was almost ready to look away now, but first, she forced herself to focus on a hospital complex in Santa Monica, in a tiny room where Orpheus Washington lay gasping amid the blips and bleeps of monitors, reaching out across a spider's web of tubes and wires for the hand of his oldest goddaughter, Lily, who by now was practically middle-aged herself, and who held on to him as long as she possibly could because she was more his than anyone else in the world—even her own parents admitted this indisputable fact, often and freely. And Bev saw his eyes glaze over and turn toward the sky, and it was as if he was looking directly at her.

And now she was so far away, she could see the entire city at once: indescribable, unquantifiable, contrarian L.A., an improbable pastiche made up of untamed wilderness, cultivated parks, gleaming celebrity mansions, crumbling housing projects, business towers reaching for the sky, strip clubs that barely got off the ground, pristine beaches broken up strategically by acres of shiny metal pipes (what the hell were they? *desalination plants*, came the answer with unexpected readiness), luxury automobiles, industrial ships, brightly colored buses, a surprisingly elaborate grid of subway lines, and people—so many different kinds of people—thrown together in a mishmash of neighborhoods with no heart because its heart was everywhere: a sum greater than its parts. How could she have missed this before? How strange the idea of missing anything was already becoming. She could see . . . *everything* now, and though she'd never seen it before, it looked oddly familiar—recognizable even, because it looked like something she'd been seeking her entire life.

It looked like the one.

THE ACKNOWLEDGMENTS

FIRST, THE FRIENDS: Mariam Al-Foudery, Abby Ex, Dayna and Ember Frank, Paul Fruchbom, Barbara Graves-Poller, Mac-Kenzie Huynh, Tia Maggini, Alex Mircheff, Dantram Nguyen, Radhi Thayu, and Julie Wie. Thank you for reading various drafts of this novel, many of you when it was still in its larval and pupal stages. An additional thanks to a handful of the above for inspiring various elements of this story. You know who you are (or at least I hope you do . . .), and you are family.

Next, the guys at Circle of Confusion: Lawrence Mattis, for forcing me to move to Los Angeles in the first place, the Davids, Alpert and Engel, for giving me my first home when I got here, and Bryan Millard, for being an ideal workmate all decade long.

Bring on the professionals: my indomitable agent Alexandra Machinist, who stood by this manuscript for a protracted and uncertain period like the fierce and loyal advocate she is, till finding the perfect home for it at HarperCollins, where I have felt supported by the team in general. Thanks in particular to Jonathan Burnham, who was an early advocate of this book, and to my editor, Maya Ziv, the rare soul with a knack for bringing out the best not only in stories but in people, too. Maya, I was so lucky to be able to hitch my wagon to your train of goodwill, dedication, and unflagging enthusiasm. A special thanks to Kathy Schneider, whose enthusiasm has pervaded this process from beginning to end; she has truly been my champion. Thanks also to Dorian Karchmar and Andrea Walker, who both provided vital expertise in some of the more preliminary stages of this tortuous (not to mention torturous) process of bringing a debut novel to fruition.

Now the relations: my sister Taryn, who was always my hero growing up, both for her overall strength of spirit and unfailing loyalty to me; my sister Kelly, whose lifelong commitment to the arts has been an inspiration for as long as I can remember; my brothers-in-law Alex and Josh; my nieces and nephews Séquoia, Siméon, Charlie, and Lilah; the Milches (Nora, Hannah, and Tom); and the Divolls (Vicki and Janet). Do I really have to say it? I love you all.

Time for the ones who lie so close to my heart it's difficult, or at the very least mildly absurd, to acknowledge them so formally ("Nelly, I am Heathcliff!" etc.). Thank you to my parents, Daniel and Maureen Donovan, for showing me what it means to build a life made out of love, and for the courage to say such sentimental things often and aloud. Thank you to my husband, Adam Milch, for choosing to build a life with me made of the same material, and for the steadfast support of a fellow writer and fellow human. You make me better.

And finally, the only one who I can't thank face-to-face, so this will have to do: Margaret Biegen (formerly Kemper, née Burns), who didn't get to read this book, but who prayed every day for its success when she learned I was trying my hand at writing. While I believe in immortality only metaphorically, I happen to believe in metaphors unreservedly, and have no qualms declaring that her loving support of me hasn't abated one bit since her passing. If anything, it's stronger. Thank you, Grandma.

ABOUT THE AUTHOR

KEMPER DONOVAN has lived in Los Angeles for a dozen years. He attended Stanford University and Harvard Law School before working at the literary management company Circle of Confusion, representing screenwriters and comic books. His first client wrote the feature film *Hanna*, released by Focus Features. He is also a member of the New York Bar.